EXOTIC GOTHIC 4

Exotic Gothic 4

Edited by Danel Olson

Exotic Gothic 4
Copyright © 2012 Danel Olson

Cover Art
Photograph Title: "Bella Muerte"
Photography, Body Painting: Apolinar Lorenzo Chuca
Hair & Makeup: Shay Prator
Model: Anna Flores

First published in Great Britain in 2012 by PS Publishing. This paperback edition first published in January 2014 by Drugstore Indian Press, an imprint of PS Publishing Ltd. by arrangement with the authors. All rights reserved by the authors. The rights of the authors, to be identified as the Authors of this Work have been asserted by them in accordance with the Copyright, Designs and Patents Act 1988.

"The Look", by Reggie Oliver. First appeared in Mrs. Midnight and Other Stories *(Tartarus Press, 2011).*

First DIP Edition

ISBN
978-1-848637-06-1

Design & Layout by Michael Smith

Printed in England by T. J. International

PS Publishing Ltd
Grosvenor House
1 New Road, Hornsea
East Yorkshire, HU18 1PG
England

e-mail: editor@pspublishing.co.uk
website: www.pspublishing.co.uk

CONTENTS

Preface: On Dark Gifting

Danel Olson

> *. . . Queen Cleopatra's skull,*
> *'Tis cloven and crack'd,*
> *And batter'd and hack'd,*
> *But with tears of blue eyes it is full.*

—Thomas Lovell Beddoes, "Old Adam, the Carrion Crow" (1825)

THE RAPTUROUS COVER IMAGE FOR *EXOTIC GOTHIC 4* reminds me of a Gothic compliment an artist once gave a woman of dark regard. It was Diego Rivera who said to Mexico's first film star with global appeal, Dolores del Río, 'Skulls as beautiful as yours never grow old.'[1] Having gazed a while on this matinee idol's glamour stills from the 1920s-1950s, I can see Rivera had a point. Something arresting as death and reimagined as desire pulls at us in the sculpted screen siren's perfect cranial, cheek, chin and jaw bones. Something fey in del Rio's geometry of bone fetches. The lines have allure, just as they do in the young woman who recently daubed body paint and clasped her throat for our cover, Anna Flores, gorgeously photographed by Apolinar Lorenzo Chuca, Jr. I believe that the skull beneath her skin will never grow old either.

[1] Quoted by Carlos Fuentes, interviewed by Alfred MacAdam and Charles E. Ruas, "The Art of Fiction No. 68," *Paris Review*, Winter 1981, http://www.theparisreview.org/interviews/3195/the-art-of-fiction-no-68-carlos-fuentes (accessed 1 April 2011)

Granted, skull appreciation *can* be a bizarre, conversation-halting, and mostly unwholesome fascination to share with women, save for those wondrous ladies of the World Horror and World Fantasy Conventions. They are the unwelcome and slightly obsessive words to bring a draft of mortality to the chat, a hint of perversion, a silence to laughter, a crossing of knees and a looking-away. They are not quite understood. They discomfit all with a nervous Poesque observation, a "Berenice" chill, even evoking the unstoppable and horrid passion within Nancy A. Collins's instant bone-classic from 1993, "Aphra". Such words make the champagne in our flutes go instantly flat.

But could there be any more sincere love than *skull-love?* To say one fancies a woman's spider-'n-web tattoo is one thing, but a bone plaudit pledges so much more: it says that beneath all—*really under it all*—she is eternally beautiful. And what compliment goes under the skin more boldly than that? Cranium praise, then, is as guileless and potent and true, as deep a declaration of beauty today, as when the muralist Rivera uttered it over half a century ago.

Likewise, Gothic fiction—that genre of things wrongly hungered for and things wrongly alive—collects and parades its skull trophies, too. The one thing I've noticed about skulls is that they're always smiling, always inviting you in, just as the Gothic smiles at us, at first anyway, and tempts. It is the literature evoking the combined force and surrender to beauty, passion and horror. It reaches to kiss whatever is eternal, infinite, archetypal. Within its plots that dissemble and terrify and seduce, and its characters who follow desire (burying misdeeds and people, or disinterring and resurrecting them as in that flawless Kelly Link story of boneyard boo-boos from 2007, "The Wrong Grave"), the Gothic lets the dead walk with us a little and talk. The Gothic invites the deceased to pull us their way, away from all the pedestrian realities that could dull us or leave us satisfied with less. Following insane desire, stripping the symbolic or literal flesh away from reality, what exactly will you find from these dead ones? You will find stories like these.

Though they aim for re-invention and new culture infusion, some element of the traditional Gothic will always float over the twenty-five neo-Gothic tales herein. What the mysteriously durable Gothic has always done is to supply a curse, bad or absentee parenting, damaged or hidden heirs, shocking human coldness, and murderous disputes over legacy or land. What else the Gothic does is well illustrated recently by my colleague Jerrold E. Hogle in *The Cambridge Companion to Gothic Fiction*. The Gothic, to paraphrase Prof. Hogle, traditionally leads us to an antiquated or seemingly antiquated place (castle, palace, abbey, ruin, prison or dungeon, crypt, woods or moors or sea, ancient city or culture, underworld, factory, laboratory, or theatre). Within this space are hidden some secrets from the recent or long ago past that haunt the visitors physically or psychically. The hauntings take many forms—they may be voices, visions, ghosts, transformed beings, monsters that rise from within or invaders that come from without, all manifesting in unsolved, unending crimes or conflicts that will no longer stay buried from view. The released threats to sanity, safety and life result in violence, grotesquerie, dissolution, or revolting revelation.[2]

Many of the writers within the pages of this *Exotic Gothic 4* will escort us to such menacing places of revelation, but with 21st century renovations. To tell the same Gothic story, in the same locale and structure, would be as pointless as it is unchallenging—it's all been done well (or abysmally and melodramatically) too many times before. As Count Earl ironically says in the 2001 video game *Cel Damage*, 'We classic monsters are all the same.' Such a bland or disappointing repetition, and all plunked right back into the Gothic UK homelands, is undesired. A redefinition of the Gothic is hungered for. Part of the dark delight anticipated for readers is watching the Gothic move out of its mouldy grave on this rare moonlit night, and all the never-seen horrors it will visit upon the nearby inhabitants. For example, the infamous private 'filthy workshop of creation' from the days of *Frankenstein* becomes in our anthology a shared St. Petersburg university laboratory with an interest in cancer growths. Mixing Shelley's revitalization

---

[2] Jerrold E. Hogle, Introduction to *The Cambridge Companion to Gothic Fiction*, Ed. Jerrold E. Hogle (Cambridge, UK: Cambridge University Press, 2002), 2-3.

preoccupation with Poe's mania for possessive romance, Moscow-born Ekaterina Sedia floats a rumor of an amorous tumor in her Russian mad science tale "Helena". Her story may be the best example in fiction I know to prove a line of Roland Barthes that has stayed with me long: 'The hallucinatory psychosis of desire not only . . . brings concealed or repressed desires to consciousness, but, further, represents them in all good faith as realized.'[3] Ivan Sechenov the researcher gets what he wanted, but more than he can control, and that's the damnable Gothic fix. Oppositely, thwarted sexual desire is a theme of Nick Antosca's new story of mind altering chemicals, "Candy". And like one of the maddest of its Gothic progenitors—*The Monk* of 1796 from Matthew Lewis—the wild end for the increasingly unstable protagonist in "Candy" takes place at the water, though in this case at a series of swimming pools instead of the swelling river at *The Monk*'s close, where Lewis's Ambrosio falls from precipice to precipice, first being taunted and scolded for pages by an insatiate daemon, and *then* dropped from a great height, falling mangled all the way.

In his original "Celebrity Frankenstein" contribution, famed *Gothic* and *Ghostwatch* creator/screenwriter Stephen Volk has medical science create a neo Frankenidol for his media-creator, agonizing not all over Antarctica, but a much colder place, *Hollywood*—the city of wayward agents, dashed callback hopes, broken studio promises, and subpar creative instincts to make movies and TV the same but different from whatever is the current box office or network bash. A black and baleful monster you've probably never seen, and would cause other monsters blob-envy, hungers for you in Simon Kurt Unsworth's hot and dusty African tale, "The Fourth Horse," along with old-fashioned Gothic longing and lust for a woman who's no good for you, and the question of who will inherit the land. And while it is hellish enough to face monsters who stand (or roll) in front of you, it is more diabolical to contend with those monsters who are inside you, as we encounter in an unsentimental and unsparing new story of old New England from Scott Thomas, "The Unfinished Book."

[3] Roland Barthes, *A Lover's Discourse: Fragments*, Trans. Richard Howard (New York: Hill and Wang, 1979) 187.

As promised in the timeless schoolyard taunt rhyme K-I-S-S-I-N-G, we spy in Lucy Taylor's animalistic Namibian narrative "Nikishi" some fateful kisses; then comes love for a real doll in Stephen Dedman's jaw-dropping "The Fall" of Japan; an easy marriage, but a devilish morning-after manifests in Margo Lanagan's relentlessly absorbing "Blooding the Bride"; then come the babies from Cherie Dimaline's First Nation-inspired "Wanishin," little ones for which no parenting class could well prepare you; and in Anna Taborska's haunting "Rusalka" comes a final cradling. 'Whatever love may be,' as the poet Howard Moss once admitted in "At the Algonquin," 'it's not child's play.'

Just as Rivera's skull-exclamation was a dark gift to his old friend Dolores del Rio—an artist's sigh at the windswept curve of her cheekbone—the newfound Gothic between these covers offers lots of unexpected presents just for you. Del Rio's fantasy-launching bone structure was simply a chance gift of her parents' union, that random DNA combination they formed that would bless her career and fill the hearts of lovers and audiences worldwide. I suspect that the connection between most of these twenty-five stories is a more deliberate one. They all choose to meditate on dark gifting. That is, they explore what it means to get a something you don't know how to use, and didn't ask for, and which may put your mind, body and soul in peril. This isn't exactly new. We all know well that haunting subtitle to *Frankenstein*. We all remember that Victor Frankenstein was symbolically a new Prometheus who gave a new kind of fire, a sin for which (like the old Prometheus) he would suffer horribly, and which would present a host of unintended consequences for us.

What is fresh is the form these presents take, and how the characters either search for or give up on redemption after getting and acting upon these odd treasures. Some of the gifts are knowledge that resolves one doubt but raises another, over who your mother or father or in-laws really are, or who your baby is, or who your spouse or neighbors or colleagues or teachers or students are—as in the case of the heartbreaking and heartstopping stories from Tunku Halim ("In the Village of Setang"), Adam L.G. Nevill

("Pig Thing"), Joseph Bruchac ("Down in the Valley"), David Punter ("Carving"), Brian Evenson ("Grottor"), and the aforementioned tales of Margo Lanagan and Cherie Dimaline. So often these invitations in the preceding stories are to stay a while in an otherworldly spot, though you can't at first for the life of yourself say why. But other gifts are inscrutable things. Outside of these freshly created stories, consider for a moment a few of the strange gifts presented in outstanding Gothic novels and novellas since 2000: the strangely scented, rather countryish dark suit that comes in the mail (from Joe Hill's *Heart-Shaped Box*), a feather and bones (Louise Erdrich's *Four Souls*), a short metal bar (James Lasdun's *The Horned Man*), an endless variety of ice (Dan Simmons' *The Terror*), a rotten pumpkin (Nancy A. Collins's *The Pumpkin Child*), a picture of a dragon (Elizabeth Kostova's *The Historian*), or a body part or two from a dead prostitute (James Reese's *The Dracula Dossier*). Another Gothic gift is willing victims, or characters who stay too long or voluntarily return to the locus of horror, that gifted site of gruesome transformation and death, and they enchant another genuinely daring artist of ours, Adam L G Nevill. Nevill terrifies with tales and novels of non-conformists or anti-socials seeking the reward of refuge, but they always choose the wrong sanctuary —going into hallways with hidden light switches and unquiet, teak-floored flats in London, or the witchy tunnels and Brown Man-haunted beaches near St. Andrews, Scotland, from his unputdownable *Banquet for the Damned* (2004). In response to my argument that what the Gothic most gives is a whole swag-bag of phobias we didn't know we had, Prof. Glennis Byron (co-creator of the impressive "The Gothic Imagination" website out of Scotland's University of Stirling) added,

> The idea of dark gifting is intriguing—I think you've really hit on something important there. Other examples came immediately to my mind, and not just from texts included here (the book and the pen in *Shadow of the Wind*, the guns in Piñol's *Cold Skin*) but many from books published even more recently—like the Barrington House flat in Adam Nevill's

Apartment 16 (2010). No doubt there's a PhD in this for someone![4]

In their own peculiar way, the narratives you're about to read often feature the non-returnable gift of a damning glance, that one look that nets the eyes: for a start, that glimpse of fabled creatures in Isobelle Carmody's moving "Metro Winds" and Paul Finch's devastating WWI "Oschaert"; or a historical picture that kills in Robert Hood's Mexican revolutionary tale, "Escena de un Asesinato"; or an intimate past in either Genni Gunn's tearful "Water Lover", Reggie Oliver's calmly cruel and caustic "The Look", or Terry Dowling's head-twirling "Mariners' Round".

So much depends on what one does with these presents. This is the emotional and intellectual bridge that these neo-Gothic tales bid you to cross . . . What should *you* do with these gifts? How will the experience change you? Would you ever leave behind what you witnessed? Could you live with what you did? I reckon you won't believe how these characters use their presents.[5]

Coming to the end of compiling and editing this book, I asked, *What is the Gothic for anymore?* It would captivate me to hear what readers of this new collection say. Is it to romance? To imagine swoony and ripped, but rather unscary lovers? That has been enormously popular lately, and Stephenie Meyer has a lot to answer for. The commercial success of all tame vampire and werewolf lovers could turn scores more novelists and screenwriters to churn an anemic and undemonic Gothic that has lost its roots of mayhem and debauchery. Where is the necessary premeditated sin and

[4] Glennis Byron, "Danel Olson interviewed by Glennis Byron Part 2," 15 Dec. 2010, http://www.gothic.stir.ac.uk/interviews/danel-olson-interviewed-by-glennis-byron-part-2-2/ (accessed 1 April 2010)

[5] A postscript to Gothic gift-giving is a memoir I taught recently that asks a troubling question: What would you do if you received a lampshade made out of human skin? Bury it, verify it, place it in a dumpster, throw it out a window, sell it, take it to a holocaust museum, or live with it? This gripping memoir is called *The Lampshade: A Holocaust Detective Story from Buchenwald to New Orleans* (2010), and is narrated by a good-hearted *New York* magazine editor named Mark Jacobson who considers all those options I listed above, travelling around the world to find an answer, including a visit to Buchenwald. In a New Jersey spiritualist's parlor, in the dark, he is told by the medium that the lampshade is speaking, and that '. . . he trusts you. You're the only one he has now' (4). As a Gothic side-note to a postscript, we might remember that Albin Grau was held at Buchenwald, the man who produced the 1922 silent classic, *Nosferatu*.

delayed guilt, parental recklessness, desperate materialism and ill-gotten wealth, devil deals and moral buy-outs, murderously wicked estate or territory battles, and unwilling seductions? When the über figure of the Gothic—the vampire—has been reduced to a softhearted and mumbling boy, and quite capable of love, maybe even a purer love than our mortal kind (enter Edward Cullen), then we are in big trouble. We then have no great monster story but a little romance, and a shamefully abstinent one at that! What is to dread about friendly monsters? Sanitize the diseased Gothic with a purer love-story, about some queasy boy who sits at the edge of your bed at night to look at you, and all the meaningful and shocking stages of G-horror die. Killed off is the significance of sexual temptation and fall, grotesque revelations and unlost monsters, the fight for one's soul and for sanity, and the long effects of trauma and sorrow and unforgiven deaths. How cathartic may a Gothic story be, if it is afraid to get a little bloody and bone-crunchy?

Perhaps the best Gothic exists now to chill, make us fear, make others fear by doing a little haunting of our own, to scandalize, to anger, to titillate, to question, to cry, to make insane, to warn, to identify oppressors and trespassers, to provide omens, to show off the monsters, to arouse unspeakable hungers, to make us love to the point of madness and despair, or to make it seem as if the top of our heads have just fallen off. Or is reading the Gothic novel like watching someone blush, revealing in that involuntary response something duplicitous or secret in our midst, as it does in poet James Lasdun's perfectly slippery neo-Gothic novel, *The Horned Man* (2002)? Might this obsessive sub-genre, at its most terrifying, be doing all of the above to us? One grand collector of horrors and secrets—two key elements of the Gothic tale and novel—is London teratologist Stephen Jones, showcasing the monsters in *The Mammoth Book of Best New Horror* series now for over twenty years. Jones shows no sign of embracing 'horror lite' or 'pillowtop Gothic', and provides a needed corrective to the worrying trend the *Twilight* pall casts. The stories he chooses have dependably sharp claws and filed teeth—the antagonists have spikes which they may hide or not, the plots are dangerously unpredictable, and the streets and paths still seem potently and engagingly malevolent, enough to endanger any protagonist. One perfect original story of teetering, unexpected Gothic victimhood and intoxicating sensuality he debuted for another collection is Sarah Pinborough's "The Bohemian of the Arbat" (in *Summer Chills*, 2007), which re-shuffles the Gothic cards masterfully. This tense study of a young, privileged, experienced, and beautiful married woman's doomed visit to Russia, and the artistic monster of Moscow who refashions her, has become a cautionary favorite of mine and my Gothic fiction students, especially those who have ever considered modeling.

Naturally, much of what each reader gets from the Gothic depends on the culture he or she lives in, and how the Gothic reflects the trauma of our times. Right now, for a North American reader, the Gothic story seems almost a chronicle of what we are enduring—a sympathetic expression to the violent extremes, and the resulting rage and mourning and helplessness, at the abductions and ransoms, rapes, and executions near the U.S./Mexico border. My students now call Juarez, Mexico (just on the other side of El Paso, TX), the City of Missing Women, and they are not terribly surprised that its staggering violence has inspired a couple of video games. They and I wonder at the secrets behind the still unsolved slayings (and sometimes the torture and flaying) of 500 young women or *feminicidios*, whose bodies have resurfaced in the vacant lots and desert areas near Ciudad Juárez, which now has the highest murder rate in the world.[6] The psychological Gothic, that paranoid kind, the type that looks into the passion and pathology of power is invoked by such savage and unprosecuted crimes. And the classic Gothic distrust of authorities (which has been alive at least from Lewis's *The Monk* onwards) is reiterated by a recent United Nations investigation into the Juarez

---

[6] Dudley Althaus, "The Tortured Women of Mexico," *Houston Chronicle*, 19 April 2010, http://www.chron.com/ disp/story.mpl/world/6964669.html (accessed 2 April 2011). Moreover, Tim Padgett in "Day of the Dead" for *TIME*, 11 July 2011, describes Juarez's murder rate as 'more than 200 per 100,000 residents, which makes it the most dangerous city not just in Mexico but the world' (26).

murders of girls and women which highlighted the 'inefficiency, incompetency, indifference, insensitivity and negligence of the police who investigated these cases.'[7]An incapacity to properly investigate the crimes and to punish the guilty is one thing, but what's worse is the stinking Gothic suspicion of cover-up. This is a dread echoed in an American official's disturbing conclusion: that 'Chihuahua state police officers, the same public servants charged with solving the women's murders, were likely behind numerous rapes and killings.'[8]

True horrors came from 'Chihuahua state policemen ... [attending] sex parties [that] could have been initiation rites for soldiers and policemen into the ranks of organized crime.'[9] This according to renowned Philadelphia forensic artist Frank Bender, whom the FBI recommended to model victims' faces from skull pieces in Juarez. Gothic scandal seems truly alive in the world[10] with Bender's next comment, 'You got to prove yourself to work for these people, so they have these wild parties and [the authorities] rape and kill a woman and then earn their keep in the cartel.'[11] Bender's claims of snuff orgies enjoyed by Mexican police and soldiers alike do not stand alone. El Paso author Diana Washington Valdez and Mexico City writer Sergio Gonzalez Rodriguez have both reported independently the existence of such death-orgies in the past.[12] Eventually, the rattled Bender, subject of the memoir *The Girl With the Crooked Nose*, ended up sleeping with the recovered skulls of five murdered women at his room in Juarez's Hotel Lucerna. I imagine him trying to envision who they were, to get

---

[7] Althaus, "The Tortured Women of Mexico."

[8] Oread Daily, "Women Still Being Murdered in Juarez," The Juarez Project, 18 July 2008,http://www.thejuarezproject.com/ (accessed 2 April 2011).

[9] Daily, "Women Still Being Murdered in Juarez." See also Arlene Getz, "Forensic Sculptor Puts Face on the Dead," *Newsweek*, 16 June 2008.

[10] http://www.newsweek.com/2008/06/15/facing-the-dead.html (accessed 1 April 2011).

[11] The Gothic often cautions what a terrible thing it is in actual life to have complete dominion over another.

"Absolute freedom of the human creature," as Argentine author Alejandra Pizarnik warned in her historically inspired tale of Erzsébet Báthory's sacrifices of young women titled "The Bloody Countess", is "horrible." Alejandra Pizarnik, "The Bloody Countess," in The Oxford Book of Gothic Tales, ed. Chris Baldick, (Oxford: Oxford UP, 2009), 477.

[12] Daily, "Women Still Being Murdered in Juarez." See for much more detail the true-crime account of Frank Bender by Ted Botha, *The Girl with the Crooked Nose: A Tale of Murder, Obsession, and Forensic Artistry*, (New York: Random, 2008).

emotionally close to them, to know from these bone fragments something of the living women, who had families who loved them before the vanishing. Maybe he was trying to hear what the skulls had to say? Bender only confessed, 'I started imagining these women alive. They almost started interacting to me like they were on a metro together on their way to work in the morning. They started like getting a life of their own at that point'.[13] And now Mr Bender, whose intuitive face-reconstructions of three of these skulls led to identifications of the unknown victims, joins the ladies in whatever comes after. He died himself on August 25, 2011, as I wrote this preface.

When grinning skulls start getting 'a life of their own' for you, as can happen, open up Exotic Gothic 4 and read. It's what I do, and is a less crowded way of conjuring and communing with the dead than sharing a room with them nightly, and will make friends worry less. Through the following creeping Gothic narratives we can assume roles, enter the victim's consciousness, and often the victimizer's. We can experience emotional thirst and sexual hunger, nightmare and separation, violation and retribution, and then linger with all the desolate ghosts of the undead past, easily in the space of thirty minutes. Who can guess what ways these world authors coming from nine different countries and two Native nations will remake the Gothic? They are as a new generation of painters capturing moonlight, and something disturbing the moonlight, on a darker shore. Unto the last sentence, through all the black lies and ciphers of this loneliest fiction, we may still learn the truths of radical evil in the moonrise. Such truths may be what the beautiful skulls have been whispering to us all along.

---

[13] Daily, "Women Still Being Murdered in Juarez."

DANEL OLSON, *Editor (b. Brainerd, Minnesota, USA, 1965)*
dates his passion for Gothic conflicts, characters, and settings back
to a broken place of lost dreams and loster minds. It was where his
Mom, all in white, occasionally took him to as a little boy when
there was no one else to watch him—her employer, the Brainerd
State Hospital, a mental asylum now mostly in disuse. Through
slow winter mornings and longer summer afternoons, he waited
near the gigantic kitchen for her shift to end. A memorable babysit-
ter is the State. He remembers drawing and reading comics and
eating waffles with strawberries as he overheard patients' declara-
tions and conversations over the dining hall tables. Stories infer-
noed with fear and anguish, crying, long pauses, real demons,
movement disorders, shouts, but then inexplicable laughter were
the order of the day at the psychiatric hospital caf. And so close to
the madness of these committed strangers was the sweetness of his
Mother's love.

As evidenced by Exotic Gothic 4 *and in true Gothic style,*
Danel now finds himself compelled to reenact the past . . . he is
still learning the gory and melancholic details of the latest story,
and still collecting the uncanny, distraught, fevered tales for oth-
ers to this day.

Other fresh fiction anthologies Danel is exploring with North
American and European publishers include Nunleashed:
New Stories of Religious Orders vs. Ungodly Monsters; Reel
Moments: Original Dark Fiction Inspired by Movie Stills;
and MONSTERS? Famous Fiends Have Their Say in 25 New
Tales.

Film books Danel recently edited include The Exorcist: Stud-
ies in the Horror Film *(Centipede Press, 2012, 516 pages) and*
The Devil's Backbone and Pan's Labyrinth: Studies in the
Horror Film *(Centipede Press, 2013).*

A more formidable gathering of Gothic surprise and criticism
that Danel piloted was joined by eight brave writers from Exotic
Gothic 4, *to which he will ever be grateful—Brian Evenson,*
Tunku Halim, Robert Hood, Adam L G Nevill, Reggie Oliver, David
Punter, Steve Rasnic Tem, and Lucy Taylor. It is 21st Century

Gothic: Great Gothic Novels Since 2000 *(Scarecrow Press, 2011, 710 pages)*. *Prefaced by S. T. Joshi, and flexing fifty-three articles averaging 5000 words each, this beefy reference guide establishes a Gothic canon for the new millennium, touted by* Weird Fiction Terminus *as "an absolute must for university library collections".*

Commentary on the Exotic Gothic series: *In 2006, I floated a concept I created called* Exotic Gothic *to over seventy publishers around the world. It was an experiment in growing neo-Gothic stories: to keep one or more traditional tropes of the old genre in each new story, but add much that's culturally different, and set them all outside of their original birthlands of the UK, Germany, and France. Since then the series has had four volumes, the first three from Ash-Tree Press of Canada (which with regret was unable to produce the fourth due to unforeseen personal commitments and time constraints), and the current from England's PS Publishing (whose name to carry the series was suggested by many of the writers within this all-new collection).* Exotic Gothic 2 *was a Shirley Jackson Award Finalist, and* Exotic Gothic 3 *a Shirley Jackson and World Fantasy Award Finalist. Many of the series' harrowing and sensual tales now reappear the following year in* Best Of *and themed collections. PS presents an all-new* Exotic Gothic 5 *in 2013.*

My favorite of the four Exotic Gothic *titles? The one you're holding. Hats off to the imagiers herein! For news, reviews, interviews, and excerpts from this trademark literary venue for never-before-seen Gothic fiction, visit my sites exoticgothic.com or exoticgothic.org.*

EXOTIC GOTHIC 4

Remembering
CARLOS FUENTES
(11 November 1928 — 15 May 2012)

For your buried mirrors, Chac-Mools, burnt water,
Gothic doors, and *Aura*, this is your book.

Blooding the Bride

Margo Lanagan

L OVE BEGAN BETWEEN THEM. LORIANE WATCHED IT GROW, as perhaps her own child would grow one day. Before she met Lucas, she had resolved not to bear children; she must never subject another to the terrifying mysteries and abandonments of childhood. But now this resolution, along with others born of her old fears, dissolved and fell away. It was possible, suddenly, for children to be a joy—Lucas's children, her sons and daughters by Lucas. What a good father, what a good grandfather Lucas would make! He would barely change, with time. His dark curls would first frost and then whiten; his smile would mellow from its present earth-conquering brilliance; he would need stronger and stronger glasses, and would keep having to dip his head to look over them at people in that daffy way of his, ready to be charmed or touched. He would be one of those long, lean, smiling old men, stooping ever more kindly over his family and fellows.

He was the best thing ever to happen to her. She could pour out her most tangled and terrified self, and he would hold her hands and listen. Sometimes he would stop her, ask her questions, prompt her to consider other things she might have done, other positions she might have adopted towards the situation besides stoic endurance. She did not have to stay as she was, she began to think, holding herself together so tightly, always protecting herself. She might become more Lucas-like, and dance through adversity, or out of its path entirely. Hopefulness and calm flowered from him— other people straightened, and laughed in surprise, and took heart as hopefulness and calm passed into them. Might she not straighten too? Might she not laugh?

He stepped down from a paint-spattered ladder. He was spattered himself, from painting a cornice in the women's-and-children's house they were helping repair. Loriane had held the ladder steady and watched. His brushwork had been painstaking but efficient; leaf by leaf he had covered and brightened the old Victorian trim, flower by flower. Now and then a droplet of Egyptian Red, fine as a pin-prick, had fallen to her upturned face.

At the bottom of the ladder he put down his paint-tin and took her hands. 'Let's be married,' he said. 'Let's be husband and wife.'

'Yes, let's,' she said, with the calmness he had brought to her, and then she wept, and laughed as he held her, because it was too good to be true, and yet it *was* true. How could she possibly deserve such good fortune? She had done nothing, yet still it was given her.

She woke through a level of dream: wind poured past a rattling window, rain thrashed a metal roof. In the middle of the room a person, suspended in an excess of white cloth, swung slightly, cold in the coldness. Two white ribbons dangled from the woman's waist to the floor, brushing, pausing, brushing the other way.

Out of the weather-noise, Loriane surfaced. Birdsong lightly stitched the silence. The roof ticked and cracked, warming with the morning. She stirred; she was stiff all over. She had not moved all night on this unknown bed. Her heavy eyelids almost grated on her eyes. Her mouth was dry, dry, and lined with bitterness. The wedding champagne, last night—it had not been poured foaming from the jeroboam with the other glasses. It had appeared, tranquil, finely beaded and insistent, on a tray between herself and Lucas at the high table. That was the taste in her throat: not the wine itself, but whatever had been added to the wine. She had drunk it willingly, and been brought here insensible from the feast. By whom? And why? And where was Lucas?

She swung her feet down to the bare boards and stood. Her bridal gown rustled and settled about her. She smoothed the heavy cream silk of the skirt, but it would not make sense under her hands. She walked into the hall, and the gown and its petticoats slowed her, made her stately, like a queen stepping onto a balcony with a waiting crowd below. There was no crowd. There was no one. To her right the front door was ajar, and sunlit veranda-boards showed beyond; to her left the uncurtained windows made rectangles of sunlight against the wall, half paneled, half papered.

She took herself in her glowing gown deeper into the house, past other rooms like her own, past a branching hallway, past French doors behind which an empty ballroom opened out, to distant windows, tall and filled with clear sky. The hall widened beyond the ballroom, leading to a large kitchen. A big black range presided there, below a silver hood. Cupboards and empty dressers lined the walls, all finely filmed with dust, and a long table ran down the middle, perhaps twenty chairs pushed in closely around it.

She walked down the kitchen, opening cupboards as she went. All she found was a half-bottle of linseed oil, a rag beside it dried into the tortured shape of its last being wrung, and between two cupboards a straw broom worn almost to the stitching. An axe leaned beside the open door to the kitchen yard; a half-empty matchbox lay on a little shelf above it.

A basket sat on the table-end nearest door. Under the red gingham cloth she found a loaf of bread and a paper-wrapped cheese. She was hollow with hunger all at once; the rich wedding feast was long ago, and she remembered it with a bruised feeling under her ribs, as if she had not kept that food down. She tore the end off the loaf, pinched out some of the softer bread and put it to her lips.

But there was an odor to it, bitter, quite unbreadlike, familiar. She licked it with the very tip of her tongue, and held the taste in her mouth—then swiftly went out, and spat and spat into the pot of grey dirt beside the door step, where herb-plants for the kitchen must once have grown, or bright geraniums, perhaps.

The cheese under the cloth had the same odor. The bottle of cordial she did not even bother to unstopper. She crossed the yard to the rain-tank, the ground hot and hard, the dead grass sharp. She ran water into her cupped hand, tasted it, and let it fall, spat it out, her tongue and teeth coated with the taint.

Back she went and stood in the doorway. The food-that-was-not-food looked lovely, and her hunger would only grow until she ate that bread and cheese despite the taste, and her thirst would make her drink the cordial or the tankwater, not caring that it poisoned her.

Out to the toilet hut she carried basket and bottle. She dropped the loaf and the cheese into the pit, unstoppered the bottle and emptied it after them. Returning to the tank, she turned on the tap and let it run. Was that her very life, snaking darkly across the yard, flowing away under the house?

Seated on the kitchen step, Loriane pushed her skirts aside to examine her satiny wedding-slippers, to brush some little stones from the soles. The slippers were almost danced through, from only one night's use. She remembered the dancing; like one of those dowagers along the ballroom wall, she watched the memory of herself dancing. A whole little orchestra had played, just for her and her wedding-guests. The ceremony, the photographs, the meeting and conversing with Lucas's relatives, the speeches—she had been so grateful to have it all done with that remembering the dance-steps had been almost a pleasure, not the ordeal she'd feared.

And Lucas had been there, delighting in her, all proud smiles among his friends and family. His father Henry, almost as handsome as the groom, had danced a measure with Loriane, and made some remark about married life that she had not heard over the party. Even his grandfather, sprightly still at eighty, had waltzed her around the floor several times. *Ah, to be so young!* he had said, and she had laughed, because he had seemed so unencumbered by his age. *To be so fresh and beautiful!*

He had deposited Loriane beside his wife and gone to fetch champagne. *A lovely bride, having a lovely time!*—had there been an edge to the grandmother's exclamation? Loriane could not quite hear, through the memory of her own breathless laughter. She had searched the woman's face, the white hair coiffed stiffly above it, the bosom below upholstered in oyster silk, laden with pearls and silver. Beyond her, Lucas's mother Cordelia had stared fixedly at Loriane. It's only jealousy, Loriane had told herself. This is my night, and they have not had theirs in so long; it's making them sad, and perhaps a little sour.

But now . . . Loriane brushed the breadcrumbs from the table top into her hand and threw them out into the yard. Let birds eat them, and die of them. Let ants carry them away. Back down the house she went, her hems sweeping and her slippers crushing the dust and leaves blown in over the years. At every window she paused and gazed out, but always she walked on disappointed, for there was no life outside but untidy eucalypts and shrieking birds and wild grasses, and in the distance a blue line of ocean. No roof gleamed in the valleys; no livestock wandered the hills. And no road led out of this place, that she could see.

The veranda was thinly shaded, and scattered with leaves and twigs and seedpods. She walked the length of it kicking the rubbish aside so it would not hurt her feet. At the end she turned, and stopped. Far off among the folds of gold-grassed land lay a lake, quite broad, and it seemed not to be connected to the sea.

The tall grass crowded right up to the house. She stepped down into it and pushed towards the gate. The morning was still fresh— how different it was, to be outside! The skin of her face and arms came alive in the salt wind.

Unlatched, the gate swung a little way open, then was halted by the grass. Loriane sidled through. The house gazed out over her, to east and north, not at all prison-like or sinister, but only part of the uncaring landscape, which might contain her or might not; it did not signify either way.

The field brimmed with yellowed weed, the dry hair of the country sprouting and seeding. As it resisted her, as she pressed on through it, Lucas appeared in her mind, now smiling, now somber. She remembered him at a distance, waiting for her in the café, absorbed in a book, all coat and spectacles and lively hair. Her fingers—*these* fingers, so slender and white, still trembling from the drug—remembered the warmth under that hair, at the back of his neck. Lucas's hand could encompass hers entirely, warm and strong. She could lean against him with her hand gone into his and the voices that had plagued her all her life would fall blessedly silent.

Breaststroking through the grass, under the oblivious sky, she remembered his stride, the *life* in him, the decisiveness and the joy. His cares never seemed to oppress him as hers did her. How they had talked, long into the nights in lounges and tea-palaces, or walking the city streets, or back and forth around the bay; how they had turned the world over and looked at it from all sides, applying their small experience to it, their two bookish minds! Lucas had studied longer than she had; she laughed sometimes at his stuffy-academic turn of mind, but admired the cool intellect overlying his warm heart. She, though, had been more watchful of people, and knew they were not the rational creatures he supposed. Hatred and greed and rage drove their actions, as well as love and hope, and reason often ran a poor second to these grand and petty emotions. If Lucas calmed her, she enlivened him with her refusal to live entirely in the mind.

They were *married*, she remembered, with a shock. They were husband and wife. How had it been engineered, this separation, on the very night when their union ought to have been complete? Had Cordelia locked him up? Had she drugged him, too, with the other wineglassful? The poison still muffled Loriane's feelings, but when it eased this small flame of outrage sprouting within her would bloom and spread. It had fuel enough from events of the past twelve hours; just think how brightly it would burn, once she added her childhood's worth of fears and humiliations!

Parting two sheaves of grass, she found at her knee the simplest of grave markers, a round-topped tablet of sandstone. It bore no dates, but the letters of the name were so weathered that perhaps a century had passed since they were fresh-carved: ROSINDA.

'Rosinda.' Loriane's voice died among the weeds. Her dream came to mind, that cold girl hanging in the winter room, her white ribbons. 'Don't be *foolish!*' she told herself. She bent and laid a hand on the stone, seeking a solider truth than the dream. The grass bowed and whispered around her. Rosinda stayed mute below.

At last Loriane reached the lake. The water tasted purely of earth and sky. She crouched a long time at its muddy edge, her slippers and skirts gathered into her lap, patiently scooping up handful after handful of water, drinking herself back to sanity, cleansing herself of the wine that had weakened and stupefied her.

The beach was farther from the house than it looked; she reached a little hill perhaps halfway before admitting that she would not achieve it. Her legs ached from forcing the dress on through the grass. Casting longing looks ahead and unwilling ones behind, she stood a long time on that hill. The wind batted at her skirt and pushed her hair about. The sea bore slow lines of foam towards her across its creased blue surface, silent beyond the dunes.

The veranda boards stung with sunlight, a smooth relief after the cutting grasses and the sharp surprises of stones. So weary was Loriane, she leaned against the shady wall, then sank to sitting in a nest of skirt and petticoat folds. Her stomach chirruped with hunger; her bones felt aerated, like a bird's. Not a breath of breeze now stirred the heat.

She must have heard it without realizing, for she lifted and turned her head to listen harder. The sound had funneled down the hall, dissipating into room after room along the way, so that only the faintest remnants floated out the front door. She must hear several of them before she could fix on the source: somewhere at the back of the house, a girl wept broken-hearted.

Loriane sprang up. She ran in, along the smooth filthy boards of the hall, her slippered feet soundless, her petticoats and gown a frantic rustling.

She paused just past the ballroom, afraid she had made a

mistake, invented the weeping out of her own hunger and weariness. Her skirts stilled, and she breathed carefully.

A sob came. By the sound, the girl was seated on the kitchen step. By her muffled crying, her face was in her hands or pressed to her knees. Loriane stood poised to run and give aid, terrified of finding herself alone again.

And as she hesitated, a sphere of light eased through the closed French doors of the ballroom, like a great blurred, slowly rolling chandelier, wrapped thickly in bright gauze—sunlit, it seemed, although that was impossible at this noontime.

This bride—for the light was a glowing bridal gown, hooped and embroidered, pushed out of shape by the girl's being on her knees—this bride crawled slumpingly out the ballroom door, shoulder to the doorpost and head swaying low like a cow's. A silver comb was slipping from her hair, and curls dangled from her half-ruined coiffure.

The bride pulled herself upright up the doorpost, her slender frame burdened with the rich cloth and her head with the dressed hair. Her gaze slid up, her eyes clarified to a sort of seeing; her face was slack and bruised.

She did not acknowledge Loriane, but she took a step towards her. The arch of her bare foot was striped with blood. She took another step; her other foot was shod in a white wedding shoe, kitten heeled. Dark trickles from above had soaked into the satin upper, and spread there.

The girl on the kitchen step kept weeping, as though she voiced *this* bride's suffering, who was as yet too shocked and intent on escape to weep for herself.

'Rosinda?' Loriane's voice was breath only.

But the two spirits heard her nonetheless, and ceased instantly. Nothing remained of them but the echo of the sobbing, however real that was. Fear took Loriane low in her back, and washed upward, up her neck and over her scalp so hard and fast that she sank against the wall herself, searching the floor before her, the doorpost, for a trace of what she had just seen—a smudge of blood, a shining of eyes, a shadow of fine embroidery on the air.

Nothing. Silence.

Loriane pushed herself off the wall, strode forward, flung open the ball-room doors. Her grubby finery fussed and quieted around her. The room magnified her gasps, gasping back at her, making fun of her fear. The sprung boards spread wide to the paneled walls; above the dado was painted an elaborate structure of white and gold lattice crept-over with vines, against a ground of eggshell blue. In the far corner, above the orchestra platform, a huge, dusty mirror hung, in a frame of giltwood horns and flourishes.

She swung away to look for the weeping girl, but the distant door was empty of all but the blaze of the yard and outbuildings. Slowly Loriane walked up the kitchen to the sunlit stone step, hollowed with wear. Her chill feet took up its warmth, and the sunlight almost clashed, like cymbals, on her head and shoulders; her own pale dress blinded her. Still her spine felt cold, her limbs stiff. This dread-filled nothingness was worse than any sobbing, bleeding presence.

In the vast hot silence outside, hundreds of insects clicked and hopped in the grass. A flight of cockatoos screeched over the distant hills, invisible. Where was Lucas? She missed him. He would have made things right, her sweet strong man and hers alone, keeper of the secrets of her heart. All she could conjure of him in her mind was his profile, laughing at the wedding with that judge, with that judge's wife impeccably dressed in the pale green slubbed silk; he would not turn and look at Loriane. What did it matter where he was? He was not here. She stretched her cold arms out into the sun. The rings shone on her finger—the radiant-cut diamond, so much admired by the women of his family, and the new white-gold wedding band. They meant nothing when she was here alone in the deathly heat, in the empty house within the empty landscape, under a sky burnt clear of cloud or bird.

*L**et me apologise in advance for my parents,* Lucas had said to her in the taxi, the night streets flowing past them glamorous with rain. *Apologise?* She had smiled at him, only delighted to have him at her side. Even his discomfort made her smile. *Should I be afraid?* She had laughed.

He had squeezed her hand and looked away, at the window newly spangled with the upthrown water of another taxi's passing, at the bright gas-lit shop-windows and a hunched man running past them to shelter.

They're strange, stiff people, he said. He might have said more, but turning to meet her waiting gaze, something else struck him, and he kissed her instead, quickly, open-eyed.

I'm somewhat strange and stiff myself, she said.

You? He had sat back to see her better through his disbelief. *Quiet, perhaps. Self-contained. At most a little shy. But 'stiff' I would never call you.*

She was wearing the indigo satin gown. It was simple and well made; it held her closely but gently; it was exactly right for the occasion. She could not imagine being old, not having this shape, this posture, this excellent health.

But here they were, at the gates. The liveried gate-man admitted them, and in they drove, the gravel noising under the wheels like a wind. Up to the portico they swept, where other women, each a different-colored swathe of rich fabric, each uniquely bejeweled, were being handed from the cars' varying clouds of steam and smoke.

Loriane had floated into the splendid house. The interior was carefully lit, finely detailed, draped and polished and finished and trimmed and hung with trophies and artworks. Its soundscape was so orchestrated, from clink of crystal to chime of cultured laughter, that all she could do was listen in wonder; to add her own voice to the mix seemed impertinent. She found the other guests to be quite foreign creatures, their cares pitched so differently from her own that she could barely understand their conversation. She stayed close to Lucas all evening; with him near, perhaps she would not float utterly away on the strength of her own astonishment.

L ightheaded with hunger, Loriane idled back into the ballroom, rustledout into the middle of the wide shaded space, turned there,turned and turned until it felt as if she was the still point, with her slippered toes spinning the room around herself, a giant carousel flashing with window and mirror-light.

She slowed herself gradually out of the spin and, staggering a little, set off for the orchestra platform. There she stepped up, and across to the mirror. She was about to write *Lucas* with her finger in the dust—but the dust was already disturbed there, with more recent dust laid thickly over the disturbance. Gently she blew on the place. Out of the deepening hollows of the reflection grew a faint word, written by another maiden's finger: *Henry.*

She stepped back. The ballroom had not quite ceased to spin, and the name skated away, and away again, from under her gaze.

There is much to endure in a marriage, Cordelia had said in the parlor, to Loriane alone, on the day Lucas announced their engagement. *One must . . . enlarge one's sensibilities, to allow it to assume its proper shape.* Her eye had glinted at Loriane. *And there are rewards,* she had said, *for enduring what we must endure, as Greaves, as Greaves wives.*

It had been as if a painted portrait spoke, Cordelia sat so still, and so calculated was everything about her appearance: the cut of her jacket and skirt, the restraint of her jewels, the precision of her French-rolled hair. This was the woman who had sent her son away to boarding school when he was seven. She gave the impression of never blinking; she had all of Lucas's decisiveness, but exercised it much more grimly.

What is it, particularly, that we have to endure? What had Cordelia endured, Loriane wondered, to become so unblinking, unsmiling? *Any more than other wives do, I mean?* She was jittery in the aftermath of the announcement, unhappy being alone with Cordelia, Lucas's oldest enemy, and perhaps hers now, too.

Cordelia had met Loriane's gaze. For an instant her eyes had held something, someone, and Loriane had been able to imagine her youthful, and in love. Then . . . She had *shriveled,* was how it looked. She seemed to forget that Loriane was there, and her composure faltered. Her face was all bone, her mouth all doubt. And then she had drawn a long harsh breath as though to

counteract her own shrinking, and Loriane had watched her
reconstruct herself: realign her vertebrae, draw her unblinking
mask again across her feelings. She had not answered the question,
and Loriane had not had the courage to press the matter.

Henry, Cordelia had written with her maiden fingertip in this
mirror-dust, imprisoned here in her wedding finery just as Loriane
now was in hers. Behind the ghostly name, the ballroom opened
out reversed in the dulled glass, and the bride silhouetted against
it stood featureless and silent, hardly more than a ghost herself.

The walk to the lake was easy, dream-easy; the grasses parted for
her and the ground beneath was as flat and soft as carpeted
floor. She carried a fishing pole, the line plaited of her own hair,
with a hairpin hook and a scrap of cloth for bait. When she reached
the water she waded in to her knees, skirts and all, and she cast,
with what felt like a practiced movement, though in life she had
never done so before.

Immediately something took the bait. A song swelled on the
dream-water, weird and minor-keyed, of many voices. Loriane
wound the weight in calmly, quite as if she knew what she was
doing. Closer and closer it came, fighting and turning in the
water—its flank shone pale; its silver-lit tail flicked droplets.

But when it reached the shore, it was no live fish but an object
wrapped in wrinkled white cloth. *Oh good,* her dream-self thought.
I have so little here; I'm sure I can use this cloth for something. She
touched it, and it gave and rolled on the water, and the white
bodice turned uppermost, busily stitched and spangled to show
off the body it encased. The skin of the bosom and the dead neck
glowed no less white. The face looked to the rising sun, grey eyes
open, water running from the mouth and nose. Some of the sodden
black hair was still arranged as for a wedding; some spread
snakelike on the water.

Loriane crouched by the girl's head, the water wickedly,
dangerously cold against her chest. She whispered into her ear,
Tell me!

But the bride did not wake and turn, and her lips stayed cold, mauve and motionless. She lay like an upturned figurehead, curved over on the water, gazing out. Clouds crowded the greater part of the sky. The cold solidified around Loriane, the water pressing, prickling, as it froze. The song, a thick drone now of bass and baritone, built towards a shout.

Loriane woke shivering into the warm afternoon, into a strong sense of the house being occupied, the singers gathered in the ballroom, expecting her. She sat up so that she would not fall back into the dream. The heat pressed through the windowless western wall; her discarded petticoats lay by the bed as if fainted there. She stood and hurried out through rags of sleep, the song persisting in a prickling all over her skin, men's voices summoning her to some vital duty.

The knob of the French door was stiff, and its rattle broke through the voices, their grandeur and their urgency. By the time she had forced in, the ballroom was empty of all mood and remembered sound, a decorated silence, dusty, expecting nothing. She walked deeper in, testing the air. It was stronger towards the mirror, that smell, that burning as of incense, but with a darker danger ready to flare out from behind it. She stood wondering as it faded. She *must* have invented it along with the rest, for there was no flame, no charred wood, no incense smoke floating in the room, only dust in the sunbeams making their slow way across the dance floor.

She must find some occupation, to distract herself from the cramping of her empty stomach. She fetched the stub of broom, and began to sweep the orchestra platform. It was a small task, something achievable in this acreage of dirty floorboards. She dug the dust out where the skirting board met the floor, scoured it from each seam of the floorboards. She did not think, only absorbed herself in the task; while she worked, she could not be distressed. *Good girl!* said some past schoolmistress warmly in her memory. *Loriane has been most diligent,* Mr Bounder told the gathering in the office for her pre-wedding morning tea, *in seeing that our clients received the best-timed, most practical assistance.*

As she finished, the sun crept over the platform riser and shot a beam across the swept boards. Oh, it still looked terrible, so dry and dusty! She brought the linseed oil and the twisted rag from the kitchen cupboard; she managed to soften the rag somewhat with the oil and began to rub the boards. Immediately they rewarded her, darkening smooth red-gold. What kind of wood was this? She would like to think it was mahogany, some spicy tropical import. She bent herself to the task, eking out the little oil she had, and the sun lit and admired her work, her bringing life and color to the neglected boards. She forgot herself in her predicament, absorbed in visions of the sun-slanted mahogany forest, and the tiny figures of men come to bring down the wood, and the great machines with their pennants of steam, on their rails or tractor-belts or afloat on the ocean, that strove to bring the wood across the world to this house, to be laid down under the musicians' feet.

When she had it all a-shine, from the risers right to the skirting boards, the sun was almost gone from it, climbing away up the dusty paneling; most of her achievement lay glossy dark in the dimming room. She had sweated into the bodice of the wedding-gown; it was uncomfortable for such work. Her knees had made grey marks on the front of the skirt, crawling back and forth across the boards. Everything was darkening and dirtying again. Night was coming. Anxiously she watched the windows. There was nothing she could do to hold it back.

S he woke pinned down in the reddened darkness. The man-choir's drone slid and mounted and fell all around, without rhythm or any sense beside a building menace. The house was thronged with men; she *smelt* them, though she had never known that men had a particular smell before. Their robes dampened the sound, though it rampaged free along the high ceilings. A weird glitter afflicted the air, like flights of darts.

One man held her shoulders down; another, behind him and invisible, pressed her ankles to the bed. The closer man was tall, spindly and strong. His hair curled up like horns. His face was all points—nose, chin, ear-tips. His pale eyes were wide with rage. He was hot with it, aglow; his palms burned against her shoulders. Beyond his shoulder hung the bride from Loriane's dream, her wan ribbons wafting in the man's heat.

He lay upon Loriane and pressed his lips hotly to hers. This was not a kiss as she knew kisses. Her lips, flattened bloodless, made a poor barrier to his, to the horrors of the mouth behind them. She must breathe the man-sweat of him, the sharp smoke, if she were not to smother. She might have fainted from the smells, but she refused to; she would rather lie crushed here, clamped closed against him, aware of everything, her smarting eyes glaring into his own. He was no great size, but he was *heavy*, as if his bones were iron, or as if men pushed down on him from above.

'Why is she not ready?'

The closer men shifted in consternation; the others maintained the song.

He pushed himself back from her, but still his hipbones bore down on hers, and his member pressed against her pubis, held away only by the gown's silk, by the fine bridal underwear. He could burn those cloths away in an instant, she was sure. She pressed her thighs as tightly together as she could. 'Why are you not opened to me, virgin?'

'Opened?' Her voice was a mere whisper, her hands ineffectual against his chest. Her thighs hurt, she clasped them together so hard; he would have to burn his way through their flesh to reach her.

'I was promised this.' His spittle burned needle-holes in her cheek. 'I have kept my part of the bargain.'

'What bargain?' she said. 'I have promised you nothing!'

'You?' His laughter scorched her face, sucked away her breath. 'Girls make no bargains. Girls are the bargaining *pieces*, passed from one man to another.'

If only he didn't reek so, didn't push at her so alarmingly from below, she might have room to think beyond keeping from swooning.

Bargaining pieces? Things that are passed? With the last of her working mind she felt the little bud of her own flame, her own rage, struggle to blossom. Darkness was closing in; the expensive silk was beginning to char and tear.

'Girls are no such thing!' she managed to flutter out, before the breath was crushed out of her.

But he did not crush. The man-choir woke her with their shout of rage, and they were gone, and he was gone, that demon.

She flung herself from the bed, across the room, her back to the wall. They had trampled the petticoat flat; it smouldered by the bed. But she, Loriane, though she panted and sobbed out to all corners of the darkness, she was not flattened yet.

She could not stay in the house, though. And she hardly needed its shelter, with the sky so clear and the night so warm. She took up the blanket from the bed. Barefoot she fought away from the house, down the hill, stumbling and falling among the sheaves of grass. The gravestone rose before her, its ROSINDA barely visible in the starlight. She spread her blanket, pillowed her cheek on her hands, and there they lay, the two ragged brides, companioning each other in their different kinds of rest.

She listened to her heart awhile, pushing the memories from her mind. The stars' magnificence spread above her, each body working along its particular round so slowly that it seemed motionless, a seed-pearl sewn to midnight silk for no greater purpose than prettiness. The stars put that man, that demon-man, in his place with their beauty and their constancy, their distance from the house and their caring not a whit what happened in it, which girl strove against the beings there, or failed before them or triumphed over them.

And Rosinda below was a comfort too, her imagined warmth, which was Loriane's own warmth caught among the grasses, which was the warmth of the night. Which bride was Rosinda—the hanged one or the drowned one, the weeping one or the one with the bloodied feet? Was she yet another bride, even, not yet shown to Loriane? Whichever she was, she had done as she was bid; she had prepared the house, and eaten what she was given, and been *ready* when summoned.

Why are you not opened to me, virgin? While Loriane had clenched herself and blocked him, Rosinda, half-insensible, had been opened, had been robbed of the power to refuse.

And submitting to him had broken her, as surely as it would have broken Loriane. Rosinda had died, if not of the act itself, of the madness that followed. *One must enlarge one's sensibilities,* Cordelia had said, but Rosinda's and others' sensibilities had shattered instead, when they realised what was expected of them, or when they saw what the demon had taken against their will.

In return for what? All that money, Loriane supposed. Diamonds the size of small grapes on the betrotheds' fingers, pearls looping the necks and swaying on the silk bosoms of Greaves matrons; houses, motors, private airships, gyros, and the very best of schooling for their son.

She remembered the grandfather, his flirting, his sprightly step on the dance floor, his confident holding and spinning of her. Health, the Greaves men might receive, as well as wealth, in exchange for their wives' wedding nights. *Oh, he's charming, all right. Never be alone with him, though,* Lucas had warned her, *or leave a maid alone, especially a young one. Can't keep his hands off them. Loves to corrupt the innocent, that man.*

She wanted to console herself with thoughts of Lucas, but how much did he know of this? How far had he been warned? How knowingly had he led Loriane to this house, and left her here? He had told her—he had shown her—that he loved her, but she could no longer be sure of him. If such a gigantic deception had been practiced on her, how could he not be a party to it? She wanted him to be blameless, but her memory was alive now with seeming clues to his knowing, all along, of this house and the poison, of her coming exile and assault. When he had lifted his glass to her at the wedding feast, when he had slid the wedding band onto her finger—when, indeed, he had turned paint-spattered from the foot of the ladder, and taken her hands and asked her to be his wife—he might have known that he was delivering her into the demon's bed.

How many times had she mourned to him, *I was wrong to trust them, I was a fool*? How many times had he reassured her, *But your*

faith in people is a wonderful trait! I love your expecting the best of us!
Well, of course he did, she thought bitterly, too pained and appalled
by her own stupidity to weep. She had trusted again; she had been
a fool again. Her whole life had been a succession of gullings, and
now she had been gulled so far as to *marry* one of her tormenters,
to promise herself to him until death.

Exhaustion calmed her eventually. She slept well enough, under
the impassive stars, with Rosinda's warmth below. In the brief
coolness of dawn, she woke in her blanket-floored room, with its
breeze-rocked bleached-grass walls and its sky ceiling. For a
moment she was utterly ignorant of all that had gone before, and
then it crept back, piece by piece, and sickened and frightened her
again.

She knelt, then stood clear of the grass-heads. The house and its
evils squatted at the top of the hill. Her shoes, such shoes as she
had, were up there, but she would manage without them.

She turned and walked down to the muddy lake shore. There she
stumbled and stuck—dying, she thought, of hunger. She crouched
in the mud, and drank and drank of lake water.

When she was quite full, she walked on along the shore. A
pelican glided out of the distance towards her, a winged airship.
How would she hunt such a thing—knock it out of the air with a
stone? She snorted; she might as well attempt to fly herself.

The bird came slowly towards the water, changed direction
slightly, coasted down the air. Quite close to Loriane, it alighted
on the water, pulled a large fish from beneath, and lifted off with
it. But, perhaps because she was so unnervingly near, it had not
quite secured the fish in its beak-bag, and the silver thing tipped
and struggled free of the clamping beak. It fell not far from her,
and onto mud.

She ran and flung herself down onto mud and fish, hearing the
clap of the pelican's beak above her, and the sweep of its wings as
it flew away frightened. The fish bit and writhed and croaked
underneath her skirt-fabric; it stilled, and thrashed and stilled, and
again struggled. She waited. Near a quarter-hour it must have taken
to die, its throat all the while rasping on the unnatural air.

When, with caution, she rose from it, her dress was muddied and fish-slimed; the mud was all through her fingers, and some dangled in her hair like plumb-bobs. But the fish gaped there dismayed, a wondrous, generous thing, the iridescence dying on its flank. She would not starve yet.

She picked it up and climbed through the breeze and the sunshine back to the house. She took the axe and matches from the kitchen, and set and lit a fire in the brick-built fireplace out in the yard. Around about the hilltop under the trees, she found and fetched wind-fallen branches and let the fire feast awhile on those. She opened the fish as gently as she could with the axe-edge, scraped out what she could of the innards and flung them to hiss and shrivel on the fire.

She cooked the fish over the coals; it was almost cozy, sitting here waiting for her meal. The daylight bleached away the terrors of the night; the cook-fire burnt off the residue. The iron-boned demon, the broken brides, they were hunger-dreams, surely? The blood-stripes like a red comb down the girl's white instep, the man's pale eyes lit with outrage, the smell of him, strong sweat and fire— well, how vividly the imagination played, when a girl was alone and unfed! This she told herself for her own comfort, though she only had to glance down at her dress, the yellow singe-marks, the dark-brown burn on the skirt, to see her reassurances for the lies they were.

On the strength of the miracle fish, Loriane reached the sea. The long dunes were kind to her feet after the weed spikes and ridges and hidden stones of the fields. The morning sun lit every corner of the world, every sliding grain of it and every flying ocean-droplet, every bob of wave and rush of foam. The green and white sea was like a milling crowd. The gulls passed amiably by in flotillas on the waves, the cormorants hung out their ragged wings to dry, the pelicans cruised slowly overhead.

She would wander here, become a madwoman by the sea rather than a bargaining-piece up at the house. The seething water would rinse away the memory of the tin roof ticking, the dry boards cracking, the weird song of the demon's men, his stinging spittle, his burning weight.

And so she did stay, all of that day. Not knowing how safe the waves were, she did not swim, but only washed off the mud in a rock pool, and paced the wet sand, and let the waves do their hypnotic work.

She slept away several hours in the fields' pillows, lying along the shadow of a tree-trunk, moving as it moved. When she woke the sun was tipped over from the zenith, and she grew anxious even then, in the bare, bright near-noonday, at the knowledge that night would come again.

The afternoon heat stilled everything: the grass fainted every which way, the leaves hung still as chandelier-drops on the trees, the fence-posts laboured and leaned under their burden of wire. Four ravens came to the trees, and gave woeful cry, glossy feathered, fearless eyed, strong beaked.

The hot air began to beat; at first she thought her own heart was failing her somehow, but then an insect-movement above the house-hill caught her eye, and then her brain re-scaled and saw the insect for the helicopter it was, gleaming black, lowering towards the house.

She plunged into the grass and struggled up the hill. The thing whirled down—now she saw the gold crest on its door, like the one on the family's sleek black motors, and pressed into the thick paper of their stationery. The helicopter hovered—where it might rest on the soft slope? It settled, tipping very slightly, adjusting itself, emitting a white puff of steam, a black one of coal-and-petroleum exhaust.

Loriane was a field and a half away when the shining glass door split from the machine like a ladybird's wing casing. She stopped fighting forward. It wasn't Lucas who clambered down but Cordelia, dressed in a tailored suit as if for a morning walk. Another woman from the wedding (an aunt, was she?) climbed down behind her, outfitted more for bushwalking, in khaki men's clothes and proper walking boots. Yet another relative followed, in a trouser-skirt, holding onto her hat.

Loriane drew back, her snagged, stained skirt dragging in the weeds. They had seen her; they were plunging towards her. She had been a fool to hurry here expecting Lucas and rescue, and let herself be seen. She should have stayed down by the lake, hidden behind the trees, or sunk in the water among the reeds.

They came at her with ridiculous urgency. Behind them the pilot dropped neatly to the ground under the stilled rotor blades. He spared a glance at the three women wallowing away from him, before turning to attend to his machine.

'Stay right where you are, young lady,' cried the aunt at the fence, but Loriane was not going to make a double fool of herself by fleeing. A familiar resignation rose like sickness in her throat; she stood as tall and with as much dignity as she could muster. She had a wistful thought of the sea, its crests and birds and its caring-for-nothing; the lucky fish flashed through her mind, and the bird that had brought it; Lucas as she once had seen him, once had believed him, smiled on her out of the past. This was her own fault for trusting, for not being watchful enough. Lucas had seen her for the naïve she was, and swooped in to take advantage. It was only to be expected.

Then the women were at her, all breath and hands, grasping, manicured, middle-aged.

'Look at the state of you.'

'Up to the house.'

'What do you think you're doing, wandering about out here?'

The three of them together were easily strong enough to move Loriane. She hardly seemed to step; they forced her and her dress along and her feet did as they might below.

'Is Lucas here, then?' said an aunt, to the others.

'How could he be? There's no road in any more.'

Through the fence they organized her: 'You push her dress through.' 'Mind her hair, there.'

Loriane tried to resist at the veranda steps, but the three women forced her on. She had no resources left; she had used up all the strength her lucky fish had given her, and was weak again with hunger.

And they were prepared.

'Give it to her now. We can carry her the rest of the way. Or drag her.'

'No, get her inside, so Hans doesn't see.'

The front doorway drew closer, and reared over them. 'No, no!' Loriane cried out, not at what they might do, but only from fear of the evil spaces beyond the threshold.

'Oh, but *yes*.' They brought her inside in a rush, and pinned her to the wall. An aunt stabbed at her and something stung her neck. A coldness spread up into her head, down into her body, deadening, unfightable. She gave in to it for a moment, slumping in something like relief. She could *taste* the taint in her throat. Her legs struggled below, not yet overpowered, but they were far away and growing farther.

The two aunts took her arms over their shoulders. They carried her tottering down the hall. The drug swept through her mind, flattening everything; it dragged in her eyelids, her jaw, her flopping hands. She felt it hit her heart and rush outward from there. Her legs went, her eyelids sank closed, her toe-tips dragged across the floorboards.

The ballroom was cooler, its drafts more general and its echoes stronger. They laid her down in the smell of linseed oil, neatened her this way and that.

'What's she been *doing*, all this filth?'

'It doesn't matter, the clothes. He won't be concerned with that.'

'Did I give her too much, do you think? He'll want her at least *awake*.'

They struck her face, struck it again. Loriane tried to open her eyes, to protest with her sluggish mouth. Above her swam the mirror's dusty eye, with Cordelia moving vaguely in front of it, frowning down at her.

'Now what?' said an aunt.

'We hold her down. Until he comes.'

Her words darkened the air, softened the mirror. Even through her eyelids Loriane saw these things.

'Must we be here for—all of it?' said the other aunt.

'Pull yourself together, Tasma,' said Cordelia. 'You've been through this yourself. Just *watching* cannot hurt you.'

'Still . . . ' How fragile her voice was! It hardly registered, against the weight and danger spilling forth from the mirror. Unable to fear for herself, Loriane found a moment's pity for this woman, her relative by marriage. Poor fools, both of us, she thought, sentimental from the poison now a heavy syrup all through her. She was a bargaining-piece indeed—anyone, any beast, any demon, might treat her as they chose. *Girls make no bargains*—that was so true! Why had she not seen it before? How could she have thought she knew better than that thin man of iron, whose burning scent now began to tease her nostrils? And it was true not just for Greaves women but for all girls. If drugs did not keep them powerless, their men did, or people's readiness to laugh at their efforts, or their want of money or schooling. It was all so clear—

The floorboards rumbled. The darkness rushed out overhead. Loriane lay readied; the other women gazed out, lumped shadows against the larger storm assembling in the middle of the ballroom.

Within the onrush, figures took shape, at first in a golden mass with a single will, shot with red, then separating into bodies robed in gold and red, growing feet below, heads above. All men, they all sang—but their voices were barely audible in the squall of the demon's approach. Smoke swirled low above, lit with orange flashes, blotting out the ceiling's insipid decorations. Haloed with the flaming imprint of what he had shrunk from, naked but for a loincloth, his flesh bright red with compressed heat, great ram-horns curling about his fiery face, the demon strode down from the darkness between the walls of the choir.

She saw this clearly too, that his vastness must be sung down, sung earthly-sized, or the contact would kill these women, would kill any mortal. This made perfect sense to her in her stupor; the stupor, indeed, seemed more a gift than a punishment, the drug more a revelation than a poison. Of course she must yield; look at the power that desired her! She could see why the women had come, why they were enforcing this; this was an honor, perhaps the greatest honor that could ever be bestowed on a woman. They had undergone it and found glory; they wanted only for Loriane to be glorified too, to belong among them, this very particular family. And to *keep* her with them, for she would not be one of those girls who died of being so elevated; she would be cold like Cordelia, and endure, and thrive in all the ways it would still be possible for her to thrive, after this ceremony, this immolation, this gift.

Then he was too close for her to do more than observe him. His priests either side presented him, arms raised and mouths open in song. The Greaves women fell together, caught between groveling and reaching for him.

He descended towards her. His glossy horns glowed against the storm. Between them his face was a gargoyle's, his tongue like turning lava in his open mouth, his eyes wide, with irises of gold, centred with red pinholes expressive of nothing but the flame suppressed within him. Loriane's body lay soft and lax as it should. As his heat pressed down, she saw how her stupefaction gave him ingress into her mind, allowed him to manifest there with greater truth and vigour. Before, he had been not much more than a man; now, he was clearly not much less than a god, momentarily compacted into passably earthly form. And he had belittled himself purposely to possess Loriane, to take from Lucas the gift that could be given only once, and from Loriane herself the choice of giving it. Why should such a small thing occupy the mind and intentions of such a creature? And yet it did, and it had come to this: he would invade her, a god inside a woman. It should never be, yet here it was. He would put *that* inside her—for the loincloth had gone, and against the darkness the sex of him glowed red, and smoked, and flamelets ran along it from root to tip.

In her swoon, she felt the women move her skirt about. They drew her legs apart, and the demon's heat radiated down on her. She could not throw the women off, or resist him, or move in any way of her own volition, and she no longer wished to. All was as it should be; let him lay waste to her, let him burn her entirely away.

But a body—heavy, clumsy, not divine—flung itself on her. With a crude, blunt, unflaming voice, this man cried protest into Loriane's neck. The demon hesitated, blurring and reconstituting himself, glaring down on this being interposed between himself and his goal. The women shrieked and tore at Lucas, but he turned over, and fought them away. Each kick and punch drove him bruisingly back against Loriane, forcing air from her lungs. She gasped for the next breath automatically, too bargained-away to feel afraid.

Lucas lay on top of her, facing upward. His hair annoyed her nostrils; she managed to roll her stone head aside. He proclaimed, and his voice sounded in the back of his skull as a series of muffled booms, while through the floor she could make out his tone—firm, calm, and without a trace of anger—over the faltering chorus and the fading roar of fire and wind. Through the eye not obscured by Lucas-curls she saw Cordelia and an aunt, thrown back against the ballroom paneling and clutching each other. Cordelia's eye was swollen and purpling, and blood ran down her cheek. Her face showed no distress beyond its ashen cast, but the aunt emoted for her, her mouth distorting from teeth-bared rage to a gape of despair.

Lucas rolled off, lay beside Loriane, put an arm and a leg over her and held her tightly.

The demon commenced departing; his true self poured aflame out the back of the compressed version he had assembled for the visit. The tall windows rattled with his going; the house quaked, the choir's song roared on, but the fire that was the demon streamed up, and the red-streaked golden robes followed, melting together, and the smoke-storm took them into its dark fist then folded that fist away and away, along its curved arm, back into the mirror. The breach repaired itself, blinked back the mirror's hardness and dust-muted shine, restored the real world's ceiling, white and gold lattice crept-over with vines, on a ground of eggshell blue.

A woman's voice clamored; another wept; ballroom-sized echoes rang around them, and never had a ballroom seemed such a small space, so hut-like and constricted. Cordelia spoke bitterly, and Lucas levelly answered. Loriane neither understood nor cared what they said; she had seen a god today, and the affairs of men and their mothers distressed her not at all; she was reluctant to admit that they concerned her at all, that she would have to return to them. She curled up, let go the world and abandoned herself to the task of working the poison from her system.

One other moment only did her memory ever keep from that time, billowing open around her. It smelled sweetly of grass, and sharply of Lucas, who cradled her, and earthily of the horse that rocked them downhill from the house of the brides, while the three Greaves women beat away through the air above.

MARGO LANAGAN *(b. Newcastle, Australia, 1960) is the author of the dark fantasy novels* Tender Morsels *and* The Brides of Rollrock Island *and four collections of short stories. Four times a winner of the World Fantasy Award, she has also been twice shortlisted for the Shirley Jackson Award, and once for the Bram Stoker. Margo lives in Sydney, Australia.*

Commentary on "Blooding the Bride"*: I imagined the story as taking place at Lake Tyers on the coast of eastern Victoria in Australia. It refers to the popular belief in* Ius primae noctis, *a medieval law under which 'the lord of the ground shall have the maidenhead of all virgins dwelling on the same.'*

PIG THING

ADAM L. G. NEVILL

DARKNESS THEY COULD TASTE AND SMELL AND FEEL CAME inside the house. Peaty and dewy with wet fern, it came in damp and cool as the black earth shielded by the canopy of the mighty Kauri trees, as if rising upwards from the land, rather than descending from a sinking sun. The branches in the forest surrounding the bungalow became skeletal at dusk, before these silhouettes also vanished into the black of a moonless country night. Had they still been living in England, it would have been an evening when bonfires were lit. And to the three children, although these nights were frightening, they had a tinge of enchantment in them too, and were never that bad when their parents were inside the house. But tonight, neither their mother nor father had returned from the long garden which the enclosing wilderness of bush tried to reclaim.

Dad had ventured out first, to try and get the car started in a hurry, shortly after nine o'clock. Twenty minutes later, her face long with worry, Mom had gone outside to find him and they had not heard or seen her since.

Before their mom and dad left the house the three children remembered seeing similar expressions on their parents' faces: when Mom's younger sister caught cancer and when Dad's work closed down, just before they all travelled out to New Zealand in the big ship for a fresh start on the day after the Queen's Silver Jubilee. Tonight their parents had done their best to hide their expressions. But the two brothers, Jack who was nine, and Hector who was ten, knew the family was in trouble.

Together with Lozzy, their four year old sister, Jack and Hector sat in the laundry room of the bungalow with the door shut; where Mom had told them to stay just before she went outside to find their father.

Jack and Lozzy sat with their backs against the freezer. Hector sat closest to the door by the bottles and buckets that Dad used for his home-made wine. They had been in the laundry for so long now, they could no longer smell the detergent and cloves. Only in Lozzy's eyes was there still some assurance of this situation becoming an adventure with a happy ending, and them all being back together again. They were large brown eyes, still capable of awe when she was told a story. And these eyes now searched Jack's face. Sandwiched between his sister's vulnerability and the innocence that he could still recognise in himself, and his older brother's courage that he admired and tried to copy, Jack found it his task to stop Lozzy crying.

'What dya reckon, Hector?' Jack said, as he peered at his brother while trying to stop the quiver on his bottom lip.

Hector's face was white. 'We were told to stay here. They are coming back.'

Both Jack and Lozzy felt better for hearing him say that, although the younger brother soon suspected the elder would always refuse to believe their Mom and Dad were not coming back. Like Dad, Hector could deny things, but Jack was more like his Mom and by making their voices go soft he and Mom would sometimes get Dad and Hector to listen.

But no matter how determined anyone's voice had been earlier that evening, their Dad could not be persuaded to stay inside the house, and had always rubbished their stories about the bush not being right; about there being something living in it, about them seeing something peer in through the windows of the two end bedrooms of the bungalow overlooking the garden and deserted chicken coup. When their dog, Schnapps, disappeared, he said they were all 'soft' and still needed to 'acclimatise' to the new country. And even when all the chickens vanished one night and only a few feathers and a single yellow foot were left behind in the morning, he still didn't believe them. But now he did, because he had seen it too. Tonight, the whole family had seen it, together.

For months now, the children had been calling it *the pig thing*: Lozzy's name for the face at the windows. She saw it first when playing with Schnapps at the bottom of the garden, in the dank shadows where the orchard stopped and the wall of silver ferns and flax began. *It* had suddenly reared up between the dinosaur legs of two Kauri trees. Never had her mother heard Lozzy make such a fuss: 'Oh Jesus, Bill. I thought she was being murdered,' she had said to their Dad, once Lozzy had been taken inside the house and quieted. Up on the hill, east of the bungalow, even the boys, who were putting a better roof on their den, had heard their sister's cries. Frantic with excitement and fear, they had run home, each carrying a spear made from a bamboo beanpole. That was the day the idea of the pig thing came into their lives. And it had returned. It was no longer a children's story.

But this was the worst visit, because earlier that evening, as they all sat in the lounge watching television, it had come right on to the sundeck and stood by the barbecue filled with rainwater to look through the glass of the sliding doors, like it was no longer afraid of their Dad. They could tell, because the pig thing had come out of the darkness beyond their brightly lit windows and momentarily reared up on its bony hind legs to display itself, before dropping and quickly moving back into the shadows of the Ponga trees at the side of their property. It could not have been on the deck for more than two seconds, which had stretched into an unbearable and unbreathable time for Jack, but the power in its thin limbs and the human intelligence in its eyes glimpsed through the glass, frightened him more than coming across one of the longfin eels in the creeks would ever have done.

'Don't. Oh, Bill don't. Let's go together, Bill, with the torch,' their Mom said to their Dad, once he decided to get the car started.

They were so far from Auckland that had either of the police officers based at the nearest station been available that evening, it would have taken them over an hour to reach the bungalow. Their dad had told their mother what the police operator had told him, after he called them and reported an 'intruder', some kind of 'large animal or something' trying to get into their house. He couldn't bring himself to say *pig thing* to the operator, though that's what it had been. Lozzy had described it perfectly. Maybe it took a four year old to *see* it properly. It wasn't quite an animal, and was certainly not human, but seemed to have the most dangerous qualities of each in that moment it rose out of darkness, bumped the glass, and then vanished. But the two police officers had been called away to a big fight between rival chapters of bikers on the distant outskirts of the city. With *it* so close and eager to get inside with his family, because it had looked terribly keen on achieving just that, waiting was not an option even entertained by their father, or open to discussion, after he hung up the phone.

Their nearest neighbours, the Pitchfords, lived on their farm two miles away and hadn't answered their phone when the children's dad called them. They were old and had lived in the national reserve since they were both children; had spent the best part of seven decades within the vast cool depths of the bush, before much of the area was cleared for the new migrants. Mr Pitchford even had hunting rifles as old as the Great War; he'd once shown Jack and Hector, and even let them hold the heavy cumbersome guns that stank of oil.

After the children's father ended the call, he and their mother had exchanged a look that communicated to Jack the suspicion that the pig thing had already been to visit their neighbours.

Going cold and shuddering all over, Jack believed he might even faint with fear. And all that kept appearing in his mind was the vision of the creature's long torso pressed against the window, so it's little brownish teats in the black doggish hair on its belly squished like baby's fingers on the other side of the glass. The trottery hands had merely touched the pane briefly, but that was sufficient to make it shake in the doorframe. There was nothing inside the house, not a door or piece of furniture, that could be used as a barricade. He knew it. Jack could imagine the splintering of wood and the shattering of glass, followed by his sister's whimpers, his Dad shouting and his mom's screams, as *it* came grunting with hunger and squealing with excitement into their home. He had groaned to himself and kept his eyes shut for a while after the thing disappeared back into the lightless trees. Tried to banish the image of that snouty face and the thin girlish hair that fell about its leathery shoulders.

And then their mother had said, 'Bill, *please*. Please don't go outside.' The children knew their Mom had put her hand on their Dad's elbow as she said this. They didn't see her do it because, by that time, they had been herded into the laundry room where they had stayed ever since, but they could tell by her voice that she had touched his arm.

'Ssh. Jan. Just ssh now. Stay with the kids,' their Dad had said to their mom, but once he was outside no one heard the car engine start. The Morris Marina was parked at the bottom of the drive, under the Wattle tree where Hector once found a funny-looking bone that must have come from a cow. And they had heard nothing more of Dad since he went out to the car.

The sudden gravity introduced into their evening had increased with every passing minute as a stillness inside the house, a heaviness that made them all aware of the ticking of the clock in the hall; it was the very thickening of suspense around their bodies.

Their Mother eventually opened the laundry door to report to the kids. She was trying to smile but her lips were too tight. On her cheeks were the red lines made by her fingers when she held her face in her hands. Sometimes she did that at night, sitting alone at the kitchen table. She did it a lot when Dad was out looking for Schnapps, day after day. And Mom had never liked the new house in Muriwai or the surrounding countryside. Didn't like the whistles and shrieks of the birds, the yelps in the night that sounded like frightened children, the animal tracks in the soil beneath her washing line that spun around in the fierce winds, the fat five-foot eel they had seen by the creek with a lamb in its mouth, the large sticky red flowers that nodded at you as you walked past, the missing dog or the stolen chickens . . . Mom didn't like any of it. Mom doubted she could ever become a Kiwi. She came here for their Dad; they knew that. And now she was missing too.

Holding Lozzy's Wonder Woman torch, because their Dad had taken the big rubber flashlight from the kitchen drawer where the matches were kept, they had heard their mother calling, 'Bill. Bill. *Bill!*' in a voice with a tremble in it, as well as something else trying to smother the tremble, as she went out the front door and then walked past the side of the house toward the garden and the car. Her voice had gone faint and then stopped.

And the fact that both of their parents had vanished without a fuss—no shout, or cry, or scuffle had been heard from outside—first made the two boys hopeful with the possibility that their mom and dad would soon come back. But as the silence lengthened it made their hearts busy with a mute dread that whatever had taken them was so quick and silent, you never had a chance. Not a hope out there in the dark with *it*.

Lozzy had sobbed herself into a weary silence after seeing the pig thing on the sundeck, and had then begun whimpering after her mother's departure. For the moment, she had been placated by each of her older brother's reassurances, their lies, and their brave faces. But her silence would not last for long. Lozzy stood up. She was wearing pyjamas. They were yellow and had pictures of Piglet and Winnie the Pooh printed on the cotton. Her hair was tousled and her feet were grubby with dust. Her slippers were still in the lounge; Mom had taken them off earlier to remove a splinter from her foot with the tweezers from the sewing box. Although the soles of the children's feet were getting harder, from running around barefoot all day outside, the children still picked up prickles from the lawn and splinters from the sundeck. 'Where's Mummy, boys?'

Immediately, Jack patted the floor next to him. 'Ssh, Lozzy. Come and sit down.'

Frowning, she pushed her stomach out. 'No.'

'I'll get you a Tip Top from the freeze.'

Lozzy sat down. The freezer hummed and its lemon glow emitted a vague sense of reassurance when Jack opened the lid. Hector approved of the ice-cream trick. After a deep breath, Hector looked at Jack and then returned his stare to the laundry door. He sat with his chin resting on his knee and both hands gripping the ankle of that leg, listening.

Committed of face, Lozzy tucked into the cone, loaded with Neapolitan ice-cream.

Jack shuffled up beside Hector. 'What dya reckon?' He used the same tone of voice before he and his brother crossed a waterfall in the creek, or explored the dark reeking caves up in the hills that Mr Pitchford had told them to 'steer clear of, lads', or shinned across a tree fallen over a deep gorge in the piny vastness of bush surrounding their house. The forest stretched all the way to the crazy beaches made from black volcanic sand, where the blowholes and riptides prevented them from swimming.

Hector had no answer for his brother about what to do now that he, the eldest, was in charge. But Hector was thinking hard. His eyes were a bit wild and watery too, so Jack knew he was about to *do* something. And that frightened him. Already, he imagined himself holding Lozzy when there were only the two of them left inside the laundry room.

'I'm gonna run to the Pitchfords,' Hector said.

'But it's dark.'

'I know the way.'

'But . . . ' They looked at each other and swallowed. Even though Jack hadn't mentioned the pig thing, they had thought of it at the same time.

Hector stood up, but looked smaller than usual to Jack.

Peering between his knees, Jack kept his face lowered until the creases disappeared from the side of his mouth and around his eyes. He couldn't let Lozzy see him cry.

Before his brother left the laundry room and then the house too, Jack longed to hold him for while but couldn't do it and Hector wouldn't want it anyway; it would make his leaving even harder. Instead, Jack just stared at his own flat toes spread on the lino.

'Where's Hegder going?' Lozzy asked, just as a bubble popped on her shiny lips.

Jack swallowed. 'To get the Pitchfords.'

'They have a cat,' she said.

Jack nodded. 'That's right.' But Jack knew where Hector would have to go first before he even got close to the Pitchfords' place: he was going into the forest with the clacking branches and ocean sounds when the wind blew; along the paths of damp earth and slippery tree roots, exposed like bones, that they had run and mapped together; over the thin creek with the rowing boat smells; across the field of long grass, that was darker than English grass and always felt wet, where they had found two whole sheep skeletons and brought them home in a wheel barrow to reassemble on the front lawn. Hector was going to run a long way through the lightless night until he reached the Pitchfords' house with the high fence and the horseshoes fixed around the gate. 'To keep things out,' Mrs Pitchford had once told them in a quiet voice when Hector asked why it was nailed to the dark planks.

'No. Don't. No,' Jack hissy-whispered, unable to hold back when Hector turned the door handle.

On the cusp of his brother's departure, that Jack knew he could do nothing about, everything went thick and cold inside his chest. Welling up to the back of his throat, this feeling spilled into his mouth. It tasted of rain. And this time, he couldn't swallow. Inside Jack's head was the urgency of desperate prayers trying to find words. He squinted his eyes to try and push the thoughts down, to squash them down like he was forcing the lid back on a tin of paint. Did anything to stop the hysterics he could feel storming up through his entire body.

'Got to,' Hector said, his face all stiff but still wild-looking.

Lozzy stood up and tried to follow Hector, but Jack snatched her hand and gripped it too hard. She winced, then stamped, was tearing up again.

'Jack, don't open the door after I'm gone. OK.' They were Hector's final words.

The laundry door clicked shut behind him. They heard his feet patter across the floorboards of the hall. Then they heard him turn the catch on the front door. When that closed too, the wind chimes clinked together and made an inappropriate spacey sound. There was a brief creak from the bottom step of the porch stairs, and then the silence returned for a while, until Lozzy's sobs made an unwelcome return inside the laundry room.

After comforting her with a second ice-cream cone, Jack unplugged the freezer. Quickly but carefully, so as to make less noise, he removed the rustly bags of frozen peas, steaks, stewed apple and fish fingers. He put the food in the big laundry sink that smelled like the back of Gran's house in England. Then he stacked the white baskets from inside the freezer against the side of the sink. Around the rim of the freezer cabinet he placed plastic clothes pegs at intervals, so there would be a gap between the grey rubber seal of the freezer lid and the base. Then they wouldn't run out of air when he shut them both inside.

'Come on, Lozzy,' he said, hearing some of his Mom in his voice. And he felt a bit better for doing something other than just waiting. He picked Lozzy up and lowered her into the freezer. Together, they spread Schnapps's old blanket over the wet floor of the cabinet so they wouldn't get cold bottoms and feet.

'This smells. His fur is on it. Look.' She held up a tuft of the brown fur the dog used to get stuck between his claws after riffing his neck. Their Mom and Dad had been unable to throw the dog's blanket away, in case he ever came back to lie on it. So the blanket had stayed in the laundry where Schnapps had ended up sleeping at night. Their Dad's idea of dogs sleeping outside became a bad idea after Schnapps began all that barking, whimpering, and finally scratching at the front door every night. 'He's soft,' their Dad had said. But tonight, it all made sense.

After handing the tub of ice-cream and the box of cones to Lozzy, Jack climbed into the freezer and sat beside her. She reached for his hand with her sticky fingers. As he pulled the lid down over their huddled bodies, he secretly hoped that the cold and wet of the freezer would stop the pig thing from smelling them. He also wondered if those trotter things on the end of its front legs would be able to push the lid up when it stood up on those hairy back legs, like it had done out on the sundeck. But he also took another small comfort into the dark with him: the pig thing had never come inside their house. Not yet, anyway.

M rs Pitchford entered the house through the empty aluminium frame of the ranch-sliding door; the glass had been smashed inwards and collected in the mess of curtains that had also been torn down. She favoured net curtains behind all the windows of her own home; she didn't like the sense of exposure that the large windows gave to the new homes the government had started delivering on truckbeds for the migrants, who were settling all over the area. She also found it hard to even look at the red earth exposed beneath any more felled trees and cleared bush. The appearance of these long rectangular bungalows with tin cladding on their walls never failed to choke her with fury and grief no good for her heart. And who could now say what kind of eyes would be drawn in to these great glassy doors if you didn't use nets? *You couldn't then go blaming them who was already here.*

All of the lights were still on. It felt warm inside the house too, even though the cold and damp of the night air must have been seeping into the living room for at least an hour after that big pane of glass was put through.

She looked at the brown carpets and the orange fabric on the furniture, was amazed again with what the English did with their homes; all Formica and white plastic and patterned carpets and big garish swirls in wallpaper the colour of coffee. Shiny, new, fragile: she didn't care for it. They had a television too and a new radio, coloured silver and black: both made in Japan. They mesmerised her, the things these soft-muscled, pale-skinned Poms brought from such faraway places and surrounded themselves with; but anyone could see they and their things didn't fit with the old bush. It had ways that not even the Maoris liked, because there were *things* here before them too.

Glass crunched under her boots as she made her way further

inside the house. The kitchen and dining room were open-plan, only divided from the living room by the rear of the sofa.

Unable to resist the lure of the kitchen area, she went inside and stared, then touched the extractor fan over the stove. It was like a big hopper on a petrol lawnmower, for collecting cut grass. She marvelled again at what young mothers considered necessary in the running of a household these days. And here was the food mixer Jan had once showed her. Orange and white plastic with *Kenwood Chevette* printed along one side. A silver coffee pot with a wooden handle; what Jan had called a 'percolator', beside the casserole dishes with their pretty orange flower patterns. Mrs Pitchford ran her hard fingers across the smooth sides of all the Tupperware boxes that Jan had lined up on the counter; they were filled with cereal, rice, something called spaghetti, bran, sugar. You could see the contents as murky shadows through the sides. Everything in her own home was wood, pottery, steel, or iron. And she remembered seeing it all in use when she was a little girl and helped her mother prepare food. Hardwoods and metals lasted. Whereas plastic and carpet and 'stereos' hadn't been much use to this family tonight, had they?

The sound of the car engine idling outside returned a sense of purpose to her; her Harold had told her not to get distracted. She turned and waddled out of the kitchen, but her eyes were pulled to the sideboard beside the dining table; at all of the silver and ceramic trinkets kept behind its sliding glass doors. Little sherry glasses. Small mugs with ruddy faces on the front. China thimbles. Teaspoons with patterns on their handles. She had her own things for special occasions; all a lot older than these things the family had brought with them from England.

They also had a washing machine in the little laundry room beside the 'dining area', and a freezer too. Jan had been horrified to learn that Mrs Pitchford still washed clothes in a tin bath, used a larder for food, and still preserved things in jars. *The bloody cheek.*

Mrs Pitchford went inside the laundry room; it smelled of wine, soap powder, and urine. All of the food from the freezer was melting and softening inside the sink. The lid of the freezer was raised and there was an old blanket inside the white metal cabinet that hummed softly. It was still cold inside when she leaned over. And it puzzled her why the food was stacked in the sink, and also how the food inside the plastic bags and paper boxes was even prepared. They had no mutton, no venison, no sweet potatoes that she could see. She looked under her foot and saw that she was standing on a yellow plastic clothes peg.

Inside the unlit hallway that led down to the four bedrooms, she paused for a few moments to get her eyes used to the darkness. It was a relief to be out of the bright living area, but she would need more light to conduct a proper search. Ordinarily, she could have found a sewing pin on the floor by the thinnest moonlight, because around here there were plenty who could see better at night than others. But tonight there was no moon or starlight at all and the curtains in the bedrooms were drawn; it would be terrible if she missed something important. She found the light switch for the hallway.

The family had no rugs; they had laid carpet all the way down the passage and even inside the bedrooms. How did Jan get the dust out of them, or air them in the Spring like she did with her rugs?

Shaking her head in disapproval, she went into the first room. Jan and Bill's room. Two suitcases were open on the large bed and full of clothes. The headboard was softened with padded white plastic. Mrs Pitchford reached out and pressed it.

The next room was for the little girl with all of that lovely thick raven hair. Dear little Charlotte. The light from the hall revealed the dim outlines of her dolls and toys, the books on all of the shelves, the bears in the wallpaper pattern. 'Darlin',' she said, quietly, into the darkness. No answer. Some of the teddy bears and stuffed rabbits were on the floor; they had been pulled off the shelves. Mrs Pitchford had a hunch a few would be missing too.

She carried on, down the passageway to the two end bedrooms: Jack and Hector's rooms. Hector was safe at their home. How he had managed to scuttle all the way to their farm in the dark had surprised her and her husband. But little Hector had come and banged on their door, then fallen inside, panting and as pale as a sheet. She and Harold hadn't wasted a moment and had swept him into their arms, before spiriting him across the yard to Harold's workshop.

'That kid was as slippery as an eel and quick as a fox,' Harold had said, his eyes smiling, as he came back into the kitchen from his workshop, and removed his sheep shearing gloves and leather apron before getting their coats off the pegs. 'Come on, mother. Better get our skates on.'

And Hector had been so concerned for his younger brother and his sister when he arrived at their farm, that she and Harold had sped to the bungalow in the old black Rover that someone else had also once brought over from England. Harold had taught himself to drive the car, not long after acquiring it from an elderly couple with those Pommy accents that miss the *H* in every word.

Harold would dress Hector when they returned with the other two children, if they were still around. That didn't seem likely now to Mrs Pitchford. The family's bungalow was deserted then, like all of those bungalows on Rangatera Road, waiting for other Pom families, or Pacific Islanders, or even more of those bloody Dutch Dike-Duckies. Poles were supposed to be coming too. *What next?*

The two end bedrooms were empty of life, but she smelled what all life leaves behind. Then she found it on the floor of one of the boy's rooms overlooking the wattle tree. Kneeling down, she tried to scoop it into her salt-white handkerchief. It was ruddy in colour and smelled strong; the fresh stool of excitement, the stool of too much fresh blood gulped down by a very greedy girl. There was too much of it.

She stripped a pillow case off the bed. 'You've been at it here, my little joker,' Mrs Pitchford said with a rueful smile. *She* must have hunted right through the house until she'd found the other two kiddiewinks hiding; under the beds maybe, or in that hardboard wardrobe with the sliding doors on the little plastic runners. 'What a rumble you've had my girl.' This kind of house couldn't possibly make a family feel safe; it was like cardboard covered in thin tin. *She'd* at least had the sense to take Jack and little Charlotte outside the house first, like Harold had shown her how to do. Otherwise, they'd have to burn out another of these bungalows to incinerate the leavings, and that was always a flamin' mess. 'One more and it'll smell funny,' Harold had warned after the last one they lit up.

Mrs Pitchford went back to the laundry room and found a scrubbing brush, detergent, and a bucket. She filled the bucket with hot water from the tap in the laundry, then went back to the boy's room and scrubbed the rest of the muck out of the carpet. While she was doing this, Harold had become impatient outside in the car and sounded the horn. '*Hold* your bloody horses,' she'd said to Harold, who couldn't possibly have heard her.

When she was finally back inside the car and seated, a pillow case in her lap, the contents wet and heavy, plus three Tupperware containers inside a brown paper bag clutched in her other hand, she asked Harold, 'You want to check the creek?'

'Nah. *She'll* be right. Long gone. *She'll* be up in them caves by now, mother.'

Mrs Pitchford smiled, wistfully. 'She got carried away again, my love.'

Smiling with a father's pride, Harold said, 'She's a big girl, mother. You've got to let them suss their own way in this world. Be there for them from time to time, but still . . . we've done what we can for her. She has her own family now. She's just providing for them the best way she knows.'

'We've been very lucky with her, Harold. To think of all them sheep Len and Audrey lost last year with their girl.'

'You're not wrong, mother. But when you let a child run wild . . . ' Harold rolled his eyes behind the thick lenses in the tortoise-shell frames of his glasses that he'd taken off the old Maori boy they'd found fishing too far downstream last summer. 'It's all about pace, mother. We showed our girl how to pace herself. A chook or two. A dog. A cat. And if dags like these Poms are still around after that, well it comes down to who was here first. And who was here first, mother?'

'We was, dear. We was.'

ADAM L G NEVILL *(b. Birmingham, England, 1969) grew up in England and New Zealand. He is the author of the supernatural horror novels,* Banquet for the Damned *(2004),* Apartment 16 *(2010), and* The Ritual *(2011). He lives in London and can be contacted through www.adamlgnevill.com.*

Commentary on "Pig Thing": *I thought I was in a Johnny Weissmuller* Tarzan *film the day I arrived in New Zealand, after a one month voyage at sea to get there. I was a boy and my juvenile senses, formed in the post Industrial city of Birmingham, England, were swiftly overwhelmed by the songs of tropical birds, the buzz of cicadas, the sight of deep fragrant forest (known as the bush), and a humid heat I'd never felt before on my pallid Pommy skin. In my imagination, anything could exist within those miles of shadowy national forest on the North Shore of Auckland, that reached from around our house to the sea. The house was even a building made from wood and built on stilts to make it earthquake proof; a veritable tree house. Even my primary school was built inside the national park. I had to be reassured several times that there were no giant man-eating snakes* out there *in that magical, captivating, terrifying bush. Once I asked my Dad what our plan would be if something came out of the trees at the bottom of our garden and looked at us through the ranch sliding doors (made of feeble glass), and he said, 'We'll give your mother to it and while it's busy with her we'll make our escape'.*

There followed a childhood of adventure within that peaty, frond-choked immensity of bush that Huck Finn would have approved of. Within months of my arrival, the soles of my feet were like leather. Bare feet in England was a rare summer treat; in 1970s NZ it was standard for kids to be unshod. And my bare feet wandered for miles and miles on and off beaten paths in the Kauri Park National Reserve. They followed giant eels down to the sea, climbed prehistoric looking trees, scaled sandstone cliffs full of wild ducks and wasps, waded across creeks in mangrove swamps and left small footprints in mud and sand upon shorelines with no public access. My brother and I led expeditions, armed with homemade spears, that could take an entire day to complete. Beyond where my physical form could travel, my imagination roamed even further. And brought back things you would consider the stuff of nightmare.

Maori legends about child eating bird women and dragons—Taniwha—were embellished by what I read (Robert E Howard's Conan stories) and what was read to me (M R James and Tolkien amongst others), until I could frighten myself witless when alone amongst the trees; I sometimes wondered if the last Moa (a giant flightless bird)—or was it a child-eater with a feathered face?—had just parted those ferns, or stepped upon a twig, behind me. And then I never ruled out an encounter with the giant wild pigs with tusks we had heard about existing in deep country, especially the one that actually broke the back of a family friend's hunting dog. Because it was not unusual to find curious bones out there either. In fact, during one family holiday, my brother and I found the skeleton of a dead cow in the bush, that had been picked clean, and brought the entire thing back in a wheelbarrow to reconstruct it on the lawn of a holiday home. We were allowed to keep the skull and take it home—and had several goat skulls under the house too. To my delight, I found that with an animal skull perched upon the top of my head, whilst my upper body was covered by an old sack, I could catch my sister's friends unawares, scattering them amid their screams. . . . I reminisce.

It is no surprise to me that I would one day return to that time in my youth and try and recreate that sense of dread-magic that I can but glimpse these days as a middle aged man. It was a magic that continuously spellbound me as a child. The very size and diversity of the Antipodean and sub-tropical terrain was not only capable of stretching my physical endurance to the limit, but that of my imagination also. The age of that land's forests, its strange music, its call to the most primal yearning inside a boy to wander and quest and to not stop, its suggested terrors, and my wonder and awe before it, was as Gothic in spirit as anything I have experienced in the old world of Europe.

The Lighthouse Keepers' Club

Kaaron Warren

On Peter's list of what to take to the lighthouse, he had 'magazines'. It meant a certain kind of magazine, the sort you wouldn't necessarily want your mum sending you. He packed the few he had and planned to buy some new ones. Really he only did it to feel part of the team. Mostly he read music magazines like *Composer's Monthly*.

He also packed the lighthouse keeper reports. He'd read some of them already but wanted them with him. There was so much he didn't under-stand.

The mayor arrived, delivering gifts to him. 'It's a good thing you're doing for the town,' she said.

'I'm only going for two weeks. Two weeks out of a whole life time.'

'Then off to University? Perth, is it? Same state, at least.' The mayor nodded; she'd known many like him. She'd send another off next year for the yearly lighthouse maintenance.

'I want to be a musician. A composer.'

The mayor nodded again. 'There's nothing like time in the lighthouse to give you a push ahead.'

You could see the lighthouse from many positions in the town. Far out it was, on the shaggiest, sharpest rock along the coastline in that region. The lighthouse stood like rock itself, reaching up like a long white finger. Kids would stare at it without blinking on a clear night, trying to see the prisoners inside. *Can you hear them crying?* On those still nights, the children sometimes imagined they could.

But the prisoners couldn't stand tall enough to reach the windows.

LIGHTHOUSE KEEPER'S REPORT, 1880

It's a lonely job, keeping the bones.

In those early days, a keeper would be out there six months but the inmates needed more attention then.

They were a long-living people in Peter's town, though they'd lost the skills to render immortal. The women who knew how to preserve all died off without passing on the knowledge. Bitter old bitches, they were. They said it was to be used for the good, not for punishment. Used for the betterment of mankind, not for increasing suffering, and they used Billy Barton as their example. The last preserved one. Peter went to visit him, resting in his soft bed, 'The Little Drummer Boy' playing. Peter had already heard it five times since sitting by Billy's bed.

'Change the music,' Billy whispered. 'I can't stand to listen to this again. Again and again.'

He was almost forgotten. Needing no real care, no real food, he lay alone until someone wanted to ask him a question. There were cobwebs in his hair, stretching to the bedpost.

He moved very little. Each breath was torture to him.

'Will the others be like you? The men in the lighthouse?' Billy was parchment-skinned, brittle-boned, grey-toned.

Billy Barton's face contorted. It was odd to watch anger move so slowly across a person's face. 'They are not "others". They are the evil ones.'

It was frightening what Billy knew. 'We had the power, and we used it the right way. It was used wrongly in the past and there were terrible times. The human body is not meant for immortality. Any such a thing is an aberration from God.'

'Why don't you ask to die?' Peter asked him. The old man shook his head. 'Never surrender. Never give up. That's what I say.'

Lighthouse Keeper's Report, 1912

I would not have liked to see the men when they were first preserved. They would have been more solid, then. Louder. They would have looked more like men and less like husks. They're not a happy bunch. They were given the choice, life imprisonment or eternal life. They choose eternal life. But were they shown the results? Did they see our own Billy Barton? Did they talk to a man who's been given the treatment, see what he thought of it?

No one should have to be around them. Those Eastern Staters, they sent all their worst to us. Always the way. Over the Nullabor, out of mind.

We sealed them into this old lighthouse. Took ten years to build the thing, then it's in the wrong place. Builder dead in the floods so not even him to blame.'

Peter could see the lighthouse from a corner of his window, and some nights it seemed to glow. It was a constant reminder of the income it provided, with the government still paying for each and every prisoner's continued care.

There was always talk amongst the young ones about innocence and guilt. 'Who's to say what anyone deserves? Who's to decide?'

Peter had no problem answering.

'The law decides. That's who. That's what it's there for.'

It used to be a big competition for the job. All the boys lined up for it after finishing high school. But now, so many of them had moved away to battle the big city. The only ones left behind were like Peter, happy to be near home, not desperate to get away.

He had to go through many physical tests. There was a time a couple of years back when one of the boys ahead of Peter in school got rejected on health grounds. No one knew what it was and they didn't want to find out. He killed himself because of it, and everyone said it was for the best. Even his mother agreed.

'It's like protective custody,' the doctor told Peter. 'We can't let the inmates get sick.'

LIGHTHOUSE KEEPER'S REPORT, 1921

This week I took in a visitor. They told me not to but she was so nice. Older woman and all that. 23, she is. Nice and smooth as any woman you ever saw. I thought she was coming for me, but she told me she wanted to see her grand-father. She wanted to see him for her mum, because he was locked up here before the mother even turned one year old. He's one of our lot, you see.

She tried to tell me he was innocent. That he was a good man. No one had told her otherwise, the weak creatures. Tell them the truth, I say. Children need the truth, young women need the truth as much as we do. I told her it. That her granddad killed her own auntie and many more and was sentenced to death and beyond. He's trapped here. Forever. There was plenty of evidence.

She stood right in front of him and she didn't flinch from how he looked. She said to him, "Grandad, did you do it? Did you kill Auntie Missy?"

He took a great snarl at her. No love there at all. Broke my heart to see her recoil.

They whisper. 'I'm innocent.' They all whisper it.

They are trapped. But not in a jail. In their own desiccated bodies.

Peter's friends banged at his door, wanting to take him out drinking. 'It's only two weeks I'll be gone,' he told them.

'Two weeks and you'll be off your tree at the end of it. No good to anyone. Come on, spend those wages before you get 'em. You'll be finding treasure out there, no doubt. You know you're coming back rich!'

He put aside the reports. He'd read 1932 when he got home.

What happened at the lighthouse wasn't a secret. They all knew about it, and knew the hefty payments arriving every month, were reliant on that money. It didn't hurt to send the young men out there for a fortnight at a time, anyway. Was a cautionary tale for them. Didn't they have the lowest crime rate in Western Australia and far, far beyond? Didn't they have journalists, scientists, sociologists, coming to look at them for that as well as the fact they lived long?

That old craggy rock. No island to walk on. All the reports spoke of that. How much it could add to your isolation. Your desperation. How the only walking you'd have was up and down the stairs.

Peter didn't get home till 4 in the morning.

LIGHTHOUSE KEEPER'S REPORT, 1932

*M*ost *of us get over here and before long think about helping the pris-oners. 'So long ago,' they whisper. 'All that happened so long ago.' Sometimes it sounds like rushing leaves. They whisper, 'We can forgive. We sit here and let it wash over us. We're a peaceful lot. Listen to the waves pounding the arse of the lighthouse and let it wash.'*

That idea of helping soon got knocked out of me. They can't move much, this lot, but they can move if they have enough time. I arrived to find them at the door, arms raised to drop a heavy object on my poor head. The effort of it meant they couldn't move another inch, though, and I knocked them down easy.

It's a lonely life out here. Even for two weeks. But it'll scare you off a life of crime. That's for damn sure.

Peter's father woke him early, fingers tapping on the door. 'Wake up, maestro! You're missing the best part of the day.

LIGHTHOUSE KEEPER'S REPORT, 1953

I brought a girl here, thinking to get her all scared and needy.

Last shred of human in these men and they use it to say, 'Fuck her here, in front of us.'

It was tempting. 'It's awful here,' she said, tight as a limpet on my side. I could feel her pelvic bone against my thigh, she was grinding into me so hard.

She said, 'Can they see or anything?'

I told her, 'They've got all their senses. But they don't feel pain. Not much, anyway.'

I showed her what other lighthouse keepers had done. The cigarette burns. The names drawn into skin. She was shocked but I told her to read her the files and she wouldn't be sorry for them. They've all got a little picture of their heads, them doing something nice.

She said, 'Look, this one liked horseriding. Where would he ever find a horse?'

'How would I know?' I told her, 'Maybe he thought he was a Mongol.'

His hair, brittle, long, white, snapped off if you lifted it. I gave her some to take home with her.

She sneezed all over them, my girl did. And you wouldn't believe it but one of them got sick. Yes he did. Not that you'd know the difference. 'Poor bastards.'

Peter didn't imagine he'd have any sympathy. They must be more dried up by now. Even less like humans.

LIGHTHOUSE KEEPER'S REPORT, 1973

What these people did . . . they deserve eternal suffering. The skinniest one, pretty well a skeleton with skin stretched over it, he kept a daughter in his cellar for 30 years. Never taught her how to speak or read. All she knew about was oral sex and silent fucking. He brought men back for her and then he'd kill them. He was unrepentant. And there were the grandchildren, too.

This one, he's got a lean to him, as if his arse cheek hurts. Sometimes he'll push himself upright, but it takes him weeks, literally weeks. I like to tip him over again.

'Innocent innocent.' I wish they'd keep quiet. And those bloody women, too, wanting us to let them go.

One of the women actually rowed across the water. They do this sometimes, get themselves across. Not the ones who brings us provisions; they just drop and run. But every single time a woman stays, things go wrong. They know there's a taboo on it. In '21 there was an outbreak of *flu that killed, what, half the population? Or there might be a terrible storm, like there was in '53. We lost some people then, they tell me, but I wasn't born yet. Any woman on the rock means danger for the town so they should stop doing, I say, or be locked up.*

This one landed.

The noise rose. 'She's here again, she's here again, she is.' One of them had a view of the water. He kept the others informed.

'Who's here?'

'You should have fucked her when she was young. Old and ugly now. Got a kid with her, or a dwarf.'

'Innocent we're innocent we've paid the price let us go.'

She banged on the door down below. What was she using? A rock? I dropped rocks down at her until she went away. Her fault about what happened to the school after. The way it burned down sudden. We all know that. She said she'd been here in 1953 and there was a great flood that year, too. I said to her, you tell people not to come back here uninvited.'

Peter wasn't born in 1973, but he'd been told about the fire in the school. You could still see the scorch marks on the wall and there were the names of the children who died, around the base of the oak tree in the courtyard.

Lighthouse Keeper's Report, 1992

What made me think reading Dostoevsky here was a good idea? Jesus. Makes me think too hard about crime and punishment and what these losers beg me to do. 'Release us, kill us, release us.'

How would I kill them, anyway? Every lighthouse keeper must consider it.

Surely the crimes are paid for by now, comes the thought. Shouldn't they be given the blessed relief of death?

Not so. They chose this. Eternal life over the death penalty. They were tricked of course.

Three things stop me from setting them free. These same three things have stopped all before and will stop all after. It's our job and what we're paid to do. They deserve it for what they did. And the town would fall apart if we had no prisoners to look after. Once that money goes, the town is done for.

It's against the rules, but I like to read them the news. Mostly they are deaf, aural nerves long since dried up. But a sentence or two seems to penetrate the buggers. . . .

SUMMARY OF CONDITIONS: *I found the prisoners to be well-nourished and of sound mind. Requests were made but not met. Prisoners appeared distressed on waking and have trouble sleeping. Prisoners experienced dry skin, chronic pain and halitosis.*

All normal for this report.

Peter was invited to visit the Lighthouse Keepers' Club. It was set way back from the road, and his guide, a lighthouse keeper from 1989 said, 'We often think a golf buggy would be good to get us to the front door.'

Peter laughed, but he had never seen such a big house. Inside, it smelt of leather and good aftershave. The grey carpet was thick under his feet, and the walls covered with artwork. He knew nothing about art.

'Can you be trusted to keep the secret?' a lighthouse keeper from 1972 asked as they sat in deep, dark armchairs. 'There's a lot of us moved away, but our community is tight, no matter where we live. You'll be one of us, soon, as long as you can keep the secrets. Won't find a tighter group of men, Peter. You really won't.' They gave him some expensive whiskey he didn't want and said, 'You'll be one of us when you get back.'

All prosperous men, and their families, too. We choose well, they said of each other. Lighthouse men know how to make the right choices.

Peter ate vegetable soup and his mother's rock hard bread. Soaked up the soup and the loaf was still chewy, but he took pleasure in it. It was only two weeks he'd be gone, but he knew he'd be changed when he came back. Some of the men never enjoyed food again, he was told. They said the taste of it was like dust.

He packed his notebooks, his flute, his guitar.

'You'll get a lot of work done there,' his mother said, taking some choco-late biscuits out of the oven. 'All that peace and quiet away from town. No girls to distract you.'

He blushed. Hated it when she teased him about girls. They really weren't into him. Wait until he was famous, though. Then they'd see. They'll be playing his music and remembering him.

His younger brother walked past spinning slowly, opening his mouth and eyes wide, closing them. 'I'm a lighthouse,' he said.

'Peace and quiet'll be a welcome change,' Peter said. He zipped his bag and left it at the front door.

It wasn't much of a send off. The old women shouting at him to set them free, give them rest. His Mum, with the tin of biscuits and an extra bottle of wine she'd saved for him. The lighthouse keepers, throwing advice at him about how much sleep to get, and where he'll find the key to the library, which was up on the top floor, behind the highest cupboard.

The previous lighthouse keeper rowed him out to the rock. That was the routine. Peter would row the next man out, though that seemed an impossible time in the future. The man rowed with his back to the lighthouse. 'You don't want another look?' Peter said.

'I don't mind it from afar. Up close, it's different, isn't it? Don't go too soft in there. Don't listen.'

'I'll keep my headphones on.'

The lighthouse keeper nodded. 'Good plan. They'll whisper to you. They'll whisper whatever they think will set them free. But they don't know how we think. What would we do with them? That's where they belong. They've got to take their punishment. And who's supposed to look after them, anyway? If we took them back to the mainland? I know my missus wouldn't want to.'

'We're doing it for the money, right? For the town,' Peter said.

'You'll go quiet in there, like we all do. Wanting to be sure about them. But there's nothing in their files to cast any doubt. Read 'em. It'll give you something to do.'

'I'm a composer,' Peter said, holding up his guitar. 'I'm going to be doing that most of my spare time.'

The great light at the top hadn't worked for many years.

The clouds hung low and it looked as if a giant troll squatted over the lighthouse, hunched over, his clawed hands and feet digging into it. His yellow toothed smile teasing and tempting.

Peter pulled his jacket closer. It was much colder out here. 'They told you to bring a lot of warm gear, didn't they? You can have my fleecy if they didn't. You'll never feel such cold as in that place. Up on the top floor, where the windows are, that's warm. But it's a long way away from your duties so you don't always get a chance to get up there.'

Peter thought about his thin coat, the two knitted jumpers his mum had given him. 'Yeah, can I take the coat?'

The previous lighthouse keeper handed it over. 'Give us it back when you're done. I'll pick you up two weeks. Barring accidents.'

As they approached, Peter could see that the walls were caked with sea creatures, sea plants, the splattered bodies of a million insects, the shit of ten thousand birds. It was craggy. Untended. Bleeding rust around the bolts.

Peter unloaded all his things, and the man helped him with the food. Four buckets of slops for the prisoners included.

'I'd help you get it upstairs but it's outside my prerogative,' the man said. 'Anyway, it'll keep you busy for a while. You got any deliveries coming over?'

Some of the men arranged for the ladies to bring over baskets of food. They'd lean out of the boat, place the basket of biscuits and cakes and jams on the rock with a *coo-eee*, then head back for shore.

Peter shook his head. He was looking forward to the solitude.

'Very, very good luck to you,' the man said, and he rowed away.

Peter clambered over the five metres of rock to the front door of the lighthouse. There were a lot of very small caves, nooks and crannies. He wondered what sort of creatures lived in them.

Someone had made a sign for the lighthouse. 'The Breatharian Institute.' Peter laughed at that. He shouldn't. It wasn't really funny that the prisoners lived mostly on air. But he admired the humour it took to put that sign up.

The key was hidden under a rock. Why they bothered locking it was a mystery, but part of the routine. The routine was very important. He had his list. His process. He pushed open the heavy door, resisting the temptation to call out, 'I'm home.' The foyer was ankle deep in dust, paint flakes, pieces of wood, a few desiccated rats.

First duty was to sweep it up. 'Might as well do it before you head up the stairs,' his list read. 'You'll need somewhere to put your luggage down, anyway.' His note was typewritten, with comments by the lighthouse keepers added along the way. These to be typed in each year, another of his duties. He planned to put into onto his computer, irritated that none of the others had done it

'Watch out,' the lighthouse keeper of 1934 had written. 'They might try to whack you with an object.'

He didn't say with what the prisoners would whack him, but there were a lot of flat rocks lying outside the lighthouse, and more inside, piled up under the stairs as if saved for a siege.

The generator was there on the ground floor, so he set it going, then took the first armful of things upstairs. It would take him five or six trips, he thought. There was drinking water to bring up. He was looking forward to not showering unless he wanted to. Wearing the same clothes day and night.

The next floor up the food was kept, and the small kitchen.

Above was the bathroom and the bedroom.

Then there was the floor where the prisoners were kept.

His list suggested that he get himself settled before he saw to the prisoners. 'Put your things away, make yourself a cuppa tea. There's always whiskey under the sink.'

He did that, and slept for twenty minutes, sitting up. He'd been partying so much the last few days that even the cold of the lighthouse didn't keep him awake.

His next job was to read the files. The crimes were very old; some of them he didn't even recognize, such as embezzling naval stores. These were men who'd been transported from Britain, then committed worse crimes and been found guilty again.

The cover on the files read, 'These are the nastiest arseholes of their time. Think Stalin. Think genocidal maniacs. Think baby biting freaks. And worse. Read the files, but remember, you'll never be able to wipe them from your mind.'

Peter already decided he didn't want to read the files. He didn't want to hate these prisoners; he wanted to treat them with as much coldness as he could muster. He didn't want his music cluttered with darkness; he wrote light pieces, things which helped the soul to soar, not sour.

He walked upstairs, cautious again about the warning of the prisoners behind the door. 'They have no strength, none at all, but together they can sometimes manage a feeble attack,' 1892 had written.

There was no distinctive smell in the air. The sea salt came in, strong as it was in his own home, and the lighthouse wasn't new, he could tell that. But it didn't stink.

He pushed open the door.

He had read as much as he could about what he would find when he reached the prisoners. The other men had prepared him; they are ugly, he'd been told. All dried up. But no stink anymore. You'll feel more pity than you've ever felt in your life, but they don't smell bad.

No one had prepared him for the noise of it, though. The clamour when he entered. Wild noise, *help me help me* and moaning, groaning.

The prisoners sat propped up against the walls. Twenty-six of them, lined up, with little pictures above their heads.

They were shrunken, desiccated, wrinkled. He'd been warned of this. He hadn't been warned about just how close to death they appeared.

There was the last remnant of bright red hair on one of them.It must have been gorgeous once. Peter imagined how he'd used this red hair to get away with things. The inmate had a picture of a sailing boat over his head. Peter had visited his grandmother twice in the old people's home she'd been locked up in. The prisoners reminded him of the residents there. Those elderly had photos on their doors, simple pictures depicting them in moments of happiness. They were trapped in their own failed bodies and their own narrow self-description. They were fed mealy food. Peter couldn't stand to be there. All those bodies strapped in, kept alive just for the sake of it. He'd always said he'd rather have an indulgent last 3 months than a restricted final 2 years.

Peter knew the prisoners didn't really need to eat, and that it hurt them, but they couldn't help but eat if the food was there.

Their eyes followed him, unblinking.

The rations he'd been given felt like they crawled in his hands, but he tipped them out into each filthy plate. 'Don't bother washing, they don't care,' his list read. 'Just give them their food. You'll do it every morning till you leave and that will do them for the year. They don't really need the food. They live off mould spoors.'

They bent over to the food and ate. There was no pleasure in the eating at all.

Peter smelt their mouldy breath. Eating was an old instinct they were allowed. Forced to endure. To remind them they were human, in case they had forgotten. Ensure they still suffered. Some of them whispered as he fed them. 'I'm innocent. It's been too long. You have to help me.'

Peter was going to put his headphones on but decided to share the music. He set up his MP3 player, played something he considered soothing but his mother hated. He watched their shoulders move up and down, as if they were dancing on the inside. Walking around, he could see that they had shifted. They again looked him in the eye, and he could see how dry their eyeballs were. He wondered how much they could see. His instructions read, 'They'll get themselves into a new position and they don't like being moved back again. They think they have the right to choose where to sit but they don't. They don't have freedom of movement. That's not one of their freedoms.'

'We'll be right,' they said as he carried them. 'We don't need moving. Leave us be, leave us where we are.'

But his list read they needed to be in their place, so he did it. Some were lighter than others and they said and did nothing. The heavier ones had a faint pulse. One of them he thought had toothmarks along his arm but Peter didn't want to look too closely. He noted the cigarette burns, the flattened limbs. The lighthouse keeper of 1961 had done this. He loaded bricks or rocks onto the prisoner's arm until it flattened.

Would have been painful if the prisoner had any sense of feeling.

Peter hated the feel of them under his fingers. 'Don't let them grab at you. Hold their wrists together like you would a crab's claws. They have strong fingers,' he'd been warned.

'I've sat here 150 years. I want a turn near the window,' one of them said. There was a constant hushing sound, underneath the sound of water washing up against the walls below. 'Unfair' and 'Tricked' and 'Innocent'.

Number 22 reached his arm out. He always stretched his arm out; reading back on the reports there were jokes about using him for a coat rack. Peter wouldn't do such a thing. He had nothing to hang up.

Peter made his bed up, the sheets slightly damp. He warmed his food over the small kerosene stove provided, and settled down to let the sounds wash over him. He had his guitar ready, but he didn't want to play. He wanted to be disciplined about it, to let the sounds and the senses fill him this first night, let it out all together rather than in dribs and drabs.

He slept well. His mother had told him being so close to the salt air would do it; they lived in air-conditioned comfort and rarely let the real air in.

———

Next on his list of duties was to clean up. 'Won't be much,' the list read. He took the dustpan and broom with him upstairs. 'Friend, friend,' they called out to him. 'My friend, my friend, you can help us. Help us to die. Leave us near the window, at least. Drag us downstairs and let the water take us.'

He wasn't supposed to touch them beyond shifting them sideways to sweep up the debris they left behind. Skin flakes, hair, all of it gathering beneath them in balls.

He cleaned up their waste, the tiniest dried pellets. Like rat shit, he thought, and that made him nervous. He hadn't seen any live rodents yet but that didn't mean they weren't around.

There were plenty of flies, though, weirdly iridescent things he'd never seen before. Half the size of his little finger, they were bright green in the middle, like a pistachio. Soft looking. Mossy. They were very shiny in the rear, like fake snakeskin. Rainbow coloured.

Huge alien-shaped eyes.

There was no meat for them. They rested on the prisoner's faces, looking for a tiny amount of sweat. If the men forgot to blink, the flies sat on their eyeballs.

For dinner that night, Peter caught fish and threw the carcass out of the window once he'd cooked and eaten his fill. The flies followed the carcass down to the rocks.

Peter set up his recording equipment, placing it right in the centre of the prisoner's room.

'What is it, what is it?' they whispered. 'What's he doing?'

They couldn't move fast enough to get to it. He'd be back in six hours. You never slept more than six hours in the lighthouse. They couldn't reach it in that time.

Peter walked into the room the next morning eating toast. Noses to the air, they sniffed at him. 'Toast!' they said. 'Who smells toast? Who remembers toast?'

'Does no one else eat in front of you?'

There was laughter. 'Who would eat in front of living corpses? What sort of man?'

'My dad drinks his cup of tea while doing a shit. We're not bothered,' Peter said. He didn't like eating in the small kitchen. Someone had painted a large picture of the lighthouse, with the troll he imagined crouching over it. It made him nervous and he preferred not to look at it. He played back part of his recording. Mostly it was moaning; the men were in constant pain. He heard them complaining to each other, whining voices, each louder than the next.

They cried: *he's not going to help us. He's like the others. He won't help.*

He fiddled with the controls to make music out of their voices. He was so thrilled by it, he couldn't wait.

'That's us! We didn't sing but we're singing!'

'He's a bloody magician.'

'I'm just a musician,' Peter said. He knew how fake the humility sounded but he didn't care. He played his guitar for them, the time passing so quickly it was more than an hour before he stood up.

'You know where there are wondrous sounds? The likes of which you'll not find elsewhere? Up above. Up top. Spend a night up there and you will be surprised. Music of the gods. Of the stars. Music of the sea and of the dirt. Music of the air. You will hear words you thought long lost, hear notes never heard before.' They wanted to help him, but he knew they were mostly trying to ingratiate themselves. It wouldn't work. Peter wished he was recording the words, because they were the most perfectly poetic lyrics he'd heard.

He hadn't been up there; had been warned that it was rarely touched, it was dusty and possibly dangerous and that no lighthouse keeper worth his salt had any interest in looking out to sea like that.

Others had told him that the beauty of the view was worth all danger. 'You feel king of the world up there. It's all possible. You can do anything.'

Before he walked up to the top floor, he had to tap their chests, looking for infection. Some sounded hollow, some sounded solid. He had no idea what to do if he found infection; the instructions said this was just a precaution and that there would be no disease found, so long as he was fit. If he wasn't fit, he shouldn't be there and it would be on his head.

He wanted to ask his mother for advice but there was no phone access. No internet, no cell tower. No access at all but the boat coming, in 12 days time.

He did climb up, too curious not to. The library was up there, and he took the key he'd found behind the troll picture, where it should be. Up there were piles of rocks, stacked up like some religious offering. One lighthouse keeper had carried them up for exercise, up and down. Peter dropped one out of the window right at the top, to watch it shatter. He could hear music, so clearly, so beautiful, it made him feel inadequate. But it was warm, at least. Much warmer than it was below.

He stayed there till evening, recording the music. He sifted through the books in the library, many of them notated with crudities or yet more advice. A recipe book from the Northern Church of the Ascension (*Cook this one for your girlfriend and she'll show you how much she likes it*); a collection of short stories from 1972, heavily edited so that every adjective was replaced with an insult; many battered *Reader's Digest* magazines and a 1951 History Book, back when they wrote history differently.

He was careful coming down. They'd told him he'd have to go down backwards and to be careful of those creeps. Once, a lighthouse keeper had been grabbed by the ankles. Weak man, that one. The prisoners tapped his ankles and tipped him over, and they almost had him down the stairs and tied up for ransom when he woke up and smashed their jaws.

The strongest prisoner was the grandfather of the girl who'd been out to the island in 1921. The picture over his head showed him with a young girl. Standing with his hand on the girl's head. It looked to Peter like he was holding her down, pressing her down. He was the one most capable of conversation. He said, 'Just take us outside for a bit. Just to breathe the air. See the light. We'll go outside now for the shortest time.'

'How could I do that?'

'You'll carry us. You know how light we are.'

Peter knew from reading the reports that everyone had had this conversation. That all of them had resisted it.

It felt to Peter that the men spoke as one, that sometimes they had one voice.

'I always thought there were hundreds of you. Hundreds and hundreds.'

'No, just us. Always been just us. We are immortal as jelly fish. We won't die through natural causes but can be killed. We can get very sick. That one over there, that pile of bones. My granddaughter killed that one. She didn't mean to. I wisht she'd done it for me, too. But I was always healthy. I never got ill no matter what. You can take us out of our misery, though, those who want it. And if you were a kind man you would do it. Others have done it before.'

'That's not what the reports say.'

'Of course not. You are paid to keep us. Paid by the prisoner. Which mouth should starve for the truth, do you think? I think you're different. I think you're the kind with questions.'

Peter laughed. He'd been warned about the flattery, the trickery. 'See what sort of slippery bastards they are. They'll try to find your weakness and they probably will. They've learnt a lot over the years.'

Peter thought, *What harm could this old, old man do? He's weak, he's got nothing.* The old man's teeth seemed huge in his head. Most of them had teeth like that, as if their faces were shrinking around the molars.

'Take me to the shore. I want to feel the earth again. Just hide me in your suitcase, it won't hurt. It really won't.'

Peter sat, staring at him. He could imagine clearly this: the old man biting his throat out part way across, biting out the boatman's throat, then rowing slowly, inexorably, to the mainland shore.

His list read, 'Save this for when you feel you need it. There's a report, for your eyes only. If you ever tell anyone what you have read, the wrath of the lighthouse keepers will come down on you. And we are a powerful lot. You know that . . . '

This was true enough. Most of the ex lighthouse keepers were rich and at the top of their careers—corporate lawyers, lobbyists, hedge fund managers, with a sprinkling of CEOs and politicians among them. Success was the power of keeping a secret, Peter thought.

He found the special notebook hidden in the library in the sunny room.

It told him, 'In their chests lies a stone. It grows and grows over the years. When you take it out, it'll grow back. You take it out, you'll be lucky for the rest of your life. Even if you don't deserve it, you'll be lucky. You'll have it all. It forms in their bodies. You cut it out and keep it. They'll be weaker for a while, but that stone will grow back. It won't kill them. This secret you must keep. And share it grudgingly. Part of the secret is selfishness.'

Tap their chest to see who's got the biggest one, the notes said. And see if they've grown back.

He did. He tapped their chests, and they tried to writhe away from him. 'Don't do it! Don't take our essence!' and they cried, dry rasping tears.

It was the grandfather who had the biggest stone; he could tell that by tapping. 'It'll grow back,' Peter said. 'I need it more than you. It's your thank you, for me looking after you.'

The man tried to pull away but Peter easily held him down. Twisting his head away, the man's fingers clawed weakly at Peter's arms. 'Don't do it, mate. Leave him be,' the other inmates called.

'It'll be you if it's not him,' Peter said, and they quieted then, all of them tucking their chins down onto their chests, closing their eyes.

The grandfather tried to hunch away. Peter thought he saw tears and he said, "Don't be a sook."

Out of kindness, though, he covered the man's head with a cloth.

Peter used his left forearm to hold the old man still across the neck and the shoulders, and he hefted the knife, treated the chest as he would a tough carp caught at the end of the season.

There was a small amount of pale pink blood, like meat cooked for ten minutes or more. He saw the stone near the surface; it was grey, lumpy and had a soft, sticky surface. He pulled it out, trying not to retch at the feel of it. Tucked it then into his pocket, and put his fish knife away . . .

Peter climbed onto the rowboat. 'How'd you go?' the sailor said. 'All good? Sorry we're running late. Let me get your case. Jeez, it's light? What'dya do, run out of food and eat your clothing?'

Peter suddenly remembered that he hadn't cleaned the kitchen.

'Don't worry mate. The rats'll do it. No fridge, is there? This is why there's no fridge. Because we often forget. You don't want to open a fridge after a year, do you?'

Peter could hear a tinkling in the movements of the water, as if his ears were more sensitive. He heard music, sweet music. Clearly heard the notes and knew how to write them down.

He recorded it; it was the music that made him famous, 'The New Rock of Ages.'

LIGHTHOUSE KEEPER'S REPORT, 2011

SUMMARY OF CONDITIONS: *I found the prisoners to be well-nouri shed and of sound mind. Requests were made but not met. Prisoners appeared distressed on waking and have trouble sleeping. Prisoners experienced dry skin, chronic pain and halitosis.*

All normal for this report.

KAARON WARREN *(b. Prahran, Victoria, Australia, 1965), has lived in Melbourne, Sydney, Fiji and now Canberra. She writes fiction inspired by outrage and delight, and has three short story collections:* The Grinding House *(CSFG Publishing, 1995),* The Glass Woman *(Prime Books, 2007) and* Dead Sea Fruit *(Ticonderoga Publications, 2010) and three novels: The multi-award winning* Slights, *the award-nominated* Walking the Tree, *and the recently released* Mistification, *all from Angry Robot Books.*

Commentary on "The Lighthouse Keeper's Club": *The story came to me when I was feeling extremely emotional and distressed about the circumstances of my elderly neighbour, who had been placed against her will in a high-level dementia ward by in-laws. She is an eccentric woman and this ensured her placement. The home she lives in is clean, the food is fine, the staff very kind and caring. But it is truly, truly awful. People are treated the same; old and senile. There is no evidence of their young selves, beyond a single selected photo outside their bedrooms. One man has a boat; another stands by an airplane. One woman holds a cat, another holds up a blanket. It breaks my heart.*

At the same time, I became fascinated by the sea forts of Kent; wondering what these abandoned structures would be like to explore. As the story developed, I decided to set it in a lighthouse instead, and fill it with the tragic, eternal inmates who echo the people I see living in my neighbour's dementia ward.

THE LOOK

REGGIE OLIVER

I

THREE WEEKS AFTER I HAD ARRIVED IN NAIROBI IN JANUARY
1976 my father wrote to me. I took it to be a sign that he was
reconciled to the fact that his only son had decided to join a theatre company in what he called 'the back of beyond.' 'It won't even
advance your *theatrical* career,' he had told me in England before I
went, the emphasis implying that he had still not lost hope that
another 'proper' career might be pursued. But I was young enough
to believe that adventure should take precedence over career con-
siderations; and of course I was right.

In the last paragraph of his letter he wrote: 'I've just discovered
that an old friend of mine lives in your present part of the world. His
name is Jumbo Daventry—I believe his real Christian name is Hugh
but everyone has always called him Jumbo—and he was a POW with
me on the Railway in Burma. He was a good man then and a good
friend: one of those who behaved well.' My father almost never
talked about his experiences as a prisoner of the Japanese in the
war, but one of the few observations he would make on the subject
was that: 'there were those who behaved well, but there were a few
who didn't, and in the circumstances I can't bring myself to blame
them.'

'I used to see quite a bit of Jumbo just after the war,' my father
went on, 'but then we lost touch and I gathered he went to Africa

69

to farm. I only recently discovered through another POW chum that he was in Kenya and got hold of his address. I've written to him and told him about you, so don't be surprised if you are suddenly contacted by a chap called Jumbo. He really is a good man; though I gather he married a rather ghastly woman, as good men have a fatal habit of doing.'

This last remark intrigued me. My father was a solicitor, and his pro-fessional deformity was discretion. For him to make such a decisively derogatory statement was a rare occurrence, so I took notice of it and waited for Jumbo to contact me with some apprehension. My father had given me his address, though, and I liked the sound of it. He lived in the Aberdare Mountains North of Nairobi and the name of his house was Cloud's Hill.

II

The Broughton-Erroll Theatre in Nairobi looked from the front like a run-down old art deco cinema which I believe it had once been. Shortly after the war Dick Broughton, a wealthy Kenyan coffee merchant, had bought it for his wife Samantha. Samantha Erroll had been a promising young West-End actress before she married Broughton and was carried off to Kenya. Having the sense to realise that his talented wife would be bored without some sort of artistic stimulus, Broughton set her up as the Queen of Nairobi Theatre, a position in which she continued to reign supreme after his death. She hired actors from England, promising them little money but, by way of compensation, excellent parts in an exotic location.

I knew, even before I went, that the theatre had seen better days. Samantha Broughton, though approaching her sixties still insisted on playing most of the leading roles and, in addition, directed in a perfunctory but autocratic manner. She liked whenever possible to line her fellow actors across the stage with herself slightly upstage of the rest of us.

The audience consisted mainly of the white community, and the plays were the kind of drawing-room comedies and thrillers that had been the staple diet when Samantha was a rising West End star. Occasionally she would do a Shakespeare or some other classic for the benefit of the schools, and on those occasions the theatre would be filled with a sea of young black faces, a rustle of excited anticipation. Those were the high points for me.

She had many regulars who would go to all the shows, whatever they were, sometimes two or three times during a run if they took a fancy to the play. One the most unusual of these regulars was Mrs King.

She generally occupied a small box close to the stage, so that the actors could see her all too clearly. She was in any case distinctive enough in appearance. She was in her sixties and Indian, possibly Eurasian. She had obviously been a beauty and maintained its memory by the wearing of bangles and colourful saris and the lustre of her dark eyes.

She was a friend, some might say a protégée, of Samantha's and could often be found back stage. Whenever choreography was required in a production she was called in as she had apparently been a noted dancer in her youth, but she was not much help. Her instructions were too oracular and impractical. This mystical cast of mind was reflected in her other backstage activity which was fortune telling.

I gathered that she was not well off because she always charged for her services, or rather asked for a 'token of appreciation', and the suggested amount was not modest. Her methods of divination varied: tea leaves, palms and cards were all used, and several of the girls in the company said she was 'amazingly accurate'. I suspected that this amounted to her telling them that they were fond of travel and felt things more than most people, but I was more of a sceptic in those days than I am now.

Sometimes she would sit with us in the Green Room during the interval, sipping instant coffee and telling us stories about 'the old days', the colonial era before Kenyan independence. I gathered that her own social position had been somewhat precarious. While claiming that she had been a 'good friend' of this or that notable figure in Kenyan society, she described many of the main social events of the era at second hand, as if she had not actually been present. She implied that this was due to her appearance and ethnicity. Being Asian she belonged to the third and most ambiguous section of the Kenyan nation: neither native, nor European ruling elite. The fact that she had married an English doctor had not qualified her for full white ruler status.

Surprisingly, she did not find her questionable position a source of much distress. Had she been less full of herself she might well have done, but her self-esteem knew no bounds. According to her, most of the male section of the Kenyan elite had been 'madly in love' with her, while she was, apparently, equally popular with their womenfolk to whom she acted as confidant. A photograph that she showed us of her as a young woman was enough to demonstrate that the vaunted adulation need not have been entirely a fantasy of hers. She had been strikingly beautiful.

There was an occasion on which I saw the facade of her serene self-satisfaction crack a little. One night in the Green Room one of the actors started to ask her about 'the Hartland Murder'. She seemed disturbed, even offended, by the question, and rapidly changed the subject. She then spilt coffee over her sari and left before the interval was over. When she had gone I asked the actor about the Hartland Murder and he expressed surprise that I had not heard of it. Apparently it had been a great cause célèbre of the late 1940s among the white elite. He would say no more about it so I left it at that.

After this incident Mrs King did not make an appearance back stage for almost a week during which I had a telephone call. Shortly before the performance one night I was summoned from my dressing room to answer the phone at the stage door. It was an unknown voice, but it was imm-ediately clear who it was.

'Hello, Jumbo Daventry here. You're John's son, aren't you . . . ? Good show! John was one of the best, believe me. True blue all through. Look, my better half Freda and I are coming to the show on the Saturday night. Now, if you have a toothbrush and a few necessaries packed, we'll whisk you off after the curtain and you can stay through till Monday at Cloud's Hill. I've squared it all with Samantha who's an old chum. How does that sound?'

I said it sounded splendid. The truth was, I was pining to get out of the heat, the dust and the hooting traffic of Nairobi, but had not yet summoned the courage to find out how to do so. My flat, provided by the management, was Spartan and noisy; what leisure I had to date had been spent learning lines and trying to keep cool.

'Good egg! Expect to see us after the perf. Over and out!'

On the Saturday evening before the show I was standing in the wings when Samantha came up to me. I was a little surprised because till now she had been rather aloof towards me, as a very junior member of her company. I remember the play was a Somerset Maugham adaptation by Guy Bolton called *Larger than Life* in which she played a star actress and I was cast, rather inappropriately as Sir Charles Temperley, one of her elderly admirers. I remember I had given myself a moustache, greyed my hair at the temples and thought I was looking very distinguished.

'So you're off to stay at Cloud's Hill this weekend, are you, you lucky boy?'

'I gather you know Jumbo Daventry, Samantha.'

'Oh, yes. Known him for ages. Everyone loves Jumbo.'

'And his wife? Freda, isn't it?'

'Ah, Freda! To use the phrase beloved of Edwardian dramatists, "she is a woman with a history".' With that Samantha gave me a last meaningful look with her dark eyes and swept away from me, as if she had just delivered an exit line from the play.

Mrs King was briefly in the Green Room that night. For the first time she appeared to take an interest in my presence. She fixed her lustrous eyes on me with the look of someone who expects to fascinate. I smiled back.

'Tell me, young man, what sign were you born under?'

I told her.

'Ah! I thought so! A dreamer and visionary. Beware, young man. Your ascendant planet is Mercury. Saturn aligns with Mars. You may see more than you would like, and understand more than you expect to. That is often dangerous.'

I hope my response to this nonsense was polite. I believe it was.

After the show Jumbo Daventry came round to collect me from my dressing room. He wore a khaki shirt, a neat pair of khaki shorts with knee length woollen socks and brightly polished brown brogues. I could tell at once why he had been given his nickname. He had the thickest legs I had ever seen on a man: they looked like young pink tree trunks. The rest of him was big too and though middle age was beginning to thicken his waist, he still looked powerful. He had sandy hair, a toothbrush moustache, blunt features and bright blue eyes. I liked him immediately.

'Jolly good show,' he said. 'Thoroughly enjoyed it. I think the wife enjoyed it even more. She loves that sort of witty, sophisticated stuff, you know.' He winked, then, recognising that her absence from the dressing room required some sort of explanation, he said: 'Freda's waiting for us, guarding the old Land Rover. You ready and fit?'

The Land Rover was parked just outside the stage door and we set off as soon as I was in it. I was in the back seat, so my first view of Freda Daventry was of the back of her head and her profile as she turned to address a few words to me.

'Adored the show,' she said. 'An absolute scream. Too killing.' She talked with a lazy aristocratic drawl that spoke of an earlier age of cocktails and country house weekends. It was a quite different sort of upper class from Jumbo's clipped, military accents: more privileged, and to me less trust-worthy. In the flickering yellow Nairobi streetlights, I could see that her features were thin and fine, her skin pale and wrinkled from long exposure to the sun. It was hard to tell in that light whether her hair was white or a pale platinum blonde.

We said little while Jumbo drove hard along dusty, bumpy roads North from Nairobi into the Aberdares or the White Highlands as they still were sometimes called.

'Can't see anything now,' said Jumbo at one point, 'but you'll love the countryside when you see it in the morning. Like Scotland only a dam' sight hotter. Eh? Eh?'

He laughed and I laughed with him. I saw Freda's lips twist into a tight smile. It was obviously a remark she had heard him make many times.

It was a long journey during which I think I must have dozed off several times despite all the jolts. Finally we were coming down a long gravel drive towards a building that looked like a gigantic suburban bungalow built out of yellow stone.

'Welcome to Cloud's Hill,' said Jumbo.

As we came to a halt in front of the house, a Somali servant who had been sitting on the steps of the front porch rose to greet us. Like most of his race, he was a tall, dignified looking man, very smartly turned out with a spotless white tunic and a green fez. I felt decidedly underdressed in his presence. He took my miserable little holdall and carried it in as if it were a precious cargo. I began to wonder desperately if they still dressed for dinner here.

While the Somali stowed my bag, I was shown into a long low sitting room where, from in front of a blazing log fire, two huge tawny Rhodesian Ridgebacks rose lazily to greet their master and mistress. The decor was almost aggressively English and Home Counties: glazed floral chintz on the sofa and armchairs, Persian rugs on polished floorboards, coloured prints of racehorses and hunting scenes on the walls. Apart from a couple of small hunting trophies there was nothing of Africa in the room. Presently, another Somali, attired like the first, brought in a tray of sandwiches and a soda syphon to accompany the whisky, a decanter of which was imprisoned in a Tantalus on the sideboard.

While Freda was making a fuss of the Ridgebacks, Jumbo took a key on a chain out of his shorts to unlock the Tantalus. Meanwhile the first Somali, having rid himself of my bag, entered the sitting room and took his place patiently beside the other servant.

'You put it in the back bedroom?' asked Jumbo. The Somali nodded and I noticed that Freda looked up, startled. 'All right, you two. Thank you. That will be all for tonight.'

I heard the two servants leave the house. Evidently they did not live on the premises.

There were a lot of sandwiches, very good ones too, but we managed to consume them all, Jumbo and I doing most of the work. In the whisky and soda stakes, however, I lagged far behind my hosts. They were both in their sixties and seemed in good condition, he beefy, she lean with a remarkably good figure for her age. She was wearing an immaculately cut cream trouser suit, and pearls did their best to cover the wrinkles at her throat. Her eyes were hazel, deep set, heavy lidded, watchful, enigmatic. To call them 'bedroom' eyes would be crude and misleading, but there was a strong sexual allure about them which hinted at the 'history' Samantha had alluded to.

Jumbo was good at overcoming my shyness and Freda showed a genuine interest in my descriptions of theatrical life in Nairobi. Two hours went by very cheerfully and there was only one mildly awkward moment. I had started to talk about the eccentric Mrs King when I saw Freda look away from me and start to clink the ice in her whisky. Jumbo said: 'Yes, we know all about Sabrina King,' and then abruptly changed the subject. Not long afterwards Jumbo said:

'Well, I don't know about you chaps, but I'm for my bed.'

This call to order was welcome because I was beginning to feel very tired. It was almost two o'clock in the morning. Jumbo led me to my room at the back of the house. I had expected 'the back bedroom' to be rather small. On the contrary it was almost as spacious as the sitting room with a double bed and an en suite bathroom. Metal framed French windows opened onto a veranda. It looked to me like the master bedroom. My pyjamas had been neatly laid out on the bed and my other clothes hung up in the wardrobe.

'Well, here we are. Hope this suits,' said Jumbo.

I expressed my admiration and thanks at which Jumbo seemed rather embarrassed.

'Yes. Well . . . We're down the corridor at the front of the house. If there's anything you need, just holler. Sleep well. Lie in as long as you like. I'm around fairly early, but Freda's a late riser. 'Night, old chap.' With that he left.

I did not immediately shut my bedroom door, so I was able to hear Freda and Jumbo talking at the other end of the house. Their tone was urgent. I could not catch all they said, but I heard her say:

'Why did you put him in *there*, for Christ's sake?'

'He'll be fine, old girl,' Jumbo replied. 'Didn't you notice? The poor chap looked all in. He'll sleep like a log.'

There were further urgent mutterings which I could not make out, except that I thought I heard the name 'Sabrina' mentioned once or twice. I closed my bedroom door gently.

Jumbo was right: I was 'all in'. As soon as my head touched the pillow I was asleep. It was a dead, dreamless sleep, so that, when I woke suddenly, I had no idea how much time had elapsed, but it was still dark. The room was stiflingly hot which was odd because it had been a cool night when we came in, and there was no radiator or heater that I could see in the room. I put on slippers and a dressing gown and went to the French windows that opened onto the veranda. They were locked and the key was nowhere to be found. I then tried the window which was a metal framed casement and opened outwards.

Though the air was cooler outside it did not seem to permeate the room, so I climbed through the window and onto the veranda. The sky was clear and moonless, the stars were out and there were odd patches of mist which covered the lawn in front of the veranda and even one end of it. Its roof was supported by brick pillars but the rest of it was of some dark, stained wood, cedar perhaps, or teak.

It was quite silent. For the first time since coming to Africa I heard nothing. The mist at the end of the veranda seemed to be moving and forming itself into something, but, as it dissipated again, I persuaded myself that I had been the victim of an illusion. Just then I heard a muffled cry which sounded as if it were coming from the other side of the house.

My senses by this time were fully alert and I felt no urge to return to my bedroom. Quietly I descended the steps of the veranda and began to walk round to the front of the house. At one corner of it I saw a lighted window. I moved a little away from the house so that there was less likelihood of my being seen from the window and observed.

It was, as I had expected, Jumbo and Freda's bedroom. I nearly turned away then and there, but something about the scene I saw held me. The only excuse I have is that it was not quite real to me, like watching a film or a peep show. I moved closer.

Freda was kneeling naked by the bed, her back to me, like a little child saying its prayers. Jumbo stood over her in his blue and white striped flannel pyjamas. In his hand was a long bamboo cane with a split at the end of it. He was beating her, on her bare back, not in a frenzy, but pausing very deliberately between each blow while she sobbed at the pain of it.

After each blow she cried out. It was not an inarticulate noise: she appeared to be shouting out a word or a name. I thought at first it might be 'stop!', but it sounded more like 'Shock', or perhaps 'Jock!'

I sensed that I was witnessing a fairly regular occurrence. Her white back was criss-crossed with red weals. After the sixth stroke Jumbo said: 'All right, Freda old girl, that's enough for tonight.' Freda, still kneeling, turned her weeping face towards Jumbo and kissed the cane in his hand. Jumbo went to a drawer in the bedside cupboard, took out a tube of ointment and rubbed some of it into her back, then he patted her gently on the bottom, at which, quietly and humbly, she got into bed. Jumbo then went to a wardrobe and put the cane in it. I noticed that there were several such instruments in there, all arranged in an orderly row. Before he turned round I had slunk away quietly. I crept round the house and returned to bed.

Despite not having had much sleep I awoke refreshed. I told myself that I had witnessed nothing the previous night and almost believed it. I dressed and as soon as I had left my bedroom I was greeted by the Somali who been on the porch the previous night. He bad me good morning and told me his name was Abdullah. Then silently, by means of gesture, he showed me to the dining room where on a sideboard under covered silver dishes, breakfast had been laid out. There was the traditional, almost Edwardian fare of devilled kidneys, bacon, sausages, scrambled eggs. There were also glass bowls full of fresh slices of pineapple and papaya.

Jumbo was seated at the head of a long dining table making his way through a heavy plate of eggs and devilled kidneys. He waited until Abdullah had left the room before addressing me.

'Morning, young feller-me-lad! Sleep well?'

I was at the sideboard helping myself from the silver dishes. When I turned to face him, I saw a searching, penetrative gaze. I told him I had slept very well. After a moment's pause he nodded curtly.

'Well, then, tuck in! Tuck in! Afraid Freda's feeling a bit under the weather this morning, and she's having a lie in. So you'll just have to put up with me. Like a tour of the estate?'

Jumbo farmed sheep and cattle over a considerable acreage. The night before he had said that the Aberdares were like Scotland; and I suppose there was a certain similarity, the same expansive and slightly hostile grandeur. I thought rather of the Wiltshire Downs magnified to a surreal scale, under a dome of sky, intensely blue, in which a few clouds floated unnaturally far above. It looked to me that morning like a paradise, but a dangerous one.

As he drove me round Jumbo explained the management of his estate and the tribal differences between the Kikuyu and the Masai who worked for him. The Somalis, he told me, made the best indoor servants: they were nearly all Moslem, an intensely proud people who considered themselves far more civilised than the native Kenyans and never downed your whisky on the sly.

Often Jumbo would stop the Land Rover to talk, in fluent Swahili, to individuals or groups of people. It was clear that 'Bwana Daventry' was immensely respected, and if I felt slightly uneasy at the unembarrassed way in which he accepted deference and humility, then perhaps my prejudice rather than his was at fault. However, I was surprised that such feudalism had survived independence. I think I managed to ask some oblique question about the Mau Mau and Kenyan independence because I remember Jumbo's comment which was typically laconic and forthright.

'Most of the people who had behaved well managed to get through the crisis pretty well intact.'

I noted that Jumbo had used the phrase which was a favourite of my father's. To me it had always seemed inadequate, even slightly cold; but I was beginning to wonder if it was simply used to disguise something more profound to which people like Jumbo and my father would be embarrassed to lay claim. Then I remembered what I had seen in the night: had that been 'behaving well'?

We returned to Cloud's Hill at lunchtime and found Freda looking as svelte and soignée as she had been the previous day. We lunched in the dining room off a selection of cold meats and the usual papaya and pineapple. I wondered why we were not eating on the veranda with its splendid view of the garden, but I did not ask. When lunch was over Jumbo announced that he had business to attend to that afternoon and that he was leaving me 'to the tender mercies' of Freda.

When Jumbo had gone Freda said: 'Now you're going to go on *my* tour of inspection' and rose abruptly from the table. She did not look to see if I or her two Ridgebacks were following, but we were. She marched out into the hall, picking up a riding crop from a side table as she went, and led the way out into the gardens that surrounded Cloud's Hill. 'They're my pride and joy,' she said to me in an unexpectedly mournful tone. I expressed my admiration as they were indeed magnificently laid out. Freda explained that because the earth was rich, and there was no dormant season, the garden could always look at its best, 'so I have no excuses.' She needed none. The lawns were immaculately green, the wide borders a riot of scarlet canna, frangipani and bougainvillaea. There were beds of subtle, tender English roses, long-stemmed lilies and fuchsias. In the air was the scent of jasmine, mimosa and hibiscus.

As we went on our tour I noticed at least half a dozen boys at work, water-ing, clipping, weeding. She spoke to one or two of them, but in a markedly different manner to the way Jumbo addressed his tribesmen. Her orders and admonitions were harsh, and mostly delivered in English. To one of them who appeared to be idling she gave a smart tap on the shoulder with her riding crop. The boy reacted, but silently and I saw fear on his face.

At first I felt uneasy in her presence, but when she found I was able to share her enthusiasm for gardening, her manner became less brittle. Our stroll through the shady avenues of jacaranda slowed to a leisurely pace while the Ridgebacks gambolled around us. Freda's conversation looped away from garden matters towards Kenya in general and Kenyan society on which she made a number of trenchant comments.

Suddenly she asked: 'How well d'you know Sabrina King?'

'Not very.'

'Has she said anything to you about me?'

'No.'

'You don't want to believe a word she utters. She's a terrible fibber. According to her, she's had everyone from the Governor General downwards. Mind you, that may well be true, but the rest is lies.'

After that the conversation reverted back to the gentler topic of gardens. On returning from our walk we had tea in the sitting room while Freda introduced me to various card games, including one called 'Honeymoon Bridge', a kind of Bridge for two people. As I knew Bridge I could play it, but I did not care for it much.

It only struck me as curious much later on that, during the time we spent together, there were no telephone calls for her or talk of visits to or from other friends. Shortly after five Freda had her first drink, a gin sling, and from then until dinner she drank steadily without apparently getting drunk. When Jumbo arrived shortly after six, he observed her intake, but made no comment.

After dinner Jumbo set up an appropriately marked green baize cloth and a half size roulette wheel on the dining room table and we played for a while with tiny stakes. The only evidence that Freda had drunk too much were the excited little squeals she emitted whenever she won anything. Jumbo did his best to keep the occasion jolly, but I found it all rather false and enervating. I could imagine how in the past there had been roulette parties at Cloud's Hill, with dinner-jacketed men and diamond encrusted women clustered round the turning, clicking wheel, and it had all been 'a terrific hoot.' Our game was no more than a pale ghost of what once had been.

At ten thirty, quite suddenly and without any prior warning

signs, Freda passed out onto the floor of the dining room. Jumbo did not seem too dismayed; it had obviously happened before. He said: 'Not to worry. She'll be right as rain on the morrow.' Then he clapped his hands for the two Somalis who, without a word, carried her off to her bedroom.

'Well,' said Jumbo, 'it's been a long day. Time we all went down the wooden way to Bedfordshire, eh?' He winked at me and I smiled back. Then he put an arm on my shoulder. 'Never had a son myself,' he said. 'Rather missed out on all that. Your father John's a lucky beggar.'

That night I kept the window of my bedroom open and heard, as I had not before, the sound of a Kenyan highland night. I listened for a while to a nightjar and the strange musical tapping of ground hornbills, like several tight-skinned little drums being played in perfect syncopation. Once I think I caught the distant cough and roar of lions. Very soon these had soothed me to sleep.

I woke out of a confused dream and it was still dark. I believe I had been woken by the sound of several muffled bangs, like a car backfiring, but when I was fully awake I heard no further disturbance, so it may have been an illusion. Certainly no-one else had been roused. I went to the window and looked out. All was quiet. Even the nightjar had gone to bed, but there was something on the veranda. I would investigate.

I began to climb through the window as I had the previous night, but some impulse told me to try the French Windows. I turned a handle and the doors opened. They must have been unlocked.

The same mist that I had seen the previous night had gathered itself

on the veranda, about five yards away from me, but this time the upper part of it had assumed a recognisable form. The form was a face, a mask with eyes, no more than that; the rest was vague. It was a young woman's face framed by a suggestion of pale, lustrous hair. The features were well-chiselled, the lips sensuously curved, the eyes heavy lidded, but it was the look that held me. Tilted downwards it seemed to stare at something that would have been at its feet if it had had them. The look itself was very particular, but hard to describe: a kind of hungry fascination, I suppose you might call it, with a slight smile on the lips as if pleasure were being taken from something that pleasure should not be taken from. The look had a certain beauty, because the features were those of a beautiful woman, and there was a rapture in it, but it filled me with fear and despair. I realise that I have been avoiding the use of the word 'evil' because I do not know what it would mean in this context. It is too general. This was a look that belonged to a particular person at a particular moment, a moment of ecstatic degradation.

I could not take my eyes off it. It must have lasted no more than half a minute until it began to waver and dissipate like a blown ring of tobacco smoke. Very slowly the mist sank and seeped away from the veranda leaving behind it only a slight luminescence and a faint perfume. Jasmine, was it?

The look was gone but it was lodged in my mind. I realised that there might come a time when I would believe, or want to believe, that I had only dreamed it, but that did not matter. The look was still the look. I could even identify the spot on the floorboards of the veranda on which the eyes had been fixed. On examination it turned out that this was where a section of the boards about five feet by three had been removed and replaced by a new segment. The substitution had been so skilfully disguised that one would not have noticed unless one had been looking for it.

III

The following morning was an exact copy of the previous one. Jumbo was, as usual seated at the head of the breakfast table devouring devilled kidneys.

'Morning, young feller-me-lad! Sleep well?'

I said yes, but avoided his penetrating glance. Jumbo told me he would drive me back to Nairobi later that morning and, just as we were about to leave, Freda appeared. She was immaculately dressed as usual but looked haggard. When it came to say good bye she kissed me full on the lips. I was conscious once again of the powerful sexual being that she was, but it still surprised me. When one is twenty one assumes, like Hamlet, that for the over sixties 'the heyday in the blood is tame.'

On the drive back Jumbo asked me if I had enjoyed myself which I said I had.

'Good show,' he said. 'We hope you'll come again. Freda enjoyed having you. She likes the cut of your jib.' I had no idea what this meant and was far too shy to ask.

On my return to Nairobi I wrote two letters, one to thank Freda Daventry for her hospitality, the other to my father. I gave few details of my trip to Cloud's Hill, and naturally excluded any mention of my more improb-able experiences which would only have provoked incredulity and distrust. I told my father how much I liked Jumbo and added, with what I thought at the time was a great show of maturity, that I did not think his wife Freda was 'ghastly,' as he had described, 'just very sad, and probably very lonely too.'

My father wrote back, as he always did, punctiliously with a letter full of rather dull news about the fox he had seen in his back garden, a rotary club dinner and his latest golf scores. Towards the end he wrote: 'You appear in your letter by implication to rebuke me for calling Freda "ghastly" when I had not met her.' It used to strike me as strange that my father, the most conventional of men, could nevertheless read my mind unerringly when he wanted to. 'But I did not make the comment ill-advisedly. I suggest you go to the offices of a local newspaper—say the *Nairobi Messenger*—and look up the Hartland case in their archives. The relevant date to start from is, I believe, January 24th 1947.'

My father added a P.S. which read: 'Jumbo has written to me and told me about your visit. I gather you made a very favourable impression and that you behaved well.' Praise from my father was so rarely bestowed that even this scrap of oblique approval made me glow inside.

For the next week or so I had very little time. Samantha had given me what she called in her old-fashioned way 'the juvenile lead' in the next play and I was very busily occupied in rehearsing and learning lines. I was very conscientious. I wanted to make a success of my first major role, even in Nairobi where nobody of importance to my career would see me. However, as soon as I felt safe in my part and had a free moment, I paid a visit one afternoon to the offices of the *Nairobi Messenger*. When I asked to see the back numbers from January 1947 nobody seemed very surprised by my request. One of their office boys fetched the relevant bound volumes and left me in a little room to study them.

The reports began on the 25th of January with a front page headline:

HARTLAND SHOT DEAD ON CLOUD'S HILL ESTATE

A brief few paragraphs in heavy type told me that in the early hours of the morning of the 24th of January Mr Henry ('Harry') Hartland, the millionaire business man and property owner was found shot dead at his home Cloud's Hill in the Aberdare Mountains; that police suspected foul play and were actively pursuing enquiries. Accompanying this was a studio portrait photograph of the victim, a balding, middle-aged man with heavy features. The eyes looked out somewhat aggressively.

Reports on subsequent days yielded further details. Hartland had been shot several times in the head and body on the veranda of Cloud's Hill. No-one had witnessed the murder itself, but two figures had been spotted running away from the scene. Hartland's wife, a Mrs Freda Hartland 'who is well-known as a leading figure in Kenyan society', had not been at Cloud's Hill at the time but had been staying with a friend in Nairobi. The photograph of Freda Hartland showed a strikingly beautiful, blonde woman with chiselled, sensual features. That picture gave me a double shock. I recognised at one and the same time the face of Freda Daventry and the look that I had seen on the Cloud's Hill veranda.

Two days after this came the announcement that an arrest had been made. Police searching the hut of Ibrahim, one of Hartland's Somali servants, discovered a .32 Colt revolver hidden under a mattress. This gun was shown to have been fired recently and its ammunition corresponded with some of the bullets which had been found in Hartland's body. It added, for the first time, that police believed that Hartland had been shot eight times, five times by a Colt .32, and three times by another revolver of unknown type. The report concluded that a few days before the murder, Ibrahim had had a violent disagreement with his master after being beaten for an offence connected with some missing silver forks.

There was some sort of paragraph on the Hartland Murder each day in the *Messenger* after that, but little was added to the stock of hard facts until about a week later when the police stated that the ownership of the Colt revolver had been traced to one Lord Glenross, 'the popular socialite and white hunter.' Lord 'Jock' Glenross told the police that he had noticed that his Colt was missing several weeks before the murder when he had been visiting Cloud's Hill. He had not reported the gun's absence at the time because he just thought he had 'mislaid' it. A picture of Lord Glenross showed a man in an African bush setting with one foot planted on the head of the lion he has just shot, a rifle carelessly slung across his back. The face, partly shadowed by a solar topee, is grinning broadly.

Another week passed before there was another front page headline:

LORD GLENROSS ARRESTED FOR HARTLAND KILLING

Again, the paragraphs below supplied very meagre additional information, beyond the fact that Ibrahim had been cleared of all charges because it had been shown that he was 'elsewhere' on the night of the crime, and it was now believed that he had been 'deliberately and falsely implicated.' It was also stated that: 'Lord Glenross had been a close and intimate friend of Mr Harry Hartland and, more particularly of his wife Freda Hartland.' Inside the paper the editorial section contained a rather windy piece of comment on 'the low standard of morals prevailing among the wealthy elite of Kenyan society where adultery is looked on as a casual pastime, to be indulged in without thought, like gambling or excessive drinking.'

At this point I looked at my watch. It was getting late and I must go to the theatre. I would have to wait another day for the trial reports—if there had been a trial.

That evening my mind was so possessed by what I had read that it took some effort to put my researches to one side and concentrate on the serious business of light comedy. I was not helped by the fact that Mrs King was in the Green Room during the interval. She smiled at me with more than her usual complacency.

'So,' she said. 'I hear you spent a weekend at Cloud's Hill.' I nodded. 'I often used to stay there myself, you know. In the old days. I know a great deal about gardens. Freda never failed to take my advice. She was born under Aquarius, always a changeable sign. Are the gardens still exquisite?'

'Superb.'

Mrs King seemed disappointed. 'People can be so ungrateful,' she said. 'Don't you agree?'

I smiled, muttered something about checking a prop and left the room. The following afternoon I was back at the *Messenger* offices.

The trial was preceded by the dramatic discovery of love letters from Freda Hartland to Lord Glenross. Though they did not directly incriminate her, they provided incontrovertible evidence that the two had been conducting a passionate affair. She was interviewed on a number of occasions by the police, but stuck to her story that she had no part in the murder and that she was in Nairobi at the time. 'This alibi,' wrote the *Messenger*, 'has been confirmed by the person with whom she was staying, Mrs Sabrina King, widow of the late Dr. Conrad King, the distinguished Nairobi osteopath.'

A partial palm print corresponding to that of Glenross had been found on the Colt .32 which ballistics confirmed to have been one of the weapons used in the killing. Witnesses came forward to testify that they had seen Glenross at Cloud's Hill on the night of the murder. There was talk of a second killer with a second gun, but neither could be identified or found.

In May of that year Jock Glenross went on trial for the murder of Harry Hartland at Nairobi's Central Court. I did not pore over every detail of the judicial process, as recorded by the *Messenger* but it would seem in retrospect that Glenross was doomed from the start, despite the best efforts of a flamboyant KC hired from Johannesburg to defend him. Glenross probably delivered the fatal blow to his own case when, half way through the trial, and against his counsel's advice, he decided to change the entire basis of his presumed innocence by claiming that he had killed Hartland in self-defence. Glenross alleged that he had quarrelled with Hartland over his affair with Freda and Hartland had threatened him with a revolver. There was a struggle and both guns had gone off accidentally. But why had there been eight bullets in Hartland's body, and where was the second gun?

Freda Hartland had gone into the witness box as a grieving widow 'dressed', according to the *Messenger*, 'immaculately in black with a spotted veil and a diamond Cartier pin on her lapel.' Opinions differed as to her performance. Some said it was courageous, stoically grief-stricken; others claimed it was a heartless and calculated charade. She had admitted to her passion for 'Jock', but denied all knowledge of the murder either before or after the fact.

Despite the pressure of evidence many had apparently believed that the all white jury would acquit Glenross, or that he could be found guilty of some lesser offence. It would appear that for most of the trial Glenross too shared this sanguine point of view, though, towards the end he was overheard 'by our reporter' to say to his defence counsel: 'They don't hang whites in this country, do they?'

The verdict was guilty and, despite many petitions for reprieve and appeals for mercy, Lord Glenross was hanged, almost a year to the day after he had committed his crime.

I emerged from the *Messenger* offices that afternoon in a daze. My mind was so immersed in the events of the trial that I was nearly run over as I crossed the road to get to the theatre. The vehicle in question was a Land Rover being driven at high speed. I recovered my senses sufficiently to notice that the driver had been Freda Daventry and that in the passenger seat beside her sat Mrs King.

IV

A few days later something happened which I had been dreading: Jumbo rang me up at the theatre asking me to spend another Saturday to Monday at Cloud's Hill. When I hesitated, he said: 'Freda and I so much enjoyed your previous stay.' A note of pleading was detectable, and I felt under an obligation. When I agreed Jumbo's normal clipped tones were resumed.

'Good show! Pick you up from the theatre on Saturday night as usual.'

On the Saturday night, in the wings before the show, Samantha said to me: 'So we're off again to the fleshpots of Cloud's Hill to be waited on hand and foot, are we? You lucky boy!'

Ignoring this, I said: 'What happened to Freda after Glenross was hanged?'

'Oh, so you've found out about that, have you? I wondered what you'd been up to in the *Messenger* offices. Well, you know, after the execution there was a great wave of sympathy for Jock Glenross in spite of everything. Someone told me that he didn't behave terribly well at the end: kept snivelling and shouting out Freda's name, you know. Which was rather a shock because everyone thought he'd go like the officer and gentleman he supposedly was. I remember him only vaguely, but though what he did was pretty foul obviously, he had been an attractive sort of scamp. All the charm in the world; and plenty of people beside Freda had been in love with him. Naturally they started to blame her for the whole thing, saying she had been at the bottom of it all, led him on, that sort of thing. She'd been a big cheese in Kenyan society, queen of the Muthaiga Club. All that. Suddenly she was persona non grata. Practically everyone was giving her the cold shoulder, except Sabrina of course, but then she didn't count. People began to notice the colour of her skin, so she was out too. Well, Freda couldn't stand this, so she went off to South Africa. She didn't sell up as I would have done: Freda always had a bloody minded streak. Well, in Durban she met Jumbo and by the time she came back to Kenya she was married to him. Of course, at first everyone thought Jumbo had just married her for the Hartland millions she had inherited, but very soon they realised he was as straight as they come and they began to make overtures to them both. But Freda wasn't having any of it. I told you she was bloody minded. She thought they had betrayed her in her hour of need and she didn't want anything to do with the swine. So she's remained pretty isolated ever since. And now, if you will excuse me, I am about to play Judith Bliss and you are supposed to be my young admirer Sandy Tyrrell. Shall we now address ourselves to Mr Coward's *Hay Fever*?'

When Jumbo came round to collect me after the show, he was unusually taciturn. Freda was not waiting for us in the Land Rover. Jumbo remained somewhat brusque as we drove out of Nairobi, and I was beginning to won-der if I had offended in some way. Then, just as we were passing the junction of the Karen and Ngong roads, he spoke.

'I think I ought to warn you, young feller. Sabrina King is currently staying with us.'

'Ah.'

'Yes. You may well say "Ah"!'

My laconic answer for some reason put him in a better frame of mind, and for the rest of the journey he was almost his usual self.

On our arrival at Cloud's Hill we found Freda and Mrs King in the sitting room with the Ridgebacks. Freda was nursing a drink and seemed with-drawn; but Mrs King, in a gold-edged purple sari, her coffee-coloured arms ringed with bangles, burned very bright.

'Welcome back to Cloud's Hill!' She said, then to me: 'Hello again, young man. And how was the *Hay Fever* tonight? Not too severe, I hope?' She accompanied this dreary little joke with a tinkling laugh, like Samantha whenever she delivered a witty line. She was behaving as if she and not Freda were the hostess of Cloud's Hill. Jumbo snorted and went for the whisky decanter.

'Care for a snifter?' he said to me.

'Thanks.'

'Now, we don't want you two boys to drink yourselves silly,' said Mrs King, wagging her finger and smiling roguishly at us, 'because

Freda and I have a plan. We're going to play Bridge, Freda and I against you two. Girls against boys.'

'Now hold your horses, madam,' said Jumbo. 'In the first place this young man has not had his sandwiches, and is probably done in after all that acting. In the second place, how do you know he plays the wretched game?'

'Oh we know that. Last time he was here he played Honeymoon Bridge with Freda and beat her hollow. Isn't that right, Freda?'

Freda merely nodded. Her eyes were following Mrs King as she darted and glittered about the room like a dragonfly. Jumbo looked at me enq-uiringly. I smiled and shrugged in acquiescence. Just then Abdullah entered with a tray of sandwiches.

'We can eat our sandwiches at the Bridge table,' said Mrs King. 'See, we've got it all laid out for you.' She pointed to a corner of the room where, under a standard lamp, the card table and four chairs had been set up, complete with two packs of cards, score sheets and pencils. 'Shall we say one Kenyan Shilling a point?'

Jumbo looked at me with a concerned expression. I was young and I felt that my nerve was being tested. I nodded soberly; he winked and gave me the thumbs up sign. Inside I felt very hollow.

In those days I was a fairly competent bridge player, and I had a feeling that Jumbo might be a good one too. Freda and Mrs King were unknown quantities, but I was reasonably confident that we could match them. All the same, I could barely afford to be even a few hundred points down by the end of the session. Besides, I have always had a deep aversion to gambling for high stakes. In that respect, if in no other, I seem to have inherited my father's genes of cautious respectability.

When we began playing it soon became evident that the two partnerships were quite evenly matched, with the advantage perhaps slightly on our side. Jumbo's and my play was solid and we rarely overbid a hand; on the other hand Freda and Mrs King had flair and pulled off a number of spectacular slam bids. Freda continued to sip steadily. She was a naturally sharp player but, as the evening went on, she made one or two careless and costly mistakes. Mrs King was perhaps the most keyed up of all of us. She counted every point and tried to keep her partner's drinking under control. Mrs King herself did not drink and only ate one sandwich, but on the table she kept a little silver case which contained a supply of strange lavender coloured sweets that she would occasionally take out and suck but never offer to anyone else.

Her gamesmanship was masterly and subtle. If Jumbo or I played or bid a hand less well than we might have done, she would always explain, with a great show of kindliness and patience, precisely how we had gone wrong. Though I don't think these attempts to demoralise or irritate us were particularly successful, I noticed, as the evening went on, that 'the girls', as Jumbo called them, were beginning to go uncomfortably ahead on points. It was not that Jumbo and I were playing any worse than them, but the run of the cards did seem to be decisively in their favour. I noticed that this was especially the case when Mrs King was dealing. I don't think I suspected foul play at that point—the idea was too preposterous— but I did dislike the exultant glitter in her eyes as she pulled off yet another spectacular slam. When I looked across at Jumbo I saw an unfamiliarly dark expression on his face. He was controlling himself by concentrating furiously on the game.

Suddenly, just as Mrs King had begun to deal for a new rubber, Jumbo leaned across the table and his great pink hand closed itself around one of Mrs King's slender brown wrists. Mrs King shrieked; Freda looked stunned.

'Oh, no you don't, my lady!' said Jumbo.

With the other hand he picked up from the table the silver case in which Mrs King kept her sweets.

'Madam,' said Jumbo in a strange, cold voice. 'You have just dealt my wife a card from the bottom of the pack. And I notice,' he continued, flourishing Mrs King's silver case, 'that you placed your little sweetie box directly beneath the pack as you dealt, so that you could see where every card went, reflected in the polished silver top. Do you take me for a complete fool, madam? Did you spare a single thought for this young lad who couldn't possibly afford to pay you his share of the money you've attempted to swindle out of us?' Jumbo brought his great red face up to Mrs

King's and growled: 'Sabrina King, you are a damned cheat, and you always have been!'

Mrs King protested shrilly against Jumbo's allegations, but she did not directly deny them. Freda left the table and poured herself another large whisky, her back to the company. When she turned towards the rest of us again, having swallowed a large mouthful of spirits, she began to stare at Mrs King with a kind of detached fascination. I recognised the look.

By this time Mrs King had backed herself into a corner of the room, like an animal at bay. She said: 'You talk to me about cheating! You're all hypocrites. You wouldn't be here. None of you would be here if it wasn't for me.'

'What rubbish is this?' said Jumbo.

'Oh, don't ask *me*, Jumbo. Ask your darling Freda. I'm amazed she hasn't told you. Didn't you tell your Jumbo all about it on the wedding night, Freda?'

Freda was staring at Mrs King, still apparently unmoved by what she was trying to say. Finally she drawled: 'Oh, do shut up, Sabrina. Nobody's interested in all that old stuff, and your stupid lies.'

'They're not lies, and you'd be surprised how interested people are in the old times. Only the other day a nice man from an English publishing company was contacting me about writing my memoirs.'

Freda said: 'Sabrina, darling, that is such a damned lie. Nobody is interested in you and your dreary reminiscences.'

'Oh, they would be interested to hear my story of the famous Hartland Murder. How you came to my house in Nairobi late that night. Why did you beg me to lie to the police for you and say you had been with me all night, Freda?'

'You bitch! That's a filthy lie! You haven't a shred of evidence for any of this.'

'I've still got the gun, Freda dear. The other gun. The Smith and Wesson that you used to shoot Harry while "darling" Jock used his Colt. You brought the Smith and Wesson to my house and asked me to get rid of it for you. Don't you remember, dear?'

'But you promised me, you—' Freda's voice faltered when she

realised she had betrayed herself. She frowned, as if trying to concentrate. The full enormity of the situation was still being anaesthetised from her by drink.

'I said I had thrown it in Thika Falls, but I did not. I kept it. I too need my security.'

Mrs King picked up her bag off the floor where it had been resting beside her chair at the Bridge table. It was a large capacious affair, sewn together, I suspect by Mrs King herself, from patches of embroidered Chinese silk and other rich fabrics. From it she drew out an ancient Smith and Wesson revolver and lowered it onto the Bridge table.

This ought, I suppose, to have been a moment of supreme drama, but somehow it was not. We were all too drained by the night's events to rise to the occasion. For what seemed like minutes we stared stupidly at the object without saying a word.

Finally Jumbo said: 'Well, I don't know about you chaps, but I'm for my bed. I'm all in. We can discuss this in the morning when our heads are clearer.' Then he turned to me. 'I've put you in the same room as you were in last time. Hope you don't mind.' I believe he even winked.

I kept my windows shut that night which was why I was only vaguely aware of some muffled bangs like a car backfiring at about five in the morning. I was woken some hours later by a commotion outside my window on the veranda. I opened the French windows and stepped out into a tableau of figures.

Jumbo was fully dressed, as were the two Somali servants who were talking volubly. A little apart stood Mrs King in a dressing gown of flame-coloured silk, staring blankly at the naked body lying on the veranda.

It was Freda, with a great bloody hole in her chest. The Smith and Wesson was still clutched in her hand. Rigor mortis had set in. The sight might have seemed more horrific had it not been for her face. It was pale and almost innocent of wrinkles and other ravages of age. Her fine features looked as if they had been carved in Carrara marble. Her eyes were closed and her look was serene. She might have been sleeping.

V

After a short service in a nearby church Freda was buried in the garden at Cloud's Hill, as she had requested in her will. The funeral was very sparely attended and of the few who came nearly all mentioned to me at some stage during the proceedings that they were there purely 'to give Jumbo moral support.' The exception was Mrs King who was pointedly shunned by the rest, as she was by Jumbo who nevertheless, for reasons best known to himself, tolerated her presence. She stayed by the grave after everyone else had gone into the house for refreshment. While Jumbo and the others were downing gin slings and whisky sours in the sitting room, I watched her through the window.

Mrs King had gathered Jasmine blossoms from the garden and was slowly, rhythmically, scattering them on the naked red earth of Freda's grave, as if performing a ritual of her own devising. Her great dark eyes were dry and she looked down at the soil which covered Freda with a kind of ravenous fascination, a slight smile on her lips. I recognised the look.

REGGIE OLIVER *(b. London, England, 1952) has been a professional playwright, actor, and theatre director since 1975. Besides plays, his publications include the authorised biography of Stella Gibbons,* Out of the Woodshed, *published by Bloomsbury in 1998, four collections of strange stories, and a novel,* The Dracula Papers: The Scholar's Tale—*the first of a projected tetralogy. An omnibus edition of his stories entitled* Dramas from the Depths *is published by Centipede, as part of its Masters of the Weird Tale series. A fifth collection of his tales,* Mrs Midnight, *is out from Tartarus in September 2011. In 2010/2011 his farce* Once Bitten *was a Christmas season sell-out hit at the Orange Tree Theatre, Richmond. Original stories he contributed to* Exotic Gothic *2 and 3 are "A Donkey at the Mysteries" and*

"Meeting with Mike," with the former reprinted in Stephen Jones'
The Mammoth Book of Best New Horror: Volume Twenty.

Commentary on "The Look": *It is inspired by, but not based
on, a famous scandal which took place in Kenya in the 1940s. I
had the good fortune to meet some of the people who were mar-
ginally involved. It was their conflicting impressions that intrigued
me and made me think about the nature of good and evil. We talk
about people being 'good' and 'evil', but I incline to the view of the
ancient Greeks and, for that matter, Henry James, that evil is a
'miasma', a kind of metaphysical infection.*

NIKISHI

LUCY TAYLOR

EASICK AND SHIVERING, THOMAS BLACKSBURG PEERED out from beneath the orange life boat canopy, watching helplessly as the powerful Benguela current swept him north up the coast of Namibia. For hours, he'd been within sight of the Skeleton Coast, that savage, wave-battered portion of the west African shore stretching between Angola to the north and Swakopmund to the south.

Through ghostly filaments of fog that drifted around the boat, Blacksburg could make out the distant shore and the camel's back outline of towering, buff-colored dunes. To his horror, the land appeared to be receding. Having been brought tantalizingly close to salvation, the current was now tugging him back out into the fierce Atlantic.

A leviathan wave powered up under the boat, permitting Blacksburg a view of houses strung out like pastel-colored beads. Impossible, he thought. This far north, there was nothing but the vast, inhospitable terrain of the Namib desert, an undulating dunescape stretching inland all the way to the flat, sun-blasted wasteland of the Etosha Pan.

Blacksburg calculated his options and found them few. So suddenly and fiercely had the storm struck the night before that no distress call had gone out from the ill-fated yacht Obimi. With the captain knocked overboard and the boat taking on water, Blacksburg and his employer, Horace DeGroot, had been too busy trying to launch the life boat to radio for help. The Obimi wasn't expected in Angola until the following Friday. No one was looking yet. When they did look, there would be nothing to find. He was the sole survivor.

The settlement in the dunes appeared to be his only chance.

Checking to make sure the leather pouch strapped across his chest was still secure, he dove into the water.

Hours passed before finally he hauled himself ashore and collapsed, half-dead, onto the sand. The fog had lifted, revealing a narrow beach hemmed in between two vast oceans—to the west, the wild Atlantic and, to the east, an unbroken sea of dunes that rose in undulating waves of buff and ochre and gold. Silence reigned. The hiss and thunder of the surf was punctuated only the cries of cormorants and the plaintive lamentations of gulls.

Believing that he'd overshot the settlement he'd glimpsed from the boat, Blacksburg trudged south.

Fatigue dogged him and acted on his brain like a psychedelic drug. Retinues of ghost crabs, fleet translucent carrion-eaters with eyes on stalks, seemed to scurry in his footprints with malevolent intent. Once he thought he glimpsed a spidery-limbed figure traversing the high dunes, but the image passed so quickly across his retina that it might have been anything, strands of kelp animated by the incessant wind or a small, swirling maelstrom of sand that his exhausted mind assigned a vaguely human form.

The hyena slinking toward him, though, was no trickery of vision. A sloping, muscular beast with furrowed lips and seething, tarry eyes, it angled languidly down the duneface, its brown and black fur hackled high, its hot gaze raw and lurid.

Blacksburg took in the clamping power of those formidable jaws, and dread threaded through him like razor wire.

He bent and scooped up a stone.

'Bugger off!' he shouted—or tried to shout—what emerged from his parched throat was a wretched, sandpapery croak, the sound a mummy entombed for thousands of years might make if re-surrected.

The hyena edged closer. Blacksburg hurled the rock. It struck the hyena with a muted thunk, laying open a bloody gash on the tufted ear.

The hyena's lips curled back and it uttered a high pitched whooping sound so eerie and wild that the temperature on the windswept beach seemed to go ten degrees colder. He heard what sounded like a Range Rover trying to start on a low battery, but this false rescue was only the guttural cough out of the spotted hyena's broad muzzle. With a final saw-toothed snarl, the pot-bellied creature—which was 70 kilos if it was 10—wheeled around and loped back into the dunes that had spawned it.

Exhaustion had so blunted Blacksburg's senses so that he almost sleepwalked past the grey, wind-scoured facade of a two-story house whose empty window frames and doorway stared down from atop a dune like empty eye sockets above a toothless mouth. Climbing up to investigate, he found a gutted shell, the bare interior carpeted with serpentines of sand, roof beams collapsed inward to reveal a square of azure sky. Gannets nested in the eaves. On the floor, a black tarantula held court atop a shattered chandelier.

Spurred by a terrible intuition, he struggled up another dune until he could look down at the entire town—a pathetic row of derelict abodes, a sand-blasted gazebo where lovers might have lingered once, a church whose steeple had toppled off, the rusted carcass of a Citroen from some forgotten era.

The hoped for sanctuary was a ghost town. A graveyard of rubble and stones.

Stunned, despairing, he roamed amid the wreckage.

The wind shifted suddenly and he inhaled the mouth-watering aroma of cooking meat. The hot, heady aroma banged through his blood stream like heroin. Saliva flooded his mouth. Half-dead synapses danced.

Stumbling toward the scent, he crested another dune and looked down upon the beach to see a sinewy, dark-skinned old man using a stick to stir the enormous cast-iron potjie that rested atop a fire. The old fellow wore frayed trousers, a yellow ball cap, and a short-sleeved pink shirt. His left hand did the stirring. The right one, flopping by his side, was lacking all its fingers.

Behind him, a girl in her late teens or early twenties was pulling a bottle of water from a canvas backpack on the ground. She uncapped the bottle and poured it into the potjie. She wore an ankle-length tan skirt, battered high-tops, and a billowy red blouse. A brown bandanna around her head held back a crown of windblown dreads. An old scar zigzagged like a lightning bolt between her upper lip and the corner of one eye.

With feigned heartiness, Blacksburg slid and trotted down the dune, crying out, 'Uhala po'. It meant good afternoon in the Oshiwambo tongue, but judging from the old man's reaction, it might as well have been a threat to lop off his remaining fingers. The old man's eyes bulged and he let loose a shriek of mortal fear. The woman had considerably more sang-froid. She held her ground, but snatched up a sharpened stick.

'My name is Blacksburg,' he croaked, holding up his hands to show he meant no harm. 'I need help.'

The old man commenced a frenzied jabbering. The woman chattered back, and an animated exchange took place, virtually none of which Blacksburg understood. Finally the old man fell silent, but he continued to appraise Blacksburg like a disgruntled wildebeest.

'Excuse my uncle,' the woman said, in meticulous, school book English. 'You frightened him. He thought you were an evil spirit come to kill us.'

'No, just a poor lost wretch.' He gestured at the empty water bottle. 'You wouldn't have another of those, would you?'

The woman took another bottle of water from the backpack and handed it to Blacksburg, who gulped greedily before eyeing the potjie. 'Fine smelling stew there,' he said. 'What is it, some kind of wild game, stock, chutney, maybe an oxtail or two?'

Using her stick, she speared a dripping slab of wild meat.

Blacksburg fell upon it like a wolf. The meat was tough and stringy as a jackal's hide, but, in his depleted state, he found it feastworthy.

Between mouthfuls, he gave a version of his plight, detailing the sinking of the Obimi and the loss of her captain, but speaking only vaguely of the one who had chartered the boat, his boss Horace DeGroot. The woman told him that her name was Aamu, that she and the old man were from an Owambo village to the east. 'We'll take you there tomorrow. A tour bus stops by twice a week. You can get a ride to Windhoek.'

DeGroot's largest diamond store was in Windhoek. Blacksburg had no intention of showing his face there.

'But what are you doing in a ghost town cooking up a feast,' he said to redirect the conversation. 'Did you know that I was coming? What are you, witches?'

The girl snorted a bitter laugh. 'If I were a witch, I'd turn myself into a cormorant and fly up to Algiers or Gibraltar. I'd never come back.'

Something in her vehemence intrigued Blacksburg, who was no stranger to restlessness and discontent. 'Why do you stay?'

The bite in her voice was like that of a duststorm. 'Do my uncle and I look rich to you? We live in a tiny village where the people raise cattle and goats. A good year means we get almost enough to eat. A bad year . . . '

Blacksburg saw no evidence of food shortage in the overflowing potjie, but saw no need to point that out.

With greasy fingers, he gestured toward the forlorn remnants of the town. 'This place, what is it? What *was* it?'

Aamu foraged deeper inside the backpack, bringing out a couple of Windhoek Lagers. 'No ice,' she said. 'You drink it warm?'

He grinned. 'I'll manage.'

'Come walk with me. I'll tell you about the town.' She took off at a brisk pace, high-tops churning up small clouds of sand, hips fetchingly asway.

Walking was the last thing he wanted to do, but Blacksburg wiped his hands on his trousers and headed up the dune behind her. It was a star dune, one of those sandy forms created by wind blowing from all directions, and it had Blacksburg's eye. Suddenly, with an agility and vigor that caught him by surprise, the old man lunged and seized his biceps in a fierce, one-handed grip, babbling wildly while pumping his mutilated hand.

'Nikishi!' he repeated urgently.

Blacksburg, a head taller and twenty kilos heavier, shook him off like a gnat.

'What's wrong with him?' he asked, catching up to Aamu.

'He's warning you about the evil spirits, the ones that take animal and human form. They like to call people by name to lure them out and kill them.' She rolled her eyes. 'My uncle's yampy. In our village, people laugh at him. Last week he grabbed a tourist lady's Ipod and stomped it in the dirt, because he thought that evil spirits called his name from the earbuds.' She took a swig of Lager, grimaced. 'Can't stand this stuff warm.'

She took off abruptly again, climbing nimbly while Blacksburg labored to keep up. They navigated a surreal dunescape, where decaying buildings pillaged by time and the unceasing wind stood like remnants of a bombing. The larger buildings, the ones the desert hadn't yet reclaimed entirely, indicated a degree of bourgeois prosperity that must have, in its heyday, seemed incongruous, perched as the town was on the edge of nothing, caught between the hostile Namib Desert and the pounding surf.

Aamu must have read his thoughts. 'Forty years ago,' she said, 'this was a busy diamond town called Wilhelmskopf. Water was trucked in once a week. There was a hospital, a school, plans for a community center, even a bowling alley. Everybody lived here—Afrikaners, Germans, Damara and Owambo tribesmen.'

'What happened?' Blacksburg said, although he could guess. Many of the smaller diamond towns had petered out by the middle of the previous century, eclipsed by the huge discovery of diamonds in Oranjemund to the south. Of these, Kolmanskopf, a ghost town just outside Luderitz, and now a major tourist attraction, was the most well-known.

Aamu's answer shocked him. 'In the late '60's, there were a lot of violent deaths, people found with their throats ripped out, torn apart by animals.'

Blacksburg thought of the hyena that had menaced him on the beach. 'Hyenas? Jackals?'

'Certainly. But fear spread that a nikishi and its offspring lived among these Wilhelmskopf people, changing into animal form at night to prey on them. A few superstitious fools panicked and turned on one another, accusing each other of sorcery. Eventually the town was abandoned. Can you believe such bosh? Now it belongs to the ghost crabs and the hyenas.'

Blacksburg finished off his beer and flung the empty bottle across the threshold of a faded cobalt house with sand piled inside up to the turquoise wainscoting. Lizards stern and still as ancient gods stared down from a piano's gutted innards and perched atop a cracked and broken set of shelves. A shiver rustled his spine. He looked away. Down below, in the purpling twilight, he could see the old man reaching into the potjie with his stick, stabbing slabs of bloody meat and flinging them out across the sand.

'Hey, he's throwing away the food!'

Aamu looked away, embarrassed. 'I told you he's mad. Years ago, my uncle was here collecting driftwood after a storm when he was attacked by what he thought was a nikishi. He claims it called his name, and when he answered, it bit his fingers off and ate them while he begged for mercy. His mind hasn't been right since. He says the nikishi told him he must come here after every storm and make a spirit offering of meat and beer. To thank the nikishi for not eating all his fingers.'

'Waste of good food,' scoffed Blacksburg. 'This transforming rot, you believe it, too?'

She looked affronted. 'Of course not. I'm educated. I was sent to Swakopmund Girls' School. I studied German and English, some science, learned about the world. That's why it's hard for me to live in an Owambo village. I know something bigger's out there.'

Blacksburg bit back a sarcastic jibe. What would someone who considered schooling in Swakopmund to be a cosmopolitan experience know about the wider world? This Owambo girl inhabited the most barren region of one of Africa's least populated countries. In Blacksburg's view, she was a half-step above savagery.

'How did you and your uncle get here? Trek across the desert?'

She arched a kohl-black brow. 'No, we rode our camels. Look!' Grabbing his hand, she pulled him along a passageway between a debris-strewn house and a derelict pavilion and laughed.

For a second he almost expected to see two tethered dromedaries. But it was a black Toyota Hilux, sand-caked and mud-splattered, that was angled on the slope behind the buildings.

Blacksburg gave the Hilux a covetous once-over.

'Nice-looking camel, this. Where do you gas it up?

'There's a petrol station for people going to the Etosha Pan about forty kilometers from here. And the safari companies that fly rich tourists in from Cape Town and Windhoek, they have way stations through the desert. Before he became ill, my uncle used to guide for one. That's how he got the jeep.'

'I need to get to Angola,' Blacksburg said. 'What say I buy it from you?'

She eyed him scornfully, his ragged, salt-caked clothes, bare feet, disheveled hair. 'And use what for money? Shark's teeth? Ghost crabs?'

'No need to mock me. Let me explain . . . ' He felt a sudden, irresistible urge to touch her, as though some electrical energy pulsed inside her skin that his own body required for its sustenance. A few strands of hair had whipped loose from under the bandanna and he used that as an excuse, reaching out to tuck the hair back into place. To his dismay, she flinched as though he'd struck her.

'Sorry.' He held up his hands, contrite. 'Look, about the jeep, I can pay you well.'

'The jeep isn't mine. It belongs to the village.'

'Loan it to me then. Go with me as far as Luanda. After that, I'm on my own.'

'But why should I help you?'

'A fair question that I'd expect of you, a graduate of Swakopmund Girl's School. Here, let me show you something,' His smile was confident, but his stomach corkscrewed at what he was about to do—betting everything on this girl's gullibility and greed.

'You say you want to see the wider world. What if I told you you could go anywhere you wanted and live like a movie star? What would you say to that?'

'I'd say maybe you swallowed too much seawater, Blacksburg. That you're as crazy as my uncle.'

'Crazy, huh? Look here.'

With a showman's flair, he reached inside his shirt, unhooked some clasps and pulled out a leather wallet protector. Unzipping it, he produced two plastic baggies.

'Cup your hands.'

He unzipped one baggy and spilled into her palms a treasure trove of uncut stones. Even in the dimming light, they glittered like a fairy king's ransom. Aamu's breath caught. She cradled the diamonds as though she held a beating heart. Her voice, when she finally spoke, was a reverential whisper.

'*Ongeypi?* What are you, a jewel thief?'

'I'm a diamond dealer,' he corrected brusquely. 'I was transporting these to a buyer in Luanda.'

He scooped the stones back into the baggy and opened up the next. These were a few museum quality pieces from DeGroot's private collection, several of which had been loaned out over the years to South African celebrities headed to New York and Cannes. Enjoying himself now, warming to his role, he plucked out a dazzling yellow diamond on a platinum chain. When he held it up, the sunlight put on a fire show, the facets blazed.

Aamu's dark eyes widened as he fastened it around her neck. In her inky irises were gold glints, a few grains of sand out of the Namib desert.

'It must be worth a fortune!'

'A bit more than a used jeep, I imagine. If you get me to Luanda, it's yours to sell. Do we have an arrangement?'

She frowned and chewed her lower lip. 'What about my uncle? We can't let him go back to the village. Everyone will know I took the jeep and went off with an *oshilumbu*.'

Blacksburg cringed a little at being called 'white man,' and looked down onto the beach, where the flames under the potjie still danced. The old man paced a furious circle around the pot, raising his arms in wild supplication to whatever dark gods fueled his imagination. Silhouetted against the blood red sun, the mutilated hand looked like a misshapen club.

He took Aamu's hand and brought her fingers to his lips, tasting the meat and salt under the nails. 'Right then, let's leave your uncle to his demons.'

She laughed and pulled away, trotting along an alleyway between a half-dozen tumbled-down buildings, beckoning him to follow. When he caught up with her, she was framed in the empty doorway of a small stone house where, with a dancer's grace and the lewdness of a seasoned whore, she slowly peeled off the scarlet top and beige skirt.

'At the school in Swakopmund,' she said, letting the blouse fall, 'the priest said I was too wild—too hungry for excitement, for boys and beer, for freedom. He said it's wrong to want too much, that it's a sin to be too hungry.' In the fading light, her black eyes made promises both heartfelt and indecent. 'What about you, Blacksburg? Are you too hungry?'

For the first time in months, Blacksburg permitted himself a laugh of real delight. For a giddy moment, he actually romanced the notion of the two of them leaving Namibia together, a fantasy that Aamu's reckless passion only fueled.

She rode him with a mad abandon Blacksburg had experienced in only a few women—and then always prostitutes high on serious street drugs. If it was sex she'd been talking about when she asked him if it was a sin to be too hungry, then both were surely hell-bound.

Their rutting was as much attack as ardour. Blacksburg, glorying in pain both given and received, devoured her. Past and future fell away, until all that remained was her thrashing body and feral moans, the sea-salt scent of her, and the fierce and biting sweetness of her teeth and tongue. He drank in the musky sweat that ran between her breasts and down her prominent ribs and tangled his hands in the lush snarls of her dread-locked mane. And when they rested, panting, sated, Blacksburg knew only that he wanted more.

Later, she spooned her limber body around his and chuckled in his ear, 'Where will you go after you sell your diamonds? Don't lie to me. I know you're running. You wouldn't be so quick to trade a diamond for a jeep if you weren't a desperate man.'

He was surprised when truth slipped out. 'England, maybe. My mother always said we had relatives in Cornwall. I might go there.'

'Cornwall.' She pronounced the word like one uttering an incantation. 'Maybe I'll go with you, my handsome Blacksburg.'

And, for a few ecstatic moments, the idea of an impromptu adventure with this exotic woman moved Blacksburg deeply, fed into his desire to see himself as noble, heroic even, a survivor conquering the world by dint of ruthlessness and valor and self-will. The man he truly was, rich and powerful like DeGroot.

Later, as he drifted toward sleep, he saw filaments of moonlight slant through the empty window and spill across her face. She was lovely, even with the scar, but what mesmerized him, what he could not tear his eyes from, was how the yellow diamond glimmered around that dark as bitter-chocolate throat.

Blacksburg dreamed about his mother. She stood outside the cottage in Cornwall before a running stream that he had seen in photographs. No longer gaunt, used-up and grey as he remembered her, but young and spirited. Her voice was high and lilting, clear as birdsong, infused with a calm serenity that in her life he'd never known her to possess. She called to him, not in the sharp haranguing style that in life had been her nature, but with a serenity and sweetness. Blacksburg almost loved her then, an alien emotion he had seldom felt for her in life, for this woman who had been an Afrikaner whore.

He woke up to the unholy cackling of hyenas and the taste of charred meat on his tongue.

Aamu was gone. For a second panic gripped him. But the diamonds, still secure in their plastic baggies, were undisturbed.

He pulled his pants on and went outside into a night no longer flecked with stars, but murky, swimming with long, damp tresses of fog. He felt like a diver floating along the bottom of the sea, enveloped in an endless, choking school of pale grey, tubular fish.

Peering down onto the beach, he tried to spot the old man's fire and thought he glimpsed the orange flare of a few remaining embers, but no sooner had he started to descend the dune, than a low, contralto rumbling halted him. The sound came from a dozen yards away, where the fog-swathed columns of the pavilion jutted from the gloom like a ghostly Parthenon.

As he approached, he saw a nest of shadows, low to the ground, diverge and reconfigure, then caught a glimpse of a pink shirt and let himself exhale. The old man was asleep in the pavilion, the noise he'd heard undoubtedly was snoring. More movement— undulating, languid. He saw what looked to his uncertain eyes to be a wild crown of Medusa dreads whipped back and forth—a host of unwelcome images besieged his mind—but it was the hyena's glaring eyes and not its mane-like, ruffled tail that finally made the scene before him recognizable.

The hyena's eyes flashed, then vanished into the fog only to reappear a few feet away. The grumbling, growling intensified. Blacksburg, shocked motionless, counted five sets of eyes.

A frightful snarling commenced as two of the hyenas, snapping wildly, fought over a choice morsel. Bits of skin and gristle flew. Blacksburg glimp-sed a ragged nub of bone attached to a scrap of pink cloth.

His breath caught in a stifled gasp. A hyena's head jerked up, and it raised its gory snout to test the wind.

Blacksburg shoved away from the pavilion and plunged headlong into the fog. He tried to remember the location of the jeep, thinking he might be able to lock himself inside, but the drifting mist cast a surreal opaqueness across the dunescape. Nothing that he saw was recognizable, the blank facades of the buildings as alike as weathered tombstones.

Ahead the murky outline of a crumbling two-story building floated up out of the fog. An empty window gaped. He hurled himself through it, tripped, and landed atop the piano he'd seen earlier—its ancient keys produced a wheezing bleat.

Behind him a sagging door led into a low hallway. The darkness was crypt black. He groped his way along, stumbling over obstacles—a plank, an empty drum of some kind—until he half fell into a small enclosed space, a storage room or closet. He huddled there, heart galloping, listening for the murderous whoops of the converging pack.

Blacksburg?

His own name sounded suddenly as alien and frightful as a curse. It floated on the hissing wind, at once as distant as the moon and close as his own breath, Aamu's voice or maybe just the scrape of windswept sand. He cleared his throat to answer and found that he was mute.

They call people by name to lure them out.

Although never in his life had Blacksburg been superstitious, now some atavistic fear crawled out of his reptilian brain and commandeered all else.

He tried to tell himself his frantic mind was playing tricks, but an older knowledge told him what he feared the most, that what called to him was no hyena but a shape shifter, a nikishi, that would split him open like the old man, from groin to sternum and feed while he lay dying.

Blacksburg!

The piano suddenly coughed out a great, discordant cacophony, as though four clawed feet had leaped onto the keyboard and bounded off.

The door he'd come through creaked, and then a single animal sent forth its infernal wail into the hollow building. At once a clan of hyenas, some inside, others beyond the walls, took up the ungodly cry.

Knowing he was seconds from being found and trapped, he bolted from his hiding place, raced up the hallway and hurled himself through a window that was partially intact, crashing to the sand amidst a biting drizzle of shattered glass.

Without pause, he got up and pounded down the duneface, arms pinwheeling, skidding wildly.

The hyenas converged around him.

The largest, boldest of the beasts feinted once before going for his throat. Its teeth snagged his shirt, taking with the fabric a strip of flesh from Blacksburg's ribs. He fell to one knee, one arm up to guard his jugular, the other to protect the pouch across his chest—even knowing, beyond all doubt, that both were lost to him.

The ecstatic yips of the hyenas were suddenly drowned out by the roar of an approaching motor. The Hilux teetered at the top of the dune, then careened straight down the face, sand spewing out behind the tires, high beams punching through the fog. It slammed onto beach, suspension screaming, bounced off the ground, and veered toward the hyenas. The pack scattered. Blacksburg staggered to his feet, as the jeep skidded to a halt beside him.

'Get in!'

Aamu flung the door wide, and Blacksburg launched himself inside, the jeep lurching into motion while his legs still dangled out the door. A hyena leaped, jaws snapping. He screamed and kicked out. The hyena twisted in mid-air and fell away. Blacksburg muscled the door closed.

Aamu gunned the engine and the jeep tore away through the fog.

She drove like a witch, outdistancing the pack by many miles, before she turned to Blacksburg and said gravely, 'I looked for you on foot at first. I called your name. I knew you were close by, but you didn't answer.'

'I didn't hear you,' Blacksburg lied, shame making him curt, resentful of her. They both knew he'd been afraid to answer, that in that desperate moment, rationality had failed him. He'd believed the hyena pack to be nikishis and one of them was mimicking her voice. He was a fool and a coward, just as all along he knew his boss DeGroot had judged him privately to be. In that moment, when he felt as though she'd seen into his soul and found him wanting, he made a harsh decision.

He told her to stop the vehicle and switch places. He would drive.

L ater, when the mid-day sun was high and blazingly hot, Blacksb urg decided they'd come far enough. He'd been driving for hours while Aamu slept. Now he halted the Hilux in the middle of a sun-blasted stretch of desert bleak and desolate as a medieval rendition of hell, shook her by the shoulder, and said, 'Get out.'

She sat up, blinking groggily. 'What . . . what are you talking about?'

'It's simple. End of the line. Get out.'

'I don't understand.' She looked around at the miles of barren, retina-searing whiteness. 'Is this a joke?'

He barked a bitter laugh. 'Did you really think I was taking you with me? I can get to Angola on my own.'

'But . . . I'll die out here.'

'Yes, I imagine so.'

For a woman contemplating her very short future, she appeared strangely unmoved. 'But we are going to Luanda.'

'One of us. Not you.' He held his hand out. 'And by the way, I want my diamond back.'

'Then take it and be damned!' Before Blacksburg could stop her, she yanked the diamond from around her neck and hurled it out the window as casually as if she were discarding a wad of gum.

He swore and struck her across the head. The bandanna came off. He saw the dried blood in her hair, and the fresh blood flowing from the wound at the top of her ear. He stared at his hand, where her blood stained it.

She dragged a finger pensively along the scar that ran along her cheek. 'You know how I got this? My uncle cut me with a knife. But I was merciful and let him live. Last night I was merciful again. I killed him before I fed his flesh to the hyenas.'

Using sheer force of will, Blacksburg hauled himself back from the brink of panic. 'You think you scare me? You're crazier than your uncle was. If I can kick my old boss out of a dinghy and into the sea, I can damn sure get rid of you. Now get the hell out of my jeep.'

She didn't budge. Wild hunger, wanton and insatiable, raged in her eyes. Her lips curled in a soulless smile. 'Yesterday I could have killed you on the beach, but I was curious about what kind of man you were, about what was in your heart. Now I know. And now, you know me.'

Her voice was lush with malice. Her face, as she commenced her changing, was radiant with cruelty.

'See me as I am,' shrilled the nikishi

At once, her slashing teeth cleaved the soft, white folds of his belly. She thrust her muzzle inside the wound, foraging for what was tastiest. The salty entrails were gobbled first, then the tender meat inside the bones, his life devoured in agonizing increments.

Hours later, a hyena pup following a set of jeep tracks came across a human skull. It seized the trophy in its strong young jaws and headed back denward to gnaw the prize at leisure.

LUCY TAYLOR *(b. Richmond, Virginia, USA, 1951) is acclaimed as the most "highly regarded American woman writer . . . [of] graphic erotic tales of terror" (*St James Guide to Horror, Ghost, & Gothic Writers*). Her sensual prose of spiritually way-ward characters, shocking revenge, and sudden insight has turned heads since her novel debut,* The Safety of Unknown Cities *(1996), won a Bram Stoker Award for Superior Achievement. In novels and short stories since, her philosophic probing of pas-sion—the shameful, the blissful, and the perverse—garnered a Dealthrealm and three International Horror Guild Awards. Her novels include* Dancing with Demons *(1999),* Eternal Hearts *(1999),* Nailed *(2001),* Saving Souls *(2002), and* Left to Die *(2004, written under the pseudonym Taylor Kincaid). Five allur-ing story collections from 1984–2004 are* Close to the Bone, Unnatural Acts, The Flesh Artist, Painted in Blood, *and* A Hairy Chest, A Big Dick, and a Harley. *A passionate traveller, she sometimes sets her tales in the places she adventures, recently writing in the* Exotic Gothic *series of Namibia (in "Nikishi"), Iceland (in "Tívar") and Japan (for "The Butsudan", read* *poignantly by the author at http://faculty.lonestar.edu/dol-son/podcasts.html).*

The Overlook Connection Press has recently re-released her novel The Safety of Unknown Cities *and the collection* The Silence Between the Screams *in e-book form (www.overlookconnection.com). Another collection* Unspeakable and Other Stories *is available at www.smashwords.com. Her story "The Plague Lovers" will appear in* The Mammoth Book of the Best of Best New Erotica, *to be published by Running Press in 2012.*

Commentary on "Nikishi": *About a dozen years ago, I visited Namibia on a cruise down the coast of west Africa and found the bleak and eerie coastline surreal and fascinating. With its endless, undulating dunes that mimicked the ocean swells, the Namibian coast was as barren, fogbound, and inhospitable-looking a place as I had ever seen. Perfect, in short, to serve as a setting for a Gothic tale!*

In the story, Blacksburg encounters Aamu and her uncle in a deserted diamond town that I modeled on Kolmanskop, a real life ghost town outside the city of Swakopmund and a popular tourist destination. Although I wasn't able to visit Kolmanskop, I read about its sad decline from an affluent and bustling diamond center to a forlorn remnant of its former self, its once magnificent buildings and busy streets buried under shifting sands. The history of Kolmanskop provided much of the background for my fictional ghost town.

While researching the story, I also learned that legends of shape shifters, including werewolves and werehyenas, can be found throughout Africa. In Angola and Namibia, they're called Kishis or Nikishis, two-faced demons who seduce the unwary and gullible (if they don't make a meal of them first!).

Whether on the African continent or elsewhere in the world, the prevalence of shapeshifter myths seems to me to speak to the fear we may experience in acknowledging that most people, ourselves included, present two faces to the world, the public one we craft to make a favorable impression, the private one that's closer to who we really are. Being confronted with the truth about one's traveling companion, whether on a honeymoon to Vegas or in the middle of the Namib desert with a stranger, can lead to all sorts of unpleasantness—from confrontations and disappointments to even a hideous demise.

One just never knows.

Add the legend of the Nikishi to the ghost town of Kolmanskop, with a dash of lust and betrayal thrown in, and you have the ingredients for my story "Nikishi".

THE FOURTH HORSE

SIMON KURT UNSWORTH

'HEY, STOP!' ATKINS CALLED, AND STARTED ACROSS THE road towards the battered Land Rover. Although the driver's window was open, the crook of a tanned and brawny arm showing, the vehicle didn't slow down and Atkins had to run to catch it as it moved away from the kerb. He came up alongside the horsebox and was going to bang on the side when he saw, lost in the African shadows of its interior, a large chestnut horse. Not wanting to startle the animal, he jogged faster, the sweat trickling down his brow. Reaching the rear of the Land Rover, he banged on the roof, calling, 'Hey,' again.

This time, the vehicle jerked to a halt in a gritted and rusty squeal of brakes. Atkins stopped, taking a deep breath of air that was too warm to refresh him, leaning over slightly and resting his hand on the roof of the vehicle. The once-white metal was hot enough to hurt his palm.

'What?' said that driver, leaning out of the window and peering at Atkins. He was younger than Atkins, with skin the tanned white of someone who spent a lot of time outdoors, and his face glistened with sweat. His voice was ex-pat English, the original accent, from somewhere in the midlands Atkins thought, threaded with the cadences of Africa. Atkins wondered if he sounded similar, his own Welsh lilt corrupted by the alien rhythms of his adopted country, and suspected it was. The years were blurring his edges, he thought, unmaking him and creating something new.

'What?' asked the driver again. Atkins sucked in another breath, as airless as the first, and replied.

'You've got a pipe loose,' he said, 'underneath. It'll tear loose if you carry on driving on these roads.'

'Fuck,' said the driver conversationally, and climbed out of the vehicle. He was taller than Atkins, bigger up and across and layered with muscle. Atkins took an automatic step back, removing himself from the man's shadow and out of his reach. His size was intimidating, his solidity casting pitch shadows across the vehicle's interior. The man saw Atkins' discomfort and smiled, revealing even white teeth. His smile was friendly, open, and seemed to shrink him down to a more manageable size.

'Thank you,' the driver said, crouching and looking under the Land Rover, and then 'Fuck,' again.

'Is it bad?' a new voice asked, female. Atkins looked over the bonnet of the vehicle to see a tall, slender woman emerge from the passenger seat. She was as tanned as the driver, her hair bleached a straw blonde by the sun and her eyes a faded blue. She smiled at Atkins and then disappeared from view as she, too crouched. Atkins bent down by the man, pointing unnecessarily at the pipe that was dangling loose behind the radiator. Fat liquid dripped from the torn maw of the pipe, pooling darkly on the pitted road.

'Oil cooler,' said the driver and rose. Atkins followed. Across the road, three of Colonel Nicholas' soldiers, dressed in ill-fitting uniforms and with weapons hanging at their hips or over their backs, were looking at them disinterestedly. One of them looked barely old enough to shave, but held his AK-47 with a practised ease. There was a barracks nearby, an outpost from the larger detachment in Kabwebwe, and the soldiers were on rotation from there. They changed every few weeks, although there had been more of them over the previous months, their number increasing slowly and steadily.

'Can you fix it?' asked the woman, also rising, her head appearing in the frame of the passenger window like a straw sun.

'No,' said the man. 'I've got spare oil but I can't repair the pipe.'

'Fuck,' said the woman. 'We need to get him there, Mark. We only have three days.' She looked over at the soldiers, who were still staring across at them. One of them smiled at her and she smiled back with her lips but not her eyes.

'I know that, Victoria,' said the man, Mark. 'I'm aware of our deadline, but this gentleman's right; if we drive like this, at best we'll break down and at worst we'll burn out the engine in the middle of fucking nowhere.'

'There's a supplier in Chingola,' said Atkins, 'that'll probably have the pipe, but it'll take a day, maybe two, for them to get it here I'd imagine. Where are you going to?'

'I'm Mark, and this is Victoria,' said Mark, holding out his hand and ignoring Atkins' question. 'And you are?'

'Atkins,' Atkins said, taking Mark's hand and shaking it. It was warm and dry.

'Just Atkins?' asked Victoria over the Land Rover's bonnet.

'Richard,' said Atkins, letting Mark's hand go. 'But everyone calls me Atkins.'

'I think,' said Victoria, 'that I may call you Richard. "Atkins" sounds very impolite. So, Richard,' she continued, walking around the vehicle and coming to stand next to the two men, 'what do you do?'

'That's why I was looking at you, because of the horsebox,' said Atkins. 'I own a gymkhana a few miles from here.'

The inhabitant of the horsebox was one of the most beautiful horses Atkins had seen, almost as tall as him at the shoulder, chestnut around its head and forelegs, dappling to a light tan over its haunches. It was a contrary one, though, and at first, wouldn't move from the horsebox, remaining motionless even when Victoria took hold of its bridle on and pulled.

'Should I help?' Atkins asked.

'No, thank you,' said Victoria. 'He's being difficult to make a point but he'll come because he knows who his bosses are. He's called Ore, and he's bred from German stock.' She tugged again at the lead and finally the horse began to move, stepping delicately down the ramp at the rear of the box and onto the ground.

'Strange name,' said Atkins, walking ahead of the woman and the horse to one of the empty stables. Behind him, he heard the measured clip of the horse's hooves as they struck the concrete floor. It seemed very loud, somehow drowning out the sound of his own feet and those of the woman. The sun, behind them now, cast the shadow of the horse's head on the ground in front of him so that it appeared to be entering the stable block first, surrounding him. Elongated, the shadow of Ore's ears curved up like horns emerging from a head the size and shape of an enormous cockroach.

'It's kind of a joke,' said Victoria. 'His full name is much longer and harder to say, and very old, so we called him Ore because we got him from a mine in Kitwe.' She walked Ore into the stable as Atkins poured water into a bucket for the animal and pulled in some straw from the bale in the corridor. In a stall opposite one of the others, probably Chime Bar, snorted quietly and stamped his feet. Ore stood quietly as Victoria removed his bridle. She didn't stroke or talk to him, Atkins saw, touching the animal as little as possible. The horse didn't move at all, showing no interest in the woman or his surroundings or the feed that Atkins offered him. Finally, Victoria backed out of the stall and closed the wooden half door. Strips of leather, tied into the animal's platted mane, swayed on either side of his neck as he finally turned to look at Victoria over the stable door. Another, thicker, strip was threaded through his tail and he had what looked like bracelets tight around his fetlocks, something Atkins had never seen before and he wondered if it was a custom local to Kitwe.

'He's very beautiful,' he said as Victoria slid the bolt across to fasten the door.

'Is he?' she said. 'I wouldn't know. He's just something I have to deliver.'

After settling Ore, Atkins drove Victoria back to where Mark was waiting with their Land Rover. They arrived to find him in the middle of a small crowd of soldiers, trying to explain why he was waiting on Mayondo's only street.

'You were seen earlier,' Atkins heard one of the soldiers say as he and Victoria pulled up behind the wounded vehicle.

'Stay here,' said Atkins, turning off the engine and opening his door to climb out.

'No,' said Victoria and climbed out after him.

'Hello, Sergeant M'Buzu,' said Atkins. Mark, taller than the men around him, shot Atkins a glance, the expression on his face impossible to read. 'Is there a problem?' M'Buzu was the head of the barracks in Mayondo, and although Atkins disliked him, he had been careful to cultivate something that might appear to be friendship with the man, if neither of them looked too closely.

'Mr Atkins!' said M'Buzu, his voice cheerful with the hollow *bonhomie* that surrounded the aggression at his centre like dough around a lump of ragged stone. 'Do you know this man? My men tell me he has been lurking here all day, making calls from the payphone in the bar. He is up to no good, we think.'

'Hardly lurking, if I've been out in the open,' said Mark but Atkins shushed him. One of the other soldiers, one of the new ones that Atkins didn't know, stepped forward and knocked Mark in the chest with his rifle, pushing him back against the Land Rover. Mark winced but stayed, thankfully, silent.

'Perhaps it is a clever trick, to pretend not to be lurking when you in fact you are?' asked M'Buzu, his voice dangerously conversational. 'And who is this with you, Mr Atkins?'

'This is Victoria,' said Atkins, his tone dismissive, *This is men's work, pay no attention to her*, and hoped that Victoria would understand. She remained quiet, and he was grateful. Already, several of the soldiers had moved their attention from Mark to her, were eying her like the lions that he sometimes saw staring at him when he rode Chime Bar out from the Gymkhana and into the open bush beyond his home. He had learned to judge when the lions had fed, knowing when it was safe to continue or whether he should turn and retreat before entering their killing zone; he wished he had learned the same trick with humans, whose lusts and drives he remained unable to judge. Their eyes were on her, crawling and lingering.

'These people are my customers, sergeant, but their transport hasn't stood up to our roads,' Atkins said, trying to make his voice calm and businesslike. *Look at me,* he wanted to say, *look at me and forget the woman and the suspicions that you don't have, but whose existence you're using as an excuse for your aggression.* All that violence, simmering in the African afternoon, clad in khaki and smelling of sweat and dust and gun oil and baking earth, and somehow he had found himself in the middle of it. He held out a placatory hand to the sergeant, the edge of a folded Kwacha poking out from his thumb and palm. 'I'm sure you and your men must be thirsty, it's a hot day. Please, have a drink on me, and I'll help my guests get on their way.'

'You have to be tough out here, eh? Africa is not kind to you if you underestimate her, her roads or her wildlife, yes?' said M'Buzu, shaking Atkins' hand and removing the note in a single gesture, clapping him on the shoulder with his other hand. 'Customers, yes? Are you sure? She is a looker, my friend! Perhaps you hope to be her customer? I'll bet you have to pay her, my friend, although not too much, eh? Not too much!'

Atkins felt Victoria tense beside him and spoke before she could say anything. 'Ha, sergeant! She is out of both our price ranges, I suspect, but we can dream, no?' He heard himself mirror M'Buzu's hearty tone and careful speech patterns, heard the soldiers laugh around him and felt himself begin to relax even while he disliked himself for playing the game. The note, spirited away now into a pocket somewhere in M'Buzu's fatigues, had bought them peace.

'My friend Mr Atkins has explained,' said M'Buzu loudly, peering around his men. His face had a clumsy, too-false expression of understanding on it, a bad actor playing a poorly-written part. 'There is nothing for our concern here.' With a final, hard stare that took in Atkins, Victoria and Mark, M'Buzu walked off across the street, his boots dragging tiny zephyrs of sand and dust with them. His soldiers followed, most throwing looks back at Atkins and especially Victoria as they went. He did not completely relax until they had all disappeared into the darkness of the nameless tavern fifty yards down the street.

'Thank you,' said Mark after they had gone. 'I've been here all this time, years now, but I've never got used to it.'

'It's just Africa,' said Atkins. Most expats understood that, the phrase they used to convey their helplessness in the face of corruption and violence and poverty and heat and dirt and brutality. *It's just Africa*, and walk away and don't rise to it and lock the doors between you and it and look at each other knowingly and say again, *It's just Africa* on a kind of disgusted, downbeat exhalation. Africa, in the hands of people who had no idea, control slipping away from the old masters to the new, and wouldn't it be better if things could be different?

'Yes,' said Mark, with the same tone 'Just Africa.'

'They're getting worse,' said Victoria, and spat into the dust at her feet.

'Yes,' said Mark again, and then after a moment, he added, 'but not for much longer.'

Night came quickly, as ever, slipping across the land and swallowing the ground beneath it voraciously. When it came to the gymkhana, it spread itself around the stable block, Atkins' small home and the various utility buildings, held back by the light falling from the kitchen windows and the lamps that he had strung out along the fencing to keep the night's predators away. He looked out at the block now, wondering about the strange day he had had. Ore was the club's first new horse for over a year, joining its three long-standing residents, only two of whom Atkins received payment for. The third, Chime Bar, was his horse, a rescue from a farmer out in one of the provinces who had found the animal abandoned in one his fields one morning, but couldn't afford to keep it. The Kwacha that Mark had given Atkins, currently piled loosely on the table and held down under a pepper mill, would pay for feed for Chime Bar for several weeks.

If there was something that Atkins loved most about his life in

Zambia, it was the African night. It was *absolute*, crowding in on his meagre lights with cathedral vastness, spreading out and absorbing everything about it. It was so different, umbrella black and greater than anything he had experienced in Wales. If he were to go outside, he would hear it as well, hear a silence that was stately in its solidity, punctured only by the distance cries of nocturnal animals and horses in the stables whinnying and moving. Safe in the fragile bubble of his home, he marvelled at it, distant and deep.

One of the lamps on the far fence went out.

It wasn't unusual. Atkins had wired the lamps himself and the bulbs, cheap African things, went often. What was strange, though, was when the next bulb along went just after the first, leaving the end of the stable block nearest the fence in a pool of darkness. Another bulb blew, and then another, a chain reaction that spread quickly along the fence as he watched. For a few moments, the stables were outlined in brutalist shapes and then the lights behind them must have failed as well, and the building was lost to the night. He looked up the ceiling light above him, which flickered slightly as though teetering on the edge of collapsing, and then flared back to life. Looking back at the window, he saw himself reflected in the glass and was uncomfortably aware of the fact that anyone out in the darkness would be able to see him clearly. He thought about the money on his table, and the soldiers who had heard him tell M'Buzu about customers and payment, about greed and violence. Then he went and turned the lights off.

The night had made its way to the other side of the glass. In it, he could make out the faded shapes of the stables and the huts that contained the generator and his tools, but little else. There were uncountable stars above him, scattered across the heights of the sky, but they shed little light. He peered out, trying to spot movement, but saw nothing. If it was burglars, they would attack soon; home invasions were swift and blood-stained and often ended in flames that scoured the earth clean of evidence. He made no attempt to find a weapon, reasoning that any resistance increased the chances of being killed. The best he could hope for was that whoever it was would break in, tie him up and the take the money and leave; he didn't want to contemplate any of the worse scenarios.

As he waited, Atkins heard a low stuttering moan that rapidly rose in pitch until it became a shriek, layered and atonal. It was like the hooting of the klaxons heard through a storm, but the air was calm and the nearby the bushes still. Another sound joined it, a staccato tattoo like fat sticks beating brittle ones, faster and faster until it became one blended noise. Atkins peered through the window, seeing only gunpowder shades of night, hearing only that which made window itself shiver slightly.

Within the cacophony, Atkins thought he heard the ragged whinnying of horses.

'Jesus,' he exhaled, and wanted to go to the loved animals that were his livelihood, but he dared not. He was old, frightened of the people out there who were making his horses nicker, and he wanted to live. Instead of moving, he watched, expecting any moment to see the darting movements of people approaching the house.

They did not come.

The noise rose, all fractured siren wails and savage battering. Over in the stables, the horses were *screaming*, he thought, screaming in voices that were almost human. He had only ever heard horses cry like that once before, when the stables of his childhood home had burned along with every animal within. Then, the shrieks had torn the Welsh night apart. To forget the smell of charring hair and horseflesh was impossible; for years, he saw in nightmares the frenzied whirling of the creatures in their stalls as the flames beat back his father and brother, preventing them opening the doors for escape.

This was worse. There were no flames; there was simply the howl itself and the night around it and then, finally, something moved near the stables. Whatever it was, he shouldn't have been able to see it; no light remained, and yet he *did* see it, a blacker patch against the darkness, roiling out from the stable in spastic lurches. There were no details for his eyes to catch, only the contractions of the thing as it squeezed itself out from the building, the upper half of the door bending out to an angle that Atkins would have sworn was impossible. The noise increased, if that was possible, raging against the glass in front of him, formless and torn.

What was emerging from the stable finally loosed itself from the door, falling to the ground where it flipped over and scuttled towards the house. It seemed to grow as it came, and although blacker than the evening around it, part of it glowed as though lit from within by guttering embers. Atkins couldn't tell its shape, only that as it came it swelled, that it had eyes that gleamed blackly and that it danced as it moved, jittering and capering. It covered the ground from the stables quickly, rising up so that it blotted out the stars above, towering above the house and still the bellowing came, Chime Bar and the other horses screaming and screaming, and something began to chuckle, sulphurous and low. 'I'm lost,' Atkins breathed to himself, sure that whatever it was, it was the last thing he would see. The laughter became louder, loose and shifting, not drowning the horses' panic but somehow magnifying it; Atkins closed his eyes and waited for his end.

After a few moments passed, and nothing happened except the cont-inuing noise, Atkins couldn't help himself. He opened his eyes and it was there, filling the window, pulsating on the other side of the glass as though pressed against the side of the house, smothering it. Thickening, liquid flesh was churning against the window, one moment covered in hair and the next naked, now scaled and now feathered, lips emerging briefly only to sink back and be replaced by eyes that blinked and glared. The air smelled of burning stone and dust, and steam gone sour, the odour filling the room in fetid waves. It pressed ever closer against the window, and the glass shuddered and bulged, and still the horses shrieked, and then the thing fell back. The sound of it changed, the chuckle giving way to a noise like the grinding of teeth, and the house shook once, as though the thing had given the building a swift, savage shake. A blue pitcher in one of the cupboards near Atkins fell over and shattered and the kitchen table jerked, the pile of Kwacha fluttering loose as the pepper mill weighting them down fell over and rolled away. Atkins' beer bottle slipped from his fingers and broke on the floor, sending shards of glass and warm beer spattering around his feet. A metallic crash came from one of the other rooms. The thing at the window writhed around and was gone.

There was a charcoal-hued cobra on the road, just on the far side of the gymkhana gate, battered flat and surrounded by a halo of blood and intestines and loose scales like confetti after a wedding. Atkins found it, along with all the other dead animals, as he walked around the club the next morning, avoiding entering the stables. The horses had neighed for hours, finally tailing off during the night's lowest point, and all around the buildings that living abyss had pranced and jabbered. Sometimes, it disappeared from Atkins' vision, but he could hear it chortling and sniggering and feel the earth under his feet vibrate as it leapt and landed. Even after the horses had fallen silent, it had carried on, only ceasing before dawn. His last view of it had been as it squeezed itself back into the stable, pouring itself like oil into the building as the sunlight crept across the horizon.

Atkins had set a fire in a brazier behind the generator shed and he scraped up the remains of the snake and added it to the blaze, where it crackled with greasy flames. Other animals were already burning, the ones he had been able to carry. Outside the fence, which the thing had left untouched, the bushes and the ground beyond were battered down and torn. Larger creatures lay among the broken branches and foliage and once dry earth, two zebra and a duiker the only ones he recognised. Others were merely torn and bloodied piles of flesh, white fragments of bone emerging from the ruins like accusatory fingers. The destruction ran in a swathe around the club, a wide circle of torn earth that stretched several hundred yards, dotted with the carcasses of animals that had been caught beneath the dark thing as it landed, and marked here and there with indentations that might have been the prints of clawed feet or suckered tentacles or something else entirely. Atkins walked it, trying to read meaning into the marks, but could find none; he felt numb, both physically and emotionally, as though he was observing himself from a long way off and through layers of glass that were scratched and muddied. Building the fire, picking up or dragging those animals that weren't too large, kicking dirt over bloodstains that, if left, would attract the daylight predators, all these things he had done with the automaton movements of the rootless men he sometimes saw in Kitwe, drunk or in a place beyond drunk, and a long way from any kind of reality. *It's Africa*, he told to himself bitterly, *just Africa, the place where the impossible can happen, where brutality and beauty walk hand in hand. Just Africa.* Finally, when he could put it off no longer, he walked to the stables.

His horses were still alive, just.

Chime Bar lay on his side, his breath coming in ragged, foamy bursts. Blood spatters ran up the walls of the stall around him, and urine and shit were strewn across the floor. His legs were covered in scratches and crusting rips; one of them was clearly was broken. Thick strings of saliva tinged a ropey pink oozed from his nose and as Atkins looked at him over the stall door, he rolled his eye, the whites bloodshot and inflamed. In the next stall, Siesta Glow was standing but each of his legs was damaged and he had a series of cuts across both his head and flanks, as though he had tried to batter his way out of the stall. Atkins supposed he had. Opposite, Enzo had his head out over his door, his mouth dropped open to reveal bloodied teeth and a tongue that he had bitten through. Dribbles of blood hung from his lips and dropped lazily to the floor.

Beyond them, Ore stood in his stall, unharmed and motionless.

'I'm sorry,' said Victoria from behind Atkins, making him jump, although not much. His reactions were slower, less taut than usual.

'What is he?' asked Atkins, looking at Ore, at the way the horse's eyes trailed both him and Victoria, its mane swaying under the weight of the woven leather strips.

'At the moment, he's a horse,' said Victoria, placing a softly golden hand on Atkins' upper arm, caressing him gently. 'I'm sorry, we didn't know this could happen. Mark and I will cover any costs that this causes, vet's fees or compensation. Here, I'll help you clear up and get the horses sorted.'

'Vet's fees,' repeated Atkins, looking again at Chime Bar. He felt tears well in his eyes, felt the weight of what he had to do press down on him. 'No. I have something in the house that I can give him that'll end his suffering. Siesta Glow and Enzo may be okay, but Chime Bar's—' and then he was crying and couldn't carry on.

'Yes,' said Victoria, 'that's maybe best.'

'I should give some to him,' Atkins managed, nodding at Ore, his sobs hitching in his chest.

'You wouldn't get close,' said Victoria. 'If I couldn't stop you, he certainly would.'

'What is he?' asked Atkins again, but Victoria merely shook her head and said, 'Let's get the horses sorted.'

It was late afternoon by the time they had the stables cleaned and the horses dealt with, and the sunlight was the slanting yellow of a tired day. The vet, a sallow, taciturn man called Pesters, treated Siesta Glow and Enzo and had taken Chime Bar's body with him; Atkins wanted to hope that his horse would be afforded some kind of burial but he knew that he wouldn't. Instead, his flesh might be sold for meat, or simply dumped away from the town where the wildlife would consume him at their leisure. *Just Africa,* thought Atkins again, as he watched Pesters drive away, Chime Bar's head lolling over the tailboard of his flatbed truck. It had taken the three of them several hours to drag the animal from the stables and winch him into the truck, and then another hour for Atkins and Victoria to clean the stall and wash away the streaks of blood that Chime Bar had left running along the stable floor. All the time, Ore stared at them, moving only the smallest amounts to keep them in view.

When they had finished, Victoria led Atkins back into his home and sat him down on one of his chrome kitchen chairs. She bent to pick up the Kwacha, still loose on the floor, and put them on the table back under the pepper mill. Then, she took two Mosi Lagers from the fridge and opened them, giving one to Atkins and sitting opposite him with the other. As she walked past him to sit down, she trailed one hand over his shoulder and then brushed his cheek lightly.

'He can't stay here,' said Atkins eventually. 'I don't know what he is, I don't want to know, but you have to take him away.'

'We can't,' said Victoria. 'The Land Rover won't be fixed until tomorrow, and we'll take him then. Mark will come before nightfall, and we'll make sure that it doesn't happen again. Please.' She leaned forward and placed her beer on the table, reaching out to take one of his hands. He took another mouthful of his beer and looked out of the window. The sun had stripped the sky to a rich, angry red now; nightfall wasn't far away. Victoria rubbed her thumb slowly across his palm, the nail tracing delicate lines towards his fingers, and said, 'It's only another night.' She had a mixed scent like night-perfuming flowers, gardenias, cereus and jasmine.

'No,' said Atkins, feeling the pressure of her hand and fingers as a maddening tickle.

'We can take him tomorrow, we'll be gone for good and you'll never see us again, I promise. Unless you want to,' Victoria said, leaning forward. The neckline of her top bowed away from her skin, revealing the top of her bra, a froth of delicate lace swirls. 'We only need to deliver him, and then it's done.'

'Deliver him? Who to?'

'Colonel Nicholas,' said Victoria.

'You must have seen how it's been going?' Victoria asked Atkins, still stroking his palm and leaning forward so that the upper edges of her smooth breasts and lavender bra showed even more . 'How Zambia's following the other African countries? How many soldiers were there in Mayondo when you came here? When did you come here?'

'Five years ago. I took early retirement from the mine to set this place up.'

'What was it like then? The town, I mean?'

'Quiet. Small. There was a garrison here then but it was only about 10 soldiers, and we hardly ever saw them except when they came to get drunk or play football.'

'And now?'

Atkins didn't answer. Mayondo had changed, it was true, but it was only as he thought about it that he realised how much.

'How much has this country rotted? Since Colonel Nicholas' coup?'

'It wasn't a coup,' said Atkins, helplessly, feeling that he was being talked back into the corner of a room whose walls he couldn't see but could feel pressing about him.

'Wasn't it? A sudden doubling of the army numbers? A doubling again after that? New garrisons? Places like this suddenly jumping from ten soldiers a garrison to sixty? A hundred? New weapons? New uniforms? And who controls them, Richard? Ultimately? The president, or Colonel Nicholas?'

'It's not a coup,' said Atkins, watching a bead of sweat trickle down Victoria's neck and into the shadowed valley between her breasts. The side of his beer bottle trickled condensation over his fingers in sympathy.

'Maybe not an obvious one,' said Victoria, placing her other hand on his leg. He glanced down at it, tanned and firm over his knee, the nails short and unpainted. Working hands. 'No battles, no bloodshed, but the Colonel's the man in charge now in all but name. Only there has been bloodshed, hasn't there?'

Victoria's other hand had started moving now, and she leaned forwards further so that she could stroke Atkins thigh. More of her laced bra showed in the cleft that was exposed by her bowing top, and she licked her lips as she looked up at Atkins and continued speaking.

'Who's controlling the soldiers now? No one. Your friend M'Buzu, for instance? Who makes sure the bastard behaves himself?'

'He's not my friend,' said Atkins.

'No, and he's not completely controlled either, which is how Nicholas wants it. A series of local fiefdoms where the only rules are what the commander decides; where that commander has almost total freedom. Rapes and burglaries, assaults, murders, they're all up, and the only absolute is that Nicholas is commander in chief, and his peccadilloes are law. Have you ever had trouble? Been attacked? I mean you're out here alone, miles from Mayondo with just the wildlife and the dust and the horses for company.' Victoria's voice, which had becoming strident, fell at the mention of the horses. Her hand, crawling ever further up his leg, stirring in maddening rubs, stopped momentarily before starting again, each back and forth movement carrying it slightly higher.

Atkins thought of his fears the night before, of the home invasions and drunken savagery he read and heard about, of his friend Prescott who had been stamped so viciously in a fight not of his making that the image of an army boot's sole had been printed across his face in old bruises for weeks afterwards, and said 'No.'

'Why?'

Atkins didn't answer; it was a question he avoided even though he knew the answer.

'Horses,' said Victoria, and now her hand was clutching as it rubbed, the tips of her fingers brushing his crotch at the apex of each circular brush, harder and harder. 'You survive untouched because Colonel Nicholas likes horses, and the men know that, and M'Buzu knows it. But most people don't have horses, do they? They don't have anything Nicholas likes, except maybe money or blood, or a body he can use. He never comes out further than Kitwe, he doesn't need to, because he *hears*, and reaches out and acts without ever moving. There may not have been a coup, but there has been a shift in power, you know it, I know it, Mark knows it, every poor sod who's been beaten or raped or had land annexed for the military knows it. You know it, Richard. But Nicholas, he loves his horses, and he likes people who love horses, and Ore is a gift for him. We just need another day to fix the Land Rover and we'll be gone.' Her hand gave up all pretence of delicacy and jerked forwards, cupping around his scrotum and holding it in a warmth that was somehow hotter than the dying African day.

'Another day,' she repeated, and squeezed gently. 'Another night, twelve hours, and we'll be gone. Mark will take care of Ore, and I'll . . . ' she let her voice trail off and started rubbing again, this time moving upwards. Atkins looked at her, at the intensity on her face, at the deep swoop of her breasts and the sweat the trickled down between them. Her tongue flicked out and licked her pink lips.

'We have a chance, but we have to be able to control it,' she said. 'The summoning binds it for three days, but the binding's getting weaker and it can escape at night. We didn't realise how much damage it can do, but just think. *Think!* What if that was in Nicholas' compound? What if it was freed, released from the bindings on the third night to do what it wanted? We could be free of him. We could have our country back!'

'Our country?' asked Atkins quietly. 'We're guests here, nothing more.'

For a second, Atkins thought she would slap him. Her face clenched, and her right hand jerked up as though to lash at him before dropping back. 'Guests?' she said. 'Guests? Without us, the people here would still be banging rocks together and roasting grubs. *Still* in the shit. We brought civilisation here.'

'And gave Nicholas the guns to make sure everyone acts as civilised as he wants them to be?' asked Atkins.

'It's Africa!' snapped Victoria. 'Just fucking Africa! They need to protect them from themselves!'

'No,' said Atkins again. 'They need *us* to treat them like humans. I don't know what Ore is, what you've done, but I can't be a part of it.'

'You already are,' said Victoria. 'You were seen with us, and the horses won't protect you if M'Buzu or someone starts to really think about you. Just a funny old man, living by himself with just the horses for company? If a man can't make love to a woman, what is he good for anymore? You're already in suspicious company, and what if they start to think you're gay? A queer? What if I were to drop into a conversation in town that I tried my hardest to give you the fuck of your life, but you wouldn't because you prefer boys? How long will you last then, Atkins?'

He remained silent, and his silence was answer enough: *not long*. Whatever protection the horses offered him, whatever carapace of civility M'Buzu wore and made his men wear, it was brittle and weak and liable to shatter at the lightest of pressures. So far, Atkins had maintained his safety by not being noticeable, being as insubstantial in people's memories as gossamer, but what Victoria was threatening would make him solid, would give him an existence he didn't want. Would make him a target. He wondered how long it would be before his tyres were slashed when he went into town, before the whispering started and then the shouts of 'faggot' and 'queer', before the shops stopped serving him. Before men came to the Gymkhana and to his home with violence at the fingertips and on their tongues, and he knew that the answer was the same as before: *not damn long.*

There was a knock at the door. Atkins went to stand but Victoria simply called, 'It's okay, Mark.' Mark entered the house, looking at Atkins and Victoria and seeming to take in everything that had happened in one glance. He looked tired and there were streaks of grease and dust across his wrinkled clothes.

'I'm sorry it came to threats,' he said. 'That was never our intention, please believe us. One more night, and we'll be gone. I just have to bind it more firmly.' He gestured to a heavy book he was holding, bound in leather so dark it looked like aged metal. 'It's stronger than we thought.'

Victoria leaned forward again, although this time she did so without revealing her breasts or bra, and kept her hands crossed over her legs. 'I'm sorry too, Richard,' she said. 'You've been good to us, helped us when you didn't have to. Just help us a little more. Help *everyone*, let Ore stay. We'll move him tomorrow, take him as a gift to Nicholas and then we'll be gone, out of your hair for good.'

'And after?' Atkins asked.

'After Nicholas is dealt with?' she said. 'The thing in Ore has a night of freedom, those are the rules. It has one night and then at dawn it'll be gone, back to the place we summoned it from. It's freed in Nicholas' compound, it destroys it and him and everything else there, and whatever mess it leaves will be put down to the usual insurrection or infighting or revenge. In the vacuum left by Nicholas' death the government can move quickly, reassert its authority. We can go back to where we were, to being a country that it's good to live in, where we can afford to not be fearful.'

Atkins looked from Victoria to Mark and back again, and then nodded, once. What choice did he have, really? Ultimately, it all

boiled down to the same thing, power and violence and the threat
of violence, no matter who was making the threats. *Just Africa*, he
thought. *If you let this blow over you like a dust storm out of the bush,
you'll emerge dirtied and scoured raw, but you'll be alive.*

J ust after nightfall, the horses began to scream again.

Atkins was at his kitchen table, looking again at the piled
Kwacha, seeing it soiled and sweating and rank. Under the sound
of the horses, he could hear Mark chanting and, taking up the
descant, Victoria singing. When he looked through his window
towards the stables, the night's opacity was shivering around it as
though it was being disturbed by something moving under its
surface but which couldn't find the strength to emerge. Finally, a
new noise joined the cacophony, a fractured, roiling belch of a
noise, furious and frustrated and so great that it made the Mosi
Lager bottle in his hand shiver like a palsied infant.

In a life of choices made to remain unseen, Atkins had often
wondered what he would do it ever presented with a situation
where all of the solutions would make him visible. As he slipped in
through the stable door, not making an effort to remain silent
because of the noise coming from within the building, he began to
understand himself better. *I've been blessed,* he thought, surprised
at the sense of dawning revelation the thought gave him. *I was
hiding so that I could have this place as long as possible, the gymkhana
and the Africa I love beyond it.* Raising the shotgun wasn't hard.

Victoria had answered his last question, but had answered a
question he hadn't asked. He imagined the roar of the horses
magnified, made huge by the addition of more horses. How many
was Nicholas supposed to have in his compound? Twenty? Thirty?
Huge numbers, certainly; he collected them the way other men
collected old paperbacks or paintings or mistresses. And who else
lived in the compound besides Nicholas and his men? Wives,
certainly; children, probably. What would they sound like when the
thing in Ore got loose? Like the horses? Worse?

Beyond Mark and Victoria, Ore's stall was filled with flapping, with wings or claws or tentacles, with something for which Atkins had no name, long and fat and writhing. It was hoofed and sparks flew like greasy spittle when it hit the walls. Mark's chanting was ragged as he held the book out in front of him and Victoria danced in sinuous waves besides him. *Just Africa*, thought Atkins, and then, *but that's not right, not at all. It's not 'just Africa', it's God's Africa, the most luminous country there is, where the light is brighter and cleaner than any other, and if this place has a problem it's us, with our 'just Africa' and 'we know better' and 'back to what it was', all built on the backs of the poor dead bastards that we thought were in our way or that were somehow less than us.* He looked again at the thing fighting the horse's flesh, trying to escape even as Mark's chanting drove it back in and the other animals screamed around him, and he wondered how much damage it could do here if it got out. *Not much*, he thought, and sighted along the gun's barrel. It could trample the animals if it wanted, flatten the vegetation and tear the earth, but more plants would grow and the earth would heal and more animals would come.

The gun's explosion was insubstantial in the noise, but Mark's back and chest disintegrated nonetheless. Blood and torn flesh leapt out across the book and the stall beyond it in vivid strings. Victoria screamed and that which had been Ore let out a bellow. Without Mark's chanting restricting it, it was growing, metastasizing, taking a shape that Atkins' eyes couldn't hold on to. It opened its mouth: a tongue slickly massive, anchored in flesh born in some darker place, lolled. Smoke curled from it, clotting around the lights and dimming them. Victoria screamed again as the thing leaped and flowed from the stall towards them. The beautiful woman vanished into it with the sound of hair sizzling in open flames, and Atkins had time to think, *Just Africa, just the place I love*, and to regret that he wouldn't ride a horse or see the burnt-honey light of the African sun again, before it was on him, was pressing all about him and he was gone.

SIMON KURT UNSWORTH *(b. Manchester, England, 1972) came into the world on a day when, disappointingly, there were no signs or portents of anything mysterious or occultly significant happening. He currently lives on a hill in the north of England with his wife, child and dogs, where he writes essentially grumpy fiction (a pursuit for which he was nominated for a 2008 World Fantasy Award for Best Short Story) and gets older. His work has been published in a number of anthologies, including the critically acclaimed* At Ease with the Dead, Shades of Darkness, Exotic Gothic 3, Gaslight Grotesque *and* Lovecraft Unbound. *He has also appeared in three of Stephen Jones'* Mammoth Book of Best New Horror *anthologies and also* The Mammoth Book of the Very Best of Best New Horror. *His first collection of short stories,* Lost Places, *was released by the Ash-Tree Press in 2010, and his second,* Quiet Houses, *by Dark Continents in 2011. He has collections due out from both PS Publishing and Spectral Press, in 2012 and 2013 respectively.*

Commentary on: *"The Fourth Horse": When I wrote "Mami Wata" for* Exotic Gothic 3, *I set the story in Zambia for the sole reason that I have a family friend living there whose life I could plunder for details; "The Fourth Horse" is set there for exactly the same reason. The story grew out of an incident involving a horse being delivered to Joseph Kabila which was related to me by the family friend, and a sense of the kind of lengths people will go to when conspiring to change or manipulate the political systems they find themselves living under. It was one of my favourite sort of stories to write, one that changed direction in the middle and ended up at place that I'd never planned or foreseen. Atkins is, I think, one of the most heroic characters I've created, and I found myself liking him and his attitude more and more as the story developed. I wish I could have given him a better fate.*

THE FALL

STEPHEN DEDMAN

THE FLIGHT TO TOKYO HAD TAKEN MORE THAN NINE HOURS, without a chance for a cigarette, and the bus ride from the airport to the hotel took another two, through a mostly grey landscape under a low grey sky. Wilson had to walk the last few blocks in the rain, because the shuttle didn't go to his hotel, only to a more expensive one nearby. The lift groaned and shuddered as it took him up to his room, and the ride up to the thirteenth floor seemed to take as long as his flight. After shutting the door behind him and dropping his pack on the floor of the tiny room, he prised off his shoes and collapsed on the bed, face up. He drew a deep breath, then lit a cigarette and lay there for a few minutes, just reminding himself how it felt to be horizontal and motionless. Days like this convinced him that man was never meant to fly—or at least, he told himself wryly, never meant to fly economy class from Australia to Japan. He was too tired even to take any pleasure from the thought of finally being here.

It was already dark at six, when he finally found the energy to pick up the phone and call Kyoko and tell her he'd arrived safely.

Kyoko met him in the lobby. They recognized each other instantly, despite never having actually met: he was the only

Westerner around, she the only person dressed in Lolita-Punk. She rushed up to him, then stopped just short of flinging her arms around him, and they stood almost nose-to-nose for a moment. Years of smoking had all but destroyed his sense of smell, but he was faintly aware of an elusive, exotic, enticing fragrance.

'How are you?' she asked, a little awkwardly. 'Jet lag?'

'I'm okay, though my body clock's a little off. I didn't think it was night-time already.'

'It gets dark early here, at this time of year. It's fall, nearly winter. Short days, long nights,' she replied. 'But it's spring in Australia, isn't it?'

Wilson nodded. 'Where are we meeting Yoshi?'

'Ahh.' Kyoko looked even more embarrassed. 'Yoshi won't be coming with us.'

'Will he be at the meeting tomorrow?' The three of them had been working together for years on an irregular web-based comic, *The Conqueror Worm*. Wilson had written most of the story, Kyoko had translated it into Japanese and drawn the human characters, but Yoshi had designed the distinctive steampunk hardware, the elaborate deathtraps, the architecture of Hell, and most of the dreaming demons. Though he was unable to draw a living being that didn't seem to be in constant agony, his mechanical plans were so painstakingly detailed that Wilson found it easy to imagine the devices working—which, he suspected, had played a major role in attracting the attention of a publisher.

'I don't think so,' said Kyoko, uneasily. 'He's . . . can we get out of here? There's a good sushi place around the corner.'

The little restaurant was nestled between apartment buildings, and obviously catered to locals rather than tourists: Kyoko ordered for him, as Wilson's Japanese was rudimentary and no-one else in the place spoke any English. 'Have you ever heard of hikiko-mori?' Kyoko asked, once the waitress was out of earshot.

'No.'

'They're mostly boys, or young men, who don't get into university and can't find good jobs, so they stay at home, more and more, until they finally stop leaving their bedrooms completely unless there's no-one around. Yoshi's been like that for a few months.'

Wilson stared into his green tea. 'This happens often enough that you need a word for it?'

'Yes. I'm sure there are other cities where the unemployed find it hard to leave home, and are ashamed and withdraw to some degree . . . but the hikikomori are extreme cases. Yoshi still communicates in other ways—e-mail, mostly, or online chat with people he trusts— but he will not see anyone else or let them see him.'

'You knew him before we started working on the comics, right?'

'Yes, in high school. He was doing well until the exams, but after that . . . ' She paused, as the waitress returned with their miso soup, then lowered her eyes and stared into the bowl for a moment. 'He has headaches,' she continued, when they were alone again, 'sees things strangely, out of proportion, I don't know the English word . . . '

'Migraines?'

'Thank you. I know he's suffered from those for years, but they didn't stop him going to school. I think he was depressed, too, but it became much worse after his father died . . . which happened just after Yoshi failed the exams. I don't think there was any connection—Ushiba-san had been sick with cancer for some time—but Yoshi may not believe that.'

Wilson swore softly under his breath. 'What about selling *Worm*? Hasn't that helped him? I know the advance wouldn't have been enough to let him move out, but it must have made him feel better . . . '

Kyoko bit her lip, then looked at her watch. 'It did, but not in a way that brought him out of the room . . . or out of himself. Please, I'll take you to the Ushibas' house. That might be easier than trying to explain any more.'

Yoshi and his mother lived on the top floor of a narrow grey-walled apartment building that had been hastily and unlovingly built soon after World War II, and overlooked a murky canal. Kyoko pointed out the dull, dark, somehow eye-like window of Yoshi's room, then led the way up a stairwell that smelled of mildew and fish sauce.

Yoshi's mother answered the interphone, and seemed glad enough to see Kyoko, but warned them that Yoshi seemed still to be asleep. 'I hear him moving about some nights after I've gone to bed,' she said quietly in Japanese, as they removed their shoes and winter jackets. After the chill of the night, the apartment—heated by a small gas fire—seemed almost oppressively hot. 'Not often: I think he waits until he's sure I'm asleep.'

Wilson decided to let Kyoko translate for him, rather than trust to his own Japanese. 'Does he speak to you at all?' he asked Mrs Ushiba, as they sat down at the kitchen table.

'He leaves notes, sometimes.'

'Do you know if he ever leaves the building?'

'I don't think he ever does.'

'Do you ever go into his room?'

'I tried. He put a latch on the door after that. He buys things on the internet and has them delivered here.' She covered her mouth, hiding an embarrassed smile. Wilson looked at her, and said softly, in English, 'Would it be a really bad idea to ask what sort of things?'

Kyoko thought about this for a second. 'Probably,' she replied; then, in Japanese, 'Can we stay until he wakes up?'

Mrs Ushiba looked uncertain, then nodded. Kyoko took out her phone, and quickly keyed in a short message. 'If he's awake, he'll probably answer, even if he doesn't actually get out of bed.'

A few seconds later, the phone miaowed. 'Tell him I'm here,' suggested Wilson.

'He says Hi,' said Kyoko, after another exchange of messages, 'and he asks if you have a phone.'

'No; my service provider doesn't work here.'

'What about your computer?'

'I left it back at the hotel. Can you ask if he can come out?'

Kyoko hesitated, then did as she was asked. 'Yoshi says no, not while there are so many people here,' she relayed, with a slight quirk of her lips. 'He knows you've come a long way to see him, and he says he'll try to come out later . . . which means after I leave.' She drummed her black fingernails on the shabby table, then looked at her watch. 'There's a store around the corner; Mrs Ushiba and I can go there for a few minutes and have a coffee or something.'

'We can't ask her to leave her own home!'

'It's a little early for her to go to bed,' replied Kyoko. 'If we go out for, say, twenty minutes, that gives him time to get dressed and come out to see you. I'll text him when we're about to come back. Do you have a better idea?'

When the women had gone, locking the door behind them, Wilson waited in the unnervingly quiet apartment for several minutes. He stared at Yoshi's bedroom door, noticing the faint zigzag cracks in the grey walls around it—souvenirs of a few earthquakes and many minor tremors—and despite his best efforts, found himself remembering how, in *Dr Jekyll and Mr Hyde*, Jekyll had also communicated by notes slipped under a door, unwilling to let anyone see that he'd transformed into Hyde . . . then, Dracula warning Jonathan Harker not to explore his half-ruined castle . . . then to 'The Monkey's Paw', then Bluebeard. . . . By the time he heard the bolt slide back, he half-expected to see Yoshi transformed into a Lovecraftian Deep One or a similar monstrosity. Instead, he saw a plump, weak-chinned, eerily pale Japanese teenager wearing black sweat pants and a T-shirt emblazoned with a portrait of Edgar Allan Poe.

Unlike the bare-walled living room, Yoshi's refuge was lined with posters, artwork, and unstable-looking bookshelves. Reproductions of Goya woodcuts and Giger grotesques, as well as tattered and much-annotated printouts of Yoshi's own designs for weapons, framed the desk; a scroll depicting the seven hells of Japanese mythology ran above the blackout curtains and around one corner; a full-sized picture of Elvira in an open coffin was taped to the ceiling directly above the unmade bed. 'Excuse me for a moment,' said Yoshi, speaking English so quickly he was barely coherent and brushing past him as he hurried towards the apartment's bathroom. 'Go in, sit down, I'll be back.'

Wilson hesitated, then ventured inside and sat in the only chair, at the desk. He looked around at Yoshi's library, the works apparently shelved at random, non-fiction mixed with novels and manga, English with Japanese, books and DVDs with figurines. A copy of *Tales of Mystery and Imagination,* bound in fake scarlet leather, lay open, spine up, on the pillow; Wilson glanced at it, then noticed strands of black—thread? hair? protruding from beneath the rumpled quilt. Uneasily, he lifted the covers and saw dark eyes in an ivory-pale face framed by ebon hair. A faint smile played about dark crimson lips, showing a hint of white teeth.

Wilson sucked in a lungful of air and stared for a moment, waiting for a sign of life or movement; none came. He heard the toilet flush, and dropped the covers and sat down hastily in the chair.

Yoshi returned to the room a few seconds later. 'Sorry,' he said. He picked up the volume of Poe, placed it on the floor, and sat on the pillow. 'I've been re-reading this, and thinking of includ-ing some of his characters in *Worm*. General Smith, the Man Who Was Used Up, might still be alive; the old men from 'A Descent into the Maelstrom'; maybe have them find Fortunato in the vaults . . . '

Wilson realized that he was holding his breath, and let it out. Yoshi mistook this for disapproval, and his shoulders slumped slightly. 'Of course, you're the writers,' he said gloomily, 'it was just an idea . . . '

'I'll think about it,' said Wilson, trying not to think about what might be underneath the hills and valleys of the quilt. He suddenly remembered another Poe story, 'The Oblong Box', in which the central character travels with his wife's corpse in his cabin. He dismissed *that* thought—the room, and Yoshi, had a sour shut-in smell, but not so oppressive that it could have disguised the rank odour of a decaying body. 'Right now, though, the main thing on my mind is meeting with Mr Tanaka tomorrow.'

'Oh.'

'He wants to meet all three of us.' No reply. 'We're equal partners in this.'

Yoshi looked away, and was silent for a moment. 'You and Kyoko do all the words, though.' His voice, which had been animated, now seemed leaden, as though he was reading a spell in an unknown language phonetically and feared that an error in pronunciation might summon up the wrong demon.

'He's interested in your artwork, too—just as much as the words, or Kyoko's drawing.'

'But you are better with words. I can send him as much artwork as you want, but talking to him. . . . I dread it. I dread the events of the future, not in themselves, but in their results. I'm scared I'd say the wrong thing.'

'I don't think you would.'

'I would. I can't be in a room where there are other people talking; it confuses me. It's not so bad when I read, but I can't even stand music any more; I can't always tell what other people are singing or saying and what I'm only thinking. I don't think I can go,' he said, shaking slightly. 'Not yet. I have to study for my exams. I failed last time. I failed badly. I don't want to fail again.' With a visible effort, he looked Wilson in the face again. 'Not so soon. Please. This is at best but a harmless, and by no means an unnatural, precaution.'

Wilson blinked. The phrase sounded familiar, but in his jet-lagged and weary condition, he couldn't remember where he might have heard or read it before. 'What should I tell Mr Tanaka?'

'Tell him I'm not well. Tell him . . . ' He shrugged. 'You and Kyoko are writers. You will think of something. Do you want some sushi?'

When he left the building an hour later, hurrying through the rain towards the subway with Kyoko, Wilson could barely remember one word of the often incoherent conversations he'd had with either Yoshi or his mother: the vision of the strange face staring out from the shadows in Yoshi's room was still impossible to shake. He'd tried to convince himself that the 'hair' had been nothing but the fringe of some garment, and that he'd only imagined the face, as humans often did when they glimpsed an arrangement of spots and curves that might have been eyes and a mouth . . .

'I see you've met Midori,' said Kyoko, when they finally reached shelter.

Wilson turned and stared at her. 'Midori?' he spluttered.

'It's what he calls her.'

'I wasn't imagining her, then?'

'Not the way I think Yoshi does. Do you remember asking if he was feeling better since he received the advance from Tanaka? I gather that's how he spent it.'

'What is she? A mannequin?' Wilson blinked. 'Well, that's not quite as scary as some of the other possibilities that had occurred to me. I knew she couldn't be dead, and I didn't think she could be alive . . . '

'You thought he was dating a vampire?' said Kyoko, amused. 'Or a zombie?'

'No. Well, they crossed my mind, along with cataleptics and the Bride of Frankenstein, but I thought it was much more likely that I was just hallucinating the whole thing. But her face looked so real . . . I could have sworn I saw teeth . . . '

'Very likely. She's a sex doll—a top of the range one, not one of those blow-up things.' She shrugged. 'There are places in Akihabara where you can rent them by the hour, but I don't think they deliver, so he probably bought his with the advance.'

'Fuck.'

'Probably the only sort he's ever had,' Kyoko agreed, 'though that's just a guess. I almost envy him, in a way.'

'You can't be serious.'

'Not completely, though there *have* been times when my life would've been easier if I could've put my lovers in boxes when I didn't need them. But some people might say he has everything he needs.'

Wilson snorted, and fumbled in his pockets for his lighter. 'Only as long as his mother keeps enough ramen in the house.'

'He can get food delivered.'

'What if their money runs out?'

She shrugged. 'They own the building, and rent out the other two floors. It's not much—the place is a dump, as you probably noticed—but they live frugally.'

'They'll be able to live a whole lot better if we do this deal!'

'True. I guess we'll just have to hope Tanaka doesn't insist on meeting him.'

They caught the subway back to Wilson's hotel, neither of them speaking until they were alone in the grumbling lift, when Kyoko suddenly threw her arms around her co-writer and gushed, 'A TV series!'

Wilson grinned back at her; her joy seemed to flow through him, intoxicating as sake and tasting much better. 'It's really going to happen?'

'I think so. Tanaka has a good reputation, and even if it doesn't, the money for the rights alone . . . '

'I know. Even converted into dollars, it sounds like a mountain of cash.' The lift doors opened at last, and they walked to his tiny but well-equipped rooms, still holding onto each other as though scared of being pulled out of a dream. They both sat on the bed, then fell over, lying on it face to face. Kyoko wriggled up the bed until her face was level with his; then, suddenly at a loss for words, grabbed her Smartphone.

Wilson's disappointment couldn't be hidden, but he tried, 'Do you think Tanaka bought the story about the migraine?'

'With that much money, he could buy my firstborn,' she replied, but with a slight downward quirk of her lips.

'Yoshi hasn't replied?'

'No. But yes, I think Tanaka bought it—for now. But he's going to want to meet him, and more importantly, he wants the animators to meet him.' She shrugged.

'Can you think of any way to get Yoshi . . . '

'Out of his room? This might. And the exams start next week—

I hope he can make it to the exam hall, because if he doesn't, the next lot isn't until June.'

Wilson bit his lip. 'We have to do something. Not just because of *Worm*, not even just because we owe him; he's—'

'No-one's ever come up with a reliable way of treating the hikikomori,' cautioned Kyoko, 'and there's been at least one case of one who was sent to a mental hospital, hijacking a bus and running over a crossing guard when he was released.'

'Somehow, I can't see Yoshi doing anything like that.'

'Me neither, but . . . I know that being hikikomori may seem strange and scary, but that doesn't mean that we can't make things even worse. Do you know the Poe story, "The Premature Burial"? The narrator is cataleptic, but this stops when he stops obsessing about death, gets rid of his medical texts, and thinks and reads about other things instead, travels . . . and lives. The macabre thoughts became a self-fulfilling prophecy—and the reverse.'

'You want to stop doing *Worm*? Maybe I'm rationalizing, but I don't see that making him happier.'

'I don't know. It's just . . . maybe he dreams he's the artist starving in a garret, like his heroes Poe and Lovecraft. Maybe he thinks you have to suffer like that, to feel everything and nothing, to make the lasting art. But you're right, we just have to wait and hope. What else can we do?'

Wilson woke the next morning, to find Kyoko gone. He lay there, feeling completely disoriented, for more than a minute before fumbling for the light switch. He stared at the depression in the pillow next to his, then buried his face in it for a moment. That was when the idea hit him.

Yoshi opened the bedroom door when he was sure that his mother and Kyoko had gone. 'Thank you for letting me know about the anime,' he said. Though clearly excited, he also seemed nervous to be outside his bedroom.

Wilson nodded. 'Tanaka wants you to meet the animators,' he said, without preamble. 'Can you do that?'

Yoshi seemed to turn even more pale, something Wilson hadn't thought possible. 'I don't . . . excuse me,' he said, rushing off towards the bathroom. Wilson waited until he'd heard the bolt slide home, then hurried into Yoshi's bedroom and raised the covers. The life-size doll lay there, face down: Wilson grabbed it, surprised more at its weight than its lingering smile, and carried it over his shoulder to the apartment's front door. Kyoko was waiting on the landing with a large empty suitcase; she raised an eyebrow slightly when she saw the doll, but helped him fold her up until she fit inside the case. 'I hadn't expected her to be quite this big,' she admitted.

'They make small ones?'

'You don't want to know,' she assured him. 'I'm glad I thought of the case, though; I'd hate to have to stuff her into a taxi while she's naked like this.'

'She?'

'You'd better hope Yoshi thinks of her as "she", not "it",' said Kyoko. 'This isn't likely to work if he doesn't—not that I like the chances of it working, anyway.' She brushed Midori's hair out of the way of the zip, then closed the crimson suitcase. Together, they carried it down to street level, dropped it once, and wheeled it out of the alley, and stood there for a moment until Kyoko had recovered her breath enough to phone for a taxi. 'Okay,' she said, as she returned the phone to her bat-winged handbag, 'you'd better go up and tell Yoshi what happened, before he decides to leave the place by the window. I'll see you back at the hotel.'

Yoshi had retreated into his bedroom by the time Wilson returned to the apartment, and when the Australian knocked on the door and identified himself, the reply came in the form of a note slipped under the door: *Where is Midori?*

'Midori's good.'

I want her back.

Wilson considered telling him that he had his playmate, in the hope that Yoshi would open the door and speak to him directly, but didn't want to risk being caught in a lie. 'You'll have to leave the building.'

A pause, then: *Why?*

'Tanaka and his animators want to meet you.'

I can't. Not yet.

'When, then?'

No answer.

'What about your exams?'

Wilson waited, but there was no reply. Ten silent minutes later, Mrs Ushiba knocked on the front door, and Wilson let her in. Not knowing what else to say, he said thank you and good night, and left.

Kyoko phoned him the next morning, waking him. 'Ushiba-san called,' she said. 'She didn't sleep much last night: Yoshi nearly tore the house apart looking for Midori, in case we'd hidden her there. She got some sleep after she made sure he couldn't open her bedroom door. She says she's scared to stay there with him, but she's also scared to leave.'

Wilson rubbed his eyes, opened his laptop, and lit a cigarette. 'He hasn't e-mailed me,' he said, a moment later.

'He messaged me last night, and asked if I had anything to do with this "somewhat childish experiment", as he called it. I don't think he wants to talk to you.'

'I keep expecting him to demand to speak to the doll,' Wilson replied, with a glance at the suitcase. He'd resisted the urge to open it for a closer look at the toy, but its presence had made him feel weirdly nervous. 'He does know she can't talk, doesn't he?'

'I think that's what he likes about her,' said Kyoko dryly. 'One of the things, anyway. What do we do now—apart from stalling Tanaka?'

'Tell him that if he wants to see Midori again, he's going to have to talk to me.'

'Okay. What about his mother?'

'I don't know. I forgot to ask: does she go out during the day?'

'Some days. She doesn't have a job, if that's what you mean.'

'Uh-huh. What about someone she can stay with?'

'No other family . . . but she knows my parents, and they know about Yoshi, I think they'd let her stay in my room for a while . . . '

'Ask. If they say yes, let her know.' When Kyoko didn't reply, he asked, 'You both know Yoshi better than I do—'

'I'm not sure about that—'

'—and I'd never *heard* of hikikomori before. If you think this is too risky, tell me.'

'I don't think Yoshi would hurt his mother,' said Kyoko. 'Not knowingly—not physically, anyway. She means too much to him, even if no-one else does. I don't think he'd hurt anyone else, except maybe himself . . . but I think he's too scared of pain for that. Did you see any weapons in his room?'

'Not real ones. Only drawings.'

Kyoko nodded. 'He can design them—he's been doing that as long as I've known him—but I don't think he's ever used one, even if he is a ronin.'

'He's a *what*? I mean, I've heard the story of the forty-seven ronin, I know they're masterless samurai, but I—'

'Sorry. It's slang—what we call students who fail to get into uni. What do you think we should do now?'

'I guess if he doesn't come out, we'll have to tell Tanaka the truth. Do you think he'll pull the plug?'

'If he thinks Yoshi's unreliable, he might . . . and I think Yoshi will blame himself if he does.'

'"I dread the events of the future, not in themselves, but in their results."'

'What?'

'Something Yoshi said.'

They spent the day in Akihabara and Harajuku, window-shopping and admiring the cosplayers, then found a small restaurant that served inexpensive tendon and tempura. Kyoko's phone miaowed while they were ordering, sending the waitress into a fit of head-lowering giggles. 'It's Yoshi,' said Kyoko, after a quick glance at the screen. 'He says he wants to see Midori, to be sure she's okay.'

'Tell him where my hotel is.'

'He says he's not leaving the house until he sees her.'

'There's a webcam in my laptop. If he'll chat with me, I'll let him see her.'

Kyoko keyed that in. 'He says okay; call him tonight.'

'Tell him I will.'

Wilson unfolded the doll and sat her in the room's only chair. There was something disturbing about her immobile face and unblinking stare, and he had to resist the urge to close her eyes—or to cover them, as they apparently lacked lids. Instead, he grabbed the white bathrobe from the closet and dressed her in that, suspecting that Yoshi might become jealous if he saw her naked with another man in the room.

He logged on to g-chat and pinged Yoshi, who replied instantly. LET ME SEE MIDORI NOW

Wilson turned the laptop around so that the doll was staring over his shoulder.

CLOSER

The Australian shrugged, wishing that he had a cell phone that worked in Japan, then picked up the computer and placed it on the table in front of the doll. He tilted the screen to give Yoshi a full-length view, then positioned the laptop so that Midori was staring over his shoulder as he typed.

ok?

BRING HER BACK TO ME

will you meet Tanaka?

A moment's hesitation, then IF YOU BRING HER BACK AND SHE'S NOT HURT

tomorrow?

No hesitation this time. IF YOU BRING HER NOW

Wilson looked at the wan face on the screen, and decided to

trust him. I'll be right there, he typed, then shut down the computer, stubbed out his cigarette, and packed Midori into the crimson suitcase. He wheeled the case to the lift, and pressed the button for the lobby. The lift shuddered, descended—and then the lights went out as it jerked to a halt, halfway between two floors.

Yoshi sat at his desk, trying hard to concentrate on something other than the digital clock in the corner of the laptop screen, not to think that if they were going to come, they'd be here by now. His need to see Midori had become so urgent that, despite the risk of his mother coming home unexpectedly, he'd left his bedroom door open so that he'd hear Wilson walking up the stairs or knocking on the door just a few seconds sooner, and could let them in a moment earlier. He glanced at the clock again—11.49—and tried telling himself not to worry. Wilson had come here before, he knew the subway system and wouldn't get lost, he . . .

so where is he?

Wilson spoke enough Japanese to give directions to a taxi driver if he didn't want to haul the suitcase to the subway . . .

maybe he decided to keep her

He wouldn't do that! He's my friend!

then why did he steal her?

Yoshi gritted his teeth, and reloaded the news headlines. Nothing about a disaster in Tokyo that would explain Wilson's tardiness. His hands shaking, he picked up his copy of *Tales of Mystery and Imagination* in the hope of losing himself in a story. The book fell open to the first page of 'The Tell-Tale Heart', and he read 'TRUE!—nervous—very, very dreadfully nervous I had been and am; but why *will* you say that I am mad?'

He closed his eyes for a moment, then opened the book to the story that most spoke to him. I won't do anything until I finish this, he told himself. Or midnight, whichever comes later. Not before then.

———

E very few minutes, Wilson pressed the button on his solar-powe
red watch to provide a little light in the oblong box, until eventually the battery ran so flat that the watch refused to glow. By the
time the doors were prised open, he'd long since lost track of time,
and would not have been astonished to see daylight.

He hauled the suitcase out of the lift and hurried down the stairs
to the lobby, barking out a request for a taxi. He lit a cigarette as
he waited, and stubbed it out as soon as the cab pulled up outside.
He stared at the blank face of his watch, then smiled wryly. He knew
he'd have to apologize profusely to Yoshi for his lateness, but at
least he felt sure that his friend would still be home when he
arrived.

K yoko was sitting up at her computer, translating dialogue for
the next page of *The Conqueror Worm* by turning Wilson's English into appropriately nuanced Japanese. As she positioned the
speech bubbles so that they didn't obscure the elaborate steampunk architecture of Yoshi's backdrop, something niggled at her,
preventing her from concentrating fully . . . something Wilson had
said that Yoshi had said . . .

She closed her eyes for a moment, trying to remember the exact
words, then googled the phrase 'somewhat childish experiment'.
All of the hits linked to a Poe story, 'The Fall of the House of Usher'.

She glanced at the clock—12.14—and realized that she hadn't
heard from Wilson since he'd said he was taking the doll back to
Yoshi's home, about four hours ago. She checked her phone for
messages, but there was nothing. She opened g-chat, but neither
Wilson nor Yoshi were online.

She tried to tell herself that she was worrying unnecessarily, but
knew that she'd never be able to sleep until she was sure that both
of them were okay, so she called for a taxi.

Y oshi had spent many hours designing deathtraps and dungeons
for *The Conqueror Worm*, and he did a thorough job of sealing

the apartment's doors and windows with duct tape before turning
on the gas. Once that was done, he sat back in his chair wondering what to write as an epitaph. A quotation from Poe—'Should
you ever be drowned or hung, be sure and make a note of your sen-
sations'—came to him, and he deliberately typed that out and hit
save.

Wilson paid the taxi driver, then hauled the crimson suitcase
out of the trunk and carried it up the stairs. There was no
answer when he knocked on the door, so he deposited his burden
on the landing, sat down, lit a cigarette, took a deep drag to try
and soothe his nerves, and tried to think. He knocked on the door
again, harder and harder each time. 'Yoshi!' he yelled. 'I'm sorry
I'm late, but the lift in the hotel broke down. I'm here now, and I
have her with me!' He unzipped the suitcase, and lifted the white-
shrouded doll free, holding the manga-eyed girl up with an arm
around her waist, her face on a level with his, almost cheek to
cheek. He felt strangely light-headed, and short of breath. 'I'm not
leaving until you open the door, so you may as well let me in!'

Yoshi had slumped over the keyboard, but even in his oxygen-
deprived stupor, he became aware of a distinct, hollow,
apparently muffled, reverberation. Unsteadily, he tried to stand,
then, swaying gently, he slowly staggered towards the source of the
noise, his footsteps leaden. Wilson continued to pound, until his
fist smashed through the dry and hollow- sounding wood.

For an instant, Yoshi saw Midori standing outside the door, and
the redly gleaming tip of Wilson's cigarette.

A taxi stopped on the other side of the street, and Kyoko stepped
out just as the explosion blew out the windows. She watched aghast
as the once barely-discernible fissures in the cancer-ridden concrete
walls burst asunder, and the top floor crumbled into the murky
waters of the sullen canal.

STEPHEN DEDMAN *(b. Adelaide, South Australia, 1959) is the author of the novels* The Art of Arrow Cutting, Shadows Bite, *and* For a Fistful of Data, *and more than 100 short stories published in an eclectic range of magazines and anthologies. He has won the Aurealis and Ditmar awards, and been nominated for the Bram Stoker Award, the British Science Fiction Association Award, the Sidewise Award, the Seiun Award, the Spectrum Award, and a sainthood. He has previously worked as an actor, game designer, experimental subject, and used-dinosaur-parts salesman; he currently teaches writing at the University of Western Australia, and enjoys reading, travel, movies, talking to cats, and startling people. For a complete bibliography and news updates, check out his website at* www.stephendedman.com.

Commentary on "The Fall": *I first heard of hikikomori from a documentary I saw in 2009—the year I first visited Japan, and coincidentally, the Poe bicentennial.*

Because so many of Poe's characters are prematurely entombed, or willingly shut themselves off from the outside world, it seemed only natural to cast a hikikomori in a Poe homage, an updated "The Fall of the House of Usher". I considered making Madeline/Midori a faulty robot, climbing out of the uncanny valley under her own power, but setting the story that far in the future seemed needlessly complicated: besides, having a robot turn killer seemed too much of a cliché. I'd learned too much about Japanese sex dolls while doing research for another story, "More Matter and Less Art", and having Madeline/Midori inanimate meant that Wilson had to play a larger role in the story, which seemed all to the good.

Yoshi's choice of epitaph is a quote from Poe's "How to Write a Blackwood Article".

My thanks to Des Hurst for his hospitality and his invaluable assistance in dealing with the Tokyo subway system.

IN THE VILLAGE OF SETANG

TUNKU HALIM

I WAS NINETEEN WHEN MY MOTHER DIED OF FEVER WHICH she contracted after her labours in the paddy fields. Soon after her white shroud was swallowed by the crumbling earth, I received word that Mak Ina, my aunt, wanted me to move to Setang, the village where our territorial chief resided. Mak Ina worked as his head cook in what she called his 'palace' and, as she was already seventy, she needed help in her daily duties.

Setang was half-a-day's walk from the village of my birth, but because of my club foot, it took all day to get there as I hobbled down the track between jungle, gambier plantations and tin mines dotted about the scared limestone hills. I arrived with my body aching, staggering with my bundle of clothes just as the insect voices mounted a shrilling octave. Then out of minarets Maghrib prayers came echoing like a wind and descended upon the valley.

At the village check point, two Japanese soldiers leaning lazily against a coconut tree, with their khakis leggings half undone, asked me what I was doing here. I told them my business and the one that looked sulkiest and half-sick spat on the ground before waving me through. I hobbled past wooden houses on stilts, perched above their small dirt compounds of weary fruit trees and empty chicken coops. An old man, smoking a cigarette, fiddled with a wreck of a bicycle. Beside him a scrawny monkey sat, tied to a wooden post, tearing up a rotten papaya whilst its mournful eyes stared at me.

About fifty families lived in Setang, the most important of which was Dato Nan's. The territorial chief's house, I had heard, was five or six times the size of a normal one. Even as I followed the track alongside several *geta perca* trees, I could see its timber, the colour of burnt umber, spanning across the hillside like a monstrous crow nestled on a verdant landscape.

I had never seen such a huge house before and my mouth widened as I drew closer. Its sturdy dark planks, its looming walls seemed to hold up the purple sky. Sloping up steeply was a thatched roof and, above it, the evening star was winking. Was it warning me or welcoming me? I didn't know. After my mother died, I felt I had nothing to live for, but here, no matter how unpromising, a new life was beginning.

I hobbled around to the back and found Mak Ina chopping pungent-smelling red onions in the small building that housed the kitchen. She was a small and round grey-haired woman, who moved with great deliberation. After warmly greeting me, she passed me a drink of water mixed with lime juice and sat me down on a *mengkuang* mat of pandanus leaves.

'Any trouble with the Japanese?' Mak Ina asked, speaking slowly in a sing song voice. 'You shouldn't have come alone, you know.'

As she spoke, my aunt's lips and tongue were dancing flames of orangey red for they were stained from a lifetime of chewing betel leaf filled with areca nut. She once told me that it gave her not only the energy but the inspiration to cook delicious food. But that was a long time ago.

'There were some along the way,' I replied. 'But they left me alone.'

'That's good,' she sighed. 'Well, Yan, you're lucky to be working here, you know.'

'I know that, aunty.'

'I didn't really need extra help in the kitchen. I can get help from the other servants. But you needed looking after. Luckily, Dato Nan agreed.'

'I know. Thank you.' I rubbed the sweat off my forehead and retied my long hair.

'After your mother died, I knew there was no one to look after you. You and I know that marriage is out of the question . . . '

Mak Ina didn't elaborate and so I simply nodded, indicating that I understood what she meant.

She was, of course, referring to my club foot—and to the black birthmark, the size of a guava on my cheek. No boys from my village had ever shown an interest in me. Perhaps that is also why the Japanese soldiers left me alone. There was once a boy though, but he married someone else. That too was long ago.

Mak Ina continued with a cursory description of the household duties that were expected of me.

'Another thing,' she said, turning to me in almost a whisper. 'Don't venture out of here after we've turned in for the night. Even if you can't sleep.'

'Why's that, aunty? Is it the Japanese?'

She shook her head.

'Then why?'

'Just don't, Yan.' She shrugged her small shoulders. 'All we have tonight is tapioca. Now let's see you slice that one up. I want to make a boiled salad of it.'

A few days later, well after Mak Ina had extinguished the kerosene lamp and we five servants were all lying on our mats, I realised my necklace was missing. I had carelessly left it hanging on a delicate branch of the Frangi-pani tree beside the old well.

Though not expensive, it was my mother's and she gave it to me a few months before she succumbed to fever from too much labour in the rice paddies. Other than the bundle of clothes I had brought with me from my village, it was all I had.

Two of the other servants were already breathing heavily. Carefully, I got on my feet. Moonlight crept in through the gaps beneath the wooden shutters and this was sufficient for me to pad my way to the main door.

'Don't go out, child,' a voice said.

It was Mak Ina.

'I forgot my necklace,' I whispered. 'I'll be very quick. It's just by the well.'

'Get it tomorrow,' she insisted.

'It might be gone by then, aunty. I'm so worried . . . '

I heard her sigh.

'You're a careless one, Yan,' she whispered back. 'Off you go then. Get it and come straight back.'

The door creaked opened and insect shrills suddenly filled the air. The dirt compound outside was bathed in eerie moonlight. A breeze swept through my hair and rustled the leaves of the trees.

The stone well was perhaps a hundred feet away and beside it stood the twin silhouettes of two Frangipani trees. To my left loomed the long main building. Its curving shadows reminded me of a *parang*, the long knife used for many things, including slaughtering animals.

I crept down the wooden steps and hurried across to the well. The wooden bucket attached to a rope was cast carelessly to one side. A pool of dark water like freshly drawn blood floated beside it. I quickly searched the two trees, my fingers running along the small branches, feeling the rough knobbly bark.

But the necklace was gone.

Perhaps I was mistaken. Where else could I have put it? I was sure I had left it hanging on a branch, its silver chain glinting in the blazing sun.

Just as I was about to hurry back to the servants' quarters, I heard a sound. It was the snap of a twig. It was almost masked by the gush of the stream behind the orchard but I had definitely heard it. I stared hard between the tree trunks and branches of mango and star fruit trees but saw only shadows.

Then came another sound.

Something scratching the ground. I should have fled then. Instead I foolishly crept forward. Perhaps I thought it might be someone who had found my necklace. Or perhaps I was just curious. The sound of my heart hammered my ears as I moved cautiously from tree to tree.

Beyond the orchard, a stream shimmered. It made a loud

cascading sound as water flowed over small rocks which appeared remarkably white in the moonlight and resembled large eggs, some of which were broken. Then I saw it, crouched on the bank was an unmistakable muscular shape.

A tiger!

Perhaps the stream had masked the sound of my footsteps and the beast did not hear my approach. But now I was afraid to turn back, afraid that it would chase me as I retreated to the servants' quarters. So I hid behind the trunk of a rambutan tree and watched.

I saw the rhythmic movement of its body as it breathed the night air. Its ears twitched as if it was bothered by insects or perhaps, more worryingly, listening for prey. Occasionally, it would stare up at the jungle across the stream. Then, I must have glanced away for a second, for when I looked up, the tiger was gone.

I swallowed hard.

What if the beast had seen me? Smelt me? Perhaps right now it was circling behind me, stalking within the shadows of the fruit trees, getting ready to pounce?

Barely able to breathe, I stared at their misshapen silhouettes, listening hard, ready for the animal to charge. What I would do, I didn't know. I picked up a large stone from the ground as a weapon and held it close to me, between my small breasts. As I waited, the moon peeped between the branches, the stars glittered in the foliage. When I was sure the tiger was no longer waiting for me, I crept in the direction of the well.

Just as I reached it, I heard a rustle. It seemed to come from beneath the steps that led up to the kitchen building. I knelt behind the moon-washed stone work and then, abruptly, a figure stepped from the shadows. He was tall, muscular but slightly hunched. As he turned to climb up the steps, moonlight gleamed upon the long white hair that fell upon his broad shoulders. Even at this distance, I could make out his dark and angular features.

It was Dato Nan!

He was the reason we were all here. Chief of the district, this was his 'palace,' and he perhaps the most powerful man in the state, second only to the sultan.

Dato Nan was wearing his bed clothes—an orange sarong and a light blue pyjama top. At the top of the stairs, about six feet from the ground, he pushed open the kitchen door and disappeared inside. Pulling up my sarong, I raced around the side of the building soundlessly in my bare feet just in time to see him leave the kitchen building and stride along the bridge that led to the main house.

It could only be him!

His white beard caught the light of the kerosene lamp inside the entry hall as he entered. But that was not before he hesitated and glanced behind him. He stood there for a long moment. Then he turned away and firmly shut the door.

The next morning, when I was hanging out the clothes behind the servants' quarters, Mak Ina pulled me aside to ask me why I had taken so long to get my necklace the night before. She said she must have fallen asleep as soon as I had left and when she awoke I had not returned.

'I was about to go out looking for you, Yan,' she chided in a slow sing song voice. 'Then the door opened and you came in. Thank Allah you're safe!'

'I saw something strange,' I said. 'I didn't want to tell you last night. I didn't find my necklace but I saw something else . . . '

I then quickly told her of a tiger and our chief.

Mak Ina shifted her small round body beneath the scorching sun. She pursed her lips and scratched her grey hair as she listened.

'Mustn't tell anyone else about this, little Yan' she whispered. Her face was grave and beads of sweat peppered her brow. 'You shouldn't have seen what you saw.'

'But why?'

'It's a secret. Our village's secret.'

'Tell me about it, aunty. Please!'

She glanced behind her towards the house whose timber shutters stared ominously back at us.

'Long ago, child,' she whispered. 'There was a dispute between Dato Nan's great grandfather and a cousin-in-law of his. It was over who would become the next territorial chief.'

I nodded, encouraging her to continue.

'Anyway, one day when this cousin was bathing in a hut made of palm leaves beside the river, a tiger leapt in and killed him. The villagers found his torso floating down the river. The palm leaves were smeared with blood. A village boy saw the tiger wading across the river.'

'Where's this river?'

'I haven't taken you there yet, child. You'll need to follow the stream until it flows into River Setang. It'll take a bit longer than the chewing of a betel nut to get there.'

'Sometimes chickens, goats, or even cows are crept on around here—mauled, killed, pulled away,' she continued. 'If traps or hunting parties are organised by those who are ignorant, they are quickly ordered to leave the tiger alone. Many think it's some sort of sacred creature that cannot be touched. But those closer to Dato Nan's family know better. The tiger legends have always been with us.'

Her orangey red lips and tongue were fiery in the bright sunlight, then her eyes stared right into mine. 'You know, this has nothing to do with your father. That was a terrible thing. But there is no connection between Dato Nan and your father's death. You must know that.'

I slowly nodded. I did not want to speak about my father. Not now, anyway. . . . He used to kiss me on the forehead, then gently touch my cheek. It made my heart fly a little.

'Seven years ago, Yan. All history now. We learn to forgive and forget. For instance, the British were our enemies seventy years ago but today we want them to save us from these Japanese demons.

'Did you know I was only a child when the British soldiers marched up the hill into our district? They looked so fine in their hats and red uniforms. After they had left the paddy fields and marched into the jungle, our men ambushed them. We attacked them with spears and *parangs*, krisses and guns. They bleed bright, little one, brighter than a crimson sunbird. Oh, what a shameful day that was for the mighty British and their Empire! The thing is, some of their soldiers were also killed by tigers. There were two of them!

'This was all when Dato Nan's grandfather was still alive. But these British returned, this time with artillery and ten times more soldiers. They came on two sides and we were defeated. Many of us Malays died. That's how we came to be under British rule. Then, of course, the Japanese came with their planes and tanks. We thought they were liberating us—they kept insisting so—but they're far, far worse.

'As for those British, they did conduct a tiger hunt but never found their man-eating tiger. So you see, our old village has a reputation for tiger attacks. Always has. But no one has ever killed or captured a tiger. Except for that one time ... '

'When was that, aunty? What happened?'

By this time, Mak Ina and I were sitting beneath a banana tree that held on tenuously to its dead brown fronds. A black and white moth flitted over the wild grass, then disappeared as though it were never there.

'Ah, you see, child,' she said. 'There was this one time when a man moved in from another district. He had never heard of the legends, knew *nothing*. So one early morning, when he came across a tiger eating the carcass of his goat, he raised his spear and flung it at the beast.'

'What happened then?'

'Well, the next day, Dato Nan's father, returned back to the house with a gash in his thigh. Nobody knows how he got it. But everyone was whispering the same thing!'

'That can't be!'

'. . . And Dato Nan is one too,' she whispered, her eyes blazing. 'Shape-shifting passes from father to eldest son. That's the story anyway.'

'But it's just a story right?'

'Yes, yes, child, just a story. But Dato Nan has five daughters. No sons. So when he dies, his position as territorial chief will go to his younger brother. Then we won't have any more problems with tigers around here.'

The next day, as I helped prepare the evening meal, I received word that Dato Nan wanted to see me. So, from the kitchen, with my heart thumping, I followed the narrow covered bamboo bridge which connected it with the main house.

We servants used it several times a day to bring food from the kitchen. It was mostly curried or fried tapioca, sometimes with other vegetables, rarely with meat. The always famished Japanese helped themselves to all our supplies. The reason the kitchen was kept separate from the main house was in case of fire. The kitchen had been ablaze twice in the palace's hundred year history and the separation of the two buildings was what saved it. Of course, we servants only whispered the word 'palace', for only the sultan was allowed to call his home that.

I pushed open the back door and entered the main building. I stood in a narrow dark hall. Mak Ina had told me that its walls used to be decorated with family heirlooms which included Chinese porcelain, pewter plates and silvery cutlery. When the soldiers of the Rising Sun came, all of these were hidden and only a painting of Dato Nan's father hung here.

From the hall, the building divided into two. To the left was the reception room where Dato Nan would receive visitors. Beyond the reception room was Dato Nan's bed chamber.

The other half of the building was to the right of the hall and it was reserved for family members. The first room was a dining area where *mengkuang* mats were spread out for meals. This was followed by two glowing family chambers shared by Dato Nan's two spouses and children.

Instead of turning either way, I continued through the hall and out to the balcony at the front. The balcony was expansive and stretched out on both sides, like wings. This space was used for family activities and it often caught a cooling breeze from the jungle. From here, a set of stairs led to the main entrance at ground level and the thick vegetation beyond.

At the far end of the balcony, three of Dato Nan's grand-daughters played a dextrous game of hand clapping. Dato Nan was lying casually on a mat at the other end, just outside his bed chamber. His gaunt-faced grey-haired massage lady, in sarong and white blouse, was rubbing his feet. She nodded when she saw me. As I approached, stooping my body to show respect, I smelt a mix of coconut oil and herbs.

Dato Nan wore a loose sarong. He was bare-chested and his nipples were almost black. His long white hair was like sand over a small pillow whilst his white beard and thick eyebrows floated like clouds above the umber timber floors. Deep lines ran through his dark angular face.

'Ah, it's you, Yan,' he said when he saw me approach. 'Come, come closer. No need to be afraid.'

Although Dato Nan was in his sixties, the muscles on his biceps and chest were firm upon his dark leathery skin.

'I want you to learn to massage,' he said in a voice that echoed deep inside his chest. 'No use spending all your time in the kitchen. I'm getting old and my body needs more and more attention.'

Then he laughed. It reverberated up in the dusky timber rafters sending a sparrow fleeing from the balcony rails.

Without warning, his hand flashed up and grabbed the air. He was so fast, I hardly saw its blurring movement.

'Mosquito,' he said. 'They spread disease and must be killed.'

He showed me the striped body of the insect before rubbing the blood off on his sarong. For the first time, I noticed his long, sharp fingernails.

'Now, come here, Yan. You can start by rubbing my neck and shoulders. I've had too many discussions with troublesome village elders today.'

I used to massage my father before he died, so I knew the various pressure points. Dato Nan, smelling faintly of vinegar and strongly of clove cigarettes, was a lot more muscular than my father. His skin was tough and strangely warm beneath my fingers. He sighed as I pushed my thumbs into the tissues around his neck. I could feel the tension in the knots in his sinews.

As I massaged Dato Nan, I wondered if he were a were-tiger. But mostly I thought about my father, how he died and how unfair it was.

A crow cawed incessantly close by, its lonesome voice shuddering an awful darkness in my head. It sounded like a warning.

One night, not long after I began massaging Dato Nan, I heard a deliberate scratching in the dirt beneath the timber floor of the servants' quarters. I opened my eyes and listened. There was hardly a sound. Even the insects had gone quiet.

There it was again. Something dragging its sharp claws against the earth.

I could hardly breathe.

Then I heard it. A snarl, then the low slow growl of a large beast. And after, a full throated *aonnhhhh . . .*

The thought of the thing stalking just beneath me sent my heart beating like a *kompang* drum. But what events were unfolding this awful night?

I heard footsteps now—very slowly—climbing up the wooden steps. The timber creaked. It groaned as if in fear. There was a loud scratching, right against the door.

Then suddenly, silence . . .

All was quiet, moment by terrible moment.

This soundlessness went on for so long, I felt like screaming. I dared take a step forward, my club foot rolling on the floorboard. Suddenly, there was a great crash as something heavy slammed against the door. It roared like thunder.

But the door held!

Then it struck again. This time, the door crashed to the ground. A flash of white leapt in. It stood facing me, its sinewy body occupying almost half of the space in the servants' quarters. I edged away towards the far wall. I wanted to scream but nothing came from my mouth. There should be four other women sleeping here, including Mak Ina.

But I was alone.

An incandescent glow spilled in through the broken door. The tiger's fur gleamed. It was almost white in the moonlight and shimmered like some divine being. The animal's eyes shone as it padded forward. One paw delicately touching the timber floor, followed by the other. It seemed to know exactly what it wanted.

Sweat dripped off my forehead.

'What do you want?' I whispered.

Now I could see its fur orange and stripes black. The white long whiskers. Its pupils, small and black, peering deep into mine.

'Leave me alone, please!' I was crying.

Then it leapt.

It pushed me backward and toppled my body to the ground. It pawed my bare legs. I tried to crawl away on my back, using my elbows. But it clambered on me. It was heavy and smelt of blood and raw meat. Its teeth were large, sharp and dripping. I thought it was going to tear out my throat.

It growled and with the swipe of his front paws, flipped me around. With several jerking tugs, it tore off my sarong.

I do not want to describe what the tiger then did to me.

But, after several nights of the same nightmare, I had to tell Mak Ina about it.

'You should not have such dreams,' she said.

But I did. And the same dream continued.

I began to enjoy the animal's visitations. I looked forward to it. There was always a thundering fear. But fear was followed by blissful pleasure. The most satisfying pleasure I had never known.

Little did I know that these dreams were a prelude to something more, for one night just before we turned in to bed, there was a knock on the door. It was one of the servants that slept with Dato Nan's grandchildren in the main building.

'Dato Nan wants you,' she said. 'He has back pain and needs a massage.'

I yawned and rubbed my eyes.

'Come quickly,' she said.

I pulled off the rose sarong that I used as a blanket and followed her. We went up into the kitchen, then across the bridge and entered the house.

'He's in his bed chamber,' she said as we entered the hall which was lit by a single kerosene lamp. Then she disappeared.

I opened the door on my left and entered the reception room.

This was where Dato Nan would sit on a large mat for his meetings with village officials. I knew that hanging on the walls, were a collection of krisses and spears, but these were now just shadows. Beyond this reception room was Dato Nan's bed chamber.

I knocked on the door.

'Come in,' he answered.

I entered, putting my right hand forward and stooping low.

'Ah, it's you, Yan,' he said in a deep voice. 'Come over here. My back is sore.'

'Yes, Dato Nan,' I said.

He was lying on a bed. It was the only bed in the house and was a gift from the British many years ago. He turned onto his stomach as I approached. I knelt on the floor and began to massage his back.

'That's good,' he said. He gestured towards the kerosene lamp beside the wooden shutters. 'Blow it out. It's too bright.'

I did as asked and returned to kneading his back.

Then, he turned over and took my hands in his. His were large and very warm.

'You're mine, Yan,' he said. 'All mine.'

He stared into my eyes, before drawing me to him.

His hands slide beneath my blouse and he caressed my small breasts. Then he undid my sarong and pulled me on the bed.

That night, I knew that Dato Nan and the tiger were one and the same. It was not so different from my dreams.

Fear and pleasure merged and mingled as he changed his form in the deepening shadows.

There was endless cooking in preparation for our wedding. Such events were usually held in the compound outside where *mengkuang* mats would be spread for hungry guests attending the dinner.

There were no chickens to slaughter as the Japanese had taken them long ago. Instead, the kitchen staff chopped coriander and galangal, they pounded tamarind, turmeric, garlic and ginger, all for a tapioca curry. The smell of cooking scented the air. As the bride-to-be, I was not amongst them, even though I had offered several times to help.

That night, to the sound of *kompang* drums, about a hundred or so villagers, mostly relatives, sat in groups of six around the meagre dishes we offered. It was a small affair because the Japanese occupation turned everyone frugal. For the same reason, there was no traditional cock-fighting contest that day.

As I sat on a timber dais next to Dato Nan, I could not fathom why such a wealthy and powerful person could be bothered with this club-footed, birth-marked girl. What did I have, exactly? He could have anyone he wanted in the village. I wondered how many of them knew of his tiger ways.

There were rumours about the family, but who knew for sure? Was it only me, or did his other wives know his secret?

Dato Nan's radiant ex-wife resided in the village with her grownup daughter. As for his two beautiful current wives, they and their girls would continue to live in the two sleeping chambers at the other wing of the house.

Dato Nan insisted that I share his bed chamber.

'Now I can be at peace,' he whispered to me one night after the wedding. 'Now that I have a son, at last, growing in your belly.'

I spun around to face him in bed.

'What?' I whispered, staring wide-mouthed.

'I know these things,' he chuckled, stroking his beard. His white hair was draped flamboyantly over the pillow. 'It's one of the instincts tiger men have. The other instinct I had was that you were the right one for me. Ah, to have found you so late in life.'

He stroked my long hair and smelt it. 'You know, you're the only one I've appeared to in my true form. You've been very brave. I knew it that first night when you saw me by the river. You didn't run away. You stayed and watched.'

His dark face, etched with deep lines held a knowing smile. In his stern eyes, I saw a kindness I had not seen before. Then he reached under his pillow and pulled something out.

It was my necklace! He could tell I was more than pleased.

'I found it hanging on a tree beside the well,' he said. 'I didn't know who it belonged to. But when you came out looking for it, I knew. I had changed form and I was watching you from behind the rambutans.'

I could only whisper now, 'I've always heard stories of were-tigers. But my mother, she told me they weren't true.'

'Well, now you know that we're real, don't you, Yan?'

He scratched his beard and stared up at the beams beneath the roof, as though mesmerised by its structure. 'This magic is passed down through the generations to the oldest son. My great great grandfather came here from a village in Sumatra. He came on a boat, across the sea, then up the River Setang. He was a were-tiger. But he was not alone, there were many.

'There was a village deep in the jungle where all of them lived together in human form. But when they stepped out of the village, they would turn into tigers. My ancestor, for some reason I know nothing of, was forced to flee the village. And so he came across the water to this land. Tigers, as you know, swim well. It was a good thing too. For years later, all those tiger men were hunted and killed. The jungle was burnt and, with it, our rare village.

'My great great grandfather could take on human form whenever he wanted. But because he could only mate with humans, this dark gift is only past from eldest son to eldest son. With no sons of my own, I thought it would end with me. And for many years I was happy with that. Isn't magic just another word for a curse, my soft Yan? Yet, though I've tried so many nights to not succumb to the instinct deep within me, the desire to stalk and kill is so strong. I cannot resist it!

'As time went by, as my body grew old, I realised that what a loss it would be to not have were-tigers in this world. And that is why I asked Mak Ina to get you.'

'What?' I blurted. 'Bring *Me*?'

'Yes, she did. She told me about your family. She told me about you. You know, my father had a club foot too. So I just knew that you would give me a boy.'

'How? How could you know that?'

'I know so much more than that, tender Yan. Your family is from the same tiger village my great great grandfather came from in Sumatra. The magic is strong between us. Such tiger men were in your lineage too. Your family was descended from were-tigers too but the magic never passed on because your grandfather didn't have sons. Now, finally, we can start our tiger village again!'

Somewhere in the longhouse a loud gecko called out *ahhhw!*, like a stabbed soldier's last breath.

'Ah there,' he said. 'The *cicak* agrees.'

He then turned over, rocking the bed and was soon snoring.

A night bird wailed from far away but, for me, sleep would not come.

Three months after our wedding, I heard shouting and loud commotion outside. I leapt from the mat in the dining area and rushed out to the balcony.

Three villagers were carrying Dato Nan towards the house.

'Open the door!' I shouted.

A servant rushed down the steps and pushed open the front door at ground level. The villagers hauled my husband up the steps and onto the balcony.

Blood dripped from his body.

'Put him over there,' I ordered. 'Be gentle!'

I ordered the servants to bring water and towels. By this time the rest of the family, including his other lovely two wives, had congregated around Dato Nan.

His body was splayed outside our bed chamber, at almost the same place where I had first massaged him. There was a gaping wound in his chest. His wives, including myself, tried to give him comfort. He drank water then coughed it out. His breathing was ragged, his beard shuddering as his body shook.

We bandaged the wound but could not stop the blood. It spilled on the floorboard and trickled down a gap between them, falling far down to the earth below.

'Take care of our son,' he whispered to me. His eyes were watery and pleading.

'Yes, of course,' I said and held his limp hand.

I stared up at the rafters, feeling terribly helpless.

Then my husband closed his eyes and I thought I heard a quiet growl.

Not long afterwards, he was dead.

He had been out hunting the night before and had stumbled upon a camp of Japanese soldiers. Having tired of target practice on our own people, they had heard the stories about tigers in the area and had come in search of trophies. One of the guards had fired his machine gun in the dark. Two bullets struck my husband in the chest. He had spent the rest of the night crawling to get back home.

The day after his funeral, I stood in the kitchen and stared at the dirt compound. The well, the plumeria trees, the orchard beyond were covered in an early morning mist.

'How are you, child?' said Mak Ina as she boiled some water.

'I'm fine,' I said. 'It was Allah's will.'

'It was, Yan. They'll find you a house in the village for the whole family. Dato Nan's brother will move in here.'

'Yes, I know,' I was trembling a bit. 'That's how these things work.'

'They say the Japanese will surrender soon. A huge bomb exploded in their homeland. So many mothers killed and so many babies. So much life sacrificed for men.'

'I think I'll go for a walk now, aunty. Down to the river.'

'Why there?'

'I like to see the water flow. Always moving. To some other place. To some other time.'

I brushed against the gnarled branches of the Frangipani trees as I drifted past the well. I glanced back at the long, umber-coloured house. The wooden shutters seemed to shy away from my gaze.

Then I followed the track behind the orchard. It wended its way beneath the jungle trees, beside the gushing stream. It may have been saying a thousand things, but I heard none of it. The rocks that looked like large eggs in the moonlight, now resembled blood-covered fists or perhaps even giant bullets.

Insect calls led me on even as the sun glinted from behind the tumul-tuous foliage. There was a rustling in the branches. Monkeys perhaps. But I did not stay to look at them. Eventually, I found myself where the stream spilled into the wide River Setang wreathed in mist.

Here it was that my husband's ancestor had killed his cousin-in-law over the succession of territorial chief. The bathing hut made of palm-leaves was long gone but I guessed it was located somewhere along the shore I was now passing, filled with wild grasses and several hovering dragon flies. A small yellow boat was pulled up on the bank but there was no one around.

I sat on a rickety timber jetty, my feet dangling over the muddy-coloured waters. The timber was cool and coarse beneath my soft pink sarong.

I placed a hand firmly on my belly. It had grown but was not huge. I felt the stirrings of my son inside me. Felt what must have been his elbows pushing slowly, rhythmically against my stomach.

My son, who would one day be a were-tiger.

As I was also descended from them, all my son's offspring would be were-tigers too. This was my husband's wishes. He wanted a tiger-village again, perhaps somewhere hidden deep in the jungle.

What did he say?

What a loss it would be to not have were-tigers in this world.

I wiped away my perspiration with my sleeve, drew back my long hair and stared at the insects darting above the fast flowing waters. A kingfisher swooped through the air and picked up a small fish. Then it was gone. Perhaps I had only imagined it. Like the trees, the river, the wild grasses before me that were so misty-veiled. Perhaps life itself.

What were were-tigers? People who turned into tigers? Or tigers who turned into us? I didn't know. I didn't care. All I knew was that tigers ate animals and often humans too.

That was how my father died.

I was twelve and sick with fever and he had ventured out to the jungle that evening to gather camphor needed for medicine. He had collected some but needed more. He had almost reached the waterfall when the tiger attacked. They only found his severed head. It was nestled above, stuck in the aerial roots of a Ficus tree.

Did the man-eating beast play with my father's head as though it were some kind of red circus ball?

In my child's mind, I had vowed I would find the tiger and kill it, this animal that had stolen my father from me. It was a vow I had never forgotten.

What a loss it would be to not have were-tigers in this world.

Would it be such a loss?

Disfigured shadows now hid in the mist. Were these the ghosts of were-tigers emerging? My lips trembled. I watched my bare feet swaying beneath me.

Forward. Backward.

Was that a drop of rain or a teardrop?

Forward. Backward.

They had no right to exist.

Not now. Not ever . . .

My feet seem too tiny.

They are falling into water.

There is a splash and coldness grips my body.

Bubbles shoot to the surface. Except for my sarong drifting like a net, all is cloudy before my eyes.

But my mind is clear.

There will be no more were-tigers in this world.

Not a single one.
I open my mouth and drink the river.
It drinks life from my body.
My husband's ancestor had sailed up this river.
Together with my unborn son, we now float down it.
Away forever.

TUNKU HALIM *(b. Petaling Jaya, Malaysia, 1964) lives in Australia but is a frequent visitor to his country of birth. Recently his stories "Biggest Baddest Bomoh" and "Keramat" have respectively appeared in* The Apex Book of World SF *(Apex Publications) and* Exotic Gothic 3 *(Ash-Tree Press) whilst his essay on Margot Livesey's* Eva Moves the Furniture *was published in* 21st Century Gothic: Great Gothic Novels Since 2000 *(The Scarecrow Press).*

He has published two novels and five collections of short stories, the latest being 44 Cemetery Road *and* Gravedigger's Kiss. *His novel,* Dark Demon Rising, *was nominated for the 1999 International IMPAC Dublin Literary Award whilst his second novel,* Vermillion Eye, *was a study text at The National University   of Singapore. He also writes non-fiction, including* A Children's History of Malaysia *and* History of Malaysia—A Children's Encyclopedia.

Commentary on "In the Village of Setang": *As a boy, I was told about how our family had a* semangat, *a spirit, which guarded us against evil. An uncle had supposedly seen this spirit, which appeared in the form of a white tiger, prowling about Seri Menanti, our royal village. Although the white tiger appeared in my novel* Dark Demon Rising, *I had also longed to write about a village of were-tigers. The territorial chief's house is modelled* *vaguely on the old royal palace in Seri Menanti. I've also managed to add my interest in history into the narrative which here takes the form of British colonialism and the Japanese occupation. "In the Village of Setang" is, in essence, a Malay tale. Its culture, myths, traditions and rural way-of-life, so diminished in our modern society, I hope, is evident. And, ultimately, I still wonder: wouldn't it be a loss to not have were-tigers in this world?*

Carving

David Punter

I SHALL MAKE MYSELF A ROOMFUL OF CARVINGS. IT WILL not be difficult. Cousin Pao who works the Cat Street market can carve anything; he takes lumps of old misshapen redwood, rejected by the carpenters, and then tourists buy all his buddhas, sleeping lions, elephants with flattened ears. But then, Cousin Pao is not suffused with rage. He and I met last night, as we often do, near Luk Fu Street, where there are still a couple of banyan trees and the stink of the urinals in the public square makes you feel you are drowning. We ate, to the clink of mahjong pieces. There was an old man stretched on a nearby bench, his feet swathed in blanketing. Yet Luk Fu Street was a stove.

Cousin Pao talked of his sister.

She is thirteen, he said. It is time.

Time for what, I asked.

He grinned, his mouth opening to reveal raw gums.

Time to make money, he said.

Later that night I dreamed what he had said. Young Yu-mei, stretched on the bunk, her skirts ridden up over smooth thighs. And then in the morning, in her grey school uniform. I thought of her tie, thought of it knotted and unknotted. And so I went to sleep.

The carvings—my carvings—would not be of buddhas; but like those they would be rounded, swelling, blessed with richness and fruition. I know what those carvings would be; but I do not tell Cousin Pao.

Third Uncle Wan greets me in the street in the morning, but I do not notice until he knocks me on the shoulder.

You are away, he says, you are away behind yourself. I grunt and squint in the heat and light. In truth, I am half-blinded. How does it go, asks Third Uncle Wan.

It goes well, I tell him, shouldering my bag of books.

Once when we talked, I and she, the she of whom I also think, she laughed at me. Or maybe she laughed with me, I do not know. I never know. She did not laugh at my bookbag. What she laughed at was this. When it rains, she said, you Chinese hate to get your hair wet, is it not so? I stared at her glumly. It is so. And you use your books to cover your heads, she went on, laughing merrily, and so all the pages go limp. Why do you do this?

I do not know why we do this. I do not know why other people do not do this.

It is bad for the books, she said, and she laughed. She is wearing the dress; but perhaps it is not always the same dress. All I know about the dress is what I see. It is also what I dream. The dream is not like the dream of Cousin Pao's little sister. It is 'contorted with rage' (I must have read that in a poem). Would that rage be in the carvings?

That night—or perhaps it is many nights—I dream also of the carvings. I shudder.

When I arrive at the college I start to climb the stairs. The department is on the third floor. The old man, Professor Davies, is climbing above me. He goes very slowly. Under his armpits are huge dark circles; if I were in front of him I would see the v-shape at his throat where the sweat has soaked through. They say that we do not sweat, we Chinese; but they are wrong. At night, when I dream, when I dream of my carvings and when I see their rounded shapes, I wake trembling and hard, and sweating just as he is now, and it is long minutes before I can see my sleeping family around me.

I do not pass old Davies on his climb, his bald head glistening, although it means that I too have to go very slowly. I fear that he might turn, but I know that he will not. To do so would take energy, and in the heat he does not have any to spare.

He is giving the first lecture of the morning. There are many girls, sixteen, seventeen; only four of us boys. I know why. Many of my schoolfriends are here at Tung Wah College, but they are doing Business Studies; they will make money. I had tonsillitis during my exams, and therefore did not do well enough. So I study English. But it is not what I thought; we do not talk in English; we do not talk at all except when Davies and the other teachers—the Australian with curly hair and warts on his arms, the Irish priest who constantly licks his lips—when they ask us questions. And her. She says to call her Sally; but her name is Mrs McLennane.

I sit at the back of the room with the other three boys. We drink cold chrysanthemum tea and try to listen, but it is not possible. Old man Davies is talking about somebody called Jane Austen, and on the desk in front of me is her book called *Emma*. I look at it closely to see whether the pages are limp. Curled; from the rain. I can read the words, almost all of them, but that is all. This book describes some place hundreds of years ago; it is a place I have never seen and never expect to see. It is in a language I will never be able to use.

My thoughts go to Cousin Pao. I imagine him grinning at me as I sit. Do not waste your time, he says softly. You are only young once. The old have nothing to teach us. He stretches his legs, then rises; he is fat, but the cleancut Giordano jeans look good on him. Come with me, he says, I will introduce you. Skinny Li is now at his side. Skinny has a scar along his jaw; it came, he always tells me cheerfully, from a fight in Sham Shui Po, bad place, he tells me, do not go there. But anyway, says Cousin Pao with a cheery little whistle, our brainy cousin here would never go there, would he? And he chucks me playfully under the arm, but his eyes are urgent; come with me, he says, and again I see his little sister, her legs spread wide, her eyes on the ceiling while something frantic but oddly muted is happening down below.

And so, Davies is concluding, our question remains. Are we to admire Emma, or to laugh at her? Does Austen treat her kindly, as she claims, or does she use her to mock our own pretensions? I am aware that my jaw has dropped and head snapped forward. Andy Wong, sitting next to me, is carving; carving somebody's name into the ancient desk. The room is full of light; I can barely see old man Davies. But I realise from his tone of voice that he is finishing; I will not be expected to answer a question, nor to be exposed to the giggling of the girls in the front row. From where I sit, at the back, I cannot see their pert row of knees, the brown-olive taut flesh; if I could, it would not move me. It is not those I wish to carve.

That night I eat with Cousin Pao and Skinny Li and a girl called Mira at tables in Wong Tai Sin. There is steam from the noodles, steam from the reeking fires of the temple, over the street, where the fortune papers burn.

Five dollars, says Cousin Pao. Skinny Li rolls his eyes and laughs. Thirty, he says. He holds the knife loosely between his fingers. The girl Mira is not paying any attention; she has wide eyes and a delicate waist. It is a good knife, says Skinny Li, and suddenly he reaches out, grabs Mira round her slender belly and pulls her towards him. A second later the knife is at her throat, Cousin Pao takes in his breath. Now, purrs Skinny Li. The girl's eyes are frightened. She is wearing a short blue denim skirt, a white blouse. There is no blade visible on the knife, but Skinny Li's finger is pressing down on a knob on the handle. Stop it, breathes Cousin Pao, though I can see he is lost in admiration. But he does not have thirty dollars. The tourists are not all fools, after all, and only a few days ago a gang from the docks stole most of his supply of wood. He can only breathe, mesmerised, like a cat in the glare. The girl says nothing; she does not move. Skinny Li moves the blade an inch to the left, presses the stud, the blade shoots out along her neckline, without touching her, without drawing blood.

In a voice which does not seem like mine, I blurt out, Fifteen. Skinny Li, Cousin Pao, and the girl, they are all staring at me. I know what they are going to say; I can almost hear it: What would you do with a knife, college boy? In truth, I do not know what I would do with a knife; not this kind of knife. There is a moment;

and then there is another moment. Skinny Li makes the blade go back into the knife; I do not see how he does it. Mira falls back against her chair and starts to laugh, but I see that her eyes are still scared. Cousin Pao is silent. Skinny Li looks at me.

Twenty, he says, and I pull the bills from my pocket.

My class with the woman is the next afternoon. Like every other week, I do not know if I can bear it. I do not know if I can walk into the classroom. As I climb the stairs, I see her dress; this time it is eggshell blue, the skirt is long, but it is like all the other dresses. I cannot bear the fullness I am going to see. Perhaps it would be better, after all, if I went to see Cousin Pao's little sister; or there are many other little sisters, some of them in high lipgloss and higher heels, walking the streets many floors below the flat where I and my family live. They make no noise, I have been told, and they are cheaper than a knife. Cheaper than the knife which is in my pocket; cheaper also than the books which are in my bag, and even than the one which I cannot now buy, a book called *Heart of Midlothian*; all because I have bought the knife.

In the class it seems to be about half an hour before I can look up. Andy Wong is continuing to carve. He is never asked questions, when asked he only smiles brightly and says nothing; the girls laugh at him, but he does not mind, his father is rich, he gambles in Kowloon City, and there is nothing he needs. This class is on modern poetry. We are looking at a poem by somebody called Philip Larkin. After a while I am able to see it properly; I have already read it, two or three nights ago. It is about a healer, about somebody who offers a kind of love. I can see that the kind of love he offers is not clear. I can see that there is a question about whether he is a fake. I read too that he is talking about the heart, about the heart swelling, almost bursting, under the pressure of wanting to be loved. As I read this passage again I find my hand tightening on the knife, and I pull my hand out of my pocket, aghast. What if it were to spring open now? I now know how it works. I tried it last night. You have to be very careful. I do not think it would be any use for carving. Besides, outside my dreams, I cannot carve.

But as I think of my carvings again I am at last able to lift my eyes and I see what I see, every night, in all my dreams. There is a slight sweat on her, I can see it even from where I sit at the back of the class, a slight sweat which I see over the low front of her dress; and as she moves, walking up and down before me, it is as though her dress, this dress, the dress she always wears, has fallen away completely; I see her body, I see her breasts in all their fullness, I see the pale nipples, I see rosy aureoles and the tiny duct pimples around them . . . I see the page of my poetry book; there are curved dents in the edge of the paper where my fingers have been gripping. I am shaking. And sweating.

These conversations we have had, they are not so much really. Some while ago, before all this started to happen—or has it always been happening? is it just that now it is so much fiercer, so much more hopeless?—I used to stay behind a bit at the end of the class, being slow to clear up my books and papers. The others did not notice; they had already packed up their things minutes before the lesson was due to end, and they had gone before I came to my feet. Sometimes—how many times? once or twice? a dozen times?— she would then smile at me. She would offer to lend me books, other books which speak of places and times which I do not know. While she cleared up her own books she would have to lean over, and I saw the front of her dress, and inside the front of her dress, a crease of mystery and the light stippling of sweat. But that was in the days before I could see it all, so clearly that nothing would go away from before my eyes.

Mrs McLennane will go soon, so they say. It is 1997, and all the British are going soon. They too have been carving, I remember my father telling me that; these British have been carving their names and their behaviour, their impossible promises, their bad morals on a foreign land. I was small when he told me that, and I did not know what to think.

What will happen, I asked, What will happen?

We will become Chinese again, he replied, gently, but I did not understand. Now I understand. I understand partly because of the madman Yu Kwei-fong.

Yu Kwei-fong came into our lives unexpectedly. There are five of us; perhaps I should have said that before. My mother, my father, and my two younger brothers, who are still at school. It was late one evening; I myself was still at school then; I was studying at the table, while my little brothers played and my mother and father were in the kitchen. I heard footsteps on the stairs, and then a knock on the door, and then voices. I tried not to listen, but then I had to. The newcomer's voice was raised, and I scuttled to the kitchen door to hear properly, but even then it was difficult because his Cantonese was strange. He was asking for a bed; no, he was telling my father that he had to stay, he was saying that he had come a long way. When I saw him, when my father came into the living room with him, I saw that he had a wispy beard and no shoes, and that is how I knew that he was mad.

He was, he said, a distant cousin, and he brought with him a letter from one of our clan in Shantou. At that time I did not know where that was; I know now, because I have looked at maps; it is in southeastern China, and he had come on a boat, herded with dozens of others, without food or water for days, and he had been landed in a remote part of the New Territories, and had come all this way to the city on foot, avoiding the police; and now we were to have him to live with us. He made very little sense, and he only stayed for a week; I do not know how my father got rid of him, but he did. But during that time old Yu Kwei-fong told us all about China, about being poor, about what it felt like not to be able to say what you felt, about the secret police.

At the time I felt that I too could not say what I felt. My father does not know, I can see he does not know, who we should hate more, the British imperialists or the Mainland Chinese dictators. We are a people without a home; we are deluded into thinking our flats and houses are secure when really they might disappear at the wash of a tide, perhaps the filthy tide which smears the shores of Tolo Harbour.

Perhaps, I think, this is the anger, the rage. I try not to think of it, and I try also not to think about Sally McLennane's breasts, but then I find that instead I am thinking of my carvings, which would be carvings from the pink heart of the redwood, bursting with life. A life, I think grimly, which I shall never have. I clutch the knife.

I think that perhaps I have been asleep. 'As all they might have done had they been loved', I think to myself, still within the poem, as I struggle to the surface. Is it like that? But because I have been dozing, I am late collecting my books and papers; not on purpose this time, I am too confused. As I pass Sally McLennane to go towards the door, she looks up, and smiles at me brightly. Still here, she says, and then she talks to me. I do not know what about. I know only that after she has talked, it turns out that she has invited me to come and see her, at her flat in the college, the night after, because she has some books for me which, she tells me, I will enjoy; and that I have said yes. I know also that her blue dress, this time, although the colours shimmer and waver, I am sure that it is blue, is lightly stained with sweat.

That night I eat, as usual, with Cousin Pao and Skinny Li, somewhere down towards Yau Ma Tei. The air is still and stifling, but Cousin Pao and Skinny Li eat pork noodles and drink Zhong Hua beer heartily. I eat the noodles, but I do not drink. When Cousin Pao stands up, he is swaying slightly. So, he says to the two of us, we shall go now; she is there. I do not know what he means. Or perhaps I do know what he means. I have the knife. I walk with them. They are merry, chortling; I am quiet. As we climb the stairs we pass her mother. She is going out shopping. Look after her, she says to Pao, but I do not want to know what she means. I think, though, that she knows.

When we arrive in the flat, Skinny Li, who has drunk too much, goes to the bathroom, and I do not see him again that night. Cousin Pao, I know, has three sisters, but two of them are not there. Little Sister Yu-mei says hello, seeming nervous. Cousin Pao smiles at me; it is almost a caring, a tender smile. He leaves us alone. It seems then as though she changes; I think Little Sister changes, changes perhaps into somebody else. She is still wearing her school uniform, but she is smiling at me—no, not smiling, she is grinning. I do not know how to respond. After a while she shrugs, stands up and, in a matter-of-fact way, unbuttons her blouse and takes it off. She must also have taken off her tie; but perhaps she was not wearing it, knotted or unknotted. Her bra is pink. She does not wait for me. Before I can move, she pulls me over to the bed.

I do not fail her. I do not know whether that pleases me or not. After it is over, I grasp her and try to speak to her, but she laughs. Now I am ready, she says.

I am appalled, I am angry. *But* . . . I say.

Now, she says as she stands, still wearing her school skirt, but having smoothed it down into place, now I can begin. Something hot and red rises before my eyes as I see what Yu-mei is planning to become, as I see the queues of other men waiting beside this bed, the money in their hands, their jaded eyes. . . . And I see the shape of the redwood carvings. I stare hard at her bare breasts; there is sweat on them, and they are small and brown and firm. Although they moved me for a few minutes they do not move me now; nor will they ever again.

Next evening I find myself in the lift in Mrs McLennane's apartment building. I have known all along that there is no Mr McLennane; it is common knowledge. I have the knife in my pocket. My mind throws up to me beautiful rounded carvings, severed, whole, perfect. They are without attachments, they are utterly bare; there is the faintest trickle of sweat on each one. As I grasp the knife more firmly, the lift doors open; I press the bell, and she opens the door to me. A smile begins to freeze. She is wearing a dress; I think it is the same dress, for I can see through it in the same old way, although now it seems to be red; or perhaps, like the heart of the redwood, it is pink.

DAVID PUNTER *(b. London, UK, 1949), whose business card calls him the 'Professor of Dream' and who is known in France as the 'Gothic Pope', is the godfather of Gothic. His book* The Literature of Terror *(1980) kick-started a new interest in Gothic among critics and writers alike, and he has continued to publish prodigiously on Gothic in all its many tentacular forms; to encourage new writers; and, of course, to write stories and poems himself. He has published four volumes of poetry–*China and Glass, Lost in the Supermarket, Asleep at the Wheel *and the confusingly titled* Selected Short Stories–*and a fifth,* Foreign Ministry, *will crawl out of the woodwork later this year.*

He holds all these slightly ridiculous roles as, for example, Chair of the Executive Board of the International Gothic Association, and Chair of the Editorial Board of Gothic Studies; but he is really far more interested in fear, phobia, trauma; in fact, he has never really recovered from watching the original televised version of Quatermass and the Pit *from behind the sofa. He lives near Bristol, UK, with his family, two kittens and a pond. Think about that last bit.*

Commentary on "Carving": *Some people seem able to say that this or that produced this story, which of course answers the classic Literary Festival question—where do you get y/our ideas from? I prefer the Terry Pratchett answer, which is that there are ideas sleeting down all the time, and sometimes we are unlucky enough to be speared by one. This story does relate to time I spent in Hong Kong, and it does have its origin in (what else?) a dream; in any case, Hong Kong was, and remains, a hotbed of dreams. I hate this vision of violence; I hope now to be free of it!*

WATER LOVER

GENNI GUNN

M ARISSA STEPPED INTO THE AIR-CONDITIONED CHARTER, the heat and humidity of Mexico clinging to her bones. She strapped herself into her seat beside a young couple returning home after an all-inclusive holiday, the girl's hair in corn braids, the boy's muscle shirt damp against his chest. All around her, revelers whooped and laughed, bodies squeezed into halters and bikini tops, shorts and sandals, as if they were flying to another tropical destination, instead of to Vancouver in January.

The plane taxied along the shoreline, and Marissa stared out the window at the white sand of Playa de Oro and the treacherous ocean waves where, according to the onboard magazine *¡Fiesta!*, in 1862, a ship carrying gold coins had burned, and over two-hundred of its passengers and crew had drowned trying to get to shore. She clasped her hands together on her lap. She was not afraid of flying, only of *oceans, lakes, rivers, streams, brooks, lagoons, basins, lochs, pools.*

As the plane rose, the ocean formed a postcard of turquoise peaks, its dangers invisible under the surface. She wondered about the countless dead in its depths. Had they been ferried across the river Styx? Used the gold coins for passage? Drank from the water of the Lethe? Had they forgotten what they'd done, who they were? How they'd suffered? She leaned back into her seat and thought about her mother stowed in a coffin below. *Safe passage, Mother.*

187

Two weeks before, her mother had been packing in an upstairs bedroom, pleading with Marissa to change her mind and accompany her to Mexico. She had tried everything from bribes to guilt, but for once, Marissa had not succumbed. She had told her mother that she was not willing to give up her job to spend three weeks stuffed into a bus with a load of blue-haired pensioners in SAS shoes, when the truth was that her mother's insistence that they return to Mexico after all that had happened there left Marissa unsettled and alarmed. Her mother had cajoled, cried and moped, but Marissa would not relent. Her mother was barely sixty, a grim determined woman, whose distress manifested in various vague and non-diagnosable illnesses, a woman, who Marissa felt, could manage without her.

'You're such a disappointment,' her mother had said, shaking her head in familiar martyrdom. Then she had boarded the plane, with a small tight smile, and within days she was on the bus that crashed over a cliff on the Costa Careyes and left no survivors.

Marissa sighed. Out of her grey backpack, she drew out *The Lonely Passion of Judith Hearne*, a deliciously depressing novel, and a black velveteen neck pillow she had bought at the Manzanillo airport. She inflated the pillow, put it around her neck and leaned back, eyes closed. The details of the past week flitted behind her lids, disordered and chaotic. Forms to sign, the crushed Golden Tours bus, the slashed purple Ultralight suitcase, her mother's blue marbled skin. She forced herself to think of the future instead. She would use the insurance money to pay off the mortgage on the house—a two-storey mock-Tudor, with gouged hardwood floors, bubbling paint, and shabby, lumpy wallpaper peeling from lathe-and-plaster walls, a house that had fallen into ruin over the past decade, since her father abandoned them. She would be happy.

The dripping sounds began on her first night back. Intermittent, and maddeningly difficult to locate. *Drip . . . drip . . . drip . . .* It made her think *wet hair, gutters, hoses, pans, irrigation, intravenous, torture, veins, guilt.* What sounded from the attic as if someone had not turned a faucet tight enough, couldn't be: there was no bathroom up there, only a series of rafters and two-by-sixes, between which lay pink discolored insulation with mouse droppings in its creases.

Before her mother died, Marissa had been living here with her, in this house where she was born, in the room where, as a child, she'd traveled with imaginary friends to the faraway places inside her books. She had continued living here, at her mother's insistence, even when she was well enough to get a part-time job at the bookstore. That first year following that disastrous Christmas and the breakdown of mind and home, she was embarrassed to have left school so suddenly, to have to explain to her friends. She needn't have worried, because by the time she felt well enough to re-engage with her former life, her high school friends were at university, married, or in other cities. When her father left, Marissa and her mother's roles reversed, and Marissa became the caretaker for a time. She had had the odd boyfriend years ago, but her timidity had scared them off. Or so she had always thought. She wondered now if her mother had been responsible, or perhaps if what had frightened them was her own unconditional submission.

She was almost thirty now, a pale slender young woman of medium height, with dark curly hair and large brown eyes that flitted anxiously from thing to thing, from person to person, as if she were afraid to focus her attention. In a room full of people, she was unnoticed beneath the men's shirts and loose jeans she had taken to wearing. Her mother used to refer to her as 'fragile,' although Marissa knew what she really meant was something else.

The house would be an antidote to grief. Already, Marissa was planning the scraping and sanding, the hammering and sawing, the prepping and painting that would turn this house into her home. (She heard the drip, cocked her head, trying to locate the sound.) And if she ever got through every room, years of landscaping awaited in the tangled garden, from which she could see the ocean. She was fortunate to own this modest house in Point Grey, nestled between two new monster homes, on a small lot that contained an easement, and thus could not be developed further. She was fortunate to have cheated death once again.

That first night, from her upstairs bedroom window, she counted ocean liners in the harbor, their fairy lights aglow, like Christmas decorations hanging in darkness. She was alone in the house, unsupervised. The last time she had felt this unencumbered, she was sixteen, on holiday in Mexico with her parents, booked into a hotel in San Patricio, on a near-deserted stretch of beach where, each evening, when the adults gathered around the pool, drinks in hand, the teenagers roamed the back streets of the little village, their sandals raising clouds of dust. At night, in the oblong of their flashlights, the brilliant blooms of bougainvilleas and hibiscus spilling over walls startled Marissa with their casual existence, not like at home, where nature was manicured and ordered. In the *zócalo*, they sat on the cool stone parapets, and watched couples, clusters of girls, groups of boys, families in Sunday bests, all strolling around in a peacock parade, searching for friends and lovers, whispering among themselves. A trio played in the white gazebo at the centre of the *zócalo*, guitar riffs mingling with the cacophony of crickets, dogs barking, a car's security alarm beep, beep beeping, with the myriad voices in the square. Marissa was drunk with the romance of it all, and so had easily fallen crazy in love for the first time, there one night, almost instantly, in the way teenagers are smitten, her hands trembling in her lap when the boy looked at her. He was seventeen, a dark, moody creature the girls gazed at behind half-closed lids. She had felt *recognized*, and when he had reached for her hand and pulled her up amid the swirl of bodies, she had followed. From that breathless first meeting, she and the boy had been inseparable, as if they had always been severed halves, and only now had become whole.

'She's only sixteen,' her father had said to her mother back then. 'Dammit, my daughter will not make a fool of herself, parading around with a *local* boy.' He had not said '*Mexican* boy,' though Marissa heard it all the same.

What had her mother said? Why had she not defended them? Marissa stared at the harbor, and for a moment, heard the echo of her mother reminding her to go to bed, to turn out the lights, to go to sleep. It's too late, she thought. Then she remembered that it didn't matter any more. She could go to bed when she pleased, and get up at whatever hour she wanted, without anticipating the knock, knock, knock in early morning, her mother's voice urging her up, as if she were afraid that Marissa would remain in bed for a lifetime.

She stared out, imagining a new life for herself. In summer, mounds of tourists and picnickers would populate the beach beyond the road that dissected her yard from the ocean. They would barbeque on the grass, eat under the shade of pines, play volleyball on sand, race kites across the sky. There would be laughter and cheering and seagull squawks; the air would taste of salt, and echo people's joy. People she could befriend, now that her mother was gone. She felt guilty instantly, thinking this, recalling those painful years when her mother had nursed her back to health, before her father abandoned them both. It's all my fault, she thought. His leaving, her mother being on that bus. If only, she'd gone with her, if only . . . Headlights bore through the monotony of night. She lay down, turned out the lights, and in the darkness, a slow *drip . . . drip . . . drip . . .* began. She tried to imagine what it could be: a downspout near her window; a hose dripping into a bucket; perhaps the people next door had bought a rain barrel. But the sky was clear. She closed her eyes and counted backwards from a hundred, in threes. The drips fell into her dreams. They became the metronome beats of her childhood afternoons spent practicing Liszt's *Hungarian Rhapsody*; the high-heel clicks of her mother's pacing overhead; the rhythmic splash of oars against black water. They became *drizzle, dew, mist, flurry, hail, sleet, snow, rain, tears.*

In the morning, she dialed the faded phone number tucked under the fridge magnet, and within the hour, a surly plumber arrived. He found no evidence of leaking pipes in the walls, nor faulty faucets, nor dripping sounds, and she felt a fool.

No one came to the house to offer condolences, and as long as she did not go upstairs into her mother's room, Marissa could pretend her mother was still alive, lying in bed, watching TV, writing letters to City Hall about noisy, inconsiderate neighbors.

She cleaned out the kitchen, threw away old boxes of crackers, corn starch and Aunt Jemima Pancake Mix. Cans and bottled goods went into boxes for the food bank. Once she began, she could not stop. She filled large garbage bags with the contents of the fridge, the cupboards, the pantry, and set them outside. When the kitchen was completely empty, she went to Home Depot and bought two brushes, two rollers and one large can of paint, the color of which reminded her of Mexico: music and sand and the tangerine walls of the outdoor restaurant where she and the boy rendezvoused. She went upstairs to her room and found an old CD she had bought from a busker at the airport, and slipped it into the player. A haunting saxophone spiraled into the room. Such a lonely sound, she thought, propelled into that other time, the two of them standing in the shadow of a dusty palm, whose leaves were projected in skeletal patterns over the boy, the spine of a fish. His head bent towards her, his eyes intent on hers. 'Promise me,' he'd said, his hands on her shoulders. 'Together forever. Promise.' And she had, although a small fear had left her breathless.

She felt suddenly exhausted—up all day, hadn't eaten since noon, and now the windows were black maws around her. *Drip . . . drip . . . drip* . She turned her head this way and that. How could she have lived here all these years, and never noticed it before? She flicked out the light and stood in darkness, waiting. But she only heard the saxophone melody, wailing like a siren around her. She crept upstairs and lay in bed. Some nights, the drips became the ocean lapping in benign ripples on sand, then suddenly rising in gigantic breakers that smashed to shore, shaking the house in its foundation. Those nights, when water broke through the roof, and walls, she awakened in a pool of sweat.

She'd been home a week already, and still had not entered her mother's bedroom. The rest of the house she'd slowly emptied and bagged. Outside, dozens of large plastic sacks leaned against the garage, awaiting pickup. She'd emptied drawers and cupboards, closets and bureaus. With each removal, she felt lighter and detached, as if her memories too, were twist-tied into tightly-packed bags. In her room, in a box high up on a shelf, she found the snorkel, mask and flippers her father had bought her after their return from Mexico that disastrous Christmas. What did he think? That she would magically don them and . . . and what? She had never used them. She took them out of the box, tossed them into a plastic bag, and set it outside. She kept only the contents of her own room, and those in her mother's room, the room she still could not bring herself to enter.

For a couple of days now, she had been walking the beach for hours, beginning at dusk and staying on until dark, trying to re-imagine herself in a different life. She had become so accustomed to listening to her mother, to silently following her instructions, that now she felt adrift, on the edge of something both exhilarating and strange. What would she do? She sat on a bleached log, and stared across the water at the downtown cityscape in the distance, skyscrapers rising like obelisks in the mist. She could keep her job at the bookstore, she thought. She loved books, the interior lives of characters she could relate to, the adventures of people who could not harm her. She would join a health club, sell the car, buy a second-hand bike, cycle to work on dry days, and board busses on rainy wet ones. She would get a dog and walk along the beach, throw balls and Frisbees, and chat with other dog owners. She would make friends now that her mother was gone.

On that fateful holiday in Mexico, she and the boy had walked hand-in-hand on the beach, following the arc of the bay, beyond the last house. The moon was low on the horizon, and the surf up and angry, like a god disturbed. Waves advanced in dark, silent lines, building in height as they reached the shore. The boy pulled her to the edge of the sand, where all the water peaked, curled, then slapped down hard in triumphant explosions. She tried to move back, but the boy held her in the frothy water that licked up the beach, and receded, dragging them in its undertow.

He laughed at her fear, a test she thought. She would do anything for him.

When they had reached the half-way point around the bay, he led her up towards the bank, to a dilapidated building that stood alone, its back to the swamp where she'd heard Morelet's crocodiles roamed. She had seen this structure in the daytime, the graffitied concrete, the iron grate in front of the opening, the rebars protruding from the walls at odd angles; had been told it was built as a seafood restaurant but never completed. The boy unlocked the iron grate, and pulled her inside, onto the blanket he had prepared for them. They had undressed hurriedly in that darkness—she, timid, this being her first time—and made feverish love, and he had asked her to marry him, his voice rising above the pull and push of riptides.

On the beach now, in Vancouver, a red sun, low on the horizon was reflected in the multiple windows of the downtown skyscrapers, creating a burning cathedral.

The splash startled her. She turned. A man rose slowly out of the waves, a black masked figure, trails of seaweed on his back. Water *dripped, splashed, trilled, spouted, trickled, bled, wept* onto sand. She drew in her breath. It couldn't be. Her heart beat frantic rhythms in her chest. She got up and raced home, locked the doors, closed all the windows and secured them. Then, she went up to her bedroom, and looked out. In the twilight, she could just discern the man on the sand. He had shed the top half of his wetsuit, so that it hung like a second skin around his waist. Behind him, partly in water, a windsurfer, its blue sail floating on the water's surface. She sighed, let out a small laugh. She was being ridiculous. She unlatched the windows and breathed in.

Downstairs a few moments later, when she opened the door, he stood, dripping, on the wooden porch, his rubber mask dangling around his neck. 'I couldn't help noticing,' he said. He shifted foot to foot, as if trying to keep warm in the blue Teva water sandals, his skin chafed red in the January air. 'Back there . . . '

She stared at him, listening to the water drip off his wetsuit into the depressions in the porch where water clustered, forming a glass harmonica of chromatic runs, pentatonic scales, minor modes, a cacophony—

'I frightened you,' he said. 'I'm sorry.'

She took a deep breath, back to herself. 'No, no, it was nothing. . . .' And when he continued to stare at her, she added, 'An error, that's all . . . I mistook you for someone. . . .' She ran a hand through her hair, aware she must look disheveled.

He smiled and stamped his feet. A rainbow of water sprayed out of his hair, which was black and sleek as an eel. 'Are you all right?'

She nodded, uncertain. She must have appeared crazy back there. She rubbed her forehead, dredging up calming techniques. 'Think of desert islands and bright sunny beaches,' her mother used to say, as if these would calm her. But Marissa had no sense of a meditative space where she was happy. Instead she placed tiny green tablets under her tongue, and counted until the knots in her stomach and chest dissolved.

'You're the girl from the bookstore,' he said.

She frowned. *How did he know? Why was he here?* Should she close the door and throw the latch? Her hand slid around the door knob.

'I heard your mother died. I'm sorry.' His eyes were black and avoided hers.

'Yes, no, thank you. An accident.' She flicked on the porch light overhead, and he was silhouetted against a violet sky. The street was deserted.

'Well. You're sure you're okay?' His head now craned around hers, his eyes stared past her, into the living room.

What was he seeing? What was he looking for? 'My father should be here at any moment,' she lied, trying to keep her voice from trembling. Beyond him, on the porch lay bags and bags of the house interior, Marissa's old life cinched into black plastic. Safe.

'It's awfully cold out here,' he said, his voice confidential. 'My wind-surfer's broken, and my car's way off at Third Beach.'

'I'm sorry,' she said, and began closing the door, when his foot stepped in.

'Would you mind if I used your phone to call a friend to come and get me?' He smiled.

Too late, she saw her mistake. She had been right to run. His eyes, the hue of his hands. She couldn't tell whether he was alive or dead; whether she was alive or dead, then or now, his voice urging her back, her whole being wanting to surrender. 'You must go,' she whispered. 'Please.' Then she was crying against his chest, his arms around her, his words soothing, 'There. There.' Slowly, he pushed the door open and walked her inside, backwards, as if they were dancing, until he sat her gently on the couch. She was sobbing loudly now, and shivering, her shirt damp. She covered her face with her hands, and dropped her head onto her knees. She was utterly alone.

She next awakened in her mother's bed, and sat up, alarmed. She was fully dressed, and the clock on the nightstand read 7:06 p.m. Had she been sleeping an hour or a full day? The open shutters cast indigo bars onto her skin. The first thing she saw was the book the boy had given her. *Mythology: Timeless Tales of Gods and Heroes.* Her chest ached with longing, knowing how the boy had dreamt of going to university, although his parents disapproved and wanted him to work in his father's blacksmith shop. *Are your own kind not good enough? they'd said.* She opened the book, its yellowed pages, and there, on page 39, marking *The Underworld*, was the coin. In the margins of the page, the words: *Safe Passage.* She shrank from it. How did it get there? She turned quickly, as if expecting . . . whom? But there was no one. Her mother's bed rumpled, the sinister shutters half-open, her purple suitcase by the door, as though she had stepped out and would return at any moment. On the dresser the coin beckoned, the ocean roaring in her ears. *'I'm not a very good swimmer,' she'd told the boy.* Who could have known? Who could have put it there? She felt her spine tingle, pulled her sweater closer. They had talked about death, of course, in the way teenagers are drawn to the dark, fascinated by myth and legend. The coin, the boy had told her, was to pay the ferryman, Charon, for passage across the rivers Styx and Acheron which divided the world of the living from that of the dead. If one did not pay the fee, he was destined to wander the shores for a hundred years.

Waves thundered in, combined with outgoing ones, doubled in size, leapt in the air, curled and furled in madness. Her father had dragged her out of that building, half-dressed, even as she pleaded

with him. In Mexico, girls married at sixteen, she'd said. *I love him.*
But her father had dragged her back to the Villas Camino del Mar.
Only later, when everyone was sleeping, had she been able to sneak
out, paying a small bribe to the night watchman, who nodded
towards the shadows where the black-haired boy awaited.

They had returned to the run-down building, and set fire to it.
Watched the eruption of flames, smoke stinging their eyes. Then,
he had urged her into his small boat though she was terrified of
water, of the tide surging around them, the undertow. She once
almost drowned as a child, but she had followed him, nonetheless,
trembling in surrender.

'Don't be afraid,' the boy had said, rowing them little-by-little
away from the shore, waves rising around them. She shivered in the
darkness, hands clasped tightly to the boat's sides, watching the
moon's sliver of light undulate on water. She wondered if her
parents would notice her absence. She felt adrift, on the edge of
something both liberating and discomforting.

She couldn't see the expression on his face, only the dark
silhouette of his taut body against the air. When they were
sufficiently away from the lights and the shore, when the ocean
rose around them, lapping against the sides of the boat, he had
locked in the oars and thrown an anchor overboard. Then he'd
moved to the bottom of the boat, and pulled her to him.

'We're meant for this.'

She'd felt alarmed suddenly, as if she had allowed herself to step
beyond the boundaries of her own common sense, of her own fears.
She wondered if her parents were missing her yet. From this angle
inside the boat, the lights of the village and the burning building
were a distant beacon in the night sky. She could only feel the heat
of him beside her. His hand reached for hers, and placed a coin in
it.

'What's this?'

'For passage,' he said. 'Put it under your tongue.'

'I want to go back,' she said. 'My parents are worried.'

But he held her to him, fingers digging into her forearm. She
trembled, shook her head.

'Keep your promise.' His voice was harsh, and his fingers burned around her wrist. 'It's time.' He began to stand up, and the boat swayed.

'We can wait until I turn eighteen,' she said, her voice rising. 'I'll come back. No one will stop us then.' She pushed against him, frightened by his intensity, the coin pressed into her fist. What had she done? She was sweating, her whole body damp, despite the cold breeze. His hand tightened around her wrist.

'You *know* this is the only way we can be together,' he said, 'forever.' He slipped the coin into his mouth, and pulled her over the edge into the water.

At first, she thrashed horribly, fought against the boy whose hands struggled to keep her against him, before a large wave had separated them, and she had been pulled under, dragged by the weight of water. When she surfaced, gasping, she could not see nor hear him above the sound of the ocean. She had managed, by not panicking, to slowly progress to shore by floating on her back, doing breaststrokes, backstrokes, crawls, until she felt the sandy bottom against her legs.

But the boy was never found.

On the dresser, the coin was a stark reminder of their childish pact, the little vow buried at sea.

A slow dripping began again. She palmed the coin, and followed the sounds out of her mother's bedroom, down the stairs, to the gush of *freshet, rivulet, current, tide, torrent, milk, sweat, urine, blood.*

She ran across the road amid the blare of a car honk and the screech of brakes, until she saw him. He was at the edge of the bay, dripping, only half-submerged. He wore goggles and she couldn't see his face. *I'm sorry, I'm sorry, I'm so sorry*, she said. She thought about her mother, wandering the shores for a hundred years.

He opened his arms.

She stopped, uncertain, the water slowly rising, her feet digging into the sand, but he reached out and held her wrist.

'I can't swim well.' Her jeans now clung to her thighs, and her voice shook, but she followed him into the water.

The cold numbed her immediately. She kicked her feet and slid silently among the waves. Ahead, a chiaroscuro summoned. She sliced through water, head down, teeth tight, the smooth glide of waves on her back, hypnotized by the black tendrils enticing her further and further out. She felt no longer like herself.

When she looked up, the sea billowed around her. She was alone, in the middle of the harbor, amid thundering waves, the Point Grey shore now too far to reach. Here and there, the massive shapes of ocean liners mocked her with festive fairy lights.

She called out to them, trying to keep herself from panicking. 'Please, someone, help me!' She fought to keep her head above the crests, fought against the weight of water in her lungs. Then his liquid arms grasped her, *forever, forever,* and she sank against the deep, gasping, sobbing in gratitude, swimming within that tight embrace farther and farther out.

GENNI GUNN *(b. Trieste, Italy, 1949) is a novelist, poet, musician, librettist, and translator. Genni's use of her 'wonderfully quirky and rigorous imagination, her unquenchable curiosity, her poet-passion for the plasticity of language, her knack for twinning grit and intelligence' (Globe & Mail) is at work here. Her stories are explorations of emotional wilderness, and often employ realistic surrealism. She is the author of seven books that have garnered critical acclaim: three novels—Solitaria (2010), Thrice Upon a Time (1990), finalist for the Commonwealth Prize, and Tracing Iris (2002), optioned for film; two short story collections—On the Road (1991) and Hungers (2001); and two poetry collections—Mating in Captivity (1994), finalist for the Gerald Lampert Poetry Award, and the recent Faceless (2007). She has also written an original opera libretto, Alternate Visions (2007, Chants Libres), produced in Montreal, and has translated* *from Italian two books of poetry by renowned author Dacia Maraini. Her website is http://www.gennigunn.com.*

Commentary on "Water Lover": *Some years ago, I almost drowned in Kealakekua Bay in Hawaii, near the spot where Captain Cook was killed in 1779 when the Hawaiians realized he was not immortal. I superimposed that experience onto a Mexican beach, with its treacherous, seductive waves, and added a promise made to the dead. The result is an exploration of fear and guilt. In this story, the protagonist cheats death twice and survives both her mother's oppression and her teenage lover's impossible sacrifice, with haunting results.*

Escena de un Asesinato

Robert Hood

'Buy a photo?' I say without hope, talking to a rotund man in a business suit. He's stopped to check out the prints stuck on my tatty pin-board, which leans uncertainly on the wall next to me.

'I don't think so,' he mutters, on the verge of turning away. But something in the photographs keeps him standing there.

'Some of them aren't bad,' he mutters at last.

I shrug, feeling the texture of the brick wall against my back, the cold resistance of the footpath under my arse. I can smell my own sweat and despondency. '$10. Give an aging ex-photographer a break!'

'How much for that one?' He points at a street scene in a Mexican town. There are two people prominent in the foreground. One is an old woman, the other a masked visage with only the eyes showing. Though the masked man is not always in the photo, he's there now. He's rarely been so close. The intensity in his eyes is unnerving.

'You from Mexico?' I ask.

The man scowls, considering. 'My mother was.'

'Did she work for the government?'

'Yes, as a matter of fact. Not that it's any of your business.'

'You have a wife? Kids?'

He nods absently.

'I can't sell you that one,' I say, resisting the deep-seated compulsion that urges me to do the opposite. I grip the object hidden in my pocket.

'Why not?'

'The masked man in the picture means you harm.'

My potential customer scowls again, more expressively this time. He thinks I'm crazy and he might be right. Yet even if he deserves the ill fortune owning that photograph would bring, I can't do it to him.

'How about another one?' I gesture vaguely at a picture of Mayan ruins. Landscape only. No people. I've never seen anyone in that particular photograph.

The man shrugs. 'No thanks.' He flicks a coin into the empty camera case I use as a pauper bowl and takes off down the street, looking back once or twice as though afraid I'll follow him.

I feel the anger radiating from the photo of the woman and the masked man. El Roto's eyes burn with frustration.

'I won't let you kill again,' I whisper, holding onto the small primitive doll for my life.

August 1999, it's cold, and I'm in Sydney—that ex-colonial metropolis hunkering down in fin de siècle tension between rising ocean and expanding desert interior. Westward, tendrils of suburban indifference spread outward from its heart. I stare through reflections on glass at the city's patterns of artificial light, burnt into the haze and dark. I'm not feeling optimistic.

My exhibition of travel photography—*Susurros del Roto*—opens tonight. There are fewer than 30 people in attendance, one of the them an influential TV talking-head who writes for the *Herald*'s culture pages and is likely to give me a much-needed review if the work either impresses him or he thinks I'm on the rise and wants to hedge his bets. At the moment he's talking to an over-sexed, under-dressed young woman in high heels who's offering him a sultry smile. My most recent girlfriend. I'm hoping Sioni's rather crude allure will get him on side.

'That streetscape is a work of genius, Morley,' a middle-aged woman says with undue familiarity, sleazing up to me and waving her umpteenth glass of New Zealand Pinot Noir between the tips of over-painted fingers. I have no idea who she is. 'You've absolutely captured the essence of the country's post-revolutionary despair.'

The 'framed silver gelatin' (aka black-and-white) print she alludes to is one I took a few years ago in Ocosingo, a town in the Chiapas state of Mexico. I can't give an exact date. My notes are less than precise and my memory's a bag with holes. An ordinary street behind the market area, made evocative by shallow depth of field, a splash of darker paint on flimsy-looking walls, and close focus on the wrinkled features of an old woman just appearing out of a doorway. Parts of the street are suspended in her gaze. She looks as though she's about to curse.

'You think so?' I say. 'I liked the contrast of the woman's ornate wrinkles against the barren poverty of the buildings. They're akin, yet profoundly separate. Aesthetics, that's all. No politics.'

She makes a small coughing sound. 'But surely the figure emerging from the shadows at the far end of the street is part of an ongoing discourse on the Country's unresolved past?' She squints at me expectantly.

'What figure?' I say, amused. 'The street's empty. If anything about that photo is symbolic, it's the emptiness.'

'There's definitely a figure there, Mr Turrand. I can see it clearly. Not its features as such but the general shape. A desperado or some-thing.'

I turn toward the photo. 'There's nothing . . . ' The words fall away. There *is* something. Behind the face of the old woman, barely distinguishable from the blur of the distant street, lurks a human form. It's unclear whether, as I'd pressed the shutter release, the figure had been moving or was stationary, observing. Nor can I tell where it's looking, though I have an unsettling sense that it's staring straight towards the camera. I've studied that image many times as I prepared the photographs for display, and I'm positive I've never seen that shape before.

I push past the woman, who grunts her own displeasure and begins whining about artistic eccentricity to someone near her. I don't care. I lean close to the print, but the figure is real enough—not simply a simulacra, not a smudge or chemical stain. It's dressed in what appears to be a loose-fitting black poncho gathered in at the waist, with a black hood or scarf tied at the top of the head to form a mask, so that only a light smear of face is visible. It may hold a rifle.

I've seen it before, or something like it.

June 1996. I'm sitting in an ordinary cantina in the township of Ocosingo, brooding over a mug of cheap *comiteco*. I look up as a woman sits at my table. It's unexpected, because there's a sign on the door forbidding entry to policemen, dogs and whores. No one seems bothered by her presence though.

'*Buenas noches*,' she says, with a sardonic smile. She's smoking a small cigar.

'Sorry,' I say, groping for the words, 'I'm not looking for, um, compan-ionship.'

Those eyes, that were copal only a moment ago, darken. 'You assume I am a *puta*? Why? Because I sit uninvited? Because I talk to a stranger?'

I hadn't expected my crude Spanish to be understood. Her English, however, is fine. I look her over. Her white shirt is open at the neck, but not enough to reveal cleavage, just soft café con leche skin. She's wearing baggy black pants. I imagine the small hips, and the firm, reddish-tanned legs they cover. 'Are you?' I ask, reverting to English.

'Does it make a difference?'

'Maybe.'

Her eyes are darkly luminous, her hair black and cut short around her ears. No obvious make-up, but she's not colourless or plain for all that. With a hat and serape, she'd almost pass for a man from a distance, but up close, her body is distinctly feminine and her face mesmerizing: full lips slightly parted, rounded cheeks, and the centers of the eyebrows, over Frida Kahlo eyes that won't let you off too easily, raised, questioning.

'Care for a drink?'

'I don't drink,' she replies and falls silent, staring at me.

I lean a little closer, smelling scented vanilla mixed with white chocolate. 'How can I help you then?'

She shrugs and blows a cloud of smoke over my head. 'I sit. I wait.'

Now I feel discomfort, even a sense of danger, though she has made no threatening moves. Her rich, unpainted lips caress the cigar with delight, teasingly. After a few moments she reaches down into a pocket in her pants, and I inhale. She fetches some object and places it on the table in front of me. Her hand draws away, leaving it standing there.

The thing is a small rough doll, whether man or woman is unclear. About 8 or 9 cm high, it's dressed in what is meant to be a black serape, head covered in a hood except for a slit from which two eyes peer, sewn in black thread. Hands and visible face are the only white fabric—though a twine made of black-and-white yarns crosses its chest like bandoliers. In its nascent hands it holds a crude rifle made of wood.

'What's this?' I ask.

'Zapatista doll,' she murmurs.

I touch it then pull my hand back. 'Zapatista?'

She glares critically, but that only makes her more captivating. 'You are not very perceptive, are you, Señor Turrand? You photograph but you do not see.'

'Well, I don't know what you want me to see—'

'Zapatistas are rebels,' she says. '*Bandidos*, if you will. Part of the *Ejército Zapatista de Liberación Nacional*. They have opposed the oppressive Mexican state since 1994—the tail-end of a war that has gone on for many decades. To many they are heroes. The better known of them have been turned into these figures, so.' She gestures at the doll. 'It is good for tourism.'

'Is that right?' I lean closer to the doll, pondering the ubiquitous tradition that transforms social malcontents into celebrities. Robin

Hood, Ned Kelly, Phoolan Devi, Ishikawa Goemon, Dick Turpin, Pancho Villa: hero-bandits all. 'Who's this bloke?'

'El Roto.' She offers a half-grin. 'Once Genaro el Roto, Genaro the Broken, the Lost.'

'Is he particularly famous?'

'Famous for being dead. He was shot here in this town during the fighting two years ago, murdered by the government's militia. His first name was indeed Genaro. But his last was a secret, his nom de guerre El Roto, after our famous Mexican outlaw from a century ago. Others have adopted that name now. El Roto lives on in them.'

'Others?'

'The fight continues, Señor Turrand. But it is now in the hands of the new generation, with their different methods. This man needs to be freed. Vengeance does not work for the greater good, and he is become a liability. Do you understand?'

I shrug, bewildered by her words and her quiet passion.

She smiles, her sensuality warming me. 'You, too, are El Roto. I see it in your eyes.'

'If you say so.'

'I do. Take it.' She gestures at the doll. 'I want you to have it.'

What's she after? I don't know how to respond.

'Those that die without resolution often return,' she adds, 'and may not serve the best interests of the country. It can be disruptive.'

'You mean they become martyrs to the cause?'

'Victims merely. But vengeful ones.'

Her burnt honey eyes hold meaning she doesn't speak. 'So where was El Roto killed?' I ask, unnerved by the depth of those eyes, which now half close.

'The market square. Along with others.' She gestures again. 'Take the doll. It is a gift. Take it back with you when you go home, to remind you that not all find peace.'

I frown again at the insistence in her tone.

'Take it,' she repeats.

'I meant no disrespect.'

She watches with curious intensity as I reach out and let my fingers wrap around the doll. When I draw it closer to myself, it's as though she relaxes. I can feel the atmosphere around us lighten.

Her eyes rest on me gently, perhaps sadly now.

'*Más comiteco*, Señor?' Torn from my distraction, I look up into an indifferent, plump and pitted, mustachioed face—the *tabernero's*.

'No thanks, though the lady might want something.'

He looks confused. Perhaps I'd said it incorrectly; my grasp of Spanish and local dialects is horrible, frankly. 'Lady?' he queries.

'This one—' I glance across the table to where the alluring woman was sitting, but she's no longer there. Nor can I see her anywhere in the room. Only the chocolatey scent of Ocosingo's fully-bloomed ceiba flowers lingers.

'Señor?'

'She appears to have gone.'

Ragged eyebrows bend into a frown. 'There are no ladies here, Señor.' He shrugs, and adds, 'It is prohibited.'

'She gave me this.' I hold out the doll.

He dismisses it as commonplace, immediately backing away from it. I can tell it worries him.

'What's going on here?' I demand.

'Please leave.' His face is hard and serious. Then he turns and shuffles back toward the bar.

I don't bother arguing; I've had enough of this. I drop the doll on the table and head for the door.

January 1994. I'm stumbling through a street off the market square, the bullet lodged in my thigh burning as fiercely as my anger. Around me, the air vibrates with shouting, gunfire and the choking breath of my own fear. From behind, a percussive rifle shot catches up to me, overtakes and echoes along the street ahead.

'Genaro!' Acatl cries and I glance back.

He falls to one knee, hand clutching his shoulder—and beyond him several Government militia run toward us, yelling and waving their rifles. I take a hesitant step forward, aware that we are being hemmed in, but not wanting to abandon my friend. Another shot cracks and bounces off the walls to either side. Acatl jerks forward onto his face, the road surface muffling his cry.

I regain my balance and turn to run on, desperation energizing my aching muscles. Bullets explode into the ground to my right, and I leap awkwardly towards the nearest cover, behind some concrete stairs. One more step then my left thigh erupts in pain, throwing me forward. My leg collapses and I crash to the ground.

I'm aware of the thud of heavy boots drawing near. A soldier looms over me. He's breathing heavily.

I glance up at him. '*Bastardo!*' I say, a mere whisper.

The man—large and black against the sky and the eves of shops on the far side of the road—looks down in silence. His face is harsh, and his rifle poised and ready.

I hear the shot and feel near-simultaneous pain in my fore-head—a blood-flash before the bullet ruptures my skull.

August 1999, the day after my exhibition's opening night. I've been drinking for hours now, appeasing my own unhappiness through the pursuit of oblivion. The morning newspapers are strewn over the floor of my apartment, torn and crumpled.

'Had enough, Morley?'

Sioni stands in the bedroom doorway, her hair untidy and make-up smeared. She's wearing a Red Hot Chili Peppers t-shirt and nothing else. It'd make me take her straight back to bed if I wasn't so pissed.

I drag my carcass off the sofa, and squint. 'So what's with Groban anyway?' I re-fill my scotch glass. 'I saw you playing up to the bastard.'

'You told me to.'

'"More post-colonial landscapes from Morley Turrand. Yawn." What sort of a review is that?'

'Is that what he wrote? He told me he liked your snaps.'

I stand close, so close I can feel the heat of her.

'Likes my *snaps*? I guess the blow-job you gave him in the backroom wasn't up to scratch then.'

'Fuck you, Morley.'

'Sioni, it's all you're good for. Least you can do is get it right.'

She glares, her whipped-puppy eyes moist. She's on the verge. It's so damn easy.

But she fights it. I see the moment of vulnerability pass. 'Maybe it's your *snaps* that are fucked.'

Before any reactive synaptic activity can generate a response in my muscles, her fist catches my left cheek, even though she was aiming for my mouth. It wouldn't have been so bad but she's got a silver skull ring on her third finger, Keith Richards-style; one I gave her! I stumble back a bit.

After a moment she looks up at me. Tears glint in her eyes—but they're hot tears, not the lukewarm drizzle of misery. 'You want me to be sorry, Morley? Well, I'm sorry you didn't get what you wanted from me. I'm sorry about your career and I'm sorry you're an arsehole. Most of all I'm sorry I've had anything to do with you.'

Her words cut through the alcoholic haze. 'Sioni, I'm bleeding here—'

'And don't bother to apologize. I'm going as soon as I get dressed. I won't be back.'

The bedroom door slams. For a moment I fight an impulse to kick it down, but the fire dies quickly. I don't even try to talk her out of it.

She's as good as her word. Still disheveled but dressed in the red, impossibly sexy silk dress she'd been wearing last night, she emerges from the bedroom about ten minutes later. 'I *am* sorry, Sioni,' I almost bawl. 'It's the bloody alcohol, my head, that dick Groban—'

She gives me little more than a side-glance before turning away. The fact that she doesn't even have the passion left to slam the front door as she leaves paralyzes me.

So I take another swig of scotch and follow up by tossing the glass, half-full though it is, against the wall. It shatters with satisfactory violence.

How long I slump in the chair, mindless with self-pity, I don't know—but I'm pulled out of it by the phone. It's Grace Nye, the gallery owner—the last person I want to talk to. When I left the exhibition at about 11, only one or two minor unnumbered pieces had been sold.

'Not good, eh, Grace,' I say.

'Not in volume, no—and yes, I noticed Groban's comment this morning.'

Silence. I'm afraid to say anything.

'But I have one piece of good news. You sold one of the major pieces.'

'Good god! Which one?'

'*Escena de un Asesinato*. The street scene with the old woman's face—'

'Really?'

'It was Norma Rivera. You know her? She seemed to know you quite well.'

I didn't, but I get Grace to describe her and I place her at once.

'The thing is, Morley,' Grace continues, 'she wanted to take it with her. Number 1 of the run. Seemed rather obsessive about it.'

'I don't usually do that—and besides, the print was flawed.' Remembering the phantom shape, I immediately determine to check the other prints.

'Was it? I didn't notice. Anyway, she insisted. Even offered to pay more. I could hardly refuse.' Grace tells me how much more and all my objections suddenly dissipate in a cloud of mercenary relief. 'Anyway,' she continues, 'can you bring me another print? Maybe a few of them, just in case. I'll get one framed before we open this afternoon. We might be on a winner there.'

'Sure, sure.'

As I hang up, I start to shout for Sioni, to tell her the good news. Then I feel my face and remember that she's gone.

June 1996, a few days after I met the woman in the cantina. I've been wandering the countryside around Ocosingo, on this occasion photographing the nearby Mayan ruins at Toniná in a way that I hope will appeal to tourists. *Travel Scene* Magazine somehow heard that I'm here in Mexico and tracked me down to the Hotel de Destino. The editor wants me to take some appropriate shots of the area, on commission. I can use the money, so I reluctantly agree to prostitute myself. Now I'm busy playing the back-door whore. It's not hard. It's what I've always done.

The day is warm, not hot enough to irritate me. It rained last night, lightly, so the air's clear. I'm feeling almost optimistic. I take some panoramic shots of the view then proceed through random clusters of trees toward the detritus of ancient stonework and Toniná's huge central pyramid. It rises from grass and vegetation as though thrust up from underground.

Despite its openness, there's a shadowy quality to Toniná that quickly drags me back into myself after the innocence of the surrounding fields. The ancient ruins are scattered over much of the hillside like the broken corpse of a city, but as I pass a sacrificial altar isolated in an open area of grass, and climb the stairs into the ruins proper, the ornate rubble closes around me and begins to squeeze my soul.

Toniná's antique paths, foundations and walls become a maze-like complex that is, they say, oriented to the night-sky, with occasional openings thick with shadow that lead downward into the earth. But I'm so enmeshed in the details, I can't see the pattern. Friezes solidify out of the rough stonework as I move about, many of them depicting bound and headless prisoners. The most prominent is of King Kan-Xul from nearby Palenque, cowering with rope tied around one constricted arm. Among Toniná's greatest achievements were, apparently, the defeat of Palenque and the capture of the King, who subsequently suffered ten years of humiliation at his captors' hands before execution. So my guidebook tells me.

I come across a sarcophagus carved out of a single large stone, its lid missing and its mortal contents long gone. By now I've lost the bucolic peace I'd found in the green fields and darker green clumps of trees that sweep across the gently rolling land around the hilltop ruins, oppressed by an awareness that what remains longest of civilization are the scars of violence and death. I wonder if the original inhabitant of the sarcophagus is still here somewhere, unwilling to leave. As I take picture after picture, the sun gradually lowers and the light glows eerily.

A breeze picks up as the day dwindles. I've been shooting the outside of a half-buried wall topped by cacti, with three arched doorways leading below ground-level to a labyrinth known as the Palace of the Underworld. Snapping shots as I go, I approach the central opening. Thick darkness beyond it gives me a momentary *frisson* that makes my skin squirm. It's a psychosomatic response, I know, but the shiver is real enough.

Looking through my Minolta, I set up a frame that encompasses only the central archway and surrounding stonework. As the scene comes into focus I'm aware of a figure standing in the internal shadows beyond the rough architrave. I take the shot then pull the camera away from my face, blinking to peer through the lowering sunlight. The opening's about 100 metres distant, so if someone's there I should be able to see him. But I can't, only that dark gaping hole into the Underworld. Another glance through the camera's viewfinder, using a close-in zoom, reveals nothing. Whoever it was must have stepped backwards into the labyrinth.

I approach the middle doorway, but even standing right at the shadow's edge I can't peer more than a metre or two beyond the entrance. Without consciously acknowledging the fact, I am unable to enter, muscular control drained by an awareness of evil. Instead I discharge the camera's flash, splashing its garish light over the rough internal walls. At the far end of the passage is a male, almost naked, what clothing he wears tattered and meager. His eyes spark red. I gasp, and step back as the afterimage fades.

'Señor?' comes a voice from behind me. I expel a weak gasp as I turn and stumble to the side. A small man wearing farmer's clothes and a large straw hat squints up at me with sardonic curiosity, as though my reaction is an absurdity he can't quite fathom.

I apologise in my uncertain Spanish. 'You, um, surprised me. There was someone . . . In the, um . . . *en el laberinto.*'

He stares in that direction then scowls, his lips twitching like anxious slugs. *'Bandido?'*

I try to explain that the figure seemed like an ancient Mayan, like many of the friezes that depict Toniná's prisoners.

He shrugs incomprehension or indifference then steps into the dark passage. I try to stop him, but he brushes me off and disappears. I hear his feet scraping down the rough path. A minute or two later he returns. His dark pupils peek through a mass of wrinkles, enough to evaluate me.

'*Nada*?' I say.

He nods.

'Do they hide here? *Bandidos*? Do they hide in those—?' I gesture toward the darkness.

He says nothing. Either he can't understand me or he thinks me crazy.

After a few moments of silence, irritated by his inaction, I ask him what he'd wanted in the first place.

'Turrand?' The word seems distasteful to him.

'Morley Turrand. *Sí.*'

His long battered hand offers me a Zapatista doll. It looks familiar. I remember leaving it behind in the cantina a few days before.

'Where did you get this?' I ask.

'*Qué*?'

'The doll . . . Zapatista doll? Who gave it to you?'

'*Fantasma,*' he answers without a hint of irony. A ghost? He follows up with a jumble of words I'm too surprised to translate, though I gather he thinks I've been careless.

I ask if he knows who the ghost was.

He says I know her—that is what matters.

'What do you mean?'

'*Fantasma,*' he repeats, pointing at my chest.

June 1996. Sometimes *this* is how I remember meeting the woman. She sits across the table from me, smoking her thin cigarette with calm intensity. She isn't pleased. We have spoken briefly and though she denies being a prostitute I can't imagine why else she would be here.

Offering me the Zapatista doll was an unsettling moment—so familiar, giving me a shiver of déjà vu, and filled with the white chocolate-mixed-with-vanilla fragrance of ceiba. Yet her explanation fascinates me, even if it smacks of unstated intent. I should refuse it and send her away.

'Take the doll,' she whispers. 'It is a gift. To remind you that not all find peace.'

I frown at the insistence in her tone.

'Take it,' she repeats.

I grasp the doll despite myself and study the odd crudity of its making to avoid the embarrassment of having obeyed her so easily. Now, however, having accepted her gift, I find myself being drawn to the woman. My skin tingles as though her slim fingers caress my face. I raise my eyes from the doll to stare at her, imagining the small blossom of a body she hides beneath unappealingly masculine clothes. The beginnings of desire stir in my gut.

'Now you want me,' she says, 'whether or not I am a *puta*.'

'If you're a streetwalker, I'm not interested.'

Her smile is private and knowing. I feel voyeuristic merely seeing it.

'To pay for sex,' she says, 'would be an affront to your masculinity, would it?'

'No, that's not—'

'Do not fear, Señor Turrand,' she interrupts, 'I have not loved for a long time, and would not consider it now except that you interest me.'

'I *interest* you?' I say, taken aback by her forthright manner.

'*Sí*. As I *interest* you.'

I should be put off by her condescending manner, but the deep tones of her voice vibrate through my mind, overturning denial and stoking the fires of arousal.

'What's your name?' I ask.

'Once, I was called Coronela María de la Luz Espinosa Barrera. Perhaps you have heard of me.'

I haven't and she knows it. Her smile makes my heart beat faster.

'Should I?'

'If you cared for more than yourself, perhaps . . . yes. History is *importante*, Señor.'

Annoyance rises again, but it only fuels my desire for her. I frown—and the woman laughs. 'Just Coronela then.'

'Coronela.' I taste the word, letting it vibrate in my throat.

'Come!' She takes my hand and pulls me to my feet. The table rattles and the *tabernero* glances our way. I extract money from my pocket and ostentatiously place it under my half-empty glass.

'Enough?' I yell across the room.

He gestures uncertainly, a little befuddled, but doesn't pursue the matter.

Coronela leads me out into the street. 'Where are we going?' I ask.

'I do not make love on cantina tables. Or in back alleys.' She gestures. 'Your hotel, I think.'

Speechless, I follow.

After a few blocks, she indicates a large space that opens out to our right beyond the buildings at the end of a narrow road. 'That is the market,' she says. 'It is there that many Zapatista rebels died when their peaceful occupation of the township was repressed most violently by Government butchers.' She gestures around us. 'Here is where Genaro el Roto was murdered. Remember the spot. You must come back and photograph it, no?'

'I guess.'

'You will photograph it, won't you, Señor Morley?'

I stare at her accusingly. 'How do you know my name, Coronela?' I demand. 'How did you know what I do? I never told you.'

That secret smile again, advising me that she has no intention of answering my question. 'Much depends on you photographing this spot.' She grabs my arm and pulls me close, forcing me to look directly into her eyes. Their black depth mesmerizes me. 'When you do, you must carry the doll with you.'

'The doll?'

'*Sí*, you must keep it close.'

'Okay, okay, I will.'

'You must.'

She lets go.

'Also when you go to Toniná in three days time,' she continues, 'you must take care what you photograph.'

'What d'you mean?'

'There are things in that place, ancient resentments, which you must not capture with your camera. The doll, El Roto—it marks you as his and will keep the others at bay. Stupidly, however, you went there without it.'

'*Went there without it*? Look, I've never been to Toniná. I've no intention of going there.'

'You will have reason to go to Toniná—and you will go, without protection. But I have righted that error. Now you will take the doll.'

'You righted it? Even though I haven't gone there yet?'

Her eyes hold me in their silence.

'I don't have a clue what the hell you're talking about,' I say.

She doesn't smile as she takes my hand. 'Come, I will give you what you think you want. Later you may understand.'

June 1996. Toniná. Is this the way it happens? It feels wrong.

I'm photographing the ruins for *Travel Scene* Magazine, fairly unenthusiastically, I must confess. I've been at it for several hours already and am now facing a wall with three stone-framed doorways leading to underground tunnels—the Palace of the Underworld. Raising the viewfinder of the Minolta to my eye, I focus on the central passage. A lighter shadow lingers in the internal darkness beyond the rough architrave. I take the shot then pull the camera away from my face, but there's no one there, only that dark gaping hole into the Underworld. Another glance through the camera's viewfinder. Nothing.

I must be imagining things. There aren't even tourists around— I haven't seen anyone all day. Nervously I grip the Zapatista doll, which is in my coat pocket. My breathing calms and once again the day seems ordinary.

I take more shots of the ruins, even forcing myself to get a few inside the structure itself. I find no evidence of other people among its evocative shadows. When I re-emerge from the gloom the atmospheric sunlight has turned into a flat gloaming and I begin the long trek back to Ocosingo. It's dark by the time I get to the hotel.

August, 1999. When I check them, none of the other prints of *Escena de un Asesinato* show any background markings that might be construed as a human being. I take numbers 2 to 10 to Grace at the gallery and she accepts them eagerly. She's hoping that Norma Rivera's excessive enthusiasm for the picture will be the start of a trend. Even if others pay less, the commission will help reduce the loss she clearly expects to make.

'How many are there in the run, Morley?' she asks. I point toward my hand-drawn signature. Under it I've written *2 of 17*. 'Only 17?'

'That's how you make these things valuable, Grace.'

'But we usually extend the run to 50 or 100.'

'I want this to be very collectible.'

'Why?'

I frown, not having considered it before. 'I don't know. Why not? I burnt the negatives of all the exclusives. There has to be a guarantee of limitation.'

'That's ridiculous, Morley. Do you realize what we could lose on a deal like that?'

'It's how I want it.'

She gives me a side-glance sneer that says *you think far too highly of yourself*, though she doesn't articulate it further. When I don't respond she turns her gaze toward the picture.

'It's a nice shot, Morley. There's something compelling in it. Why's it called *Escena de un Asesinato*?'

'*Murder Scene*. A revolutionary was killed there in 1994.'

She nods thoughtfully. 'That explains something the Rivera woman said: *An echo of the last Ocosingo insurgents*. She reckoned there was a bandit further up the street. She was keen to show it to her husband. Couldn't see it myself.'

'You couldn't?'

She shrugs, holding up print number 2. 'Well, can *you*?'

As I leave her to her business, I feel a sense of disquiet scratching at the insides of my skull. I'm sure there had been a shape there on the street in print #1 of *Escena de un Asesinato*, the suggestion of a bandit-like spectre coming my way. Norma Rivera had seen it. So had I. Why not Grace?

J une 1996.

Do I make love with Coronela?

'You must see, Morley, and if not you, you must let your camera see what is before you.'

I peer through the lens down a shadowy street, snapping pictures as she directs.

'There,' Coronela says, *'El Roto is there. Do you see?'*

Someone is there, in the distance. His eyes are black holes—all three of them, one in his forehead. An old woman with wrinkled skin and withered lips appears in the frame. *'No camera!'* she screeches.

Click.

After we reach the Hotel de Destino, does Coronela come up to my room and with the aggressive lack of subtlety that seems typical of her, does she remove her clothes, place my hands on her skin, encourage arousal in herself and in me? I don't know. I can't remember. There are images in my head, erotic moments, heat and passion, all infused with the ceiba scent, but I don't know if they are memories or simply phantoms of desire.

'Do you seek love among the dead?' I hear her whisper in my ear. *'Futile if you don't find it first among the living. Should life get too dark, then in death there will only be profounder darkness.'*

'There! El Roto is there.'

Click.

She consumes me, draining any desire to escape. I try to push her away, but instead find myself drawn further and further into the heart of her.

I want to know who she is.

'Coronela María de la Luz Espinosa Barrera was a veteran of the Mexican Revolution of 1910,' she tells me. *'She fought with greater distinction than most men, and was awarded a pension once the fighting was done. But she became an exile in her own land, her temperament unsuited to peacetime society's inane mores. She wandered the country like a lost ghost, dressed as a man, abandoned in a time that was no longer her own.'*

'And you're this La Coronela, are you?'

She laughs. *'Perhaps. Perhaps not.'*

'What do you want from me?'

'There! He watches you from the shadows. Shoot!'

Click.

'What will I do?'

'You will take these pictures back to your land,' she says, tapping the camera on the table near me. Her voice is no more definite than breath. *'The doll will protect you, but your actions will feed El Roto's desires.'*

Click.

Click.

A black bird flaps against the window and startles me. I open my eyes to the bloody dimness of twilight as it leaks in through tattered curtains.

I'm alone. The sheets are crumpled and sweaty. I untangle myself, needing to use the toilet, and look for my pants. My camera is lying on the floor near my discarded clothes. I check how many pictures have been taken, only to discover the entire roll is spent. I'm sure it was new only an hour before.

Later, when I develop the film, I see I have taken a series of pictures in the streets around Ocosingo's market square. I don't remember doing it.

'These are good,' I mutter to myself, knowing I've found the soul of my upcoming exhibition.

August 1999, and it's the day after the opening.

In a display of useless pretension, I seek out Norma Rivera, ostensibly to give her the choice of obtaining an unblemished print for her money, just to be fair. But in truth I don't care about her or fairness. I simply want to see the thing, to assure myself that the figure we both saw at the opening is still there, and not a glitch of memory.

It turns out that Norma Rivera is the wife of Alex Rivera, CEO of *Harvest Futures*. Their mansion is on the Harbour foreshore in an exclusive northside suburb, and I can't even get past the gate. But an intercom device, its far end impersonating some sort of semi-articulate minder, finally listens long enough to discover what I want, and replies with the terse diagnosis: 'She's dead.'

'Dead?'

I pause, trying to summon either genuine surprise or a modicum of sympathy. Neither comes.

'Um, perhaps I could speak to Mr Rivera then, if he's not too busy,' I say at last, rather tactlessly.

'I'm sorry, sir,' the voice replies, 'Mr Rivera is ... unavailable.'

Now a pinprick of apprehension scratches across the inside of my belly.

The intercom coughs and faintly I hear a gruff voice: 'I'll take care of it.'

At that moment, I spot a blue flash through the bushes, down the distant end of the curving driveway. A cop car. Of course there'd be police.

'Who is this?' the voice growls.

'I'm a photographer,' I manage then add hastily, 'Not the press.'

He asks me to explain and I do and by the time I've finished there's an officer approaching the gate. I resist the urge to run, experiencing a moment of Hitchcockian paranoia. *I didn't do it,* I want to shout.

The cop opens the gate. 'Mr Turrand?'

I acknowledge the fact and he asks me to accompany him back to the house. He says nothing as we follow the roadway up to Rivera's mansion. The day has become colder, but sweat soaks into my shirt.

Something rather gothic is what I expect from the place, but the house turns out to be modern—all straight lines, glass and hard, functional edges. An incongruously soft-edged man in a dark suit nods in my direction. He approaches and holds out his hand.

'Detective-Inspector Greer,' he says. 'Thank you for cooperating, Mr Turrand.'

'Ah,' I say, shaking his clammy palm, 'I have no idea how I can help. I don't even know what's happened.'

'They're both dead.' His placid eyes stare into mine. I sense his evaluation, though not as a threat.

'That's terrible,' I offer, without much conviction. 'How?'

'Undecided. Did you know the victims?'

'Victims?'

'Did you know them?'

'No, no, not at all. The woman . . . Mrs Rivera . . . spoke to me at the opening yesterday. I didn't know who she was. And I've never met the other.'

'I see. If you could follow me, I'd like to show you something.'

At the door he gives me plastic covers to put over my shoes. 'Don't touch anything,' he mutters. 'We're still examining the scene.'

He guides me into an open area that looks out through huge plate-glass windows onto an immaculately kept and spacious yard, leading down to a small wharf and Sydney Harbour beyond. It's the kind of view you see on calendars and has to be worth millions. In the room are more cops, a forensic team with assorted gadgets and bags, and two bodies. Norma Rivera is on the floor, leaning against a white wall with her eyes staring at me, sightless—mouth open as though frozen in the middle of a passionate monologue, all secret in their meaning. There doesn't appear to be a mark on her. A man I assume is Alexander Rivera is spread-eagled on the far side of the room. There's blood pooled around him and before Greer guides me away, artfully obscuring sight of him, I realize that his head is shattered, with blood and gore forming a Jackson Pollock splatter across the polished boards.

'Is this your photograph?' Greer asks.

Norma has already hung it, giving it pride of place on an open wall beside a small bar. But the glass has been shattered and the photograph ruined; it looks as though three bullets have been fired through the print into the wall behind.

'I guess he didn't like it,' I say.

'Where was the stain you reckon was on the print?'

'There.' I point. 'Right where the holes are.'

'Do you know of any reason why the victim might have done this?'

'I told you, Inspector, I've never met the man. It was just a picture I took while I was in Mexico a few years ago.'

He nods to himself, rubbing at his chin as though what I've just said is the key to some grim insight.

Then he asks if I have any objection to being fingerprinted.

'Am I a suspect?' I ask.

He shrugs. 'I very much doubt it. But you did turn up here at the scene and there are procedures.'

As one of his underlings takes my fingerprints and particulars, Greer presses me some more, with questions relating to my whereabouts and movements the previous night, perhaps hoping I'll be distracted by the bureaucratic chores and give myself away. He takes down Sioni's contact number so she can corroborate my alibi. I wonder if she will. Finally he decides I'm either innocent or a complete drongo and gets one of his men to show me out.

In the days that follow I discover from one of Grace's PR acquaintances that ballistics indicates it was definitely Alex Rivera who pumped three bullets into *Escena de un Asesinato* #1 of 20— but no other rounds had been fired.

'What about the one that killed him?' I ask. 'He was clearly shot in the head.'

'Not so, apparently,' she replies. 'No other bullets anywhere, no chemical residue in the wound, no projectile scoring on the skull fragments. He wasn't shot, or battered to death for that matter.

They don't know what caused it. That's what's got them confused.'

'I don't understand.'

'Incidentally,' she adds, 'were you aware that he was a native of Chiapas state?'

'What?'

'Born in San Cristóbal, Mexico. Quite a coincidence, eh? Apparently his father was in the Mexican army during the 1920s and fought against the rebels. He may have been ex-militia himself. At any rate the cops suspect that Rivera was a member of one of the larger drug cartels and involved in illegal importation. They think he may have swindled his Mexican bosses. That'd be why he was killed. Retribution.'

I'm aware of someone sitting on the bench at my feet, their presence obvious to me though I haven't opened my eyes yet. *Do not resist him*, a female voice whispers. My pulse quickens. I pull my old coat off my head and push myself onto one aching elbow. The night has been cold and my joints are stiff. There's no one there.

'What d'you want of me?' I shout at the empty space, scaring a group of pigeons into panicked flight. An early morning commuter across the park glances in my direction and quickly looks away again. He hurries toward the sounds of traffic beyond the trees.

June 1996. In retrospect, I realize that I can't remember ever feeling Coronela's breath on my skin, hearing her heart beat or sensing her warmth as our bodies press together. Is she still here beside me, I wonder? Was she ever here?

'*We avenge our men and ourselves,*' she whispers. '*It may be the men who die, but it is the women who suffer.*'

I want to reach over and touch her, but suddenly I'm afraid of what I'll find. It makes no sense.

The darkness thickens and night palls.

'Why me?' I ask.

Her voice seems to linger, no longer immediate, but more like a memory.

'I'm sorry, Señor *Morley,'* she whispers.

In the morning, she's gone.

August/September 1999. A cleaner named Emilio Torres dies in his flat, his skull shattered, though from what investigating officers can't tell. Inconsistencies in the forensic detail run counter to evidence that it might have been the result of a physical blow. Torres wasn't a rich man, and had lived alone, yet he'd felt compelled to buy one of my overpriced *Escena de un Asesinato* prints. He'd limped badly—from an injury sustained during the Chiapas uprising of 1994, he told Grace. That's why he was so fascinated with the photo. She sold him one of the later numbers, unframed. It was found crumpled near his body.

A few days later Gabriel Moreno, owner of a chain of Mexican restaurants, is shot in the head in his home, though no bullet can be found at the scene and nor does forensic analysis reveal sign of a weapon's discharge. He was holding the print of *Escena de un Asesinato* that he'd purchased the previous evening. His wife and son are found dead in other parts of the house, though their bodies reveal no signs of violence at all.

Robert Ortega and his wife die under mysterious circumstances the following evening. They have also bought one of my *Escena de un Asesinato* prints. Ortega has diplomatic connections with the Mexican government, though none of my sources can discover what those connections are. Whatever his job might be, it ensures that the details of his death remain hidden from the press.

I sleep badly. In the night I dream I am running through the streets of Ocosingo, pursued by a man with no face. There is a pattern, I'm sure of that, and I also know that if I can only work out what it is, I can escape the inevitable fate that awaits me. But in my blind panic I can't see the pattern, only chaos. I try to change the dream, knowing the outcome, but am unable to. Inevitably the faceless man will catch me.

Juliana Estranez buys *Escena de un Asesinato* #5 of 17, takes it home and subsequently tries to burn it. She fails and is discovered next day by her cleaner, dead on the floor near the fireplace. There is no sign of violence. Later I learn that her father had been an officer in the Mexican army during the first half of the 20th Century.

Before too long, manic with weariness and fear, I embrace what my rational mind has been avoiding and collect all remaining copies of *Escena de un Asesinato* from Grace. She doesn't understand and I can't explain. We argue.

'At least leave me a couple of them,' she pleads.

'I can't.'

'What are you going to do with them?'

'Doesn't matter. Just push the other photos, Grace.'

'No one wants the others, Morley. They want *Escena de un Asesinato.*'

'I'm not selling any more of them. That's it.'

In frustration, she points out that this sort of idiosyncratic behaviour might be tolerated in the Greats of the Art World, but it isn't going to do a second-rater like me much good at all.

I shrug.

She cancels the exhibition not long after I leave.

I'm too fixated on my absurd belief that the prints are haunted, too terrified of the impossible, to care one way or the other. Back in my studio, I rip the remaining prints of *Escena de un Asesinato* apart, tossing the shreds into a metal waste bin and setting them alight. For a while, as I decimate the run, I don't notice the decrease in room temperature that causes my breath to cloud, despite the flames and the heated air rising from the bin. After four or five prints have turned to ash, it seems as though my strength has leaked away, weariness overtaking me and turning the deepening shadows into a weight I can barely carry. Any blood still flowing through my veins becomes lethargic.

'Leave me alone!' I growl at the shadows that seem to fill the room.

But I've been careless. I don't have the Zapatista doll on me. It lies on a nearby bench, far away, and I glance at it now, fighting despair. My muscles have weakened to the point of almost total incapacity; I fight the feeling, staggering forward with my hand extended. The remaining prints drop from my fingers, scattering across the floor. I stagger. Ambient hiss in my ears becomes louder and louder as the sound of traffic beyond the walls disappears. And then, all around me, yet dim as though echoing from far away, I hear voices shouting in Spanish. I can't make out what they're saying, but the fury they express is unmistakable.

My fingers clasp the doll. Instantly the sounds disappear and my strength returns. The atmosphere lightens.

'Just stay away!' I rasp at the room. 'I won't let this continue.'

Holding onto the doll with one hand, I scoop up the scattered prints and one-by-one drop them into the fire. Flame consumes them. But as the last blackens and shrivels, consciousness leaks out of me and I collapse onto the floor.

Living on the streets should make you feel free, but it doesn't. It's like a constant ache, a bone-cold reminder of the human connections that have foresworn you—or that you have foresworn. You are not part of the current that rushes time and the world forward. Rather, you dwell in a psychological billabong of your own, a stagnant backwater where the detritus of your past gathers to groan, to mutate, to drown you.

My life is a torrent of memories and desires, regrets and delusions. But why do the memories keep changing? Everything can't be true.

A cold wind rakes its claws through the park and I shut my eyes and hunker further into my coat. It is old and no doubt smelly, but I'm used to the stink and it's at least thick, the weave tight. It keeps out some of the chill.

Half the time now I can't remember why I burned the photos, what it was that made me imagine that posthumous resentments lingered in dark places within my mind and escaped via memory of that confused three-week visit to Mexico. The ghost of El Roto? I looked him up, back when I had internet access. El Roto—Chucho el Roto—was a bandit active at the end of the 19ᵗʰ Century. He was famous, an ambiguous hero, a lover of the theatre, a seducer, and a 'non-violent' thief, but he died in prison in Veracruz in 1885, possibly beaten to death. Not in the streets of Ocosingo in 1994. The woman I knew, Coronela—she'd said the doll was Genaro el Roto. Not Chucho. The designation 'el roto'—'broken', 'discarded', 'abandoned'—has been applied to many unfortunates, many outlaws. What does it mean? Why did he, whoever he is, pick me to be his courier, his 'people smuggler'?

You, too, are El Roto, she said.

It wasn't until much later—expelled from my studio and my apartment with whatever prints I could scavenge—when the money was gone, and I was hungry and desperate—that I decided to do what others did and sell my old, unwanted goods on the street. Some spruiked ink drawings, some old comic books, some bits of metal twisted into ornaments. Photographs? Why not? What good are they to me? As I pinned them to a scrap of cardboard in the hope that someone would buy them, one grabbed my attention. I seemed to remember it. *Escena de un Asesinato.* Hadn't I destroyed them all? One of that run, just one, had somehow survived. I couldn't recall why I'd burned the rest.

Why does knowing that one still exists give me the tremors? I clutch at the doll I keep stuffed in my coat pocket till the fear subsides.

Escena de un Asesinato has a strange possessing power, there's no doubt about that. Though I know I shouldn't, I can't help displaying it with the other, harmless prints of Mayan ruins and Chiapas countryside. An overweight man in a brown business suit is staring at me from further down the street. I recognise him, even though I see many people in a day at my railway-entrance post. He's been here before. He shuffles up, hesitant, frowning.

'That photo?' he says. 'I want it.'

I know which one he's referring to.

'It's not for sale.'

Obsession's twitching his muscles. I imagine the fire that scalds his belly and tightens its grip on his heart, so intensely I imagine for a moment that I can see the flames burning away his resistance.

'Fight it,' I say, feeling the eyes of the hooded man in the picture drilling the back of my skull.

'What?'

'It's him.' I gestured at the image. The eyes are visible through the mask; at that moment their intensity makes me pull away. 'It's El Roto,' I explain. 'He's the one that's making you want the picture.'

I force myself to stand, though I feel weak and unsteady. As I lean toward him the man draws back.

'He was murdered,' I whisper. 'His hatred runs deep.'

The man looks panicked and for a moment I believe he's about to run off again.

'He'll kill you,' I tell him. 'He'll kill your family.'

I see the moment he capitulates. El Roto's fire leaps into his eyes. He reaches out and grabs me by the coat, teeth gritted and violence turning his desire into a weapon. 'Shut up!' he snarls, and pushes me aside. I'm too weakened to resist. I stumble and fall, cracking my head against the brickwork. Commuters drift past like ghosts, some looking, conflicted, but declining to commit to helping me. I've been exiled from their stable, civilised lives and don't command protection.

Dazed, I watch the man in the business suit grab the picture, but it's too quick and my vision is too blurred for me to tell if there is triumph in the eyes of Genaro el Roto.

'Wait!' I manage, reaching into my coat and extracting the doll. 'Take this. It belongs with the picture.'

The man stares at it.

'They belong together,' I insist, desperate for him to have it. 'It'll save you.'

For a moment he clutches at his forehead, as though the pressure is already building within his skull. Perhaps, at a level beyond the control of El Roto, he knows I mean what I say, even if my words seem to be nonsense.

He leans down and snatches the rough doll from my

outstretched hand. The undercurrent of guilt that lies beneath El Roto's passion breaks through. I see it on his face.

Then it's gone. The man turns and runs.

Perhaps I saved him. I'll never know.

Three days later, I huddle in a disused sewer outfall, listening to the obsessive sounds of my own inner workings. The rush of blood through veins and the tighter hiss of its passage into smaller capillaries leading to the brain. Gurgling from my stomach and intestines, as they struggle to deal with whatever scraps I can find to send to them. The thudding of my heart. The white noise of tinnitus.

It should comfort me perhaps, this symphony of corporeal existence, but instead it fills me with dread. I don't know if they're the sounds of life or reminders of mortality.

Something—a shadow of something—has appeared in the photographs of ancient Mayan ruins that I took one afternoon in Toniná. It's a shape formed from shadows and I think it is coming closer. At first I believed it was El Roto, back to have his revenge on me. But no, this is something different, something more ancient and perhaps more terrible.

I don't know what to do. I'm too weak to resist, and Coronela's protection is gone.

Keep it with you at all times, she'd whispered.

So all I can do is sit.

And wait.

Perhaps she'll come back to me—and change my memories once again.

ROBERT HOOD *(b. Rydalmere, New South Wales, Australia, 1951) can't claim to have met a ghost–not knowingly anyway–but he writes about them often. He finds them dramatically rich and* *profoundly metaphorical. His short story collection,* Immaterial: Ghost Stories *(2002), is dedicated to phantoms of various kinds, though they crop up elsewhere as well, such as in his subtly haunted novel* Backstreets *(2000), his YA supernatural thriller series* Shades *(2001) and in* Exotic Gothic 2 *(2008). His story "Behind Dark Blue Eyes" in* Exotic Gothic 3 *(2009) dealt with a more corporeal vision of afterlife continuity—zombies—and such hyperactive cadavers, along with monsters of all kinds (including the giant-sized and the purely human), crop up throughout his fiction. He enjoys mixing genres, often writing crime, science fiction and general fantasy tales as well as horror, stirring elements of them together into an unsettling, surprising mix. Much published over the years, Rob has also gathered his stimulating and spine-chilling stories in the collections* Day-dreaming on Company Time *(1988) and* Creeping in Reptile Flesh *(2008, 2011). He has won awards for his writing, both fiction and film commentary. His website is www.roberthood.net, which will provide you a link to his monster-haunted "Undead Backbrain" blog.*

Commentary on "Escena de un Asesinato": *Renowned for its Day of the Dead imagery as well as its history of political turmoil, ancient ruins, banditos and sensuous women, Mexico has long struck me as the perfect place to set a gothic tale. That this story ended up sharing its Mexican 'persistence of memory' with another country (my own) that has had to deal with a lingering colonial past merely reflects on the universal nature of both ghosts and immigrants, illegal or otherwise. Into the thematic mix I added a question that has often struck me as relevant to ghosts; namely as they provide metaphors for the lingering effects of history and exist outside the bounds of normal temporal reality, could it be that their timelessness would make it possible for them to retroactively manipulate the events that led to the present?*

THE OLD MAN BESET BY DEMONS

STEVE RASNIC TEM

A N UNFOCUSED GROWLING CAME FROM SOMEWHERE BELOW Josiah's wreck of a chair. He'd always been cursed with poor health, but in the year since Hannah's death he'd faced a gradual loss of control over his shameful suit of fatty meat. Could there be anything worse? Hannah, with her delicate nature, had found that part of her illness almost unbearable during her final terrible weeks.

They'd moved back to Abaco after his retirement because that's what she'd so desperately wanted, into her family's old cotton candy-coloured house she'd had such fond memories of, even though to his eye it was like most poor Bahamian homes, a jumble of weathered wood plastered together with stucco, painted over in some festive pastel, the whole mess served up on a concrete slab. A fortunate thing they were blessed with such pleasant weather— such a house would never hold up in the States.

But he'd always given Hannah what she wanted. Some love demon had grabbed him when they were young, turned his head, and kept turning it until his neck was nearly wrung, all those years, like some scrawny bird cooked up in a poor islander's chowder. Now he was too frail, too poor to move back to Florida—they probably wouldn't even let him back in the country. He's spent much of his adult life pretending he wasn't Bahamian, and never made mention of his father's Haitian blood, not even to his beloved Hannah. But he would be dying on this island, of this he had no doubt, imprisoned inside this ridiculous pink house.

The streets outside vibrated with the sounds of Junkanoo. Cowbells, goat skin drums, and whistles eviscerated the peace, accompanying the drunken dancers as they snaked their way through Green Turtle Cay. Josiah had always thought it shameful, an excuse for the poor and the uneducated to get high, to riot, and on the day after Christmas, of all times! Not that he was religious, but he did believe in a certain decorum. That's what raised mankind above the beasts—not intelligence, not some crude dexterity, and certainly not religion—it was a sense of shame that made us human beings. Without shame, you were less than a savage.

Hannah had managed to enjoy such spectacle, and when she'd been alive drug him out there every year to see the 'artfulness of the masks.' Personally, he had a natural distrust of people in costume, not being able to tell who people were, or what they were up to. Sometimes you couldn't even tell if they were black, or white, or some other color entirely.

The monster that the crowd had become sounded suddenly just outside his flimsy walls. The whole house shook with their animalistic gyrations, their shoutings, their sexual moans. As if in response his own body growled out of its inarticulate illness, its failure of organ and bone.

Gradually, comprehensible words settled out of the growl. 'You know, you done shoulda slapped dum sense inna dat wicious witch.' The voice was lazy and dumb and came from somewhere below his right knee. Josiah shifted his leg to get a better look, in the process giving himself an arthritic charge.

A tiny, man-like abhorrence approximately a foot tall stood defiantly in front of Josiah's swollen legs, his red and disproportionately large head shuddering with palsy like one of those bobble-headed native dolls in the island's gift shops. 'Hello, Chief,' Josiah said. 'I don't need you here today.'

The ugly little demon cocked his head like a rooster. His smile pushed out his cheeks so far that the entire lower half of his face swelled, simultaneous with a shrinking of the upper skull that made his eyes bug out sickeningly. 'You say you don't want duh company?' He laughed. 'Now dat witch she dead?'

'Let her be. The poor woman is gone now. I won't tolerate insults to her memory.'

The demon came closer. 'You always wanted to slap dat girl.'

'That's a damn lie,' Josiah said softly, and made a half-hearted and un-successful attempt to kick the demon. He cursed his legs for not being limber enough.

For some reason, Hannah had loved him. When she said it aloud, and she did so frequently, it made him uncomfortable. He could not quite fathom it, even now. He was a bitter old snarl of driftwood, and could not remember if he had ever been any different.

'Ain't you de biggety man! I did feel you hands itch wid de wantin. I seen you look at dat girl wid yer cut eye.'

'I have a temper. I don't know where it came from. Maybe you gave it to me.'

The Chief split himself open with laughter, then vanished in a smoky snort.

Josiah tried to remember when he had first encountered the Chief. Sometime during his teenage years, he believed. When Josiah was twelve he had tripped a crippled boy on crutches for chuckling at him. The boy had tumbled down the school stairs and broken a leg. Had Josiah met the Chief by then? He couldn't be sure. What he had done had been a bad thing, but it wasn't the worst he'd ever done. *I swear you have a jumbey in you boy*, his mother used to say. She didn't know the half of it.

Josiah struggled to get up from his rickety old chair. Finally he was able to leverage himself out by bracing his left elbow and rising in a rolling motion that almost sent him tumbling. He felt no better than an old piece of furniture himself. What was it his mother used to say in her last years? 'Lissen to me, boy,' she'd say, grabbing him by the shirt and dragging him into her rotting embrace. 'Don't be gettin old.' Lovely woman. Always encouraging.

He pulled open the near-empty refrigerator and grabbed a Kalik. Besides his plentiful supply of this beer—the best thing about living in the Bahamas as far as he was concerned—there was a carton of orange juice, an old half-eaten plate of sweet potatoes, a little bit of leftover grouper and grits now turned crispy and brown lying in the bottom of a brightly painted pottery bowl. And something green that might have been anything. He hated going to the grocery store, where people judged you based on what you did or did not put into your basket. But soon he'd have no choice. The neighborhood women had stopped bringing by their covered plates for him months ago, perhaps because he'd complained to one or two of them about the spiciness—his old belly couldn't tolerate the heat anymore—or maybe because he had such a hard time saying thank you. Either way, it looked like they were now content to let him starve.

Once, maybe twice, he *had* thought of slapping Hannah. No— he hadn't seriously considered it, not really. He could just imagine himself doing it, was all. She would have been shocked to know this.

He'd always assumed most people just occasionally had these rash impulses to do the worst thing they could think of: pushing the old lady, dropping the rock on the passing car, holding the child's head underwater. And maybe sometimes the impulse took control and they acted. But Josiah didn't know for sure. He truly knew nothing about what went on in other people's heads. He didn't think he wanted to know.

'Don't kid youself, Biggety Man,' the Chief said from the top shelf of the refrigerator. 'You not fit to be wib otha peoples. You de debbil hisself.' He began to snigger and several teeth fell out, exposing his bloody gums. Josiah shut the refrigerator door on him.

The house still shook from all the noise outside, the laughter and the drunkenness, the generations-old stupidity of the natives. He himself shook, his feet unsteady on the floor, the whole world rocking back and forth as if intent on casting him out of it into some not entirely undesired nothing-ness.

Josiah fell back into his chair so hard a sharp pain in his lower spine made him cry out in a high and distraught voice he hardly recognized. 'Demons,' he choked out, as unwelcome tears fled his eyes.

When Hannah was still alive they'd spent most of their evenings here together, reading, watching the Florida stations on their small television, listening to classical music on the radio. A sedate life, not very exciting. But at least it had been calming, at least with Hannah. He always felt he owed her for that.

Now he filled his evenings with drinking and unfocused TV watching. And this routine only seemed to aggravate the agitation he'd felt since childhood: a kind of dissatisfaction beyond simple disappointment that things hadn't turned out the way he'd wanted. He didn't know what he was supposed to do, what he could do that would have any meaning for him, what could bring him contentment, or if he even had it in him to be happy about anything. He felt as if he could barely sit still, and yet he could not bring himself to get out of his chair.

The pretty heads on his television chattered away about lives so far removed from his own, yet he couldn't stop staring at the screen.

'I'm going to bed straightaway,' he said aloud, as if a vocal statement would make it happen, as if the things who tormented him might this night leave him alone.

The broad head of a blue gravity demon appeared as a slowly growing bulge in his belly, popping his shirt buttons and eventually becoming tall enough that it interfered with his view of the screen. The gravity demon's eyes opened in Josiah's skin, pale and wide and slightly crushed. 'I don't think that's going to happen,' it said in a voice like collapsing food cans.

'Nope. Nope.' The gravity demon accumulated weight by the second before it collapsed back into Josiah's chest. A sense of stoniness spread through his body, slowing his breathing and forcing his eyes closed.

For some time he floated in and out of awareness. Smallish, mutating figures climbed over him inspecting ears, mouth, nose. Sometimes they rearranged the tufts of his meagre ginger hair. Occasionally one would press its hard wrinkled knot of a face against Josiah's cheek while another took a photograph with a tiny, fake camera carved out of wood. They poked and scratched him, kicked him with their pointed, aggravating feet. No wonder his arthritis was so bad. He didn't know exactly what they wanted—he had a vague notion they wanted to use his body for housing—god knows he'd taken lousy care of it himself, perhaps they could put it to better use. He suspected he'd be vacating it soon in any case. Then they could do whatever they wanted.

'How long has it been, Josiah?' The garishly painted body of the demon Louise swirled before him like a quetzal bird. She was near-naked except for a crimson net stretched over her breasts and obscuring her lower body. An insulting caricature of femininity, she danced with abandon on top of his television.

'Not tonight, Louise—I do not have the patience. You *know* the answer.'

'Oh that's right, *years.*' She mocked, wiggling herself until he had to look away. 'How long before the old woman died did you stop having boom-boom and bubby? Was it a year, or two? Or did her sick breath bother you at all, every time you wished to kiss?'

'Shut up, Louise.'

'Did she talk dirty to you, Josi, those last few months? What did she say?'

'*Shut up! Shut up!* My wife was a lady, not a, a boonggy slut like you!'

Louise cackled. 'I know she did not attract you anymore—I mean, how could she? So who did you dream about? Was it *me*, Josiah?' She leaned forward as if to kiss him with her enormous red lips.

With superhuman effort Josiah managed to stumble out of his chair, gaining his feet in a stagger as he struggled his way toward the kitchen. He shut the door and leaned against it. Mercifully, Louise did not reappear beside him. She certainly had the capability and the inclination—she was near-insatiable.

So what if he had imagined other women when he had been with his wife? Wasn't that something all men did? Not that he was proud of it, but he thought he must be the same as pretty much every man—needing just that bit of fantasy to get through the tedium of the day. He still had always loved his wife. He had still been committed.

The realization that he was no longer sleepy but shuddering awake made him almost despair. He went to the refrigerator for some milk, thinking that might help and realized that of course he had not bought milk in a very long time.

He was struck by how filthy the kitchen had become since his wife's death—large sections of the green pastel walls filmed with gray. He searched for a cloth to wipe the walls down but the only ones he had were several wedged behind the faucet, board-stiff and ridged with blood-colored rust.

Something scraped across the wall at the back of the house. Josiah crept to the door and lifted a corner of the shade. He could see very little—the bulb out here had burned dead months ago and he'd never bothered replacing it—the only light was secondhand, borrowed from the neighbors, and from the lanterns carried by that distant tangle of revelers, reflected off a giant moon hanging over an iridescent Bahamian sea. He'd removed a large tree from the yard so that Hannah could get a better view of the ocean from their back door. He never looked at the water directly anymore, avoided even a casual glance whenever he could. From here the glittering reflections looked pretty enough, but he'd lived long enough to know they were merely decoration on the dark, immeasurable mass that spread beneath everything, and which he no longer cared to look at.

Something stirred at the corner of his vision, and he saw then how a mound of rags had gathered, and now stood hunched over one of his carefully secured trash bins. Josiah had always prided himself on how he took care of his garbage. He'd seen people here throw their trash into the street! He flushed with sudden heat, pulled open the door and stepped outside onto the open porch.

The figure jerked its head around fearfully. 'Just . . . just looking for dem leftovers, Chief. I be no tief.'

Josiah bridled at the name. He stared into the man's face, painted a demonic red. But poorly—Josiah could still see the man's frayed and careworn dark features through the gaps in the carelessly and no doubt hastily applied blood-colored paint, the eyes dull, glazed. He thought he now knew the beggar's game— these days the streets were full of these drug addicts, looking to take advantage, to steal in support of their habit. You couldn't just leave your house unlocked anymore. What better cover than Junkanoo, prancing around dressed all in red like that love demon Monsieur Agoussou?

But this was a sad-looking figure, half-starved, and weakened. Josiah felt some of the anger leaving him, but then his own personal demon, his Chief, climbed up on the railing behind the bum. The Chief's reddened hands were balled into swollen fists kept so close to his chest they might have been tumors.

'Chief?'

The bum gazed at him sideways and frowned. 'Ain't scared of you—you tink you ain't dark like me? Hey, you *blacker* dem me!' He snickered and something wet flew out of his mouth. 'An you as old as me—you ain't no better. When I slap you, you goin stay slap. You could be *me*, afore you know it.' The guy turned and started off the porch and into the back yard, his filthy hands clutching a plastic bag full of his findings.

The Chief leapt from the railing with a screech, landing square on the intruder's back. The raggedy costumed bum continued down the steps, apparently not yet aware. Josiah grew alarmed as the Chief raised his swollen fists above the bum's head, so he lunged forward and made a grab for the angry demon. The Chief eluded him, but Josiah's hands still found the top of the bum's back and shoved. The man went sprawling face-first into the grass.

Josiah rushed down the steps. 'Hey now! I didn't mean that!'

He bent to help the fellow up, then stalled, not really wanting to touch his greasy, fuzzy rag pile of a coat. The bum pushed away from him and got to his feet a few yards distance. Blood dripped from his nose, and one eye looked swollen. 'Just wanted sometin to eat, man. You jest stay where you be and I be gone.'

'I really didn't mean . . . '

'I be leavin now. No reason to call de law. Jest stay dere—don't make me do nothing.' The bum stumbled away, then gathered himself, straightening his back. He moved more casually now, almost strutting. Suddenly he stopped, glanced back over his shoulder and said, 'but to hell wid you and your fambly. You all be dead, soon nuff.'

Josiah blinked, not quite believing he'd heard this. Then he bellowed. There were a few moments of mental incoherence as he rushed at the man's back, knocking him down, then straddling him there, his hands wrapped in the long hair, beating the fellow's head into the ground.

As his head cleared, Josiah was disgusted to find both of his hands knuckle-deep in the man's filthy, oily hair. He let go, and as the skull plopped into the reddening grass and mud, Josiah saw the edge of the flat stone beneath the man's head.

He scrambled backwards off the body, sobbing. He sat very still, staring at the sprawl of rags in front of him, listening carefully, for breathing, for sounds of neighbors rousing, coming out of their houses to investigate the commotion. And heard nothing, except for the receding clamor of the revelers, intent on their merriment. His head pounded, consumed by shame.

'Oh, you done did it now.'

Josiah tried to focus his eyes. The Chief stood by the corpse, peering down, prodding it with one foot. 'You, you caused this,' Josiah said, his voice shaking, tears dripping off his face.

'I not be the one wid de bloody hands. You gots *no* self-control. Better get de stiff-toe from out the yard so nobody seen him.'

What Josiah really wanted was for the Chief to shut up, but of course, yes, he had to move. Although still so out of breath he thought he might vomit, and his muscles on fire from unaccustomed exertion, he climbed to his feet and grabbed the dead trash-picker's legs, dragging the body in a lumbering stumble through the yard. He looked over his shoulder, not sure where to take him, and saw the Chief had disappeared again. Then he saw that there was plenty of room under the porch.

Josiah could feel and hear the skull bouncing as he pulled. The body felt as if it were stretching, elongating, pulling apart behind him. He avoided looking. It wasn't until he turned around and started maneuvering it under the steps that he realized the Chief had been riding on top of the corpse. Once he got the dead man where he wanted he sat down on the ground nearby trying to catch his breath.

He was exhausted and scared, but he realized with shame that there was also exhilaration in the mix. He had acted, put down a foe, a threat. He'd taken care of someone who'd defied him.

'Cobah de po man, Josiah.'

The Chief was right in his face. Josiah could have leaned over and strangled him, but he didn't attempt it. 'What?'

'You hab to cobah him wid somethin. How bout dat dere tarp?'

'But it's so dirty.'

The Chief looked suddenly embarrassed for him. 'Don't believe de man gonna care dat much.'

Josiah made himself pull the tarp out and over the body, tucking in every place tuckable. After the package looked all neat and tidy, just a roll of old canvas tarp wedged under some steps, he ducked his head and went back out into the yard, and started up the steps to the porch.

But the Chief's icy hand on his arm stopped him. 'You got de saw? Lectric be de quickest.'

'What? Why?'

'You gonna hab to cut up de body. Dat's de only way.'

'I'm not doing that,'

'You like de Abaco jail, Josiah?'

He shook off the demon's hand. 'Then I suppose it's jail.'

He found the two bottles of Nassau Royale he'd hidden when Hannah began her rapid decline. He hadn't wanted to be drunk when she needed him most, but he knew these bottles would become an absolute necessity for him at some point. She'd never minded when he had a beer now and then, but anything more worried her. She'd hardly approve of what he was doing now, but then she shouldn't have gone off and died first like that.

He took both bottles out on to the unlit front yard and sat in the old lounge chair. He downed almost a third of the first bottle without even thinking about it, and without choking, which pleased him inordinately. His vision was blurry—all he could see were the tops of some trees, some lights, that dark and moving sky. But no ocean, thankfully.

'Josiah! Josiah!' He opened his eyes. The Chief was hovering over him. Literally. 'You gots to move, boy! You gots to take care o' dat stiff 'un afore de sun rise!'

'Ain't your boy no more dere, Chief!' He sneered, taking pleasure in his use of that stupid, ungrammatical dialect, the voice of his people. He closed his eyes again, drinking some more. And then drinking some more. Until he could no longer hear the Chief nagging him, but could hear, and see, better things . . .

He and Hannah were sitting in the living room back in their nice house in Florida. She was knitting baby booties. He had no idea why, since they'd never had any children. She'd wanted them, he didn't—what kind of father would he have been with all his demons, his anger?—but he'd always felt he'd cost her something very dear. Well, let her knit whatever she wanted. The poor woman deserved no less.

The music playing was not their usual Bach, Mahler, or Beethoven, melodies which always carried him away to some place better. This music jangled, made him want to break something. He bit the inside of his mouth and tasted blood.

'What is this, Hannah?'

'Shostakovich, dear. I wanted to try something a little different. Do you like it?'

'Maybe.' He listened carefully—something seemed discordant about the background, jangling his nerves a bit, but the music was beginning to grow on him, at least it resonated with things in his head. 'Hannah, are you an angel?'

'Oh, hardly. Angel or demon, they're pretty much the same, aren't they? Sometimes they say things that make you uncomfortable. They express what you really feel.'

'Hannah, you *can't* be a demon. You're too good for that.'

Someone else was sitting in the corner. Josiah couldn't quite see—the shadows were thick as jerk chicken smoke. 'Hannah, did you invite someone else over?'

'Now, dear, I know you don't like company, but he looked so sad and hungry standing out there.'

Josiah tried not to look. He liked looking at his dead wife instead. But this music, it seemed to be growing louder, and it was making him anxious. 'I just don't know what to do with myself since you left me.'

'Well, why don't you listen to music, or read? You know things you can do, Josiah.'

'But those things just aren't the same without you, Hannah. I never wanted to move back to the islands. I don't even like the ocean—I never have. Did you know that? It's too large, Hannah. How can you ever feel comfortable with something so large?' The music had grown still louder, and there were all these drums, these inappropriate noisy drums.

'Now, no hasty judgments, Josiah. You were always one for making hasty judgments. Have you tried a hobby? Retired people are always taking up hobbies.'

He could barely hear himself over the obnoxious drums, savage Bahamas' drums of goatskin, even donkey. His thoughts had been displaced by the discord. 'I don't want some damn hobby, Hannah! I just want to feel better about things. Why can't I feel better about things?'

'You just need something to do with your time, dear. You filled your time with our little activities together. Now you have to fill your time with other things. That's all life is, my dear, finding ways to fill the time. Isn't that right, Mister Albury?'

The figure in the corner leaned forward. It was the intruder in the red face paint. The addict who stole from garbage cans. Half of his forehead was missing and flamingo-pink brain matter was now leaking down into his mouth. 'That's right, Josiah,' he growled. 'I always tried to keep myself busy. Not that it matters now.'

Josiah started, clutching the empty rum bottle, his head swimming. It was still dark out. He was tired of the dark. After a few minutes he was able to struggle to his feet, and he leaned, as if magnetized. And then he let himself stagger off in the direction of his lean.

Trash filled the streets, as if a flood had passed through here and deposited a large quantity of debris. The trash became thicker the further he went, layering the ground, the way one might layer the bottom of a bird cage.

No one cleaned up after themselves anymore. No one bothered to simply dispose of their trash in a proper bin.

Here and there amidst the rubbish he began to notice the bodies of the drunken revelers, sprawled, sleeping. He went closer to several of them, just to make sure they were still breathing. They were. They were just sleeping it off.

He thought briefly of dragging the corpse of his intruder, that Mr. Albury, out here and hiding him among the fallen celebrants. But it was much too far to drag such a burden. After all, he was just an old man unable to fill time.

He suddenly found himself at the beach. He wanted to turn himself around, but could not. He felt an overwhelming despair. He felt unsteady in his physical body, and his feet unsteady on this land, and this land just a bit of spit floating unsteadily in a jet black sea, on a world spinning through nothing. The sand he was standing on was white, luminous, a bright ribbon that wound around to the horizon both on his left and on his right. Revelers were collapsed here as well, but with the white sand beneath them it was as if they were on display, objects of Caribbean art in their bright costumes, their colorfully painted skin.

And beyond this ribbon of sand there was this great, impenetrable wall of night. This solid darkness of the ocean. He collapsed on the sand staring into it, unable to pull his eyes away, unable to understand a thing.

Mr. Albury came and sat down beside him, his head still bloody. But of course—it would always be bloody. There was no way of washing such blood away.

'So are you a demon too, now?' Josiah asked. 'Are you now one of my demons?'

Mr. Albury appeared to be considering the idea. 'I don't want to be yours,' he finally replied. 'But I suppose I am. I don't understand it, but then I was never a very educated man.'

'Your speech is much improved, though,' Josiah replied. 'In fact you're now making sense.'

'Thank you,' Mr. Albury said, but he did not smile.

Josiah shook his head. 'I don't understand very much either. I just have no idea. When you're first born they tell you they love you. They make all kinds of nonsense sounds and they make silly faces and they give you even sillier things to play with. But you don't care for the baubles. You just know that somewhere deep inside you there's this dark place. There's this dark place and you came from there. And yet it's still there inside you and you don't want to go back there. You turn your back on it because you never want to go back and you try to pretend that place doesn't even exist. You can't put words to it, but that's why you cry all the time. You don't want to return, and you cry all the time. You made yourself forget that this dark place is there waiting behind you.

'They pick you up in their arms and there's a promise in that that you'll never go back but you know better even though you don't have the words.

'The rest of your life you pretend to know yourself. You pretend other people also know what's inside you and that they can appreciate you for it. Sometimes you even meet that other generous heart, you meet your Hannah, and you think everything is fixed. We all can know each other and love each other and feel good about it but of course it's all a lie. Sometimes we can pretend these things so well it is almost as good as if they were really true but it takes so much effort and all pretending must eventually have an end.

'The night inside us never lets us fool ourselves completely. It never lets us be anything but completely and utterly alone. It smiles and it whispers and it eats the very heart out of us, it eats our organs one at a time and even what it can't eat it poisons. Until at last we are so poisoned by its anger and its despair we are no longer able to draw a decent breath. And that's the way it is.'

'And that's the way it is,' Mr. Albury repeated, and they sat there together, and sat there together, staring at that dark ocean, filling their time, and wondering if the dawn would ever come.

STEVE RASNIC TEM *(b. Jonesville, Virginia, USA, 1950) lives in Colorado and has published nearly 400 short stories over the last thirty-plus years, earning many international awards. A stunning dozen of the stories appeared in* The Year's Best Horror and Fantasy *over its twenty-one year run, as did two more that he co-wrote with his acclaimed wife, Melanie Tem. One of their potent collaborations*—The Man on the Ceiling—*went on to take a 2001 Bram Stoker, International Horror Guild, and World Fantasy Award. Re-released in 2008, that chapbook is now in a reimagined, loosely autobiographical novel version. One of the most reliably eerie artists in the genre, Steve's novels include* Excavation *(1986),* Daughters *(2001) (with Melanie Tem), and* The Book of Days *(2002). Ash-Tree Press published a creepy cache of Steve's stories in 2001 entitled* The Far Side of the Lake. *More story collections of a haunting nature include* Decoded Mirrors: Three Tales After Lovecraft *(1978),* Fairytales *(1985),* Absences: Charlie Goode's Ghosts and Celestial Inventory *(1991),* Beautiful Stranger *(1992; with Melanie Tem),* City Fishing *(2000), along with a book of poems,* The Hydrocephalic Ward *(2003). A graphic story that began with Steve's acrylic paintings is "Shadowhouse: My Father's Heart" in* Blurred Vision 2.

Asking what it would be like to manage a remote hotel retreat for creatures dead, secretive, scorned or supernatural—and to watch your daughter grow up in such a place—is Steve's phantasmagoric novel Deadfall Hotel. *It was excerpted at the end of* Exotic Gothic 3 *and premiered as a limited edition hardcover in 2011 by Centipede Press, featuring pen and ink illustrations by the Danish artist and animator John Kenn Mortensen. Solaris Books*

follows with mass market paperback and ebook editions in 2012.
Crossroad Press's audio edition of his novel The Book of Days *re-*
leased in 2011, and his collection of noir fiction, Ugly Behavior,
appears from New Pulp Press in 2012. Steve was also recently a
finalist for the Theodore Sturgeon short story award.

Commentary on "The Old Men Beset by Demons": *After*
so many published short stories I realized I'd never written a story
about plain old-fashioned nasty demons (I wrote one and one only
about the devil, and several in which angels are involved). This
piece is my answer. The Bahamas looked like a good place for
demons. I don't like the tropics, sand, or especially islands—how
solid are they, really? (And don't get me started on fireworks or
big bands).

Atacama

David Wellington

FERMIN COULD FEEL THE MOISTURE EVAPORATING FROM his skin, as salt crystals grew in his pores. Even his eyes felt like they were drying out and turning into raisins. And he had just gotten down from the truck.

He tied a bandana around his forehead to soak up sweat and pulled a cowboy hat down low over his eyes. It was cold, maybe five degrees above freezing, especially up here in the altiplano, but the sun was fierce, a ball of burning ice that looked like it would never set. There was not a single stray hair of cloud in the sky.

'Here,' he said, handing a bottle of water to Whitman. 'Drink this now.'

'I just had one,' the scientist grumbled. He was busy pulling crates of supplies off the back of the truck. He took the bottle anyway. Water wasn't something you turned down in the Atacama.

This was the driest place on Earth. Rainfall had never been recorded in this stretch of the desert. It might not have fallen there for millions of years. Nothing lived here, not so much as scrub brush or bugs. The soil was so sterile and dry that astronauts came here to study what it would be like to live on Mars or the Moon.

A thin, cold wind came down from the hills, listlessly browsing through the red sand with its weak fingers. Having shed any moisture it might once have held on the far side of the Andes, it blew through the Atacama with no purpose and helping no one. Fermin hated this place, hated the glaring salt pans, hated the reddish-brown slickrock that crumbled under his boots. He would not have come here if it had not been for the money. For twenty years he'd been driving scientists and eco-tourists down into this desolate country, dropping them off and then coming back to pick them up when they'd had enough. It never took long. This one, this Señor Doctor Whitman as he liked to be called, looked like the kind who could take it for a week, which was about the upper limit.

Fermin just hoped he wasn't the kind who would go crazy out here and find religion. That wouldn't do at all.

Together they carried the crates up the long slope of the hill toward the place where the dead people waited. Fermin's legs ached as he clambered up the rocks—there was no path up there, no obvious way to mount the hill. Maybe that was why nobody had discovered the bodies before.

This was Fermin's second visit to the site. He hoped it would be his last. He did not like the way the rock crested overhead like a frozen wave, waiting to crash down and wipe away the little hollow near the top of the hill. Though at least the overhang of rock kept the sun off his face. The two of them clambered over a low ridge and there, on the far side, was the graveyard.

Sheltered from the sun, huddled out of the wind, a line of the dead sat with their backs against the red rock, their feet in the dust. There were a hundred and seven of them, more mummies than had ever been found in the Atacama in situ. At one end of the line, the dead had the decency to look like corpses—shriveled, screaming faces framed by long black hair that still shone. As you walked farther up the line, though, the bodies changed. Someone had taken the time to paint them black from head to toe, to cut them open and disembowel, then sew them shut again with thick leather thread. Even farther up the line were the worst of them. These had been painted red everywhere except their faces, which were obscured behind black masks of clay. Those bothered Fermin the most for their veiled eyes.

'Look at you, my impeccable beauties,' Whitman said. He dropped his crate in the sand and knelt by the closest body to peer into its shrunken features. 'Oh, somebody loved you, all right.' He took out a digital camera and started snapping pictures.

'The light here's no good,' Fermin said. He knew all about photography from the tourists he'd worked with. 'You need to use the flash.'

'Flash photography can damage the specimens, believe it or not,' Whitman told him, shaking his head.

'Really, man? These things have been here for a thousand years, they aren't going anywhere now,' Fermin said, with a laugh.

'More like . . . three thousand,' Whitman said, wiggling one hand to suggest he was approximating. 'Some of the older ones might be nine thousand years old.'

Fermin whistled in appreciation, because he was pretty sure that was what Whitman wanted from him. '*Long* time.'

'The ones at the end, the ones that were just left here—the Chinchorro didn't know what would happen. They just left them here because this was where you put your dead bodies. The desert mummified them on its own, with no help. Aridity kept them from rotting, and there are no predators here to snack on them. When the Chinchorro noticed that, they decided to improve on the process. Some of these later ones are absolute miracles of mortuary science—the skin was completely removed, the organs and the brains taken out with specially made knives. Then the skin was replaced and the flesh simulated with grass and plant fibers, sticks were used to strengthen the bones. The skin was sewn back on and the hair replaced with wigs made from the hair of the living. Then they painted the bodies, maybe to protect the skin, maybe for religious reasons we don't understand.'

'Sounds like a lot of work.'

'Absolutely. And we still know so little of why they did it. This was a culture that lived almost exclusively on fish. They had very few tools, almost no technology at all. But they developed some of the most elaborate methods of preserving their dead anyone's ever seen. All of this thousands of years before the Egyptians thought of it.'

'Amazing stuff.'

'Hmm,' Whitman said. He sat down on the rock, folding his legs beneath him. He looked like he was going to be there for a while. From his pockets he took out a notebook and a bunch of pens, a voice recorder, a jeweler's loupe. 'We're going to learn a lot from this bunch. Generations of archae-ologists will come to see this— the best preserved collection of Chinchorro mummies anywhere, and with all three periods of their culture represented! Simply amazing. I'll barely scratch the surface here myself, just cataloging the remains and identifying gross surface features. I can't wait to get started. Can you offload the rest of the gear for me? Just put it anywhere, I'll move it where I need it later.'

Fermin frowned. He had assumed the two of them would share the workload. But now wasn't the time to pick a fight. 'This must be really rewarding. You know, like fulfilling. But I bet it doesn't pay so good.'

'Hmm?'

Fermin shrugged. 'I mean, it's not like it's going to make you rich. Me, I drive a truck. I'm in debt since I was born, you know? I live on credit.'

'Are you . . . are you asking me to tip you, now? I assumed that was done when you picked me up next week.'

Fermin felt anger bristle through his back and shoulders, but he fought it back down. 'I'm talking about an opportunity, Señor Doctor.'

That got the little professor's attention. Whitman turned around and stared at Fermin with a curious look.

'There's this guy I know, I mean, a friend of mine knows him. Real rich guy who lives in Santiago, right? He's a collector, my friend says. He's got a collection. Of mummies.'

Whitman got it right away. 'Oh. Oh, no, that's not—'

'Just listen, okay? My friend says this guy will pay pretty damned good for just one mummy. Just one. And there's more than a hundred here, more than enough for your generations of scientists. One isn't going to be missed, huh? Now, I could just grab one, sure, but the *policia* keep a pretty sharp eye out for antiquity thieves. They'd catch me up right away, and I'd have nothing but a stupid smile to give them. But if you could sign some papers, say I was authorized to take the mummy to some museum or other, they wouldn't look twice. They hear some gringo scientist says it's okay, they'll believe that. They might call you to confirm, but that wouldn't be anything. You just tell them yes, and then you and I can split the money. And it's a lot of money, believe me. Even paid out three ways, you, me, and my friend.'

'Impossible,' Whitman said.

'Listen, I know, it ain't strictly ethical. But just a single one. Come on, Señor Doctor. Just one. You're cataloging them now, right? So nobody even knows for sure how many there are. Nobody ever needs to know, right?'

'You don't understand. The only reason these mummies are pristine—the only reason they haven't completely rotted away—is the climate here,' Whitman said, speaking slowly as if he were talking to a child. 'The incredible dryness. If you took one of these mummies to a more humid place—and I've been to Santiago, it's humid enough—it would start decaying almost instantly. It would simply fall apart and rot. Do you understand? These mummies hate moisture. They can't bear even the slightest trace of it.'

'I understand just fine, Señor Doctor,' Fermin said. He knew this wasn't going to work, now. But he had to keep trying. 'I figure that's not my problem. I figure that's the rich guy's problem.'

Whitman chewed on the side of his lip. It was already chapped from the dry air and now it started to bleed. 'Maybe I can show you something. Maybe I can make you understand why I would never, ever do that.'

'Never's a long time,' Fermin said. 'Especially when money's involved.'

'No, come over here. Come with me.' Whitman led Fermin down

the row of bodies. Away, at least, from the creepy red ones with the face masks. Farther down among the all-black mummies was one unlike the others, but only because of its size.

It was tiny. It would have fit in Fermin's hand. It looked like a doll compared to the man-sized mummies on either side. Yet in every other way it looked exactly like them—painted black, cut open and then sewn shut again. It even had a little wig of black hair that was teasing loose from its head.

'*Santa Maria!*' Fermin gasped, when he understood what he was looking at. 'They mummified their babies?'

'They mummified everyone,' Whitman said, in a low, reverent voice. 'They're one of the few cultures that did. You find mummies all over the world—from Alaska to Ireland to Egypt to here. But almost always it was something rich people did. Do you understand that? In our culture we give each other reassuring funerals. We have someone else embalm our dead and then bury them in expensive, sealed coffins. That's just to make us feel better, to make the dead look prettier. We accept that they're gone, truly gone. Either to Heaven, or just to rot in the ground where we can't watch.

'Cultures that mummified their dead saw it differently, though. You see how these people are sitting outside here—that's because their survivors, their descendants, would come visit them often. They would bring food up here and share a picnic with their ancestors. Because their ancestors were still alive.'

'These things,' Fermin pointed out, 'are stone dead.'

'Not to the Chinchorro. They went to all this trouble, all this effort, to keep their loved ones alive. To them, in a religious way, in a very real way, a mummified body was *still alive*. It didn't rot away. It didn't turn horrible colors or ooze nasty fluids or get torn apart by dogs and scattered across this desert. It was still with you. It would live forever. And they wanted that. People all over the world have wanted that. But in Ireland they only did it to sacrificial victims, people who were exceptionally holy. In Egypt only the rich got to live forever.

'But the Chinchorro mummified *everyone*. Every member of the tribe got this treatment. Yes, even babies—and more. That's not a baby mummy, Señor Fermin. Look closer. Have you ever seen a baby that small?'

'No,' Fermin admitted.

'No. That was a fetus. A stillbirth. Can you imagine the grief its mother must have felt? The soul-tearing anguish, when her baby was born dead, probably three months premature? But the Chinchorro had a solution to that agony. They could make the baby live. They could make the baby live forever, just like everyone else. Do you understand now? For the Chinchorro, no one was allowed to die.'

'That's—that's something else, right there, I'll agree, but—'

Whitman shook his head. '*No one was allowed to die.* And if I let you take one of these bodies away, I'd be defiling that. I'd be committing an incredible sin. So, no, I won't be part of your scheme. Now. If you could offload my things, I'd appreciate it. I only have a week up here. It's not nearly enough time.'

Fermin headed back to the truck snarling and spitting. Crazy damned scientist. He was more interested in preserving some ancient heathen bullshit than helping out a fellow living Christian? Fuck that, man.

Off the truck bed, he pulled crates and tossed them on the sand, not caring too much if they broke or not. He had a long ride ahead of him back to Arica, the nearest town, and the only place in a hundred kilometers you could get a beer. He planned of getting lots of them.

One damned mummy. Just one, and he'd be fine. He could pay off his creditors, maybe have enough left over to get a new truck. Hire a second driver—there were always gringos who wanted someone to drive them out to the Atacama, he'd have more business than he could handle. Yeah, he could start a whole tour service. Make some real money. One damned mummy and he could have a new life.

But the bastard said no.

Fermin pulled the last of the crates out of the truck and stacked it haphazardly with the rest. That just left the water tank. It was a big son of a bitch, a rusted fifty-five gallon drum with a tap on one end. All the water Whitman would need for his week-long excursion, since there was no way for him to get any more out of the desert.

Fermin wrestled the tank down from the truck bed and put it with the rest of the stuff. His muscles screamed and he was breathing hard by the time he had it in place. That was it, though, all of it—he was done. Time to get back on the road.

But then he had an idea.

Fermin had a bunch of tools in the truck—if it broke down here, nobody else was going to come along and fix it for him. He reached inside his toolbox and took out a screwdriver with a flat head and a long thin shaft.

He approached the water tank like he was going to commit a murder.

He picked a spot low on the side, where the rust was thickest. Where a puncture wouldn't look so suspicious. He glanced back up the hill to see if maybe Whitman was watching him, but no, the scientist was too absorbed in his dead people.

Fermin placed the spade-like head of the screwdriver against the side of the water tank and shoved hard. The rusted steel parted like tissue paper, and a tiny drip of water started to run down the side of the tank.

Then Fermin got back in his truck and drove away.

He didn't want Whitman to die, not at all. He figured it never had to come to that. It would probably take the scientist a day or two to notice that his water was draining away. That it was never going to last the full week. Out in the Atacama you couldn't last twelve hours without water. Whitman would recognize that. Then he would call Fermin on his satellite cell. Call and beg Fermin to come back, to save him before he succumbed to dehydration.

And Fermin would show up straight away, with a replacement tank. A brand new, rust-free tank full of precious water. And a smile.

And a sheaf of papers authorizing him to remove exactly one

mummy from the site, for delivery to a 'private museum' in Santiago.

There was no way Whitman could say no to that, right? The man would be so grateful. Fermin would save his life and he couldn't possibly say no.

Except, it didn't work out that way.

The first two days passed uneventfully. Fermin sat in an air-conditioned café in Arica and drank *chicha*, the local beer brewed from corn. He kept his phone nearby, just in case. If Whitman discovered the leak right away and called for water, Fermin would just have to play it cool and deliver as requested. And maybe that would be it.

The third day he kept the phone in his hand, ready to answer the moment it rang. Whitman had his number, he was sure of that. He considered calling the scientist to make sure, but that would be pushing things.

On the fourth day he stopped drinking. He made up for it by smoking too much.

When five days passed with no phone call, he headed out to his truck. He started the ignition and almost put it in gear. But no, he couldn't just show up and ask how Whitman was getting along. That would look too suspicious. Maybe the archaeologist had come across some eco-tourists out there in the desert. Maybe he'd talked them into sharing their water. If Fermin just showed up early, claiming he was just 'checking in'—no. No. It would look wrong.

The sixth night he slept in his truck, because he wanted to be ready to go the second the call came in.

It didn't.

The morning of the seventh day, as early as he could justify getting started, he headed out to the desert. In the back of the truck he had a full water barrel—and a good first aid kit.

He really, really hoped he had not killed the man.

If he had, there would be nobody to sign the paperwork.

Mist shrouded the tops of the mountains. Here and there a dead-looking scrub brush poked through the flaky soil. Elsewhere, the Atacama was utterly without life and unforgiving. The soil changed colors as Fermin drove, first red, now brown, now reddish brown. The sun hung over it as if it had frozen in place in the sky.

He topped a gentle ridge and could see for miles. Off in the far distance, cut into the side of a hill, an angular giant stared upward at the featureless sky, its arms raised in supplication. Fermin had heard it was a kind of calendar, that you could tell what season it was by where the sun set on the giant's crown. He had no idea why that would be useful in a place like this, where nothing could ever change.

When he reached the place where he'd left Whitman, the ancient graveyard of the Chinchorro, he leaned on his horn three times before he opened his door and stepped down onto the crunchy soil. There was no sound anywhere except the fading echo of his signal. He had hoped to find Whitman sitting by the side of the road waiting for him. The scientist would have been pissed off, sure, and called Fermin incompetent or maybe even accused him of attempted murder. But he would have been alive.

'Hey, Señor Doctor!' he shouted, cupping his hands around his mouth. 'Hey, you okay up there, man?'

He received no answer, of course. Rubbing at his lips—they were already dry and chapping in the extreme aridity of the place—he headed up the slope, toward the graveyard. Maybe the guy had found some eco-tourists after all. Maybe they'd given him a ride back to town. Maybe he was back there, laughing it up in some bar, getting free drinks for his story about how he'd survived the deadly Atacama.

Yeah, sure, or maybe he was at the police station in Arica, reporting a crime.

Or maybe . . . maybe he'd been so absorbed in his cataloging work, so intent on his dead people that he hadn't noticed his water was running low. Maybe it had all run away before he knew it was happening. Maybe he'd found out, late one night, that he was going to die.

Maybe he had headed into the desert on foot, praying he could find somebody with water. And maybe . . . maybe he didn't, huh?

Fermin tried not to think about what it would be like to die of thirst, all alone in this empty place. He tried real hard.

It didn't work. He imagined the taste of sand in his mouth. The burning of his lips and his eyes as they dried out. He imagined Whitman's tongue, shriveled and gray, licking endlessly at lips that cracked and bled. He imagined the man collapsing on some hillside, too far from the road. Too far to even crawl down where someone might find him.

He imagined the last few moments, the last thoughts. Thoughts of nothing but water, of how good it would taste, of how cool and soothing it would be as it poured down his throat.

He couldn't not think these things. He rubbed at his own lips again. He had some lip balm but it was back in the truck. He would go back for it in a minute. After he checked—after he made sure Whitman was okay.

Coming around the corner he saw the line of dead people, all sitting there with their knees up, watching his approach. None of them had eyes anymore, of course. Those went, whether you were mummified or not. Their empty eye sockets couldn't see him. He grunted and spat and tried to remember how to make the sign against the evil eye.

The ones with black-painted face masks were still tough to look at. Their eyes—their eye sockets, whatever they had—were covered and they couldn't see him, even if they still had that power. But they were facing him, turned directly toward him. Like they knew he was there somehow, anyway.

There was no sign of Whitman at the camp. All his stuff was still there—notebooks and equipment. The satellite cell phone. Fermin paged through the notebook but found nothing there, just columns of numbers and descriptions of the various mummies.

How big they were, whether they were male or female. Some of them Whitman couldn't tell. Fermin dropped the notebook on the ground and turned back to face the mummies.

'Ain't going to tell me where he went, are you, huh? Sons of whores.' He turned to spit again.

'... Ferm ... Fermin ... ' one of the mummies whispered.

Fermin shrieked and jumped in the air.

Then a wash of relief went right through him, like a wave of cold water running down his back. He raced over to the end of the line, to where one of the mummies was slowly uncoiling itself, lifting its arms.

Except it wasn't a mummy at all. It was Señor Doctor Whitman.

'Hey man, hey now, buddy, it's gonna be okay, your pal Fermin's here now,' he said, scrunching down next to the scientist. Whitman had curled up at the end of the row of mummies, curled up in a ball just like them. Crazy, Fermin thought, but he kind of got it—alone up here for a week with no water, Whitman must have been so desperate for companionship that even dead guys would do. 'Hey, take it easy.'

Whitman wasn't in good shape. His face was creased with new lines and congested with dark blood. His eyes were shrunken in their sockets. His mouth was one huge mass of blisters and he could barely mumble. His face turned very slowly to focus on Fermin. 'So ... dry,' he whispered, a sound like the wind playing with the sandy dirt of the desert. 'Dry. They ... they wouldn't let anyone die.'

'Hey, you're going to make it. Just hold in there, guy.' He grabbed his canteen off his belt and took off the cap. Lifting it over Whitman's mouth he dribbled a little water over the scientist's swollen lips.

Whitman reacted violently, spitting out the little water that made it into his mouth. 'No!' he rasped. 'Any moisture at all ... dangerous ... instant decomposition ... can't ... '

'You need this. Just little sips, okay?'

Whitman's arm came up faster and stronger than Fermin would have thought possible. He knocked the canteen right out of Fermin's hands and sent it spinning away, its precious contents splattering all over the dry ground. In seconds the thirsty earth had absorbed it all.

'No . . . water! Everyone . . . they did it to . . . '

'Jesus and Maria, man, that was—that was—hey, it's alright, I've got more. Just hang in there, okay?' Fermin said. He patted Whitman's shoulder as he rose, intending to run down to the truck and get the new water barrel. He didn't even care about stealing a mummy anymore. He just needed to keep Whitman alive. If the scientist died, Fermin would be guilty of murder. It didn't matter if nobody else ever found out. He would know.

When he stood up, something caught his eye and he stared at his own hand. It was stained red.

'Oh, mother of—' He shook his head. Whitman, he saw for the first time, was covered in bloodstains. Oh, man. Had the scientist been so thirsty he'd cut himself to drink his own blood? It was crazy. It was—it was—

It was all Fermin's fault. He raced back through the camp, headed for his truck. Along the way he got a whole new shock. He saw Whitman's water barrel. The one he'd sabotaged. He couldn't see anymore where he'd punctured it, because it had been torn apart.

Jesus, just how crazy had Whitman gotten over the last week?

It didn't matter. It was just temporary, a reaction to the stress, to the maddening thirst. Fermin was certain that with proper medical care he could get Whitman back on his feet. He hurried down the slope of the hill, skidding on the loose soil. Funny, he thought. Really funny, but not something you could laugh about. Whitman's face and his body were covered in red stains. He looked like one of his precious mummies, the way they were painted. Real fucking peculiar. Had that been intentional? Had Whitman figured he could survive, somehow, if he was like the mummies? Or had he wanted to die by the end, had the thirst driven him to suicide, but he wanted to become like the others?

Maybe it was just a coincidence.

Fermin made it down to the truck without slipping and breaking his neck. That was a small victory, and he'd take what he could get.

They didn't let anyone die, he thought. Whitman had told him that, a week ago, and repeated it now. Like it was important. The Chinchorro had mum-mified everyone, even their babies. Because they wouldn't let anyone die.

Fermin wondered why the hell that mattered now. He ran to the back of the truck and threw open the doors. The water barrel was huge, a fifty-five gallon drum, and he would have trouble carrying it all the way up the hill on his own. If he rushed he was likely to drop it and—

When the truck doors opened, water came sluicing out, rushing over Fermin's chest and legs and filling his mouth. He spluttered and grabbed the side of the truck to keep from being washed away. When he could see again—when he could think again—he looked into the truck's cargo compartment.

Inside, the replacement water barrel had been torn open. Not cut or ripped open. It had been torn nearly in half, the edges of the broken metal shiny, pulled back like flaps to let the water out.

Any moisture at all, Whitman had said. *The mummies hate moisture. They can't bear the slightest trace of it.*

Fermin reached up to put a hand over his mouth. *No. Unh-uh*, he thought. *No fucking way.*

While he stood there, wondering what the hell was going on, a new noise broke the desert silence. A huge, tearing, crashing noise. Fermin screamed and ran around the side of the truck. What he saw made his eyes nearly pop out of his head. The whole front of the truck was torn open. The hood had been bent back like the pop-top of a beer. The engine was steaming and smoking. The radiator grill was torn free and the coolant was leaking a bright blue stream onto the desert sand.

'Whitman,' he said, 'what the hell are you doing—I don't even know how you could do that, it's—it's—'

He said this because someone was standing next to the ruined truck's engine. A figure painted red and black.

It wasn't Whitman.

It had a stone knife in its hand. *They took out the organs. Defleshed the corpses. Rebuilt them with sticks and stuffing, and sewed them back up. That was how you made a mummy, that's the Chinchorro way.*

Nobody ever died in their culture. Nobody—ever—was allowed to.

DAVID WELLINGTON *(b. Pittsburgh, Pennsylvania, USA, 1971) is the author of the* Monster Island, Thirteen Bullets, *and* Frostbite *series of horror novels. He wrote an issue of* Marvel Zombies Return *for Marvel Comics which became a* New York Times *bestseller. He got his start posting his books for free online. He lives in New York City.*

Commentary on "Atacama": *The Atacama Desert in South America is the driest place in the world, an almost lifeless expanse of desert and mountains so desolate it has been studied by NASA as the closest thing to a Martian desert on earth. It is also home to some of the best preserved mummies in the Western hemisphere, human remains that have survived millenia untouched by rain and dried to perfect preservation by constant winds. It is one of the most haunting and evocative places I can imagine and I thought it would make a great backdrop for a story that focused on the scarier aspects of solitude, of being alone, totally alone, in a harsh place not meant for human comfort. I often think of the poor archaeologist in my story, all alone in those hills with no water, and the thoughts he must have had, the expansion of his consciousness as it mapped itself across that totally inhuman landscape. This is a story of betrayal but also of obligation, of fear and horror (two very different things), but mostly it is about a place, a place unlike any other.*

Metro Winds

Isobelle Carmody

for Fernanda

So there was this girl. Young but not too young. A face as unformed as an egg, so that one could not tell if she would turn out to be fair or astonishingly ugly. She came to the city as a visitor, sent by a mother in the process of divorcing a father. By them both, in fact, for the one thing they could agree upon was that the girl should not be exposed to the violence they meant to commit on their life. There was a quality in the girl that made it impossible to do the ravening that the end of love required.

'She must be sent away,' the man said in civil but forbidding tones.

'For her own good,' the woman agreed. 'My sister will have her.'

The girl stood between them, wordless and passive as a bolster. She who had lived on the remote coast of Australia in a solitary yellow timber house listening to the chilly grey sea that ran straight up from the Antarctic to the shore beside her bedroom window, was to be sent to the distant crowded city in Europe where her mother had spent her childhood.

Red nosed and blue lipped, bare armed and bare legged, she had played in rocks where crabs scuttled through pools of clouded sky, but on the day of the departure, she wore a navy blue dress and jacket, grey stockings and patent black leather shoes all of which had been purchased from a catalogue. The unrestrainable mass of silky hair, darker than red mangrove bark, had been wetted and bound tightly into two thick braids. Now she watched her white night shift being folded into a dark boxy suitcase although it had been agreed between the sisters that she would be provided with a wardrobe fitting her interim life in the city.

'She can't go with an empty case,' the woman muttered as she closed the mouth of the case. It was almost empty yet how could she be blamed for the lack of clothes or stuffed animals to pack, or pictures in frames and much read books. The child could not be forced to have accumulated such things.

She glanced at the girl and felt a pang of unease at her unfamiliar appearance, but told herself that her destination was a very old and sophisticated city, and not some dangerous wilderness, so what need was there for anxiety? She wanted to cup the girl's face and kiss the cheeks and eyelids tenderly, but only rested her hands lightly on the shoulders; felt the fragility of them; noted absently that her fingers were stiff as dried twigs.

'You will see,' she said vaguely.

There was no need to evoke good behavior, for the girl was calm and biddable and, remarkably, did not practise deceits. When a question was asked, she saw it only as a request for information. It did not occur to her to concern herself about the consequences of answering or the uses to which the information she gave might be put. Being asked, she told. If she did not know, she said. This might have made her blunt and tactless, but she seldom spoke unless asked a direct question, and then answered only what had been asked.

 What would her plump soft sister make of the girl? She had no children of her own, having never married, but rather than leaving her embittered, the lack had softened the centre of her until she was sweet enough to ache your teeth, and yielding enough to flow like tears. She had been full of delight at the thought of having a vessel into which to pour the rich syrup of her emotions.

'I shall adore her and she will be happy,' she had written.

The mother frowned at the memory, for the girl was too deep for happiness. She seldom smiled and had laughed aloud but once.

The woman had seen a storm brooding and found the girl standing at the edgy rim of the sea with her hands lifted to the bruised clouds as a child will to its mother. What sort of child is it that embraces a storm? Stepping closer she had seen the girl's teeth drawn back from her lips in a rictus that looked at first to be an expression of pain, but had been only what laughter made of her features.

The woman had withdrawn without letting the girl notice her.

No. One could not say to one's sister that the girl had a capacity for frightening joy and so she had simply agreed that they were bound to get along. That, at least, might be true.

Stowing the case in the boot of her car, the woman thought how over the years she had tried to convey to the sister in letters, her disappointment in the girl, so that the deeper details could be prised gently from her. The sister had only congratulated her on her good fortune with a cloying wistfulness than left no room for the confession of the fear that she had borne, not a flesh and blood child with sulks that must be coaxed, fits of ill temper that must be humoured and fears that must be soothed, but a sort of angel. And not the soft fat promiscuous angels of Italian frescoes, but a wild untamable creature of feathers and blazing sunlight and high wailing winds.

Neither the woman nor the man thought of the girl with intimate possessiveness. It was not in the man's nature to possess more than abstract ideas, and these only vaguely and in passing, for he was a research doctor. And the woman found it impossible to love a child who required neither forgiveness nor tolerance. The girl was the girl, and that was how they named her to themselves and to the world at large.

She sat docilely in the car on the way to the airport, hands folded loosely in her lap.

'Are you afraid?' the mother asked after they had checked the bag and learned of the seat allocation.

'It will be different,' the girl said out without reproach or sorrow.

The woman swallowed an aimless spurt of anger, and nodded because it was true.

As the girl turned to walk through the door to international departures, the mother found herself remembering with sudden shocking clarity the lumpy slipperiness as the midwife pulled the child from her womb and swung it up onto her flaccid belly; the rank animal stench of the fluids that flowed out of her, and the purplish swollen look of skin smeared with white foam and strings of bloody slime; that auburn hair and the dark bottomless eyes that looked through her skin and into her soul.

The airport doors closed with a smooth hiss, severing them from one another. The woman stood for a time looking at the ambiguous smear of her face in the dull metal surface.

The girl spent much of the journey gazing out at the sky, surprised at how substantial clouds appeared from above. For of course she had only ever before seen their undersides, which must have been grazed to flatness by the mountains that scraped at them. When the sky darkened as the plane entered the long night, a steward asked if she wanted chicken or beef. She never ate meat but the travel agent had forgotten to note that a vegetarian meal would be required when booking the ticket. It did not matter. She liked the way her belly gnawed at her from the inside like little teeth.

When she slept, it was to dream an old dream of wandering in dark tunnels searching for something she could not name, but whose absence filled her with intense grief.

The girl's aunt was tremulous and moist with emotion when her new charge emerged at last into the arrivals foyer. Yet the first sight of her caused the older woman to draw a swift unpleasant breath. A moment later she could not have said what had made her react that way. She had seen photographs so the child's appearance was no surprise. In the taxicab she fussed and tutted at the late arrival of an already late flight and told herself it was pity that had made her gasp, for the girl's clothes were so severe they only accentuated the formless vagueness of her features.

The aunt's apartment was large but managed to be cramped as well because it was so full of fringed lamps, occasional tables, frilled curtains, plump down filled tasselled cushions, painted china statues, little enamel boxes, carved animals, winged armchairs, tapestried ottomans and vases of stiff dried flowers. The floors were richly carpeted in dove grey but there were also square gorgeous pools of colour in the form of exotic rugs, ochre and henna red, so that the sound of movement was altogether smothered.

The girl slipped off her shoes and wriggled her toes, searching for the bones of the place under its fat pelt. The house by the sea had hard wooden floors that had been limed the icy hue of a bleached winter sky.

Noticing the pale slender feet, the woman decided that the girl had removed her shoes out of consideration for the carpets.

She showed the girl to a bedroom also filled with small furnishings and tiny pools of light she by lamps with blushing peach fringes. The walls had been covered in a velveted paper of palest oyster and the window and four-poster bed were draped in thick folds of matching lace, with an overdress threaded with gold ribboning.

The aunt left the girl to unpack, having noted the lightness of the case, and fearing to embarrass them both by witnessing the paucity of the possessions it contained. Removing her coat, she told herself that her sister had married worse than she had feared. She smiled in pity at the girl over a late supper laid out on gold edged plates. There was a silver pot of hot chocolate, rich cream puffs, jam horns, creamy slices and little sandwiches. The girl ate one corner of a cucumber and lettuce sandwich, and when pressed to try a pâté sandwich, explained politely that she did not eat meat.

'But these are only fish,' the aunt said. The girl did not respond and the woman ate one of the smoked salmon sandwiches but was discomfited to be so frankly watched. She was relieved when the girl asked if she might go to bed and in a gush of guilty remorse, promised a shopping expedition on the morrow.

In the room, the girl removed her outer clothes and lay them aside. She was wide awake for her body told her that it was early morning. Nevertheless she must adjust to the new time and so she struggled to open the window, which had been painted shut, before lying down.

The aunt would shut the window in a fluster the following day, warning of breezes and burglars. She did not believe in fresh air. In fact, moving air of any kind troubled her. But now it was night and a breeze stole into the room as if sensing it was an unwanted intruder. The girl watched her hair float up in a dark nimbus of questing tendrils that seemed to be as individually and blindly questing as the pseudopods of a snail or a sea anemone and remembered the way the icy wind slipped up through the cracks in the bone pale floorboards, and shuddered the window glass in its frames as it tried to get out again. Sometimes it was so strong that when you opened the drawers in the kitchen, the wind blew out into your face; so loud that people telephoning the house would be moved to ask who was screaming. If one looked through the windows at night, there were not the thousand and one lights visible from this window, but only darkness laid like a film over shadowy trees waving their branches and beyond them, the lines of foam that trimmed the relentless waves. If she opened the window, the air would fly like a dervish into her room, smelling of icebergs and open grey seas, unpeopled beaches and sodden green hills.

No human scents survived the primal nature of that wild wind, yet the city air was so heavy with the smells of people and their machines, that one could detect nothing green or wet or wild in it. She imagined it was as weary as a sick stray limping along a dirty lane. She imagined it as the breath of an old man who had lived too long.

Despite the wind, she was not troubled by the dramatic change in her life. She understood that she would find it hard to breathe or move with so many people and their lives pressed up against

her. If she may be said to have felt anything, it was that she was
interested to see *how* she would live.

The following day, the aunt kept her promise and they went
shopping. First they caught a taxi to a market of little shops,
where they brought food. This was undertaken with great serious-
ness. They went to a fruiterer. The girl had never seen
pomegranates, pears, and strawberries laid out with such reverence. The aunt discussed what she should buy with the shop
assistant and they seemed to come to a joint decision about what
should be bought. They went to a bread shop, and a cheese shop,
and again the aunt spoke with the proprietors who were courteous
but assertive. They carried nothing from these shops as it was to be
delivered to the apartment where the maid, D'lo, waited to put
them away.

They ate lunch at a restaurant where, the aunt said, a man had
once come with a gun to shoot his lover's lover. She told this
anecdote with the same relish she ate, as if the flavour of it pleased
her. The girl had no sense of the murder and wondered if the aunt
was wrong. The room they were in was decorated with huge vases
of lilies and small vases of violets set on spotless white tablecloths
which the tables wore as if they were ball dresses. The girl chose a
lemon sorbet, clear cucumber soup and bread, and a cut glass bowl
of strawberries. The aunt, heavy as a caramel dumpling, was
disappointed with her charge's poor appetite, and enjoyed her own
food less as a consequence.

Afterwards they walked along a boulevard of shops with wide
windows where lights converged to worship a single stiletto with a
transparent icicle for a heel, or a red dress or a seed pearl and
diamond dog collar. The girl was led from one shop to another
where almost identical skeletally thin women with white china
complexions and slick red mouths discussed cut and colour. The
aunt was puzzled at the girl's passivity. One would think she was
being dressed in a bazaar for all the interest she showed in clothing.
It occurred to her that perhaps the child was mildly retarded. Her

sister had not said so, yet in looking back, hadn't there been something unsaid in the letters she had sent over the years? Something struggling to be revealed?

The girl was unaware that the clothes were more important that the people who sold them. The languid gestures of the thin elegant women with their ferocious smiles made her think of a panther she had seen in a cage, lying absolutely still with a bored expression in its lovely eyes. Only the flicker at the end of their tail revealed its innate savagery. Pale, pastel-clad acolytes scurried in with this dress or that jacket or skirt, and the girl saw that despite the anonymity conveyed by identical pastel smocks, they were quite different. One had a saucy look and quick nimble fingers, and another smelled of cigarettes and yet another had eyes that had been powdered over to cover their redness.

The aunt's taste for frills and beading and what she called dramatic colours, was gently but firmly directed into more delicate fabrics, paler hues and plainer styles. But so skillfully was this done that when they were leaving the last shop, the aunt declared that it was a good thing she was firm and knew her own mind or heaven knew what would have been foisted onto them. The only thing she has resisted had been white.

'*Not* white,' the aunt had said, wondering why they could not see how it only increased the insipidy of the girl's features. Besides, the aunt thought of white as the colour poor people dressed their children in so that garments could be boiled to whiteness again and again.

Like the foodstuffs, the clothes were to be delivered; unhampered the two walked to an open air restaurant within the main park in the city.

'I thought you would like the wildness of it,' the aunt said, pleased by her own generosity since open air restaurants were not her taste. She spotted an acquaintance who was invited to join them, and who proceeded to tell a long whispered story about a man and his doctor wife.

It was very still and hot and beads of sweat forced themselves through the delicate skin in the little dent on the girl's upper lip and in her palms. She gazed out at the park where carefully edged rose beds were watched over by manicured hedges shaped into animals. On one side was a small marble fountain where a woman with bare stone breasts poured water from a jug into a bowl. The paths were made from loose crushed white gravel that radiated warmth in the heat and crunched agreeably under your sandals. Grass grew only in patches surrounded by metal chains from which were suspended signs forbidding feet. Wrought iron chairs stood about the edge of these pools of dazzling green and people sat in them and stared at the grass as if it were a pond where their faces looked back, or fish swam.

She wondered if the park had been a wilderness which had been pro-gressively tamed by the growth of the voracious city, or if it had been created as it was.

It was late in the afternoon, so apart from them and the aunt's acquain-tance, there were only a table of business men stabbing fingers into a map laid out in their midst and an elegant woman in a grey pantsuit talking into a mobile phone. After a time, a group of tourists in white shorts and bright T shirts converged on the restaurant with loud bird cries of delight.

'It's so sweet,' one said, clapping her hands together.

A waiter approached them and they opened their lips to display huge white smiles. Pink gums showed around the edges of their teeth.

An elderly man in a perfectly tailored cream suit and Panama hat entered and made his way to a table. He sat down, drawing out a long slim cigar. The waiter approached and lit it deferentially after snipping off its end, then a second waiter brought a coffee and a small glass of green liquid on a little tray without being asked. The girl watched him pour some of the green liquid into a spoon full of sugar and set a flame to it. An emerald flame swelled and hovered around the spoon like something halfway between liquid and smoke. When it had burned itself out the man dribbled the thick dark residue into his coffee, stirred and drank it.

The girl reflected that perhaps when the aunt called the park a wilderness, she had meant that it was where people came to be wild.

At length, the aunt pronounced it time to go, and refused the offer of a lift home in the acquaintance's car. They were going by metro, she explained, for she might have to go out of the city for a day or two from time to time, and the girl might want to attend the theatre or visit a gallery. She added that she would purchase a long term ticket.

'You must never to go down into the metro after dark,' the acquaintance advised. She had not addressed a single comment to the girl before this.

The aunt said, mildly peevish, that she would explain all that needed explaining in good time.

The girl had had a photograph taken in a booth for her long term ticket, and this was snipped out and slid into a laminated case which she slid it obediently into her purse. Inside the metro station, which was only a sort of corrugated tin shed with turnstiles and a ticket machine, there were windows where men and woman sat looking identically bored and annoyed. The metro platforms themselves were deep underground, the aunt expl-ained, pointing to an escalator that would carry them down to the place where one boarded the underground electric trains.

It was a steep decline and the girl held tightly to the hand rail which moved at a slightly quicker pace than the steps, so that she must keep adjusting her grip. The roof slanted down too so it was as if they were riding through an angled tube. The ascending escalator was alongside and the girl looked into the faces of people standing on it: a tired man cradling a briefcase as if it were a baby, a scruffy young couple twined and kissing voluptuously, two women in lavish silk evening gowns and a group of drunk men who were singing an apparently obscene song and leaning precariously on one another, a swarthy man with a black eye and a surly expression and a big woman with a beautiful face and a stained ecru bodice, a young woman muttering rapidly to herself.

The aunt murmured discreetly that one should not stare because aside from being ill bred, it virtually obliged some sort of intercourse. The girl did not see how any sort of exchange could be conducted with people going decisively in the other direction, but she looked down as directed in time to see the short hall between to two opposing platforms come into view. From here, one went a little way until one came to arches left and right, through which were the platforms. One going one way and one the other. Just before they reached the bottom where the silver teeth of the escalator were swallowed by a metal grille, an enormous gust of cold wind blew up into their faces from the depths as if the earth itself had sighed and the girl gasped aloud as it tugged her hair from its braids and drank the sweat on her upper lips.

'I smell the sea,' she said in wonderment.

The aunt pursed her lips and said nothing for the city was very far from the sea. She sniffed surreptitiously but could only smell the oily escalator reek, under which lay an unpleasant tang of urine. Her notion that the girl was mentally afflicted strengthened.

When they passed through the arches to the platform, there were only a few other people down the far end. Between them and the aunt and the girl, there was a man standing in a niche unwrapping some sort of instrument. He wore corduroy pants with threadbare knees, a greasy blue shirt and a Greek fisherman's hat from beneath which hung a dirty plait. A black dog with a faded bandanna knotted around its neck sat by his ankle, and the girl experienced a slight thrill to discover that it was watching her closely.

'I told you, it is better not to look at anyone,' the aunt said. 'Men like that call themselves musicians but they are beggars and perhaps worse.' She flushed slightly.

The ghostly subterranean wind blew again, and the girl's hair and clothes fluttered wildly. A moment later, the metro train, a sleek snake of silver, burst from the tunnel and sighed to a halt, its doors sliding open with a bang. The girl and the aunt entered and when seated, the older woman said that one must never make the mistake of entering the metro when people were going to or leaving work, for it was impossibly crowded. She spoke of pickpockets, but there was something more than hands feeling for a purse in her eyes. It must also be avoided when there were too *few* people as well, she added.

When they stepped out onto the platform of the station the aunt explained was within walking distance of their apartment, the earth exhaled again and again the girl smelled the distinct odour of the sea.

At the top of the escalator there was a disturbance centred on a filthy old beggar woman.

'My soup has gone sour!' she cried, pointing to the battered metal boiler in the pram. Most people pretended not to see. The crowd simply split and went in two streams with averted eyes. But several young men with army greens and shaven heads had stopped to jeer. One had a swastika tattoo on the back of his scalp.

The aunt made to steer them by, but without warning, the old woman pounced forward and caught the girl by her wrist. The aunt gave a little shriek and batted uselessly at the hand in the frayed glove, blackened fingers protruding like the nails of an ape.

The old woman had eyes only for her pale young captive. 'Do *you* know what it means when soup goes sour?'

The girl shook her head.

The old woman leaned close enough that the girl could smell her earthy reek. 'It is a sign, child. There are always omens for those who know enough to read 'em.'

The aunt wrenched her free with strength born of indignation, and when they had got out of sight of the group, took out a tiny lace edged handkerchief and rubbed hard at the girl's wrist. The old woman's fingers had left a perfect print, but the mark was queerly indelible, like a bruise.

'So many unsavory people lurk in the metro, my dear,' the aunt said and warned her never to go beyond the ends of platforms where they became narrow ledges that ran away down the tunnels. 'They are used by workmen, but the metro is very old and there are disused sections that are dangerous. People have been lost down there,' she added.

She fell silent then, thinking that perhaps after all it would not be a good idea to let the girl use the metro. It had been many years since she had done so herself, and it seemed to have been allowed to lapse into an anarchic region where decency and laws held no sway. If only the girl had the wit to be afraid, but clearly she did not.

When they emerged it was night, and the girl was surprised for when they entered the metro it had been daylight. Their underground journey had not seemed so long, but of course time must move differently with the weight of so much earth pressing down. She thought of the web of tunnels reaching down from the city well over one hundred feet into the chill dark earth, and suspected that all the wildness which had been oppressed above had not been tamed or crushed out of existence, but found its way down.

She thought of the old man in the cream suit conjuring his green flame with its dark residue and guessed that same fugitive wildness managed to rise up in threads to permeate the city and its occupants in fantastical and perverse ways.

That night, she dreamed the tunnel dream again, but somehow the old woman with her pram

had got into it.

'What are you looking for?' she asked in a raw crackle.

'I don't know.'

The woman shook her grizzled head. 'Then you will never find your heart's desire.'

'I don't want anything.' the girl said, and thought this was true.

The woman looked sad. 'Then all is lost.'

The following day, the aunt chose which of the stiff new dresses the girl was to wear with which shoes and which cardigan to carry in which bag. The girl let herself be turned this way and that by the aunt and by D'lo who had been sequestered to help. D'lo was as black as an old polished tree root, with a voice than flowed as thick and golden-viscous as warmed sap. The girl liked to hear the cook's voice.

'She fine. She sho lookin' fine,' D'lo exclaimed.

The aunt told the girl they had been invited to luncheon and suggested they walk since their destination was in the neighbourhood. They passed through a small park and the aunt reminisced about her poodle, Mikolash, who had been walked there. He had died, but the aunt called it Passed Away. The girl understood that such phrases blurred the terrible cutting edge of death, but she preferred words to be exact and simple.

The aunt dabbed at her eyes sentimentally interpreting the girl's silence as respect for Mikolash. She told herself the child was perhaps only a little slow, and that was not so detrimental in a girl as in a boy. Indeed looking at the mess her sister had made of her life, it might be said that cleverness was more of a disadvantage to a woman than anything else.

The girl was thinking about her dream, for it seemed to her that she had seen something in the tunnels just before the old woman appeared. Something huge and white.

Their hosts' apartment was lavish with marble floors that gleamed in a chilly way, and blond leather furniture. There were clear vases of yellow irises, long pale heavy cream silk curtains and paintings in muted colours, but also many blank walls which had their own beauty. Most of all, there was empty space filled with shafts of sunlight.

Privately the aunt thought the apartment ostentatiously bare, though of course she admired her hosts' exquisite taste. She preened when it was insisted that her own apartment was much nicer and cosier, for this was exactly her own opinion.

Later the woman's husband came with the daughter of the house and the girl was introduced to them both. As the husband took her hand, an odour arose from him as if he carried something old and musky in his pockets. Instinctively the girl pulled her hand from his fingers before he could press his lips to it.

It became clear that the visit had been arranged because the two girls were of same age and therefore must become friends. It was explained that father had just brought her home from her piano lesson. The daughter smiled at the girl and asked questions prettily, tossing a head of radiant honey curls fastened with a pink ribbon. The three adults smiled. The girl answered her gravely but both understood at once that they had nothing in common; under other circumstances, one would become the victim of the other.

The aunt regretfully contrasted the feminine pink and gold flirtatiousness of the friend's daughter with her sister's child. Out of loyalty, though, she murmured to her hosts that the girl was very shy, having lived in isolation with only her parents for company.

As they ate a spicy crumbly-dark fruit cake and drank raspberry syrup, the girl was asked gently inquisitive questions by their hosts. Her answers dissatisfied because she would only say yes or no, and would not be drawn to elaborate on the one thing the adults wished to know: why did her mother and father no longer wish to keep her?

'She is delightfully unspoiled,' the friend murmured to the aunt when they were preparing to leave. The aunt smiled but took this as the criticism it was and on the way home, spoke sharply and rhetorically about her friends' husband who was the president of a petrochemical firm which had been lately accused in the newspapers as having paid a politician to secure the defeat of a business restriction. She might feel the girl was lacking in certain ways, she thought to herself wrathfully, as was her right as a blood relation, but other people should be more restrained. She was now glad she had not issued an invitation to a small party in honour of the girl's birthday which was two days away, as had been her impulse.

Besides all else, given the limitations of the girl, a party could only be a social disaster.

The following morning, a box arrived announcing itself to be from the girl's father and also a parcel from the mother. They had been sent separately, but perversely, the same carrier brought them together. They were a day early, but the aunt suggested the girl open them in case they contained something perishable. Certainly the flowers must be put into water.

The parcel contained a simple armless shift dress in white silk with a pattern of small leaves sewn in white satin thread beaded with tiny pearls. It was far too young, the aunt thought. Worse, the card asked the girl specifically to wear the dress on her birthday because the mother had dreamed of her in it. The aunt thought this a ludicrous and even irresponsible thing to ask, but only admired the needlework in a lukewarm voice.

The girl fingered the dress thinking how, in her dream the previous night, she had worn such a dress.

The box contained roses. Not long stemmed roses with tender pink buds which the aunt would have deemed appropriate for a young girl, but a dense tangle of crimson buds nestled amongst dark green leaves, with stems that curled impossibly in on themselves and fairly bristled with thorns. The colour of them as well as their barbaric tangle confirmed to the aunt the foolishness of her sister's choice in a husband.

At first the roses seemed to have no scent, but when they returned from an exhibition in a gallery that afternoon, the whole apartment was filled with their perfume.

The following morning, the aunt woke in fright from a dream in which she had been running naked through a forest of wild red roses, pursued by some sort of animal. Wrapped in chaste pink linen and a soft lace nightgown, she patted her plump round belly and told herself she ought not to have drunk coffee so late in the evening. But when she opened her bedroom door, the smell of the roses was so powerful that she blamed her dreams on a lack of oxygen. Panting, she broke her own rule and struggled to open some windows.

Setting a dainty birthday breakfast table, she glanced from time to time with real loathing at the roses which had opened up in the heated apartment and now gaped in a way that struck her as frankly carnal.

Nibbling at the haunch of a marzipan mouse as she set its companions on a small glass platter, she consoled herself that at this rate, the petals would be dropping by midday, and the flowers could reasonably be disposed of by evening. Beheading the mouse with a neat sharp bite, she thought of the pictures she had seen of her sister's husband and reflected that she had always known there was something wrong with him. A doctor should look ascetic and have white slender pianist's fingers and soft limp blond hair, but the man looked gypsyish. His hands were as big and rough as a Moscow butcher's.

She shuddered to think of such hands on her body and wondered that her sister had borne it. She folded pale green napkins, and remembered her own birthday at this age. There had been an elegant party to which silver-edged invitations had gone out. She had worn pink taffeta and a matching chiffon scarf in her hair, and she had met her guests with skin as white and cool as ice cream waiting to be licked. But the boy she had hoped would kiss her had gone to the garden to wait, and when she had been delayed, had embraced another girl instead. The aunt had come out into the moonlight in time to understand that her moment of romance had been stolen, and it seemed to her now that there was an inexorable path from that night to this apartment and to this day, where she was as virginal as the girl for whom she was sugaring pink grapefruit slices.

She felt her eyes mist and wondered if she would cry for the life of connubial bliss that had been stolen from her, but then the stairs creaked and the girl appeared in her seafoam green nightgown.

The aunt could only gape for the pale, dull girl had become a bella donna with high, flushed cheekbones and heavy slumberous eyelids fringed in sooty black lashes that drooped over eyes so dark as to be all pupil. Her lips were red and swollen exactly as if someone had spent all night pressing bruising passion against them.

'You ... you look ... ' the aunt began. Then stopped in confusion.

I dreamed. . . .' the girl murmured, and rubbed at her eyes with her fingers balled into childish fists.

Remembering her own dream the aunt wondered if it was possible for a dream to have wrought this astonishing change. Then common sense prevailed and she told herself that the girl had a fever, that was all. Illness produced the hectic beauty. She ought not to have opened the windows.

The girl was thinking about the dream in which she had run and run in wind-scoured sea scented tunnels and had glimpsed a white beast running ahead of her. She had come quite suddenly to a place where all of the metro tunnels converged in one huge barrel vaulted cavern with many entrances and exits and queer niches and markings. The cold ground had been clammy under her toes, the walls stained by a seepage that oozed from high up cracks and crept downward to congeal on the floor in overlapping circles of sulphur yellow and livid purple. The smell of the sea had been overpowering there, and then came a drumming as if the cavern were actually under the ocean.

The man with the black dog had been against one of the walls, playing a mournful saxophone pitted with green warts of verdigris. The girl listened from the other side of the cavern, for she wished to respect the aunt's fears, even in a dream.

She had felt a prod her in the ribs, and found the pram woman leering. The beggar scratched her wiry, fried looking hair and gave a snort that could have been a sneeze or a laugh or something of both. 'You think you have come so far to obey the forbidding of a frightened aunt?'

The girl knew that she was dreaming, so the woman and even the sax-player knew everything she knew because they were all shapes worn by her own mind.

'Tunnels are dreams,' the old woman had gone on in the manner of one confiding a vital secret. 'The right dreamer finds anything in them.'

'Can I find the ocean?' the girl had asked. Without warning the cavern plunged into darkness and the dream broke.

After D'lo had cleared the remnants of grapefruit, croissants and coffee, the aunt suggested they dress and go to a classical concert in the afternoon as a treat. In the evening they had been invited to supper. She hoped the girl would choose one of her stylish new dresses, but obedient to her mother's desire, she donned the white dress that had been sent. When the aunt saw her in it, she felt the blood rise in her cheeks: the dress was made of silk so soft and sinuous that it caressed and outlined every muscle and gave the impression of nudity.

It might have been sown with this unearthly transformation from child to woman in mind, the aunt thought with renewed unease.

The girl noticed the fullness of her lips and the heaviness of her eyes in the hall mirror as they left, and wondered if it meant that the bleeding that she had been warned about was to begin. Certainly her body felt as if she had been filled up with fluid that lapped inside her like a warm red ocean. She was not afraid, although it was clear that girls were expected to fear the blood, what it heralded: womanhood and all of the pains of the heart and soul and body that flesh was heir to. She knew that she experienced the world differently from the woman and man that were her mother and father, and also from the other people she had encountered.

The thought came to her like a whisper, that the raggedy people who prowled the dank metro corridors experienced the world differently too.

In the taxi that brought them to the theatre, the aunt gave her two small beautifully gift-wrapped packages. The first contained a small antique bible with a leather cover and a tiny metal lock which must be for ornamental reasons for why would one lock a bible? The second held a set of exquisite pearl combs and the girl pushed the combs into her dark locks as she was bidden. It occurred to the aunt that clad thus, the girl looked like a bride.

It was very hot outside; the zenith of a string of hot days, and a record for the month. They arrived at the theatre early and stood outside to wait, for there was no air conditioning in the foyer. The building facades opposite had a bleached bone look, and the asphalt gave off a hot black smell. Women around them stood wilting in expensive gowns, while their escorts fanned florid faces above tuxedos and ties. The leaves of a caged tree hung motionless and the sky grew more mercilessly and perfectly blue. God might have eyes that colour when he sent Adam and Eve from the garden, the aunt thought dizzily, feeling her blood vibrate under her skin and hoping she would not faint.

She decided they must walk a little as the press grew. Around the corner, they came unexpectedly to a church and the aunt decided they must go in. The coolness beyond the arched stone of the doorway was so profound that she could have wept for the relief of it. They sat in the very last pew and the aunt waited until the glimmering stars that had begun to wink before her eyes, had faded. Then she glanced sideways at the girl and wondered if she had not been influenced come into the church. The child had such a dangerously potent look. Of course she was a heathen because her sister had abandoned their religion, but in the church's eyes it was better to be a heathen than the member of another church. The latter went to hell, while heathens along with unbaptised babies, went to wait in the grey eternity of limbo.

She didn't really believe in limbo any more. Not exactly. But she didn't disbelieve either. Her mind was not shaped for such decision-making. She had a nostalgic affection for the innocent rites of her childhood faith, and in old age, would be able to draw her religion tightly back around her like a beloved shawl.

The girl liked the cold smell of the church, the cool tobacco-dark shadows striping pictures of dim, tortured saints and the faint humming of the stone under her feet. She liked the little banks of candles and the font of water and the wood polish smell of the pews.

Finally the aunt touched her and motioned that they should go.

If there was a god, and the girl was in some sort of danger, perhaps He would see fit to intervene. The aunt could do no more.

The performance they had come to see was merely competent and afterwards the aunt said it was a pity but one could not be sure what one would find waiting inside. Perfection was as likely as mediocrity. But it was a pity.

Neither had the girl enjoyed the performance, finding the musical arrangement too mannered and consciously intricate. There was a wild simple music in the world which she preferred, although it was hard to hear in the city. The longing to hear the disordered cadences of the waves grew until it hurt the bones in her chest to keep in. It was the first time in her life she had consciously desired something she did not have and she wondered if wanting was something that came with the bleeding.

Outside it was hotter than ever and the sun still shone, although in was now early evening.

The aunt wished she had arranged a taxi so they could go immediately and directly to her friend's apartment. With the crowd swelling out, there was no chance of hailing one, so they walked, searching for a telephone. The aunt's eyes watered at the brightness of the sun and she flinched when sunlight flashed off an opening window and pressed into her eyes in two sharp points.

The girl was thinking that the heat was a trapped beast prowling and prowling the streets with its great wet red tongue hanging out, gasping in the exhausted air. If someone did not let it out soon, it would go mad and tear everything to pieces.

At last they found a phone box and called a taxi.

To the aunt's irritation, when they arrived at her friend's home, he announced that it was too hot to stay in. He had organised for them to eat in a nearby cafe, he said, but at least they were borne there in a car with air conditioning. The friend was very like the aunt in his plump pinkness, although he was somewhat sharper in mind and manner. His eyes were a beautiful transparent aqua that reminded the girl of the sea on certain days when an unexpected beam of light penetrated a dark sky, and they settled on her with avid curiosity.

'You are something of a beauty,' he told her. He looked at the aunt with amusement. 'You did not say she was beautiful.'

The aunt was almost suffocated with all the replies she might have made, from the inappropriateness of telling impressionable young girls such things about themselves, to the strangeness of the fact that she had not been beautiful until this morning. Fortunately a waiter chose that moment to lay a starched cloth in her lap, preventing any response.

'This terrible heat,' she said, when he had departed with their orders.

But her friend ignored the warning tone. Or perhaps he did not notice it, for he was still studying the girl. 'It is interesting to think that with lips a little less full and eyes a tiny bit closer together, you would not be beautiful,' he said. 'Such a small amount of difference between ugliness and beauty.'

'Beauty is in the eye of the beholder,' the aunt said firmly. But her friend gave a laugh.

'Yes and inner beauty is more important that outer fairness. I know all of that and of course it's true, but, my dear, the child is exquisite, and her life will be shaped by that because regardless of what people say, humans revere beauty. Something in us is thrilled by it. Aren't *you* thrilled by her?'

The aunt looked involuntarily at the girl and thought that she was more frightened by her impossible radiance which surely had grown since the morning.

'We who are not and never have been beautiful must be a little envious as well,' the friend went on. 'Few would be pure enough to simply worship at the altar of beauty. There is some cruelty in our makeup that makes us want to shred and smash it even as we adore it.'

The aunt made a business of buttering a bun for herself and for the girl.

But her friend would not be diverted. 'You were very pretty and your sister was what one would call handsome,' he said pensively. 'But this girl surpasses all of those lesser forms. Is your father very beautiful?' He asked her directly.

The girl thought a little and then answered composedly, 'I do not think one would call him beautiful. He is bald and thickset, and he has a very big nose.'

He laughed aloud in delight. 'What a sophisticate! I had thought you might be a barbarian having been brought up in such a way and such a place. My dear, you must be so pleased.'

This to the aunt who did not know what she was supposed to be pleased about. A certain vexation began to show in the wrinkles rimming her eyes. 'How is your salad, dear?' she asked the girl determinedly.

Over dessert, the friend clutched at his chest and made a strangled noise. The aunt knew he had a heart condition and cried out for the waiter to summon the friend's driver. She did not call an ambulance knowing that he thought them vulgar and in any case they were so notoriously slow to come, one might expire beside one's mousse.

By the kerb, she massaged the friend's wrists and temples and shed a scatter of tears, and was sorry to have been angry with him. After all, it was true that the girl had by now become almost unbearably exquisite. She noticed that two storm clouds shaped like long-fingered hands were reaching out towards one another, closing the blue sky in a black grip. She had never seen such a thing and, fearing it was an ill omen for her friend, she thrust some notes into the girl's hand and bid her catch a taxi home.

'I may be some time,' she said, climbing after the friend into his black car. Only as the car pulled away and she glanced back, did the aunt see that the dark hands were clasping directly behind the girl, as if the sky itself would pray for her, or crush her. It was too late to stop the car, and she would have been a fool to do so, for of course it was an absurd fancy.

She turned with relief to wipe the brow of her ailing friend.

The girl stood watching the car go. She looked up to find the sky filling with surly cloud. A storm was close to breaking, but for the moment the heat had grown fiercer as though compressed by the dense cloud cover. She began walking and had gone a block before it occurred to her that for the first time no one was waiting for her and no one was watching over her. She could do anything she wanted, and wondered what she did want. Other girls might search for a nightclub to dance into, or perhaps a smart café bar where there was classical guitar. Or they might go to a movie. Certainly they would think of meeting a boy or even a man. The girl desired none of these things and wondered why.

She walked three blocks then five, and had an orange presse in an outdoor cafe. Nearby were two young men talking; one was half lying on his seat and the other was staring into the froth of a beer. Both smoked heavily. An older woman in a red dress batted at the grey ribbons of their smoke winding around her.

The girl felt no desire to talk to the young men or indeed to anyone. She did not enjoy conversation. Very little needed to be said in life and she did not understand why people spoke when there was no need. Weary of being surrounded by people, she made up her mind to walk back to the apartment if she could find the river to guide her.

She tried to imagine how it would be to marry one of the young men in the restaurant and let him touch her and found it impossible. But most women did marry and that was seen to be something one must do, or at least contemplate. Yet she could not imagine it for herself. Living with a man, lying beside him, arguing with him and being ignored or lectured. Yet if one did not join with a man, what else was there? The aunt's sort of life with its overstuffed cushions and chocolates, and gentle smugness, and underneath that, a kind of aridity? Or a life in which the passion of work replaced the passion for a man? Neither appealed, for she felt that her body had begun to ripen for some specific purpose. But if not a man, then who?

Her body seemed to ache, as if it understood its purpose better than she did. And in the moment her longing for the sound and scent of the sea returned with such intensity she felt nauseous. She thought then that one could be taken into the arms of the sea as of a man.

S he saw the river glimmering darkly at the end of a long narrow
street and stopped.

Between the river and where she stood was one of the glowing
Metro stop signs. There was no light at the entrance to the metro,
and she thought of her aunt's warnings, but fear would not take. As
she came closer, the girl could smell the grey-black skin of the river
beyond.

Inside, a light glowed from somewhere deeper down and she
walked forward. The endless escalators were operating, their steps
humming downward, and the girl stepped forward onto them. The
light increased as she descended until she could see that the
advertisements in their slanted billboards were peeling and
streaked with slime. It was impossible to make out what they
offered. There were no other people going down or up, and the girl
supposed she had chanced on a moment between crowds. The
escalator was longer than the others and she wondered if this
particular tunnel had been some sort of natural fissure that had
been incorporated into the metro web, for by now there were no
more billboards and only what seemed to be a natural rock wall.

She thought of Persephone who had made a bargain to live six
months of each year beneath the earth, and wondered how she
had felt as she travelled downward, knowing she would not see the
sky or daylight or the sun for another six months.

Without warning, the metro wind blew and the girl breathed in
with delight at the briny coolness of it, wondering if it were
possible that a dark ocean lay at the heart of the world. At last she
reached the bottom, and there in a corner stood the man with his
greenish gold saxophone. He played a long note that strove up at
the nether end. Then he stood his instrument against his leg,
pulled a cigarette from behind his ear and a lighter from his pocket.
The flame gave his features a reddish hue as he took a deep breath
and held it, his eyes half-closed.

As she walked past, some impulse made her fish for a coin and
throw it into his case. Only then, did his eyes open a slit and rest
momentarily on her. They were the dull colour of his saxophone.
Once she had passed him the tunnel curved bringing her out of his
sight, then straightened and ran away out of sight. The aunt had

mentioned there were longer tunnel links between some platforms and escalators, and she set out beginning to be puzzled that she was still alone. Surely the theatre shows had finished by now? On the other hand, she knew that time worked oddly in the tunnels, so perhaps only a few minutes of real time had gone by.

Suddenly a man stepped out of a pool of shadows and brandished the horrid pouting pink stump which was all that remained of his amputated hand. The girl wondered if he wanted money from her, but he did not hold out his other hand.

'What do you want?' she asked.

'Save us . . . ' he moaned and fled away into the shadows.

The aunt had explained that many troubled souls gravitated to the metro. The girl understood that the labyrinthine and subterranean maze would seem more real and relevant to them than the flat bright world above. The aunt said they slept here as well if they could evade the police who would come to flush them out when the day ended. One could imagine they might know the maze better than the police, and when all of the metro doors to the outside were secured, they could creep out knowing that they need fear no one except others like them.

She thought of the old woman with the pram wondering if she collected the unwanted food from the back doors of bakeries and patisseries and even restaurants, to distribute to the subterranean poor. It would explain why she had been so upset at the thought that her soup had soured but did it make enough sense to be the answer? Was it possible such a ragged woman would feed the hungry?

It did if the rich did not care for the poor. Then the poor must fend for their own.

As if conjured by her thoughts, the beldam with her pram appeared accom-panied by a gypsy woman who clutched a baby wrapped up in dirty rags to her sagging breasts. The old woman turned and gave the girl a level questioning look which she did not know how to answer. The woman shrugged and turned away, leaving her feeling obscurely guilty. She followed the two women, although they had gone out of sight, and came to a platform which, from the state of its dilapidation, must be one of the disused stations the aunt had mentioned. There was no sign of the two women and the baby, but sitting by a billboard was the black dog that had been with the saxophone man.

It was watching her as intently as ever, and the girl went nearer slowly when the dog gave its black tail a single flip that might or might not have been a welcome.

'What are you waiting for?' she asked it softly.

The dog did not move a muscle but the thought persisted that it was waiting for *her*.

The metro wind blew again and this time it smelled of the storm which must be breaking in the city overhead. The girl's hair flew forward like twin black flags and she turned her face in time to watch a train punch from its tunnel and howl past the platform. The girl glimpsed the driver looking out, his mouth opened in an *O* of surprise. Then she turned back to the dog, but it had gone. Before she could make anything of this, as in her dream, the lights went out and she was standing in inky blackness. She did not move, thinking they would go back on, but the dark remained, settling like a dust cloth thrown over a couch.

Reaching into her pocket, the girl found the key-ring with its tiny attached torch that the aunt had given. A narrow pencil beam of light sliced the blackness. It was so slender as to be virtually useless in such massive darkness. Without knowing why, she turned it on herself; saw the hem of her birthday dress, its winking beads and pale sequins; she wondered if Persephone had been forced to dwell six months in total darkness, or had been allowed a candle.

Playing the light carefully backwards and forwards she looked for a sign pointing to the escalator. They would probably be switched off at a disused stop, but she could climb up to the surface.

More by luck than design, the beam fell at last onto the sign and she took her bearings. But after some minutes walking, it was clear she had missed her way again. She turned and began to walk back playing the beam about. Black graffiti appeared on a cement wall on one side, but when she looked at the other, there was only blackness. It took a moment for her to understand that this was because there was no other wall. She had walked right past the end of the platform and was now making her way along one of the narrow ledges that ran inside the metro train tunnels.

She stopped and from behind her came muted laughter or screams or crying, which her footsteps had muffled before. She felt cold and wondered if that was fear. She listened again and thought there was not one voice but a babble of them approaching.

When she turned to face the voices the metro wind blew so hard she rocked on her feet.

Another train? She heard a tremendous clattering as if a great number of cows or goats were being herded along the tunnel. But the cacophony resolved into the hoof beats of a single beast, with a loud accompaniment of echoes and something appeared in the torch beam, which could not be contained or encompassed by it. The only certainties were a massive whiteness and a bruise-black eye rolling in terror. The girl swung aside with instinctive grace else she would have been trampled and something huge passed her so closely that she felt the roughness of its pelt on her cheek and the damp heat of its fear.

A horse, she told herself, hearing it gallop away back towards the platform. Or maybe a bull, but bigger than any bull or horse she had ever seen. Impossibly big. How had it come down here?

The voices were louder and now she could make out shouting and laughter and grunts and cries and shrieks and even what seemed to be discordant snatches of song. Instinctively pressing herself to the wall, she switched off the torch and let the crowd pass. In the light of dull lanterns that barely lit their faces, let alone the way ahead, she saw that they were all human, although some were so hairy and hunched as to look like beasts. Many carried loops of rope and it came to her that they were some sort of hunting party, and that the white beast that had thundered by her was their quarry.

The girl thought she saw the face of the man with the amputated arm, but it was now hard to know anything.

When the noise had faded, the girl flicked on her torch and her heart leapt into her throat and almost choked her for looming in its thin stream was the wild tormented eye of the white beast. Somehow it had evaded the rabble and had doubled back. It was trembling and she sensed it was about to plunge away from her into the darkness.

'Don't be afraid. I won't hurt you,' she whispered, holding out a hand.

It shifted uneasily but stayed as she moved the torch. Its beam illuminated an ear pricked forward and, fleetingly, something shining and sharp. The beast shook its mane nervously.

'I will help you get out,' she promised. She reached out with her free hand and laid it on the coarse white coat. Powerful muscles rippled under her palm as the beast gathered itself to bound or trample her to death; then all at once it became still and the violence died from its eyes.

'Come,' the girl said, and it went passively along with her. Now she could see it was definitely a horse, but its head had been deformed. For the first time she wondered if it actually belonged to the metro denizens. It was no less a freak than they, for all its strange beauty, and perhaps they were not hunting it but trying to find it. Even so, why should it be their captive or even pet, and kept in the black darkness of the metro tunnels?

She began to run lightly and the beast kept pace so beautifully that it was as if they merged into one animal. The sensation was unlike anything she had ever experienced. Waves of pleasure shuddered through her, and as they ran, her hand on its hot neck, she understood that this was the thing she had sought through all the dreams and all the tunnels, the union long awaited. This running, this sweet fear, the hot flank under the whorls on her fingertips. This is what she had been shaped for.

When they reached the derelict platform, she forced herself to stop so that she could again find the exit sign with her torch. The beast nuzzled her neck tenderly seeming to draw her smell in and she shivered and smiled with pleasure at the intimate touch of its nostrils on her bare skin.

A cry told her the crowd had turned back and was almost upon them.

'*Run,*' she insisted, but although the beast shivered, it would not go. She made herself push it away from her roughly, but it was like trying to shift a granite mountain. But the creature was not stone. She could smell the salt of its sweat.

'I can't protect you from them!' she cried to it. 'Run can't you?'

But it stayed and the dimming beam of the torch showed a pleading look in its eyes.

'What do you want of me?' she whispered.

It rested its head on her shoulders and leaned downward. The weight of the massive head, even applied gently was such that her knees buckled slowly, and when she had been forced into a sitting position, the beast knelt and lay its lovely deformed head on her knees.

'O you poor thing you must go,' she muttered helplessly, shining the torch down onto it, but the violet sadness of its eyes asked only where it could go, and there was no answer to that.

Then it was too late. There was a great hullabaloo of triumph and the ragged men and women with dirt-streaked faces and crazed eyes appeared from the darkness crowing with glee, as they caught hold of the great white beast by its mane and tail and ears. A dozen filthy pairs of hands bore it away and brushed aside the girl who tried to hold onto it without seeming to notice her. Or so it seemed, until one of the men, a great hulking hunchback with ash-brown beard, looked over his shoulder at her and said with rough gentleness: 'You've played your part.'

The girl stood boneless and willess, as they surged away and were swallowed by the dark, for it was true that she had caught the beast and held it for the crowd. Without her, they never would have caught it.

She screamed, and the sound echoed away and then was carried back at her by a surge of the metro wind which wrested the torch from her fingers. It came to rest against the wall beside a tunnel, its beam reduced to a flickering golden egg of light against the cement. As the girl retrieved it, the wind blew again, gently, a mere sigh cool and damp with smell of the sea.

It occurred to her that if she could have, she would have led the beast onto the rails and leapt with it into the face of an oncoming train. Exhaustion deep as a mineshaft had come upon her. She struggled into the tunnel where the ragged people had taken the beast, uncaring that she did not know where it led. If nowhere, it seemed as good a destination as any.

The torch light gave a sepia spasm and then she was again fallen in darkness. She let it fall from her fingers, lifted her hands, one to the front and one to the side, and walked on. Hours passed, or weeks. It seemed possible that if she ever emerged, it would be to find she was a wizened old woman. It was as if she had walked into a tunnel that had led her into her dreams, or which had let her dreams spill out and become real. All that drew her on was the salt-strong smell of the sea. If she could find her way there, she would return to herself. The beast would be safe in her dreams.

She was still walking an hour later, or perhaps years later. In the darkness, time had become elastic and then liquid. She felt her life flowing around her. Memories of the wind and the sea and of her solitary childhood punished her; the way the woman and man who were her parents made sure never to touch her; the way the aunt had looked at her face that morning.

Something happened to me in the night, she thought.

'You have played your part in this,' the hunchback had said.

At first, she thought the blue light sloping downward ahead was an hallucination but it grew and gathered definition until she saw that the tunnel ended. That turquoise light came from beyond it. She expected to find herself in a cavern filled with ghostly phosphorescence, but if it was a cave, then it was big enough to swallow a small world. Under her feet was a beach of sand so white that the light dyed it aquamarine. Or perhaps it *was*. Beyond it a sea stretched away and away to an invisible horizon, and the waves hissed as they unrolled at her feet. Some distance away, the narrow beach jutted out in a long pale finger, and at the very tip, she saw the red flare of a fire; the movement of a great mass of people. Beyond them or in their midst was the white beast, swaying slightly to and fro, its milky coat stained red and pink from the firelight.

Filled with relief, she made her way along the beach and out onto the peninsula. When she was close enough to hear the fire crackling, she stopped, wondering if it might not be better to slip away without being seen. To find the beast that had been no more than a pet of the metro hoards seemed to diminish it, and her too.

She heard a step and found the pram woman by her side. She looked younger in the moonlight though her hair lay white and shining over her shoulders and her eyes glowed like two stars. 'There are some things too great for grief,' she said, and the girl's heart clenched in her chest with foreboding for the old woman's eyes brimmed with unshed tears.

She looked over to where the animal stood, and saw what she had not seen before.

It was not a living creature that stood behind the fire but its pelt stretched out to dry, the redness not firelight, but blood. And turning on the fire were lumps of sizzling meat dripping their fat, raw and blackened in alternating patches.

The girl doubled over. She heaved until nothing more came but thin yellow bile and still she retched. 'How could you kill it?' she gasped when she could. *'How?'* She did not expect an answer for they must be mad, all of them. To do such a thing.

'Child is born out of the harrowing of woman; the tearing and hurting of her. That's the way if there are no modern hospitals and doctors. Sometimes it only comes in the killing of its mother.'

'I don't know what you are talking about,' the girl cried. 'You are monsters.'

The woman said, 'Monsters for a monstrous deed.'

The girl was faint with guilt. 'If I had not come . . . '

'It would be running and running in the never-ending night that lives in the tunnels, until it fell and broke its leg and starved to death. Or was devoured by rats.'

'I could have brought it out. It would have come with me.'

'And what would you have brought it *to*?' the old woman demanded, shaking her with wiry strength. 'Up there to the city? What would they have made of it excepting that it must be put in a glass case and gaped at until it withered and died of despair? You think that would be a lesser betrayal?'

'I helped you catch it.'

'It was needed. This,' she waved a hand encompassing the fire with its bloody lumps of meat, the rabble with their burning flames for eyes and the empty red streaked pelt, 'was needed.'

'Needed? *Needed?* Are you mad?'

'It was the only way.' It was the saxophone player. He had risen and was staring over the fire at her. He looked less a beggar now than a rough king. 'The beast could not enter that world as it was. It was a shape that could not be accepted. You saw it.'

The girl thought of the sharp gleam of a single horn. 'It was . . . '

'It was a thing you summoned.'

The girl had dreamed of something running before her in the tunnels. Was that enough to have summoned the beast? 'It was a dream,' she said.

'It was and then it was not,' the man responded brusquely. 'It was real, and its death was real and now we who caught it and killed it will honour its sacrifice.'

The girl felt thin and insubstantial, as if she were the dream. Perhaps now they would kill her and eat her too. The smell of blood was mingled with the smell of the sea so that one could not know where each left off.

Lightning cracked overhead.

'It is time,' the man said, glancing up.

The old woman reached out to take the girl's cold fingers. 'Come on.' The girl shook her head as the stench of roasting meat rose. 'You have been pure, Lovey,' the old woman went on so softly that it might have been the wind speaking. 'So pure as to have been almost a mythical creature yourself. Only thus could you have summoned the fey monoceros. Only thus could you have gentled it to you and allowed it to be taken. It was afraid. Your purity gave it the courage to be what it must be: a sacrifice. And now the very purity that summoned it must be breached that its heart can begin the healing of our world.'

The girl recoiled from the old woman's dry touch, but the memory of the beast's eyes held her, pleading. Reminding her that it had paid the price of her touch. That there was a price for all things, especially the saving of a world from the cancer in its heart.

The old woman knelt and pushed her hands into the depths of the fire and withdrew a round ball of charred mud. She lifted it up in both crabbed hands as if to offer it to the night, and lightning flashed as if in reverence. A moment later, thunder cracked. The storm above had followed her into the earth.

'Quickly,' the man said. 'The moment must not slip by.'

The old woman ignored him and bent with a grunt to crack the thick crust of mud open on the edge of a stone, as if it were a black egg. The girl felt the heat of its centre blaze out, and yet the pram woman did not flinch as she held out the half where the heart reposed, red and glistening.

Beating.

'Its heart is yours,' the old woman said.

The heat of the heart was immense and the girl's eyes watered, but suddenly she was not afraid. She thought of the beast—its heat under her palm, its head in her lap, its nostrils on her neck—and parted her lips, but when she bit down, it was not into flesh, but into the soft flesh of an enormous peach, yet it was not a peach for there was no downy flesh or spiky stone at centre. It was peach and pomegranate and mango and it was none of them. Ripe, warmed by the sun, and piercingly sweet nectar flowed down her throat.

It quenched thirst and fear and pain, and when she drew back, it was to find something burning and thudding at the base of her throat, which might have been her own heart or the heart of the unicorn.

ISOBELLE CARMODY *(b. Wangaratta, Victoria, Australia, 1958) is an Australian writer of science fiction, fantasy, children's and juvenile literature. She divides her time between a home on the Great Ocean Road in Australia and her travels abroad. Isobelle began work on the highly acclaimed* Obernewtyn Chronicles *when she was just fourteen years old. She continued to work on these while completing a Bachelor of Arts, majoring in literature and philosophy, followed by a cadetship in journalism. The first two books in the* Obernewtyn *series were short listed for the CBC Children's Book of the Year in the Older Readers category;* Scatterlings *won Talking book of the Year.* The Gathering *was a joint winner of the 1993 CBC Book of the Year Award and the 1994 Children's Literature Peace Prize.* Greylands *won an Aurealis Award and a White Raven at Bologna, while* Billy Thunder and the Night Gate *was shortlisted for the Patricia Wrightson Prize for Children's Literature in the 2001 NSW Premier's Literary Awards. Both* Little Fur *and* A Fox Called Sorrow *received BAAFTA Industry Awards for design.* Alyzon Whitestarr *won the coveted Golden Aurealis for overall best novel at the Aurealis Awards. With Nan McNabb she was the participating editor of the first of a two book collection of stories by taking a dark look at fairy tales, titled* The Wilful Eye *(Allen & Unwin, 2011), and her most recent book* The Red Wind *was shortlisted for Book of the Year and The West Australian Premier's Prize. She is currently working on the final book in the* Obernewtyn Chronicles, The Red Queen.

Commentary on "Metro Winds": *When I first travelled*

abroad, I was struck by how it felt to be someone from a place like Australia where my history is the short history of those descended from willing or unwilling invaders, coming to the Old World. We who are descended from those first settlers wear our violent, ignorant history lightly—too lightly, I think. Perhaps because it is relatively short, and perhaps because we are linked to other places by culture and language. But we wear that connection of place lightly, too. Our ancestors came from over there, somewhere long ago. We were like children who had left home and didn't want to call home. We thumbed our nose at parents that could not control us but in fact we have never cut the apron strings. Not really. Not finally. I have no judgement to make about that. Judging the world or people is not what interests me. I went overseas lightly, curiously, wearing both those thin cloaks carelessly. But history saturated them as I travelled and made them heavier. Yet never as cumbersome—as burdensome, as darkly intricate and complex as the cloaks of connection and history worn by people from all the other worlds of Elsewhere. I felt both free and yet insubstantial as the glitter of sunlight on water in spring. Again and again I found myself fascinated by my own reactions and later, by the reactions of other travellers from Australia to the older, darker, wiser and yet infinitely heavier world I found Elsewhere.

"Metro Winds" is the first story I wrote that reflected my experiences and observations. But it is also a story about what happens when something precious from one world and time must be released in another. It is a story of dark and necessary transformation.

The story will reappear in slightly different form in Australia for my Allen & Unwin collection ten years in the making, Metro Winds.

MARINERS' ROUND

TERRY DOWLING

I T STARTED SMALL, AS THESE THINGS DO, WITH A CHEAP glass jewel pried from the rump of a genuine Charles Carmel merry-go-round horse at Sydney's Luna Park one cool autumn evening in 1977. A blue glass jewel set into a gold-painted wooden harness, many faceted, the size of a king's thumbnail, a queen's ransom, big enough to be easily visible and look so precious to kids watching the carousel turn.

Easy to pry off, too, in a small enough act of vandalism by one of three fourteen-year-old schoolboys on a cool, just past summer evening.

Davey Renford wanted it, yearned for it, loved the idea of having a precious blue-glass jewel from the haunch of the magnificent white wooden horse he'd chosen. *Lysander*, the chest blazon said, and it was on the outermost of the three rings, a smooth-turning stander, not like the favoured lift-and-fall jumpers on the two inner rings that most boys preferred. The fixed ones were not as exciting to ride but, being on the outside, they had the armour and bright fish-scale saddle cloths, the mirrors and the jewels. And this, to Davey, was the finest mount of them all, picked from the forty-two others, chosen over the two chariots, the lion and the fabulous (oh-so-tempting) griffin.

There was something about its dark gaze, the arch of the neck, the way the splendid creature lunged forward to seize the night, Davey couldn't explain exactly. Stallion or mare, it didn't matter. This was his horse, his jewel, something to mark the time.

Riley Trencher couldn't have cared less, not yet. He was on an inner ring jumper, four horses ahead, yelling something back to Frank Coombs who was busy swapping horses mid-ride when the operator wasn't looking. And it was just as Davey's cousin, Frank, was swinging between a second-ring jumper and the outer-ring fixed black behind Davey's that he saw Davey reach back to run his finger yet again over the blue gem in the golden harness.

'You want it, take it!' Frank said. 'It's just glass!'

Which it was, of course, yet could never be.

'Take it!' Frank said again.

Davey couldn't.

But for Frank Coombs it wasn't an issue. He glanced at Riley Trencher sailing on ahead, then at the operator, whose back was still turned, then in seconds had his penknife out and open and the blade in under the jewel. In seconds, he was cupping the cool hard thing as it came away, then passing it forward to Davey, who took it, gaping in shock and wonder.

'What's that you're doing?' Riley called, which made the operator turn, shout an automatic 'Behave yourselves, you boys!' and ended conversation until the ride was over.

By the time the platform had glided to a halt and all the horses were fixed and still, Riley and Frank had forgotten the jewel. They were too busy hurrying off to the Ghost Train, leaving Davey to follow on, lost in a buzz of wondering if it had really happened.

It was on the way home that Riley became the closest thing to an enemy Davey had ever known. The three of them were off the train at Hornsby, walking down Sutter's Lane with the backyards of homes to one side and the vast open spread of the railway lines to the other. There was a streetlight ahead, just before the pedestrian underpass, and in the thin yellow light Frank saw how distracted Davey was.

'Hey, Davey-boy! Why the long face? You got the jewel.'

Which had Riley immediately demanding to see it. 'Hey, yeah! I wondered what you two were doin'. Show me!'

Davey would've refused, but it wasn't worth setting Riley off about anything. He was like a spring on its first flex, a firework teased with fire.

Davey took the jewel from his pocket and passed it over.

Maybe it looked precious in the light. Maybe it triggered something in Riley Trencher that had never existed before. For in a flash, mere seconds, his arm was back and he was flinging the stone out across the tracks.

For Davey it was a frozen moment, an eternity of alarm, dismay, rage beyond telling. He couldn't speak, couldn't move.

Not so Frank. An instant more and Frank had his own arm back and was punching Riley full in the face, spinning him off balance, sending him careening down the embankment. The chain-link fence should have caught him, but other kids had loosened the mesh for a short-cut and Riley went plunging through, scrambling and yelling, landing hard at the bottom on a standing length of pipe that went through his left thigh.

The yelling roused the neighbours. Suddenly there were adults there, and police and an ambulance soon afterwards. But by then Davey and Frank had been led aside, questioned and taken home.

So it is that things happen, lives are turned, debts left owned and owing.

Twenty-five years later, David Renford—Dave to his close friends, still Davey to his closest—knew so much more about the jewel, or rather the horse and the merry-go-round they had ridden that fateful night. Even before becoming a free-lance heritage analyst, even before being called in to do insurance appraisals on two different Luna Park gates and associated vintage attractions by various state governments, he had learned its origins: how it was an American three-row menagerie carousel in the Coney Island style purchased in England by Herman Phillips and brought to Sydney in 1910. How the horses had been carved by Charles Carmel, one of the greatest of the American carousel horse carvers of the early twentieth century, a student of Charles Looff himself, and who, as an independent competitor, had specialised in splendid armoured mounts, fish-scale saddle blankets and feather-pattern, jewelled harnesses.

And twenty-five years to the day of that momentous evening (though he wasn't to know *that* for another hour or so), Davey was sitting in the Trebarin in Dublin at 1:45 on an overcast Saturday afternoon listening to a five-piece band playing 'Whiskey in the Jar.' There was a petite, redheaded woman with a winsome, heart-shaped face drinking with friends and singing along who kept catching his eye and smiling the right way. Losing on-again off-again Tina had made him cautious, even shy, and he meant to wait before attempting any kind of overture. What if he were wrong?

Still, it was the first time he'd been really, truly, unequivocally happy in the five years since Annie died, and it had started with winning the lucky door prize at the local RSL: the return trip to Ireland with three weeks' accommodation and three thousand dollars spending money. He felt his life re-making itself at last.

But then—sheer astonishment!—Frank Coombs walked in, Frank or a time-worn lookalike. There was no mistaking him, though it had been ten years since he'd last seen his long-lost cousin, well before Annie.

'Frank!' Davey called above the singing, and Frank heard and turned, eyes widening in recognition, mouth falling open in an amazement to match Davey's own.

'Davey? What on earth?'

For the next thirty minutes they huddled over beers in that corner of the Trebarin just off O'Connell Street, though the surprise and delight turned to a different, darker sort of astonishment after the first few minutes.

For Frank had won his own prize at another RSL, the three weeks' accommodation, the three thousand dollars. It was unbelievable, impossible.

But more. On his way out of his hotel just forty minutes ago, Frank had been handed a most intriguing message at reception.

Your next surprise. The bar of the Trebarin Hotel, 2 p.m.

It had all been planned: the strictly fixed-term plane tickets, the proximity of their hotels, the meeting.

'What's going on, Dave?' Frank asked, more to the universe than his one-year-younger cousin. 'I thought *you* must've arranged the whole thing.'

'How I'm seeing it too, Frank. But what are the chances? Someone saw I was here and phoned your hotel.'

They spoke on, matched lives, found they had even more in common than they'd first thought.

Davey had lost Annie five years before in a car accident in Royal National Park. Frank's wife Marguerite had left him a year ago, taking their remaining child to her parents' property at Calloway Point after a house fire had caused the death of their six-year-old son Mark.

The more they talked about their lives, the more alarming the symmetry became.

Several years back, Davey had looked like becoming a favoured heritage analyst for the Australian Museum in Sydney until an elaborately staged hoax had led first to his being sidelined, then sidestepped altogether. Frank, on the other hand, had been forced to close a promising rural medical practice when a lawsuit from a woman whose cancer had been misdiagnosed led to a malpractice investigation. The pathology lab had ended up being held accountable but, country towns being what they were, Frank's reputation in the district had been effectively ruined.

'Believe in conspiracy theories, Davey?' Frank asked.

'Starting to,' Davey answered. 'It's too weird.'

The timing of this 'discovery' phase had been planned as well. Forty-five minutes after their meeting, the waitress who came to clear the glasses handed them a business card.

'A gentleman upstairs asked me to give you this,' she said. 'He's in the private lounge on the first floor. Room 10.'

No, she didn't know his name, just what was on the card. He'd booked the room, seemed a bit of a big spender. Then she hurried off about her duties before they could quiz her further.

The card gave no other identification than Blue Circle International, with a downtown New York address and contact details. On the reverse someone had written in a neat script:

There are things to discuss. Please join me for 3:00 p.m.

Davey and Frank checked their watches, saw that it was five minutes of that.

All of it planned.

But answers. Answers now at least.

They left their table and took the stairs to the first floor, continued along the hallway to the polished mahogany door of Room 10. Davey and Frank exchanged glances, then Frank knocked and they entered.

The spacious room was unoccupied but for a tall man sitting in a leather armchair before the fire. He was their age, late forties, early fifties, and had a full head of greying hair, a neatly trimmed beard. There was a walking stick by his left hand and his suit looked expensive. Two more armchairs were arranged near his, and a small table was set with an ice bucket and a bottle of champagne, three glasses, a modest if ample plate of sandwiches and cakes.

The man turned in his chair, smiled. 'Gentlemen, good afternoon. Excuse me if I don't get up. An old injury.'

'We got your card,' Davey said, settling in one of the armchairs.

'And your plane tickets,' Frank added, taking the other. 'An explanation would be appreciated.'

'Of course, Frank,' the bearded man said. 'And please help yourselves to the sandwiches. Davey, do the honours and pour us each a glass. You've come a long way and we have things to celebrate.'

'We do?' Frank asked, even as Davey twigged to it.

'Riley? It's you!'

'Indeed it is, Davey-boy. Good to see you. You too, Frank. Good of you to come.'

There was a strange silence then, absurd under the circumstances, and Davey eased them through it by opening the bottle, filling the champagne flutes and passing them out.

'Thought we should catch up,' Riley said when they all had glasses. 'Twenty-five years ago today. *Today*, you realise!'

Frank had lost things from his life. He needed to gain control here. 'Riley, none of that was meant to happen.'

'Of course, it wasn't, Frank. We were kids. I was a jerk. But twenty-five years! Different hemisphere, different country but *this* date, and here we are!'

Davey returned the bottle to the ice bucket. It was vintage Krug. 'You seem to have done well.'

'Based in New York now. Married into old money. Spend my time running Blue Circle. Mainly antiquities auctions. One of the top five auction houses on the east coast. Who would've thought? But here's to your health!'

They all drank the toast.

'So why the beat-up, Riley?' Frank said when it was done. 'It's a long way for an anniversary drink. Afraid we wouldn't come?'

Riley set down his glass and laced his fingers. 'Frank, it's more to do with completing an old formula, an old incantation, if you can believe it.'

'An incantation!' Frank was first puzzled, then annoyed. As he'd just told Davey down in the lounge, ever since the lawsuit, ever since Markie died, he'd sworn never to put up with bullshit again.

Riley smiled. 'All right. A protocol, if you prefer. How something has to be done. Davey, you're in the trade. Ever hear of something called the Chinder Commission?'

'The name's familiar. A carousel?'

'Exactly. A menagerie merry-go-round. Charles Carmel worked on it after the fire destroyed his own new carousel in 1911. His was uninsured and he lost nearly everything. But before he died in 1933, he did some work for Horace Chinder.'

Frank set his glass on the table. 'Davey, Riley, how about you talk shop some other time. I want to know why we're here.'

Riley raised a hand in a placating gesture. 'Frank, please. What happened *that* night definitely has a place in this. That jewel you got for Davey.'

Davey was restless too but saw that the best way to get answers was to play it as Riley wanted. He turned to his cousin. 'Frank, the carousel we rode back in 1977 was a Charles Carmel merry-go-round. Brought to Sydney from the US, sold back to a US company after the 1979 Ghost Train fire. We might want to hear this.'

Frank settled back, let Davey top up his glass. 'All right. But make it the five-dollar version, okay?'

Riley grinned. 'The five-dollar version it is. Chinder was a stage magician, grandson and great-grandson in a family of very successful stage magicians. He was into puzzles and tricks, creating mysterious objects and events. A bit like that Kit Williams fellow.'

'Like who?' Frank asked.

'Kit Williams. Back in the 70s he made a hare out of gold, set it with jewels, and buried it in the countryside, then published a picture book with clues to its whereabouts so a lucky treasure hunter could find it. *Masquerade*. Do a net search. Chinder was like that, only he did it with a carousel.'

'Oh, and why is that?'

For all Davey knew Frank might have been trying to behave but his words came over as sarcasm.

Riley seemed not to notice. 'Well, it's a sacred shape, isn't it? The wheel of life. Like the Round Table. No beginning or end. Anyway, you can't stoppeth one of three unless you have three to start with, yes. Just like in '77.'

'That's a Coleridge reference,' Davey said for Frank's benefit, in case his cousin didn't know the allusion. '*The Rime of the Ancient Mariner*.'

'Gee, I was just going to say that,' Frank added. 'Five-dollar version, Riley.'

'Gotcha. But it was Chinder's favourite poem,' Riley continued. 'And his favourite line was the first one: "It is an Ancient Mariner, And he stoppeth one of three." He had it inscribed on the marquee on *Mariners' Round*, the carousel he had made for him, all fancy curlicue so you can barely read it. At least it's supposed to be there, hidden in plain sight. And it's a clue.'

'To what?' Frank asked.

'Exactly, Frank.' It was comical. Riley was ignoring Frank's impatience and irritation, was treating him as if he were a fellow devotee, an interested colleague and ally. 'To what indeed? That's where you can help. I've located the Chinder Carousel. Now it's a matter of solving the clues. All I need is an hour of your time.'

Frank shook his head in amazement. 'That's it? We're here to solve a puzzle?'

Riley remained unshakeably charming and enthusiastic. 'I've done a lot of work already. I'm nearly there. It has to do with the real purpose behind the Chinder Commission. Why these particular mounts. What they were intended to do.'

'To do?'

'To make possible.'

Incredibly, there was another silence then, just the sound of the fire crackling and of traffic out in the street. Quite possibly the champagne and the warmth were having their effect, for when Frank next spoke, it was as if he had worked through the absurdities and the impossibility, had found other things to settle on for a time, other memories, possibly a clearer sense of the reality of this unique moment in their lives. 'Never thought of people having careers carving carousel horses,' was all he said.

Riley seized on the change of mood, handled Frank as he was no doubt handling them both. 'I know. And you can't imagine what a competitive, quirky bunch they were, Frank. One of them, Marcus Illions, had highly trained assistants but insisted on carving every horse head himself. Just the heads, think of it. Solomon Stein and Harry Goldstein turned out really quite frightening mounts with big heads and large teeth, quite ferocious-looking, like they were deliberately trying to frighten the children they were meant to attract. But most manufacturers just did the frames and hired carvers to provide what was needed. That one we rode as kids was a real beauty. Bit of a hybrid, not quite the usual Carmel menagerie. Mostly horses but there was a lion, a griffin and two chariots for variety.'

'We remember,' Frank said, the edginess returning.

Riley picked up his glass of Krug, though barely drank. 'Right. How can we forget? Something else was there to 'stoppeth one of three' that night.'

'Riley, we were kids,' Davey reminded him in case it was needed. 'Let it go.'

'Hey, they saved the leg. I've done well.' Riley became thoughtful again. 'But it's strange, Davey. You seem to know Carmel's work, but nothing about the Commission.'

'Just heard the name somewhere.'

'Right. But you probably know that when the fire destroyed his own carousel, Carmel was a broken man. He had to take whatever work he could get. I'm not saying it was arson, but suddenly Chinder comes along wanting a special menagerie unlike any Carmel had worked on before.'

'All conveniently omitted from the biographies,' Davey said. 'I get piecework, diabetes, worsening arthritis, dead of cancer in his mid-sixties.'

'Strict secrecy was part of the brief. Carmel went to a dockside location in Brooklyn, used only the most trusted assistants. We know so little about it, just that it had a nautical theme and took two years to complete. Chinder was very specific about what had to be included. He also provided the materials. Can you guess what they were?'

'Just tell us,' Frank said.

'The timbers from wrecked sailing ships, Frank. Every single sea-mount for the Chinder Commission was made from the bulwarks and ribbing of old trading ships, from wrecks washed ashore, buried or never appraised properly. Timbers from storm-damaged vessels or hulks turned in for salvage.'

Frank had reached his patience limit again. 'Great. So how does the jewel fit in?'

'Precisely the right word, Frank. Fit. Something being fitted. And since it has to do with the three of us, *re-fitted*. All three involved, like in the poem.'

It wasn't what Coleridge had meant at all, Davey wanted to

remind him, but he was looking out for Frank. '*One* of three, that poem says, Riley. Every three people, the Mariner would stop one to tell his story to.'

'Right, Davey-boy. A bit melodramatic pushing the image, I know, but circumstances make it relevant. You wanted the jewel back then. Frank took it. I ended up with it. Only fitting, don't you think?'

Ended up with it! was Davey's immediate thought, but his cousin spoke first.

'You threw it away!' Frank's words were too loud in the otherwise empty room.

Riley's eyes flashed in the firelight. 'Did I now?' He gave a strange, somehow nasty, possibly exulting grin; Davey wasn't sure how to read it. 'Time to put this on again, I think.'

He took a silver ring from his jacket pocket and slipped it onto his right ring finger. It was handsome but too large, too overdone. And set into the crown was the blue glass jewel pried loose all those years ago.

Davey sat stunned. Blue Circle International. That name, of course. 'But how—?'

'You bastard, Trencher,' Frank muttered, even as Riley answered.

'I palmed it! What did you think I did?'

Davey and Frank glanced at each other. The implications spun out before them.

'Riley . . .' Davey began. *He never got to tell them he had it! It happened so quickly. Too quickly. All the violence for nothing!*

'You two nearly ruined my life,' Riley continued. 'For a while I even got to thinking that maybe I should ruin yours a bit.'

'Say again?' Frank demanded.

'What's that?' Davey said.

But Riley had regained whatever composure the rush of feeling had brought undone. He reached down and laid a hand on his walking stick, then regarded the cousins again. 'Still, that was then. This afternoon I have something important to show you.'

Frank was leaning forward, hands on his knees. 'Finish what you were saying!'

'Frank, bear with me a bit longer, please. You've come a long way.

The Blue Circle offices are in New York. You should be asking yourselves why here. Why Dublin?'

'The carousel's here,' Davey said, before Frank could speak.

'Right on, Davey-boy! So think back to that night. Those horses had names. What was the one you rode? The one Frank took the jewel from? Do you remember?'

How could Davey forget? '*Lysander.*'

Now it was Riley whose face showed surprise, more than that: astonish-ment. He went very still, not blinking for ten, twenty, thirty seconds. Then he reached up and stroked his beard with one hand, almost absent-mindedly. He probably didn't know he was doing it.

'Riley, what?' Davey asked.

'*Lysander,*' Riley said at last. His manner had changed. He was still distracted, but now seemed shrewd and calculating as well.

'Yes, so?'

Riley brought his attention back to the cousins. 'Part of what got me into this. The auctions, maritime archaeology, all of it. There was a 17th Century spice trader with that name. Ninety-eight footer. Three masts. Went missing at sea in 1704 by all reports.' He took out a pen and notebook. 'Davey, how is that spelt, please?'

He wrote the name as Davey spelled it, then, saying 'Excuse me a moment,' took out his mobile and called a pre-set number. 'Beverley, I have the name. It's *Lysander.* Spelled L-Y-S-A-N-D-E-R. Within half an hour please.' He broke the connection.

Frank was still sitting forward as if preparing to leave. 'Riley, something important to show us, you were saying. I assume it's this carousel.'

'Gents, just one more hour, that's all I ask.' Riley was not only back in control but seemed to have reconsidered how much he would reveal. 'Davey, it may help to see it as Chinder must have. He pondered the old questions. What is the role of magic in a life? Not necessarily *real* magic, *working* magic, as they say, but our relationship to magic as an idea, a constant, something wished for.'

'Magic?' Davey was thrown by the sudden change of topic, then realised that the coincidence with the names had changed everything, saw too that Riley was probably working to a schedule, filling time.

'I know. Crazy stuff. But as a historical, cultural, personal thing we keep yearning for, keep returning to. The *possibility* of it.'

Frank made a disgusted sound. 'Riley, what *are* you going on about? Real magic! Working magic! What is all this?'

But Davey raised a hand this time, urging patience. 'You're saying Chinder sought more than just the conceptual kind?'

'Davey, he did. We're talking *real* magic here, I promise you. The real deal.' He turned back to Frank. 'Chinder made his career exploiting the other kind, Frank, the conceptual kind, pandering to our yearnings, manipulating our need to believe. He was an entertainer, but his papers show he actually did believe in working magic as well. He spent much of his life finding ways to use it.'

Frank breathed out heavily. 'Oh, for Pete's sake!'

But he too saw the glint in Riley's eyes, no doubt grasped that it *was* quite likely from exultation at a quest nearly completed, something about to reach its end.

'The Chinder Commission was the culmination of his efforts,' Riley said. 'Some ancient cabbalistic, shamanistic way of reaching his goal.'

Davey had to ask it. 'Which was?'

'Why, finding the heart's desire, of course. Nothing less. That's how his papers put it.'

'Which for him was what?'

Riley shrugged. 'Chinder doesn't say. And if I'm right, he never completed the process. But that's what it was. Finding his heart's desire.'

Frank shook his head in disbelief. 'Which for you would be locating this old ship. Using the bloke's carousel.'

'An indulgence, Frank. We all have them.'

Though much more than that, Davey knew, fascinated in spite of himself. After the long flight, after winning the prize that wasn't a prize, the shock of meeting first Frank and now Riley again, this was something familiar, something to anchor him. 'Riley, the Commission was never displayed. Never seen.'

'Right. It was packed up and shipped. Even Carmel never saw it re-assembled.'

'But you've located it.'

'Davey, I have. It's out in the docklands, and I've bought it. Humour me, please. Come and see it now is all I ask. Then you can both go on your way. Enjoy your holiday.'

Frank stood, stepped away from his armchair. 'Riley, I've heard enough!'

'Frank, one thing for old time's sake, please! All I ask. Just ten minutes from here.'

Frank looked down at his one-time friend. 'Oh, Jesus! For old time's sake then.'

The afternoon outside was bleak and wintry and Davey wasn't surprised to see a hire car waiting for them at the curb. They climbed in and were driven, mostly in silence, through late afternoon traffic out to a dockland, warehouse district, finally pulled over near a large brick building beside a chainlink fence.

Davey could easily imagine a menagerie being hidden away in such a structure, but the building itself wasn't to be their destination. When they were standing in the road and the hire car had driven off, Riley used a key to unlock a gate in the fence, then led them down a pass-through by a construction yard to a high fenced enclosure of a more traditional kind, a barricade of old wooden palings, sturdy and close-fitting. All about them could be heard the sounds of the Liffey.

Riley unlocked a gate in that fence as well and held it open while they all stepped through. The cousins found themselves in a large dim precinct formed by paling fences on all sides, even facing the river so there was no view at all, just the sounds of gulls, with the smell of estuarine mudflats strong on the breeze.

At first, Davey wasn't certain what he was seeing; then, as his eyes adjusted in the last light of day, he saw that it was indeed a derelict carousel. *Mariners' Round*, the faded letters on the canopy said. And, sure enough, all the worn and time-damaged mounts he could make out were things of the deep, lunging, looming, crowding over each other.

Some were based on real animals: sharks with gaping mouths, dolphins in mid-leap, whales sounding, spouting, a great squid with out-thrust tentacles, a brace of seahorses side by side, the impressive spiral of a nautilus. But others were fanciful, wonderfully, disturbingly strange: a wild-eyed kraken, a sea-serpent with a tabard of old mirrors scrolling down its chest, half-human tritons and mermaids, all with heads that seemed larger than life, more in the style of Stein and Goldstein than Carmel, with bared teeth, rolling eyes, a manic, frantic, restless quality, like gasping things dragged from the depths before their time and against their wills.

Davey couldn't help but be impressed. It did indeed seem to be the Chinder Carousel, Riley's lost Carmel merry-go-round, seized, landed and trapped here in this sad enclosure beside the Liffey.

'Not as derelict as it looks,' Riley assured them. 'There's a new electric motor installed, though the musical accompaniment will be turned right down this evening. Mustn't draw too much attention. But it'll work well enough for a little ride.'

Frank wasn't having any of it. 'And why would we want to do that?'

'Frank, please. Choose a mount and take the one ride. Just one.'

'Riley, what's to be gained?' Davey asked. 'Why does it matter so much?'

'This jewel.' He raised his ring. 'It was never meant to go to the carousel we rode in Sydney that night. Bet you never knew that, Davey. It was meant for *this* special hybrid, the Commission. There was a mix-up. Just the one jewel and it all went wrong for Chinder. Maybe a mischievous assistant palmed it, passed it on.' Riley's grin was fierce. 'Maybe it was an honest mistake. Maybe the carousel itself wasn't ready. But that's why it never worked as far as we can know. Never fulfilled its function.'

'Delivering the heart's desire,' Davey said, echoing Riley's words from the hotel, even as his mind locked on what else Riley had just now said.

Maybe the carousel itself wasn't ready!

'The heart's desire,' Riley continued. 'Something like that. But *we* found the jewel that night. I palmed it, had it in my pocket at the accident. And there was blood. It was blooded. Maybe that's it, you tell me. But the three of us were involved then; it seems right that all three have to be involved now. Chinder's papers put it like that: "All that is intended," the line goes. Well, all this was intended—*is* intended, as I see it! What we did then means it should be that way now. I'd already been tinkering with your lives a bit, getting even for what happened.'

There it was again, the hint of threat and reprisal. Frank seized on it. 'Wait! Wait! What's that supposed to mean?'

And again Riley ignored the question. 'Last year I finally located the carousel here, arranged to buy it.'

'Wait up, Riley!' Frank's eyes flashed with anger. This wasn't a hotel lounge with torpor brought on by alcohol and a cosy fireside. This was a chill, naked evening with a fine drizzle beginning to fall. 'What do you mean "tinkering with our lives a bit"?'

'Then I brought you all this way. Now we take the ride, restore the jewel one way rather than another and it's done. You can go.'

'Go fuck yourself, Trencher!' Frank said. 'What sort of tinkering?'

All through Frank's outburst, Riley seemed patient, even unnaturally calm, but Davey sensed the old Riley Trencher danger waiting there. 'Forget it, Riley,' he said, more gently than he felt. 'We've seen enough.'

Riley gave a strange smile. 'Gents, you don't understand. I have more fun and games planned if you don't co-operate. Frank, right now Marguerite is at Calloway Point with your daughter and your parents, yes? Davey, your parents are still living in Chatswood. There are things in place. I need only say the word. I think one quick ride will be worth all the incon-venience. So, please, choose a mount, finish what we started. What Chinder started.'

He left a silence then, rather something of one for it was filled with the soughing of wind about the transoms and the canopy, getting in between the palings of the enclosure. Time seemed distended, every second stretched, laden. Davey and Frank stood in the growing gloom numb with loss and grief all over again, feeling the helplessness, the rage and fury, the old embers smouldering now, re-kindled.

For the first time, Davey saw his life as something *deliberately* spoiled. Not just the hoax but—hell and Jesus, no!—the accident! Annie! Other things that had been at least bearable as part of the burden of hazard in any life. But no longer. No longer.

Frank had to be feeling the same: seeing Markie's death anew, the malpractice suit, losing Marguerite. What else had *she* been told in the careful, spiteful workings of Riley Trencher's plan?

And Riley read that moment for precisely what it was, knew where it had to lead. He reached inside his jacket, produced a handgun and aimed it their way.

'Think carefully about what you do now, gents. My associates are close by. Refuse to take the ride and you'll be shot. You'll be strapped to a mount. We'll take the ride anyway. You don't have to be alive for it. Inside or out, the blood is still there. All that is intended.'

'You killed my son,' Frank said in a whisper, a ghost's voice drawn thin.

Riley just tilted his head in a way that might have said: *Collateral damage, Frank. I merely requested a house fire.*

Davey couldn't speak at all. The thought of Annie's death, of Riley's abiding hatred, that order of single-mindedness, brought the familiar weight, the exhaustion.

Only the search for this old carousel had stayed his hand, Davey realised, had brought this respite, this interlude, this whole parody of charm and civility. There'd be no going their own way once this was done, he was sure of it.

And dying here wouldn't just end his own life, Davey saw, that was the thing. It would end Annie as well somehow, the chance to keep her in the world in some way, *any* way. Just as Frank surviving, continuing, kept Markie's memory as something at least. We end, those things end. More forgotten things, the world moving on.

The bleakness of the thought, the hour, this cold, too early evening hour, made it possible. Why not take the ride? Move it along. Bring more hazard to the mix. Why not?

He moved towards the carousel. As if on cue, three proximity floods switched on, ghost-lighting the whole macabre display. Now glass eyes glittered in the time-struck faces, teeth gnashed, flashed off-white and worn silver, tongues lolled, mouths silently screamed. Old mirrors gave the barest glints and gleams, ancient brightwork showed in swatches, snatches, hints of fraught primary colours that had not been visible before.

Davey didn't dare stop. The great squid impaled on its brass pole rolled a baleful eye, watched him approach, move past. Three mermaids offered scarred breasts, mouths flecked with old enamel.

Mount us! Mount us! Ride!

Sirens heaved, rolled, lolled in their meagre twists of surf.

No fish tails here, fancy-boy! Press close. We can be Annie! Annie!

Davey saw them through tears: flaunting, writhing, limbering.

Tritons glared, daring, warning off. One lunged—no, no it was Frank, Frank there with him now, circling the zodiac too, this wheel of lost and forsaken things.

'Davey—' his cousin began to say.

'Just do it!' Davey said with a voice, a forthrightness neither Davey nor Frank had ever heard from him before. 'Move it along!'

'But we have to—'

'Frank, he has others with him. We've no choice.'

'We don't know that! We don't know that at all!'

'Doesn't matter which ones we choose. Just pick one near mine, okay? Stay close!'

'Davey, we have to—'

'Frank, there's been enough harm. Let it go! Get through this.'

And Frank did let it go then, like a balloon deflating, emptying, moved with Davey around this ancient wheel sea-changed—no, land-changed—into a base pathetic thing. Only one mount had a legible name-plate, a *new* plate newly fitted, *Lysander*. Riley's mount this time, not his. Not now. Never his now.

Davey moved clear of it, well beyond, climbed atop a leaping dolphin on the outermost ring, one that looked less manic and blighted than the rest. Frank took the wild-eyed shark next in the row, climbed up and settled, gripped the pole.

Riley must have already been in place back there behind them for the platform began creaking, heaving, easing forward like a tide on the turn, moving faster and faster, girding itself like a king tsunami reaching to take on the world.

The music would be playing, that was part of the equation too, but was turned right down as Riley had said it would be. There was just the creaking, the straining, the flapping of the old torn canopy, just the on-shore breeze, laving, pushing, growing stronger, smelling of tidal flats, sea-wrack and early rain. So, too, set running out there was the turn, turn of the city lights a way off, and more lights from the river, scant, precious, locked in time, those things shifting to a blur as the great wheel gained speed, completing itself by the act of moving forward: animals, grotesques and halflings thrown, lunging, plunging into flickering night, snatching the life of the flow, wheeling, rushing, flinging into time and chance, purest hazard.

And caught in the sweep, that relentless rush, Davey almost saw it happen!

He came back to it, to everything, with a song, to words that went like this—

> *Hoist away and make some sail,*
> *We'll have a toast for England.*
> *Tomorrow we're away to Spain or off to Araby.*
> *A man has many chains on shore*
> *But Davy Jones has many more.*
> *He has no home, his wits are foam,*
> *He cannot leave the sea.*

—found himself in a corner of the Trebarin in Dublin on a wintry Saturday afternoon, woke to an old sea-shanty being sung as a round—a round, yes!—by two, three dozen men and women who were laughing, many with arms linked, raucously singing their parts. The pretty woman he'd seen before was still among them,

smiling at him, coaxing, inviting, daring—he couldn't be wrong!—
so clear now through the refrain.

Mariners' *Round*. Of course. Davey spared a thought for Frank
and, unexpectedly, for Riley Trencher, wondering what had befallen
them in this astonishing sleight-of-hand, sleight-of-mind, sleight-
of-time.

Because look where he was! Just look! And look at what he had!
Davey laughed, found his feet, and went to join the chorus.

F rank Coombs woke under the trees in the sea-meadow above
Calloway Point, looking out across the headland to the
sparkling Pacific. When he heard laughter, the sound of children
singing, he leant up on his elbows like some hayseed farm-boy, saw
the old farmhouse under its sheltering Moreton Bay figs. Before it
there were adults dancing in a circle with ten, eleven children—a
reel it was—while other parents and friends watched, smiling,
singing along, clapping in time.

A round, Frank realised. It's a celebration, probably a birthday,
and they're dancing a round!

'Come on, Frank!' one of the spectators called, leaving the group,
approaching. It was Marguerite, worn, dishevelled from the
festivities and another handful of years, but Marguerite! 'You took
the trouble to come,' she said. 'Least you can do is join in. Unless
you're too old for it!'

'As if!' Frank cried.

For he wasn't. You never were. While you lived, you did what you
could.

Frank laughed. There was no Markie, no, that lasting bruise on
the perfect day, but there was this and, surprisingly, it was enough.
He scrambled to his feet and went to join in, wanted Marguerite to
see him doing that. Just that.

A nd Riley Trencher? Why, Riley found himself on the ship of his
dreams, of course, on the deck of the late 17th Century spice

trader *Lysander* circling, endlessly circling, on the inner slope of a mighty maelstrom, a vast yawning gulf in the sea, at least two thousand metres across, five hundred deep, turning, roaring under a wild, leaden sky.

The decks were canted at an alarming forty degrees above that terrible drop, but a crewman used sea-lines to haul himself along the upper rail, finally arrived drenched by rain and spray. He wore the foul-weather oilskins of an older time.

'You made it!' he shouted above the roar of the vortex. 'They said you would! You've got the ring?'

'What?' Riley could barely hear his own voice. The roar numbed every-thing. 'What's that?'

'The ring, man! You've got the bloody ring?'

And when Riley raised his hand to show it, the man nodded, actually managed a ragged grin.

'Thank God! We can end this!'

'End what?' Riley asked, but knew, knew, even as the seaman gestured out at the gloom, the churning murk below.

All that is intended.

And after so many, too many, wasting, wearying years, the old ship leant harder into the wind, doors to crew quarters blew open, maps flew from the captain's cabin like doves, the twin mirrors of a sextant floated in a half-silvered sky, and *Lysander* began its final descent.

TERRY DOWLING *(b. Sydney, New South Wales, Australia, 1947) has been called 'Australia's finest writer of horror' by Locus magazine, and "Australia's premier writer of dark fantasy" by All Hallows. As well as being author of the internationally acclaimed Tom Rynosseros science fantasy saga, his U.S. retrospective* Basic Black: Tales of Appropriate Fear *won the 2007 International Horror Guild Award for Best Collection and earned him a starred review in* Publishers Weekly. *Terry's stories have appeared in*

The Year's Best Science Fiction, The Year's Best SF, The Year's Best Fantasy, The Best New Horror, *and many times in* The Year's Best Fantasy and Horror, *including anthologies as diverse as* Dreaming Down Under, Wizards, The Dark, Inferno, Songs of the Dying Earth, Ghosts by Gaslight *and the previous three* Exotic Gothic *volumes (from which he reads "Jarkman at the Othergates" hauntingly at http://faculty.lonestar.edu/dolson/podcasts.html). His most recent collection is* Amberjack: Tales of Fear and Wonder *(another starred review in PW) while London's Guardian newspaper said of his debut novel* Clowns at Midnight*: 'this exceptional work bears comparison to John Fowles's* The Magus.*' His website is www.terrydowling.com.*

Commentary on "Mariners' Round": *Untangling the threads of inspiration for the story, there are four definite elements at play: most recently the maelstrom at the end of* Pirates of the Caribbean 2 *(leading me back to the one that swallowed the Pequod in the 1956 film* Moby Dick*) that gave the story's final image, next the story's title and how it might be resolved in three different ways in the lives of three different people. Those touchstones led inevitably to a lifelong determination to set a story around the wonderful Charles Carmel carousel that once held pride-of-place in Sydney's Luna Park. Imagine (TD thought to himself, title in hand, maelstrom in mind) a lost Charles Carmel merry-go-round! What might it have been like? Why was it lost? What might it have been for? But behind that, behind everything else, crucially, there was the blue glass jewel that a thoughtless but incurably romantic teenager once pried from the back of his genuine Charles Carmel carousel mount. This tale is both to honour Mr Carmel and perhaps stand as a small act of restitution between us.*

OSCHAERT

PAUL FINCH

T HE SKY WAS LEAD GREY. STEADY RAIN WAS FALLING AND, though it was only September, the air was cool and rank with autumnal decay. On the first cockcrow, the barrack yard was empty. By the third, it was stirring to life. The execution detail filed out from the blockhouse and took their place on the concrete parade area. There were ten of them, clad as though for the front line in helmets and waterproof capes. Six Lee Enfield rifles were waiting for them in two stacks of three, alongside a stretcher with a canvas sheet folded on it.

Each man who'd been assigned to shoot picked up a weapon and checked that its single round was chambered. None of them knew which one contained the blank round. None of them wanted to know. The four men assigned as stretcher-bearers fell in behind, more thankful than they could say that the lots they had drawn during the long torturous night had been the lucky ones.

CSM Hall perambulated into view, splashing through the puddles and calling the squad to attention. Lieutenant Cavendish also arrived, his swagger stick tight in his gloved hand, his Webley revolver holstered at his hip. Last of all came the medical officer and the Adjutant's Provost, a staff-colonel to oversee. He was a thin, elderly man, huddled inside his greatcoat and looking groggy at having risen so early. The crimson band around his hat was the only bright speck in an otherwise colourless scene. None of them even looked at the heavy wooden post cemented in place twenty yards away, or the wall behind it, concealed by a great mound of sandbags.

Cavendish nodded to the CSM, who gave a bawling shout. The door to the guard-hut opened, and two military policemen emerged with Private Longshaw between them. The chaplain, his clerical collar incongruous over the top of his olive green tunic, tailed behind, reading from the *Psalms*.

Cavendish glanced at the firing squad, now formed in a rank, their rifles dressed down. They each knew Longshaw personally. They had been purposely selected from his own battalion, which the previous afternoon had been forced to stand in stoic parade while the unfortunate man was ordered to fall out and hear his death sentence pronounced. Supposedly, firing squad duty was a reward for those men whose life had been imperilled by the cowardice of a colleague, but Cavendish knew that in reality it was a warning to them: desertion in face of the enemy would mean that the next gun-barrel they stared down would be wielded by a friend. It was now two years into the war, and there was increasing resentment among the rank and file of the British Army, firstly that such severe punishments were being inflicted at all on men whose nerves had been shattered, and secondly, that they themselves were the executioners. On this occasion, the Provost had been concerned that members of the squad might deliberately shoot wide, and issued a stern warning that if any man failed to do his duty it would be deemed mutiny.

It was well known that Longshaw had shown great courage during the first and second days of the Somme advance. With men falling around him like wheat to the scythe, he'd crawled on his belly through a mire of blood and debris, to personally cut lines of wire that the artillery had failed to blast away. He'd detected landmines and guided other lads around them. He'd even tackled a German pill-box, lobbing a Mills bomb through the aperture, and bayoneting the surviving machine-gun crew when they emerged. It had only been weeks later, still under relentless fire, when his nerves had begun to fray and he'd finally been caught hiding at the rear in a derelict farmhouse.

Even now, in his shirtsleeves and braces, he was an impressive figure of a man. Twenty-five years old, tall, slim at the waist and broad at the shoulder, with a lean, handsome face and a shock of sandy hair, he walked to the execution post bravely and steadily, apparently having refused to take a single drop from the bottle of whiskey they'd sent him the night before. He stood erect and unaided while the military policemen bound him in place. He didn't flinch when they pinned the white paper target over his heart. When they offered him a blindfold, he shook his head firmly.

It was strange—not to say alarming, Cavendish reflected—how many men who'd been accused of cowardice were prepared to look their killers right in the eye just as the triggers were being pulled. For his own part, he had little real sympathy for those condemned as cowards. He'd only been drafted in from HQ and attached to this company in the last month of the Somme campaign, but he understood the sacrifices so many men were making. It simply wasn't possible to send some to certain death, and allow others to malinger behind the lines.

Sensing that everything was ready, he stepped forward and raised his handkerchief.

'Aim,' the CSM said quietly.

Six rifles came up in unison.

Just before Cavendish dropped his handkerchief, the howling began.

It was the eeriest thing—a low, mournful ululation, the sound a dog might make in the extremes of sorrow, and yet somehow 'false', as if it wasn't a dog that was making it. Cavendish gazed curiously at the prisoner. Longshaw's mouth was clamped shut, his face running with rainwater as he stared defiantly at his executioners. Cavendish glanced further afield, unable to tell where exactly the sound was coming from. Only when he caught CSM Hall watching him, one eyebrow raised quizzically, did he remember where he was—and drop the handkerchief.

The rifles reported with an echoing *crack*, which resounded around the barrack yard.

The howling continued. Cavendish looked the squad over, wondering if one of them was reacting badly to the pressure. But they'd now dressed their weapons down, and were awaiting their next order, water dripping from the rims of their helmets. From their steely expressions, they weren't even hearing the curious dirge. Again having to force himself to remember where he was, Cavendish turned to face the prisoner, who was slumped against the post, his head hanging down. Only his bonds were holding him upright. His shirt and the chest beneath had been rent apart; the sandbags behind him were patterned with blood. But the medical officer, who'd already performed his customary check, had now stepped aside and, when he and Cavendish's eyes met, he shook his head gravely.

Still unsettled by the howling, Cavendish strode forward, drawing his Webley. He barely noticed that the claret-coloured pool spreading around Longshaw's feet was now swimming around his own. Or that Longshaw, despite injuries so horrific that his shattered ribs and shredded inner organs were visible, was still twitching in his ropes. Only when Cavendish placed the muzzle of his pistol to the prisoner's left temple did the howling suddenly, very abruptly, cease.

Cavendish nodded, as if that was how it should be. When he pulled the trigger, it was the loudest noise he'd ever heard.

Cavendish's eyes snapped open.

He was in his private room, which was filled with the dim, milky light of a March dawn. The coverlet was drawn under his chin. Just below his feet, his dressing-gown was folded over the iron bedstead. Across the room, the wardrobe door was closed; inside it, everything would be in regulation order. The only other item was a chest of drawers.

Cavendish climbed stiffly from the bed. The bare tiles of the floor were ice-cold, so he cast around for his slippers. He'd known worse billets than this, but had he even had an inkling how ascetic the lifestyle of the Sisters of St. Francis, he might have resisted being brought here to their convent at Adinkerke. He shrugged his dressing-gown on, tied its cord and moved to the window, the pane of which he slid aside in its squeaky frame. Beyond the shutters, a grey mist oozed through the trees of the convent grounds.

But that didn't conceal the strange, bent figure lurching out of sight around the corner of the building.

Cavendish remained at the window for several moments, staring after it.

Whatever he thought he'd seen, it hadn't looked fully human. It had been hunched and stunted; it capered rather than walked as if it trotted on paws. In normal times the sight of such a thing would have worried him greatly, but not now—when he'd seen it so often before.

Breakfast was the usual desultory affair, most of the chaps loafing around in dressing-gowns, some sitting very still as they ate, others needing to be helped to the tables by the sisters, who spoke quietly and encouragingly to them. Beyond the serving hatch, a porter was bringing in a barrow-load of potatoes. Unintentionally, he swung the outer door closed. It echoed through the building like a gunshot, and sent several men under the tables. Cavendish himself closed his eyes, a spoonful of lukewarm porridge half way to his lips.

When he opened them again, he saw Sister Valentina emerging from the conservatory, where she'd no doubt eased someone down into an armchair, and provided him with an army newspaper. She smiled at Cavendish. She was a slim, elfin creature, with an ethereal beauty somehow enhanced by her religious garb; the distinctive blue habit and scapular, with its gray tabard and gray wimple and veil.

Unlike the Nuns of St. Francis, an enclosed order whose house was located thirty miles up the Belgian coast, the Sisters of St. Francis had an active apostolate to work in the local community, the majority of them fully trained nurses. A significant number had even qualified in the new psychotherapeutic methods. As such, when Adinkerke had been assigned as a casualty clearing station a couple of years ago, the convent here had become an obvious focal point of care for patients whose minds had been damaged as well as their bodies.

By late 1917, after the catastrophic clashes at Arras and Ypres, with rivers of maimed and wounded flowing back from the front, and hospital beds in too short supply—especially close to the lines, where regulations stipulated the shell-shocked must be treated— the sisters had graciously accepted quarters with local people, and handed their convent over to the British Army's Medical Corps, so that it might be utilised full-time as a sanatorium. They would continue to lend their own expertise free-of-charge, on a twenty-four hour basis.

Of course, there were still many in the high command who regarded the notion of nervous disease as a sham, an excuse not to fight. Thus, by early 1918, decisions had been taken to keep as many 'emotional cases' as possible with their units, so that they never grew unused to the sound of the guns and could, with a few wise words of encouragement, be rotated back into action at the first opportunity. Only those very severe cases were to be confined in special neurological centres.

'I'm not overly fond of officers,' Cavendish told Doctor Mulroony.

Doctor Mulroony watched with interest across his desk. In comparison to Cavendish, who was tall and thin, with dark hair and a dark, clipped moustache, Mulroony was short, squat and red-headed, with eyes like blue buttons behind his pince-nez. 'But *you're* an officer, Lieutenant Cavendish.'

'When I think of officers, I think of men who are upright and honest. Defiant in defeat, magnanimous in victory.'

'Surely these criteria have been evident all along the Front?'

'They have. I'm surrounded all the time by reminders of what I ought to be.'

'So they don't apply to you?'

Cavendish pondered. The office was more luxurious than any other room in the building. It had been bare when it had housed the mother-superior. But now shelves of leather-bound medical tomes lined its walls. Mulroony had even had two armchairs brought in, one placed to either side of the grate, where a small fire crackled. His Dachshund, Wilhelm, was curled like a fat German sausage in front of it.

'If I were to rank my own performance in this war,' Cavendish said. 'It would be one out of ten.'

'Why would that be? Because your company was destroyed, but you survived?'

'No.'

'Did you run away?'

'No.' Cavendish remained blank-faced, as if this question was completely irrelevant. 'But I only survived because I was fortunate.'

'It has occurred to you, lieutenant, that any soldier who survives this war will have been fortunate?' Mulroony took a wedge of tobacco from the pocket of his white coat and thumbed it into his pipe. He applied a match. 'You're thinking about Private Longshaw again?'

'I think about him all the time.'

'And the dog?'

'You mean the "dog-thing"?'

'Oh yes . . . the dog-thing. Because it isn't quite a dog, is it?'

'No, it's something worse.'

'There are many worse things than dogs. Lions, tigers, leopards. . . '

'And dog-*things*.'

'Yes, dog-things. Whatever that actually means.' Mulroony puffed out fragrant Amphora clouds with an underscent of citrus. 'Where was it this time?'

'Outside the window here.'

'I see. So it's coming closer?'

'I even *saw* it.'

'You've seen it before.'

'I *imagined* I saw it before. I saw it for real this time.'

'This is the dog-thing that was howling during Longshaw's execution?'

Cavendish pursed his lips. 'There's a problem here, which I won't deny. I genuinely don't know whether it was howling then, or not. I didn't speak to anyone about it—I hardly dared, but no-one reacted as if they could hear it.'

Mulroony's Delft blue eyes twinkled. 'And what does that tell you, lieutenant?'

'I was *not* dreaming in the middle of an execution?'

'You didn't have to be dreaming then . . . just since. When you have a nightmare about the execution, you dream about the dog-thing also. It's a dream within a dream.'

Cavendish looked thoughtful.

'Isn't it about time we talked about the thing that's really bothering you?' Mulroony said.

'It's only the dog-thing.'

'I think not, lieutenant. As long as you've been in my care, you've failed to mention—unless prompted rather sharply—the events of last year's September advance.'

'Those events are well documented.'

'But you never talk about your *personal* experience. Is that because you can't remember it?'

'No . . . I remember it.' Cavendish smiled at the idea that he might have forgotten.

He remembered the green farmland transformed to a sea of filth, of mud, blood, and the torn, poisoned flesh of innumerable puffed corpses.

Remembered the front line, that 'suicide ditch' of slit-trenches, sand-bagged bastions and low wooden bunkers, all ankle-deep in mud and manure, rat-infested, swarming with bluebottles and lice, threatening always with trench fever and influenza.

Remembered the bombardment of the German forward positions, heavy and medium-range artillery pouring the most exhausting, intensive fire into them: one cataclysmic explosion after another rending their fortifications, blood-red dawns lighting the night sky, fire and muck erupting all along the Front, leaving an unrecognisable moonscape, a trackless waste of craters and mountainous rubble, as though the very guts of the earth had been strewn higgledy-piggledy across the battlefield.

Remembered the advance. The eerie silence after the artillery ceased, his ears still ringing with the roars that had pummeled them for days. And then 'zero-hour', as Captain Frederickson drew his pistol and blew his whistle. Unlike the advance across the Somme, there'd been no idle chatter this time, no absurd confidence that everything was going to be all right. They scrambled up the firing-steps hurriedly. There was no orderly formation of companies on the top. They'd seen the result of that little farce. It was every man for himself, surging headlong, bayonets to the fore, even though No Man's Land was drifting in smoke and rank with the sulfurous fumes of cordite, meaning there was no visual sign of the enemy—at least, not for about twenty seconds, at which point Mauser rifles and *Maschinengewehrs* fired. One minute the quiet was broken only by the cursing and grunting of the men, the rattle of their harness, the crunch of their boots; the next, a howling hurricane of lead was ripping through them.

It was less easy to remember the exact details of what followed after that.

As always, no matter how many times they'd been subjected to this, the men were initially too stunned to react. Cavendish recalled seeing a couple of lads, one to either side of him, drop like pieces of wood, dead before they hit the ground. They were the lucky ones. That was the only way to view it with the advantage of hindsight.

Captain Frederickson dropped right in front of Cavendish, shot through the heart. To the other side, Private Kelly lay groveling, scooping up handfuls of his own intestines and trying to shovel them back into his ruptured belly. Corporal Lampwick was hit in both thighs, the limbs breaking and pitching him down, where he squealed like a castrated boar.

When the German field-artillery struck, bodies of men, both dead and alive, were blown around like straw. Those who survived stooped or crawled, so blackened with dirt and smoke that they were indistinguishable from corpses. The Bosch didn't worry about that. Their relentless fire swept back and forth, riddling the dead and wounded over and over.

When Cavendish reached the wire, he found it was far deeper

and denser than expected, and quickly became enmeshed. He sank to his knees through exhaustion, his hands slashed to ribbons, his uniform stained head to foot in mud and gore as debris rained over him, as bullets whistled past, whining like wasps. One glanced the side of his helmet, knocking it clean off.

He heard CSM Hall shouting. Looking round, he saw that Hall too was caught on the fencing. He was bellowing, his eyes bulging, demanding that Cavendish do something—*anything*, to get what was left of them out of there. Then Hall was also killed. Before Cavendish could reply to him, a piece of shrapnel hit him in the throat like a guillotine-blade, shearing his head from his shoulders . . .

C avendish remembered the events blurred, as if witnessing them on faulty film.

Knives and cudgels, bayonets used like spear-points. Boots stamping, kicking, hacking blows exchanged. Dirt and sweat flying; shouts and curses. A German grenadier came at him with a rifle-butt and was shot in the face. Another wrapped a brawny arm around his throat. Cavendish thrust his revolver past my hip and fired. The German reeled away, clutching a belly-wound. Cavendish put the next bullet through his neck.

'By my approximation,' Cavendish later told Mulroony, 'the last German to enter our position died two minutes after the first one. That was how quick it all was, though it didn't seem like it at the time. I managed to get hold of the Lewis-gun right at the end, and trained it on their support companies. Knocked them down like skittles.'

He blew a long stream of cigarette smoke.

'How did it make you feel?' Mulroony asked.

'Euphoric . . . for a minute. We'd beaten them off, hadn't we? For one more day, we were victorious. Or so I thought.' Cavendish smiled, and, to the doctor's consternation, it was a cold, cruel smile. 'It was part of my job to keep the men's spirits raised. Even up to your bollocks in mud and blood, you'd be surprised what a rousing speech can do. Except where the dead are concerned, of course. Even Henry V would have had trouble motivating the dead.'

'You're men were dead?'

'All of them. I actually started congratulating them . . . and then it struck me that I was the only one left.' He lapsed into silence.

Mulroony puffed Red Amphora a while, before asking: 'How about if I assigned you to gardening duty this afternoon?'

'I would refuse. . . with due respect to your rank, major.'

'You still can't go outdoors? Yet you've just given me a detailed account of the Passchendaele advance, without a hint of distress.'

'I've already explained . . . it's what came afterwards that I couldn't deal with.'

'While you were alone?'

'While I was alone.'

'Could you manage gardening duty if you weren't alone?'

'I've never been a dab hand with a hoe.'

'In that case, at two o'clock this afternoon, report for "walking in the garden" duty. Do you think you can manage?'

Cavendish didn't look convinced.

Sister Valentina had initially been shocked at Doctor Mulroony's proposal. There was enough of the nurse in her to realise that the advantages for Lieutenant Cavendish would outweigh the disadvantages for her, but she'd still found it necessary to protest that she was part of a religious order. Doctor Mulroony had waved this aside brusquely, reiterating that, of all the nurses working at the convent, Cavendish seemed to respond to her company best.

Valentina knew her allure. The Sisters of St. Francis were not allowed mirrors in their private cells, but since they'd moved to live with the townspeople—Valentina lodged with her brother, whose position as groundskeeper at the convent gave him use of one of its outbuildings—she'd caught her own reflection many times. It puzzled her that, even though she was sworn to a life of chastity, God had gifted her such blue eyes, full lips and soft honey-blonde hair.

'Lieutenant Cavendish is a bachelor, of course,' Doctor Mulroony had warned. 'He has no wife to go home to when the war is over. So you'd best be on your guard about that. But you're experienced enough to know that romantic entanglements are likely to be the furthest thing from his mind at present.'

Valentina glanced sidelong at the lieutenant as they strode together in the convent grounds. He was very upright and correct. In his regimental hat, his belted green serge tunic, tan riding breeches and brown leather boots, he was every inch the British officer. But there was a tightness around his mouth, and he stared directly ahead as though down a tunnel. Since the war began, Valentina had nursed some dreadful cases: men glassy-eyed as if they saw only nightmares; men who couldn't see at all, or who couldn't hear or speak; men persistently weeping, asking where they were, who they were, when they could go home; men twitching or laughing hysterically or driven to fits of delirium by the least sign of military apparel; men just drooling and burbling, or shuffling feebly along as though drugged.

Lieutenant Cavendish had shown none of these symptoms—not at first glance. He'd merely appeared distant and strange. But of course that wasn't the whole story.

'Don't be fooled by appearances,' Mulroony had reminded her. 'The man's agoraphobia is extreme. Take him outside and he growls, snarls like an animal, even falling to all fours. Two or three male orderlies at a time haven't been able to force him.'

'And I, on my own, will be?' Valentina had asked skeptically.

'It takes two or three male orderlies . . . or one fetching nurse.'

'That's ridiculous, doctor.'

'Far from it. It's a tried and tested method, though you won't find it in any medical manual. The important thing, Valentina, is that he *must* open up to you. He must face this outrageous fear he has *now*—while the war's still on—or he'll never be right again.'

It was a pleasant spring afternoon; cool but sunny, a pastel blue sky contrasting with the tiny green buds on the wet, black branches of the trees.

'At home, I hear you are a school-master?' she said.

'Yes ... a boys' school.' Cavendish sounded preoccupied. She knew that, for all Dr. Mulroony's faith in her looks, getting him outdoors had been something of a miracle. Cavendish strolled stiffly alongside her.

'And what do you teach?' she asked.

'Mathematics.'

They entered a narrow walk between two lines of willow. Cavendish gazed directly ahead. He didn't glance once into the woodlands to either side, not even when they passed another group of patients whom several of the sisters were supervising as they erected a tent and constructed a campfire. The schoolboy enthusiasm with which the patients undertook these tasks was pitiful, but Cavendish didn't notice.

'Were you a popular master? Or were you strict?'

'I like to think I was both. The world isn't soft and boys need to learn that.'

'My father used to say such things.'

'He doesn't say them anymore?'

'He's dead.'

'I'm sorry.'

'He was old ... I wouldn't have wanted him to see what happened to Leuven, the town where we lived.'

If Cavendish remembered rightly, the Germans had behaved like beasts in the university town of Leuven, looting and burning, killing whoever they could.

'My father spent his whole life a shopkeeper there,' Valentina said. 'A poor man, but a believer in education. He used to say that ignorance would be the end of us all.'

'Interesting idea.'

She glanced at him, thinking she'd detected scorn. 'I thought a teacher would share such a view.'

'I do ... but maybe things aren't quite so black and white anymore.'

'Yet still you will direct your boys firmly?'

'Yes, when I get home. *If* I get home.'

'You *will* get home.' She linked arms with him, drawing them closer together.

Fleetingly, Cavendish was aware of the warm, curved body beneath her simple monastic garb, her full lips, her apricot skin. His own leaner figure seemed to meld into her as they walked. There was a stirring inside him—until they came to a stream.

Valentina suggested that Cavendish go across the line of flat white stepping stones first, and he sucked in a breath so tight that it almost choked him.

When she assured him that she would follow straight after, he ventured forward. The crossing itself wasn't a problem—the stream, though fast-moving, was only about three feet deep. But waiting for her on the other side, alone, seemed to take an age. The woodland path ahead of him meandered away between deep rhododendron bushes. He gazed along it, fascinated, wondering if that was furtive movement he'd just spied amid the glossy vegetation.

The sound of Valentina's clogs clipping over the stones distracted him. He turned. She was holding her skirts up as she approached, showing shapely legs clad with grey woolen hose. She smiled at him as she reached dry land, brushing her habit down demurely, then taking his hand and walking on.

'Perhaps you should tell me about the dog-thing,' she said.

'You've heard about that?'

'If I'm to treat you, I must know everything.'

'In that case, you probably know more about it than I do.'

'Is it true he first came to you before you ever fought? During an execution, I think?'

Cavendish put a cigarette to his lips and lit it. 'To be honest, I can't say.'

Valentina wondered what troubled him more, the memory itself, or that he couldn't remember where it first came from.

'The first time he *physically* came to me . . . ' Cavendish finally said. 'We'd reached a forward position on the battlefield. We tried to hold it but they gassed us and shelled us constantly. Mounted infantry assaults . . . pretty soon I was alone.'

He glanced into the rhododendrons, which were getting deeper and more entangled

'For how long were you alone?' Valentina asked.

'A couple of days. Maybe three.'

'And the dog-thing . . . it just came?'

Cavendish glanced around, as if he'd heard a sound in the underbrush.

Valentina hadn't heard anything, so she persisted. 'The dog, it . . . ?'

'Yes.' Cavendish threw away his cigarette, though it was only half-smoked. 'As soon as I was alone I knew he was nearby. He made this low belly-growl.'

'Did you see him?'

'I thought I did. But only when it got dark. I'd been listening to him for hours by then. It was still raining, of course. Thrashing rain. Shells were falling too, everywhere. That's when I spotted him. Bounding from crater to crater, gambolling through the corpses.'

Cavendish now spoke in low monotone. His brow had blanched, sweat standing on it. Valentina wondered if she had pushed too far, but she knew what Doctor Mulroony would say. *You must get him to open up. He must face his fear.*

'Even when he was some distance off, I saw his eyes,' Cavendish said. 'Black cavities with crimson points. And his teeth—curved yellow blades, the jowls wrinkled back . . . '

He paused, as though struggling to breathe.

'Did he reach your position?' she asked.

'How could he have? I'm still here.'

'Perhaps it would help if you described this dog-thing?'

Again Cavendish seemed to hear something in the bushes.

'Lieutenant?' she persisted.

'It's grey in colour . . . '

'Field-grey?'

'No, it's not a uniform, if that's what you mean. It's covered in grey fur. Very mangy.'

'Sorry . . . "mangy"?'

'Bad fur. Rotten. It runs on two legs, like a man. Its head hangs low, but is horizontal, with a protruding snout. The body is long, misshaped, all ribs and taut sinew . . . '

Cavendish suddenly froze, his eyes fixed on the rhododendrons to their left. A low, rumbling growl emanated from them, followed by a shrill yelp. Valentina felt a pang of fright, herself. She too peered into the bushes, which suddenly quivered. There was another yelp, another growl—which intensified into a prolonged, savage snarling.

Cavendish shook his head dumbly as he retreated along the path. Valentina's hair prickled as she peered at the violently moving undergrowth. Something was forcing its way through towards them. Something that yelped and snarled.

Cavendish turned and fled. Valentina called after him, but she too was alarmed. She spun back around as a stooped figure lumbered out of the bush onto the path alongside her—only for her fear to turn instantly to anger. It was her brother, Jacob, his grey overalls covered with twigs and leaf-matter. He chuckled as he leaned on his rake.

'What do you think you are doing?' she hissed.

His smiled faded. 'What do you think *you* are doing? Is that Englishman your new boyfriend?'

'How dare you!'

'Father would turn in his grave if he knew you were walking with a foreign soldier.'

'That soldier is my patient.'

'A funny kind of treatment, taking him into the woods.'

Valentina knew that rage was a sin, but for a moment it was all she could do not to strike her elder brother. She turned and walked quickly back towards the convent.

'Where are you going?' he asked, hobbling alongside her, perhaps concerned that she would speak to Doctor Mulroony.

'I must try and undo some of the damage you've just caused . . . *idioot!*'

'You shouldn't be seen walking with any of these men.' He was shouting now, as she skipped across the stream-stones. 'Valentina, you will bring shame on our family!'

She didn't look backwards.

'Yes, yes Mulroony,' a senior British officer in a greatcoat and walrus moustache was complaining. 'I understand that the high command don't understand neurological illness, and I think that in some ways they're wrong. But you know as well as I do that half these "Not Yet Diagnosed Nervous" are malingering. It's never been an honourable way to escape battle, and for their own good it's time they realised this. In any case, it's a matter of practicalities. The Bosch are limbering up for one hell of a counterstroke. We're not exactly sure where it's going to fall, but the view is that we need every man we can muster. That means all your slight cases will need to be rotated back to their units.'

Mulroony tapped out his pipe. 'Sir, with all respect, we don't have so many . . . '

'You can hang onto your more severe cases, so long as you think they're reclaimable. But not too many, mind. And if there are any so severe that they're unlikely to be fit for further service in the field—those who are barking mad, so to speak—they shouldn't be in Flanders anyway. They're no bloody use to us, so evacuate them home. We're going to need all the bed space we've got, I'm afraid.'

The Lancaster armoured car drove away. Doctor Mulroony gazed after it, tightlipped, before going back indoors.

Jacob continued raking the grass. He didn't speak English well, but he had more than enough to understand the gist of what he'd just heard. And to decide that maybe he didn't need to caution his sister after all.

Cavendish sat upright in the darkness.

A drop of icy sweat wormed down his left cheek.

The scratching sounded again.

Even though he'd been listening to it in a fitful doze for the last few minutes, it was suddenly clear that this wasn't a rat in the attic or a bird at his window-shutter. It was claws—on the other side of his bedroom door.

'You can't come in here,' he blurted out. 'This is a holy place.' But it was already inside the holy place. And anyway, did holy places matter these days, when God's Earth had been blasted to fragments and God's children ploughed into it like compost?

A low, reverberating growl responded.

Cavendish glanced sidelong at the chest of drawers, faintly visible in the dimness. His Webley was in the top one. Persecution could not go indefinitely without an answer. He leapt from his bed, extricated his revolver and crossed the room.

The door banged open, as he yanked at it—but there was no-one on the other side.

At the far end of the corridor, a cruciform window in a high, triangular recess cast dim moonlight over the top of the stair. All the other bedrooms appeared to be closed. It was unusually quiet. Often at night, you heard moans from patients; on occasion you'd notice the distant throb of the guns. Tonight nothing.

He switched on the light in his bedroom, and examined the door, the surface of which was scraped and dented, but no more than all the doors in this Spartan building. He gazed again toward the distant patch of moonlight. And had to blink—a bent figure had just flickered through it, as though descending the stair.

Cavendish went back into his bedroom, put his dressing-gown on and slipped the revolver into its pocket. He took a second to compose himself—staring at his reflection in the smeary mirror, combing his hair with his sweat-greased fingers. His heart was trip-hammering. A cigarette might help, but there was no time for that. Quietly, he went out, closed the bedroom door and strode down the passage. There was a night-shift station on the ground level, but it was located in the other wing. One of the sisters or an orderly would occasionally make rounds with a lamp, but at the dead of night those tours were rare.

From the top of the stair, the lower floor was shrouded in blackness. As Cavendish descended into it, it seemed unnaturally cold. He halted at the bottom until his eyes attuned sufficiently to distinguish a faint blot of radiance on his left, probably moonlight from the conservatory filtering through the dining room. More puzzling was the light he could now see from the other direction.

This too was faint—but, with all the shutters on the ground floor routinely closed and fastened at night, he couldn't think where it emanated from.

He walked towards it slowly, the hand in his gown clamped on the grip of his revolver. He didn't feel bold as much as numb. That was the harsh lesson of the trenches—you had to dull it all, try to convince your body that what you were seeing and hearing all around you wasn't happening. However, when he reached the passage between the kitchen and the scullery, and peered down it, this became difficult, not to say impossible. The outer door at the far end of the passage stood open, veils of moonlit mist drifting past it.

When Cavendish proceeded again, he was so numb that his fingers and toes tingled; his face felt as if it had been stretched over the front of his skull like nerveless parchment.

Then a hand touched his shoulder.

A shout caught in his throat as he spun around, drawing his revolver and cocking it.

'N-no!' a figure stammered, backing away, hands raised.

Cavendish also backed off, training his revolver firmly on the man who had emerged from the kitchen annexe. He was short, swarthy and wearing dingy work clothes. Even in the darkness of the passage, he looked faintly familiar.

'Who are you?' Cavendish demanded.

'Please . . . please.' The man, who spoke with a phlegmy accent, indicated that Cavendish should lower his revolver.

Cavendish didn't. 'Have you just been upstairs? Have you been to my room?'

The man nodded, embarrassed but clearly very frightened.

Slowly, reluctantly, Cavendish lowered the Webley. 'You'd better have a damn good explanation.'

The man nodded quickly, as if on this matter he would not disappoint. He sidled past Cavendish towards the outer door, beckoning with a crooked finger. 'You come, uh?'

Cavendish demanded to know where, but the man had already gone outside. Cursing, Cavendish pursued warily. He was particularly wary before stepping outside, glancing left and right, but seeing only skeins of mist drifting over lawns now glinting with dawn dew. The man was already about twenty yards ahead. He stopped and beckoned again. Cavendish thrust the revolver into his pocket and continued. They didn't go far, just to a rickety shed leaning against a stone wall. Orange light shimmered from its grimy window. Cavendish followed the fellow inside.

'You're one of the groundskeepers here, aren't you?'

The man nodded. 'Is true.'

Cavendish regarded him with undisguised repugnance. The fellow smelled of sweat and dirt. He was also stunted, his odd-shaped torso tilted forward at an angle. His face was jowly, pock-marked and covered with stubble. The hair on top of his head grew in thin strands greased across a bare, liver-coloured pate.

'You forgive, yes?' he asked, the eyes oddly bright in his dark features.

Cavendish glanced around the interior of the shed. It was cluttered with gardening implements, and reeked of earth and grass-cuttings. A stool was drawn against a rough table, on top of which an oil-lantern glowed.

'For God's sake, man, forgive what?'

'I hear you say to Sister Valentina . . . about dog. Lieutenant. This dog . . . very bad thing.'

'What do you know of it?'

'Is called . . . ' The gardener lowered his voice. 'Is called "Oschaert".'

'Oschaert?' Cavendish was astonished that some uneducated lout could understand anything of his predicament, but the fact that it might have a name—the mere suggestion of a rational explanation behind this misery, even if it turned out to be terrifying (and indeed the gardener wore a grimace of horror)—sent a shiver of hope through him. 'Tell me more!'

'Oschaert is very bad demon.'

'Demon?'

'We talk old days . . . stories of *Belgae*.'

'For God's sake, man, what are you gabbling about?'

Cavendish noticed a book with a scuffed oxblood leather-bound cover lying on the table. The gardener opened it at a page he'd marked with a sliver of grass.

Cavendish found himself gazing at the colourful illustration of a man—by his habit and crucifix he was a medieval cleric—running through a tangled wood, glancing nervously over his shoulder at a shaggy, shapeless form with glowing red eyes, which followed him. The text alongside it was large and ornate, but written in Flemish. Cavendish flipped through several more pages. One bore an equally colourful image of an elf-like figure seated on a toadstool, darning socks. Another portrayed a princess gazing mournfully through the bars of a tower window.

'This is a children's book,' he finally said.

The gardener drew him back to the original page and pointed at the shaggy, red-eyed figure.

Cavendish glanced at the text. The word 'Oschaert' featured several times. 'Can you translate this for me?'

'Ahh . . . ' The gardener shook his head.

'Can I take this with me, at least?'

The gardener all but pushed the book into Cavendish's hands. 'Is real!' His smile became strangely insistent. 'Oschaert . . . is real beast.'

Cavendish knew it was ridiculous, but he'd already passed the point where logic had a role. If there was the slightest chance this book might be the key to his problem, it was worth something. The only question was who would translate it for him. Sister Valentina obviously could, but he felt sure she would refuse once she knew why. There were others in this town who might help; most of the shopkeepers had a smattering of English. But this was a children's book, for Heaven's sake! Wouldn't they laugh?

The only other person here he had acquaintanceship with was Father Hendrik, the priest at the Church of St. Cecilia.

Formerly spiritual adviser to the sister, Father Hendrik had continued to come into the convent after the war started to bring Communion to those patients who were Catholic. Cavendish didn't know the priest well—they'd struck up brief conversation when they'd happened to sit at the same table to drink spearmint tea.

Certainly, no other reason would have goaded Cavendish to expose himself to the unknown danger that he felt was now encroaching on him in the open spaces of Adinkerke town centre. When a signpost directed him down a narrow passage towards St. Cecilia's, and he found himself truly alone, his fear intensified. The passage meandered away, enclosed by tall, gloomy buildings. Stone gargoyles gazed from overhead, representing various miscreated animals—one beaked, another horned, a third tusked, and all gripping the parapet with talons as they leered downward. The one at the end trickled rainwater from its gaping jaws . . .

He hurried on, taking a footbridge over a narrow sluice, its slate-coloured waters gushing. Beyond that the entrance to St. Cecilia's was visible, its nail-studded door standing open. Cavendish entered the building with considerable relief—though inside there wasn't quite the sanctuary he'd expected. Candles blazed across the church's altar and deep into both its transepts, most probably lit by soldiers due to return to action. But they cast little light. Heavy rain trickled dark shadows down the narrow, stained glass windows.

Dim candles also burned at the rear of the church, where a small side-chapel had been dedicated to St. Cecilia, the Christian noblewoman brutally wounded by her Roman captors and left untended in a cell, where it took her three days to die. Dominating the side-chapel there was an aged oil-painting, portraying the saint as a beautiful Renaissance lady—in the style of Rubens or Van Dyck, though old and decayed, and cracked in many places. Slips of paper had been inserted into these fissures—prayers and petitions, Cavendish realised, again mostly from soldiers.

He walked down the central aisle between rows of polished pews. Overhead, seen through a gauze of incense and some noticeable strands of cobweb, the ceiling had been painted blue and decorated with stars. Against each pillar stood a painted statue—the Madonna, St. Joseph with the Holy Child, Jesus himself, his sundered heart emblazoned on his gown, his punctured palms outstretched. The pillars and walls bore lavish scenes from both the Old and New Testaments, though the most impressive feature was the altar. Its central oak table was spread with crisp, white linens. Behind that, two latticed panels were closed beneath an arching triptych detailing the road to Calvary. From the black recess behind them, there was a faint glint of gold, denoting where the tabernacle was kept.

'Are you in need?' a voice asked.

Cavendish turned and saw Father Hendrik approaching. He was a tall but gentle-looking man, with a pale, wizened, face, heavy, snow-white eyebrows and a shock of snow-white hair. Only when he came close did he recognise the visitor.

'Lieutenant . . . I think? You are looking well.'

Cavendish wasn't sure whether he looked well or not. Perhaps the priest would think the rain accounted for his sweat-damp face. Before he could respond, a hint of movement drew his attention to a high choral gallery.

For a second Cavendish was too surprised to speak

Surely it couldn't be here, not in this sanctified place? But then nothing was sanctified now. Not in Belgium. How much blood had saturated the surrounding fields—not just from this war, but from countless others: Napoleonic wars, Franco-Spanish wars, the Eighty Years War, the Hundred Years War, the wars of the Dark Ages, the wars of Julius Caesar?

'Can you translate for me, father?' he half shouted, trying to drag himself back to the matter at hand. The priest looked startled. More quietly, Cavendish added: 'I've found something written in Flemish.'

'Ah yes.' The priest nodded, but when he took the book and looked at it, he regarded Cavendish curiously.

Cavendish pointed out the page in question. 'I assure you I have good reason for this.'

Hendrik took some spectacles from his cassock pocket, perched them on the end of his nose and commenced reading.

'This is an old fable of Flanders,' he eventually said. 'Something for children. To make them behave when they are bad . . . you understand? An old story from superstitious days.'

Hendrik indicated the shaggy shape, which now that Cavendish stared at it, seemed to possess much brighter and redder eyes than before; they almost gleamed. 'This creature is called the Oschaert. It is like a thing from nightmares, yes? How you would say . . . "a goblin"?'

'How would one recognise it?'

Hendrik shrugged. 'How could one fail? It is like this. A man-beast.'

'A man-dog?'

'Yes. I suppose a dog.' Hendrik eyed Cavendish again, noting his ashen cheek. 'Lieutenant, this is foolishness—village prattle from the old days.'

'Why is the Oschaert pursuing this priest?'

'The story comes from a time of plague. You understand? The Black Death, which was a great curse here. So many died.'

Another layer of human carrion sunk into Flanders's black bowels, Cavendish thought.

Hendrik continued. 'This priest has betrayed his flock. By charging them excess fees . . . or is the right word, "excessive"?'

'Yes, yes, go on please.'

'Excessive fees . . . to bury their loved ones in the church yard and not the plague pit. This is a big crime in those days. And also it brings pestilence to the heart of the town. So then . . . everybody dies.' Hendrik snapped the book closed. 'Except the priest, who locks himself in his church.'

Cavendish was confused. 'What about the Oschaert?'

Hendrik shrugged. 'The Oschaert then comes for him. It does not pick random victims. In these stories, the Oschaert only feeds on the souls of those stricken with bad conscience. Those who are mad with guilt, you see?'

Cavendish gazed at him long and hard.

'Lieutenant, is there something . . . ?'

'No!'

The priest offered him the book back. He took it, turned on his heel and marched stiffly out.

Following him all the way back to the convent was a half-glimpsed shadow moving above the town's ancient eaves, balancing along the sagging gutters, leaping the narrow gulfs between the houses. By the time Cavendish passed through the gates onto the convent's wooded drive, his nerves were as taut as cello strings.

Nobody else was around. The rain had eased off, but the air was damp and cold, and the clouds that had lowered over Adinkerke all day were still so thick that they cast a dimness verging on twilight. Thunder rumbled in the distance, but that didn't muffle a crunching of twigs as someone slid out from the undergrowth onto the drive behind Cavendish. He hurried on, refusing to look around.

The shape of the convent, austere as a woodcut, was in view, dull lights visible in its windows. He increased his pace, but the impacts of his feet were now echoed by another's, and by a panting sound. Still Cavendish didn't run. He knew only too well what happened if you ran. But the panting was right behind him—and the tapping of paws on the gravel.

'Enough!' he shouted, with an attempted parade-ground bark. He halted and spun around on his heel.

Looking away from the lighted building, it was astonishing how dark the afternoon had become. There were flickers of lightning in the far distance, but the blue-grey dusk cloaked all except thirty yards of drive. It almost cloaked the squat, overcoat-wearing figure of Doctor Mulroony, as he came ambling up, a stick in one hand, a dog-leash in the other. His Dachshund, Wilhelm, sniffed around Cavendish's boots.

The pulse of blood in the back of Cavendish's neck was about to ignite a migraine. For a second he felt absurd, utterly embarrassed—as though everyone would know about the mistake he had just made and be up-roariously amused by it. Mulroony himself was smiling, but this seemed to owe more to his exertions.

'Brisk walk, lieutenant?' he asked.

'Sir, I . . .'

'Forgive me for running after you, but I saw you coming in through the gate. You've been into town?'

'Yes.'

'On your own?'

'The convent became a little oppressive.'

'Well of course it did, old chap.' Mulroony walked on, planting a hand in Cavendish's back to steer him the same way. 'It was designed for people who've given up on the world. Anyway, whatever your reason, this is splendid news. You're clearly on the road to recovery. That outdoor stroll with Sister Valentina must have done you a power of good.'

Cavendish muttered that it probably had.

Mulroony stuffed his pipe with tobacco, and put a match to it. 'If you want to come and see me in the morning, I'll have your discharge papers ready . . . so you can return to battalion.'

'So soon?' Cavendish tried, but failed, to keep the shock from his voice.

'You've been here several months already. Under normal circumstances I'd want to keep you for observation a little longer. But unfortunately we have a war to fight.'

'I suppose they'll allocate me a new platoon?'

'Well, they won't send you into battle alone.'

'No,' Cavendish said distantly.

'Splendid. Just shows what we can achieve when we put our minds to it, eh?'

It was very late that night when Sister Valentina finally found Lieutenant Cavendish. He was alone in the darkened conservatory. The chairs and tables were littered with newspapers, the ash-trays overflowing. Rain hammered the glazed panels as he stared towards the distant flashes of lightning and increasingly loud thunder.

'I hear you are leaving us?' she said cautiously.

Cavendish didn't look around. 'That's correct.'

'Isn't it a bit sudden?'

'I dare say it's for the best.'

'Only yesterday you were frightened outside in the grounds.' She hesitated, before adding: 'I can tell you are frightened now.'

'I doubt there's a man serving in Flanders who isn't frightened.'

'Can Doctor Mulroony not write to your commanding officer? Maybe find you a post away from the fighting . . . an administrative position of some sort?'

'No doubt he could, but I don't want that.'

'I see.'

He focussed on the distant storm.

'Are you packed and ready?' she asked.

'I have other duties first.'

'Is there anything I may do to help?'

'Not anymore.' He turned to look at her. His face was a mask of tension, his voice tight. 'It's an old cliché of course, but you've been quite the angel while I've been here. And though I didn't used to believe in angels, I do now. In truth, I didn't used to believe in all sorts of ballyhoo nonsense . . . '

'Ronald, I hoped I wouldn't have to tell you this, but . . . that noise you heard in the trees yesterday . . . that was not the thing you fear.'

'It will be when the time is right.'

'What do you mean?'

He nodded at the approaching storm. 'You hear the guns? Don't they sound closer?'

'Guns?'

Cavendish sniffed. 'At first when Mulroony said he was sending me back, I thought good . . . when the Bosch make their last throw of the dice, I can face it in the company of others. Not the company of those I'd grown used to, alas, but the main thing was I wouldn't be alone. But now, I think maybe it's better if I *am* alone. We must face our fear exactly as it is, not in some other guise. Isn't that what you and Mulroony believe, sister?'

'Ronald, I'm going to speak to Doctor Mulroony. I don't think you can go back yet.'

'The guilt is dreadful.'

'Guilt? But you served your country well.'

'Not when I was alone.' He stared out through the rain-drenched glass. 'When all the others were gone and I was alone . . . that was when this thing became real. Don't you see? Private Longshaw was alone too, when he was found in that farmhouse. And yet I never felt sorry for him. Even on the day I executed him. Even though I was warned there and then about what I was doing . . . '

There was a zig-zag flash outside, and a shocking concussion. Cavendish remained rigid, but Sister Valentina was so startled that she leaped forward and put her arms around him. In response, he slid his arms around her. She tried to disentangle herself, but he wouldn't release her—and in truth she didn't try particularly hard. She peered up at him, his solemn features running with dark shadows.

He was chilly and unbending, as so many of these British officers were, but deep down—or maybe not so deep—vulnerable. And of course unattached. When he leaned down to kiss her, she didn't instantly pull away. Only when their tongues touched did she remember who she was, and jerk her head backwards. This time he released her, and she fled.

Valentina couldn't go back to her lodging, because it only had a curtain to give her privacy from her brother with his peevish, interfering ways, and tonight that wouldn't be enough to prevent him realising that something had happened. She might have found solitude in the grounds, had it not been for the rain and wind. Instead, she tottered into one of the common rooms, which, at this late hour was empty.

There she wept, but as much with regret as with hurt and confusion. What a weak vessel she was. Now she couldn't even request that Lieutenant Cavendish be invalided home, because that would mean he'd be kept here during the interim period, which could be weeks, maybe months, and all that time her position would be compromised.

And yet wasn't that piling sin on top of sin?

Was she happy letting a man return to battle in full knowledge he couldn't cope with it? Would this be done to preserve some

idealised vision of herself? The virtuous virgin. And yet how many
nights had this virgin spent with one hand clamped on the soft
heat between her legs, with thumb and fingers working the taut
nipples beneath her starched nightgown. God demanded too
much.

She dabbed her tears with a tissue as she rushed back through
the convent, its passages moaning to the storm. The conservatory
was now empty, so she ascended the stair, only to find that
Cavendish's bedroom was also empty. On his bed, she saw his pistol
holster. It lay next to an open book.

The stamp inside the book's cover indicated that it had recently
been drawn from a library. By its vivid but simple illustrations, it
was for children. But the page it was open on made Valentina pale.

I t always seemed to be raining in No Man's Land.

Cavendish was soaked head-to-foot as he strode forward,
revolver in hand, picking his way purposefully through mud and
tangles of wire, skirting around shell-holes filled with water which
reflected blood-red in every blinding explosion. Even when forced
to crouch, he pressed on, crawling if necessary and always, when he
could, getting back to his feet. He owed it to Captain Frederickson,
to Sergeant Hall, to Corporal Lampwick, to Privates Kelly, Piper,
Frodsham, Harrison, Burling, Cook—and of course to Private
Longshaw, who had walked alone but unaided to the execution
post.

When Cavendish heard the first yipping growl, he thought he
was mistaken—all sounds were distorted by the crashing of the
guns. But the second time it was clearer: a combination of whine
and snarl, unmistakably canine, unmistakably filled with blood-
lust. He halted his advance, his revolver levelled. The rain washed
over him in sheets. All around there were impacts, flashes of flame,
detonations fit to burst a man's eardrums. He didn't flinch,
remaining ramrod straight—even though he was shaking to his
toes. His teeth were clenched so tightly that his jaw almost locked.

The next snarl came from a different direction. It was circling him, he realised. He pivoted around, his eyes trying to penetrate the murk. Another shell impacted, the gout of flame glittering on the shattered trees and gutted earth. There was no end to the howling of the wind, to the roaring of machine-guns.

But where was it?

It was close by, he knew.

And then two hands were upon him, seizing the fist in which he clasped his revolver.

'Ronald!' Valentina cried. 'What are you doing out here?'

He yanked his gun-hand free. 'For God's sake, Valentina!'

She too was drenched by the rain. Her veil had blown off, and her long golden hair was streaked down the sides of her face and onto the front of her habit. 'Ronald, it is not real. Oschaert is a fairy tale.'

'No, I've seen it.'

'You heard a silly story made up to frighten naughty children.'

Somewhere behind them, stones skittered. Cavendish spun around, but still saw nothing in the tumult—which was strange because now a grey, milky light was leaching across the land. A whizz-bang detonated overhead. The concussion was shudder-inducing. Valentina grappled with him again, trying to pull the gun from his grasp—but he pushed her away, and glanced sharply to his left. Even in the dimness of dawn, Valentina saw his tortured expression change to one of angry relief and then vicious joy. He raised his firearm.

'No!' she screamed, hurling herself onto him.

When he threw her off this time, he knocked her to the ground, driving the breath from her body, before turning fully around to confront it—his nemesis, where it perched on top of a blasted parapet, crouching amid sandbags, twists of wire and broken, tangled limbs. It leaned forward with a gruesome snarl, its pricked ears twitching, its eyes like pinpoints of fire. Its shaggy, grey body quivered with hunger.

Valentina shrieked as he took aim.

When the shot was fired, it was the loudest noise she had ever heard.

It took several frantic minutes for Mulroony and other members of staff to arrive. On first being woken, they'd been given confused reports about a gunshot in the convent grounds. Mulroony thought it likely someone had heard only the storm, but the thunder now was distant. Rain fell softly.

It was on the west lawn where they found Sister Valentina, kneeling in prayer next to Cavendish's body. His revolver was clasped to the side of his skull, through which a hole passed cleanly from right to left.

'My God . . . ' Mulroony breathed, tightening the cord of his dressing-gown. 'I didn't . . . I didn't realise he was still so traumatised.'

Valentina regarded him coldly, not blinking as the rain dripped from her lashes. 'This war, like all the killing before . . . it takes and rapes us, and leaves this evil behind.'

'What the deuce are you talking about, woman?'

'When the fighting's finally over . . . ' she was sobbing as she walked away, 'sow this country with salt.'

PAUL FINCH *(b. Wigan, Lancashire, England, 1964) is a former cop and journalist, now turned full time writer. He first cut his literary teeth penning episodes of the British TV crime drama,* The Bill, *and has written extensively in the field of children's animation. However, he is probably best known for his work in horrors and thrillers.*

To date, he's had ten books and nearly 300 stories and novellas published on both sides of the Atlantic. His first collection, Aftershocks, *won the British Fantasy Award in 2002, while he won the award again in 2007 for his novella,* Kid. *Later in 2007, he won the International Horror Guild Award for his mid-length story,* The Old North Road. *Most recently, he has written three* Doctor Who *audio dramas for Big Finish—*Leviathan, Sen-

tinels of the New Dawn *and* Hexagora. *His horror novel,*
Stronghold, *was published by Abaddon Books in 2010 and his*
Doctor Who *novel,* Hunter's Moon, *by BBC Books in 2011.*
Paul has also written scripts for several horror movies. The most
recent of these, The Devil's Rock, *was released to the cinemas*
last July. Five more of Paul's horror and thriller scripts are cur-
rently under option.

Paul lives in Lancashire, UK, with his wife Cathy and his chil-
dren, Eleanor and Harry. His website can be found at:
http://paulfinch-writer.blogspot.com/

Commentary on "Oschaert": *On one hand this story is not an*
unusual venture for me, in that it draws on an ancient mystery,
though on the other it is slightly different from the norm in that it
doesn't impose that mystery on the modern age but on another
different period of history.

In truth, I'm not sure exactly when this idea formed, though I
do remember leafing through a musty old book about the mythol-
ogy and folklore of mainland Europe and suddenly coming across
this rather fascinating being who, despite my having what I con-
sider to be an encyclopaedic knowledge of this type of thing, I had
never heard about before.

Initially I was reluctant to write the story. The First World War
is such an abject tragedy in its own right, and so filled with un-
speakable but real-life horror, that it almost seemed immoral to
introduce a supernatural element. However, I then got to thinking
in detail about war and warfare, and how it appears to surround
us all the time, and it struck me that artists and authors are not
doing their profession justice if they refuse to acknowledge this
dark spectre merely to avoid causing upset. Even those of us who
write tales of the fantastic—perhaps a frivolous past-time in the
eyes of some—are disrespecting the reality of human experience
if we suddenly decide there are no-go areas. And, the more I
thought about this, the less controversial it seemed. After all, the
movies have been doing it for years—there have been war-ro-

mances, war-musicals, war-comedies, war-actioners. Is war-horror so different?

I suppose maybe it is if what you are trying to say as a horror writer is that your horror is more horrifying than the horror of war itself. So perhaps that's something to guard against, or at least, if you can, to try and balance. Hopefully I've managed something of that nature with "Oschaert". You must be my judge.

HELENA

EKATERINA SEDIA

Ivan Sechenov probed the brain of a frog stretched out in a metal pan, weak and pale as veal, with his finger. It was amazing to him how the change of scenery made everything seem so unreal: back in St. Petersburg now, in his own laboratory at the University, there was no reason that his experiments wouldn't work as well as in Germany. And yet it felt futile, as if a memory of a dream, an impotent copy of itself.

He dropped another crystal of salt onto the brain quivering in its brain pan, and stimulated the nerve with a gentle pinch of his forceps. It was starting to drizzle outside, and the room turned gray. The frog's leg twitched, albeit lazily, and Sechenov dropped his forceps with a loud clang of metal on metal, startling himself and the dissected frog. It was the same salt, the same brain area—and yet, reflex inhibition, so well established and sensible in Germany simply refused to work in this rainy, leaden place, where sun rays penetrated as reluctantly as the light of reason.

It seemed that that particular chapter was closed, and Sechenov stared at the windowpanes, furrowed with rain tracks, and thought that perhaps he could start a new experiment, something that belongs to this place and doesn't feel like a pale transplanted ghost. He could expand his work to other animals, perhaps—surely, it wasn't just frogs who exhibited reflexes.

Cheered up, he walked out of the laboratory in quick stride, forgetting the now still frog and the pan on the bench.

The city was so familiar yet alien: it seemed unfathomable that after knowing France and Germany, he could change so much and return to this eternally same city; he recognized it but no longer felt like he belonged inside it, as if his edges wore off in his travels, his angles no longer fit into their assigned grooves—but the mismatch was merely a reminder of the time when there was a harmony. The streets were too wide and wind-blown, the blocks too long, and his legs felt useless and rubbery, as if in a dream. This city rendered everything ineffectual, even science—or rather, it demanded its own.

Sechenov did some of his early research here—his work on the effects of alcohol on human body was still a classic, both in self-experimentation angle and in its results. He shuddered when he thought back to these days when his every morning started with a glass of vodka, and when he consumed barely any food. Since that time, he couldn't stand the taste of alcohol.

He toyed briefly with an idea of vomit reflexes and chuckled to himself at the impossibility of performing self-experimentation on brain processes. And there didn't seem to be any other options, for who would let him experiment on the brain of another man? Not counting his teaching, of course.

Several weeks went by, and Sechenov's ennui grew deeper as the temperatures outside dropped and the wind from the Baltic grew more vicious and penetrating. Sechenov went to the University and met some of the newer members of physiology department—it was a dizzying experience, as everything else has been lately. The new blood talked about new science. Many had grown interested in Ringer's solutions, a science fashion exported from London (a trend Sechenov scoffed at, since he was committed to the continental way of doing things): these salts of potassium, sodium, calcium and magnesium supported growing chick embryos outside of an egg for several hours, and there was a talk about trying that with mice.

Sechenov thought whether such salts would affect the developing brain. He also wondered if his frogs with removed skulls would be able to survive longer, and perhaps his work on brain reflexes could be continued. His idle musings grew less tentative once he read that Germans were growing chicken embryos for several weeks, with simple addition of serum from horse blood. And when Gottlieb published a paper on maintaining a frog's brain, a spinal column and a leg for a week and then stimulating all three with electricity, the new direction of his studies took shape in his mind.

He started with his classes: during laboratory demonstrations, he challenged his students to dissect frogs' nervous systems, nerves ghost-white and roping, the spine translucent, softly bulging at the sides. The brains quivered, the muscles tensed and unwound, went limp and yielding, the bones nothing but mere pegs, fading into unimportance. It was all about soft tissue and flesh, shot through with the white electrical wires. Salt crystals worked again, but this time Sechenov was indifferent to their inhibitory magic. He would rather dissolve them in horse's blood serum and pour them over the still living tissue—even as he imagined the spirit departing, a faint glimmer of imitation life left flickering along the flayed nerves.

It was coincidence really that just next door, in the anatomical theater of the university, they were dissecting a cadaver. A young woman, known only by her initials of H.L., who had died from a rare cancerous tumor on her brain stem. Sechenov stopped by to say hello to his medical colleagues—although not physiologists, they were still closer to Sechenov's own heart than the biologists who populated the neighboring halls, numerous like vermin.

And he stood perplexed at the sight: a face as white as the slab under-neath, body draped in a sheet to conceal the unimportant— but the pink tumorous mass protruded from in-between the cerebral hemispheres like a swollen and mocking tongue. He couldn't look away.

Dr. Konev, the surgeon who performed the dissection in preparation for the students' arrival, laughed. 'You want this?' he said. 'To add to your frogs?'

'Maybe,' Sechenov responded. 'I think maybe I could keep it alive if you let me take it right after you're done.'

Konev rolled his eyes. 'I was joking,' he said. 'But you're welcome to it.'

A lump of tumorous tissue seemed like such an accidental find, such a whim, that Sechenov was surprised to learn that his fancy was not foolish: the tumor grew, and in retrospect it made sense—this is what cancers did, after all, in horse serum or a person's brain. It gave rise to a lattice of cells, translucent and pink like the inside of a child's ear. They shimmered in their solution and mounded up, like no cell had ever done in his experience, and even spread up the walls of their glass flasks, as if searching for escape. When Sechenov added the dissected frog's nerves, H.L.'s cells overtook them, wrapping them in soft fleshy cocoons until the frog tissue disappeared, consumed. He had to transfer some of the ballooning growths into additional flasks and then some more, until the entire surface of his lab bench was nothing but glass flasks and the tin trays with drying remains of several frogs.

It was only a matter of time before Sechenov slit open the tip of his left ring finger, the skin ridges spreading apart like lips in a slow smile. He trained himself to be resistant to pain years ago, but even he flinched as the sharp edges of the forceps seized the white thread of a nerve and pulled. It dangling tip touched the mass of cells in the glass flask, and they seemed to heave toward the nerve, coating it in a cool, soothing blanket.

And then there were flashes of light shooting up his arm, sending the wool of his jacket sleeve into incandescence, and then his whole body stiffened and glowed, and he had no words to describe it and no thoughts to comprehend it.

An experience was so jolting that Sechenov had no memory of the next few hours—he came to his senses and to the realization that he was quite cold, the air around him was dark and stung the insides of his nostrils with ice crystals, and he was standing on the stone Neva embankment, not too far from Anichkov Bridge and his home. His left hand was still bleeding, and he had left his gloves at the university—along with his coat, it seemed, since he was still dressed in his jacket. He fought the impulse to rush back, to see what the ravenous cancer cells had done to his poor disembodied nerve, and instead headed home.

Despite his distinguished occupation as a professor, he rented a small suite of rooms above a bakery, most of all because he found the yeasty smell comforting, and the constant traffic of the customers and loud workers' voices a convenient tool for measuring time. He had a tendency to get lost in thought, and the slamming of the iron gate over the bakery's window at night reminded him sharply that it is time to eat dinner, and the morning bustle woke him up in time for his classes. He was an undemanding man otherwise, and learning to fit his life anew left him little resources for other desires or aspirations.

The bakery was closed by then, and his apartment cold and dark. When he lit the candle, the flame flickered, reflecting in the dark windowpane, along with Sechenov's own narrow and bearded face—and then, someone else's. At first, he thought it was the doubling of the reflection produced by the shifting lights and the double thickness of the glass, that it was merely his own face made longer and paler and sadder by the concave reflective surfaces. However, when he turned he saw that it was another person, entirely separate, sitting on his settee.

She bore an unsettling resemblance to Sechenov, for sure, and for a moment he hesitated, thinking that perhaps she was a misplaced relative, a long-lost cousin, a niece he always had but got distracted and forgot about. But that didn't explain why she was wearing Sechenov's coat and gloves, or her bare feet, for that matter—blue and cut up and bleeding. Her eyes, blue pools with neither sclera nor pupil nor iris separate, turned in his direction but it was impossible to know what she saw.

'Who are you?' he asked eventually, after the two of them had time to come to terms with being in each other's presence.

'Helena,' she answered.

Of course, H and L were so prominent in the way she said it— exhaled it, decaying apples on her breath—that he had no choice but to recognize her.

'You've escaped from your flask,' he said.

'Many flasks,' she echoed. 'Do you know what it's like, to have your body flayed and split and splintered, to have your mind fractured so that you don't know whether you are real?'

'Yes,' he said. 'The frogs?'

'Mere food, energy, sustenance.' Her lips curved with contempt, showing a sliver of a pink, toothless gum. 'It was you—you, your electricity—that gave me the strength, the—' she paused, her fingers clutching the narrow Astrakhan collar of his (now hers) coat—'the impetus to free myself from glass. It was, after all, binding.'

'How did you find me?'

She shrugged, disinterested, and shifted on the settee, stretching her legs in front of her. 'Your coat smelled of bread and warmth, and your gloves yearned in your direction. Your fingertips are beating in my heart.'

He studied her carefully, trying not to appear as if he was staring. She looked little like the cancerous cells in the flask, and yet he could see the similarity—the almost-indecent pink of her skin, the sweet rotting fruit of her breath, the smoothness of her outline under his coat that hinted at neither joints nor sharp angles. She was undoubtedly a tumor, given life by his foolish exposure of his nerve endings, and he feared to find out what she looked like under his coat.

'Would you like a robe?' he said.

Helena stayed with him, because every other option presented an even bigger inconvenience than personified cancer curled up on his settee, pretending to read Sechenov's own monograph on inhibitory reflexes but in reality studying him out of the corner of one narrowed monochromatic eye. Taking her back to the university would surely necessitate a dissection, and Sechenov suspected that Helena would not find this possibility acceptable; he also guessed the malice that seethed so close to the surface of her impossibly smooth skin would likely compel her to commit any act necessary to prevent her further study and degradation. She seemed to deeply loathe the idea of being split into flasks and turned inside out; she had however retained her appetite for frogs, and Sechenov brought her a few every night when he returned home from the university.

If he was in a different place, he would've screamed his throat raw with frustration and the impossibility of living like this—but here, as the nights stretched well into afternoons and mornings, when the sun all but disappeared, wrapped in the dark heart of winter, he felt only mild despair. By the time New Year's came and went, he wanted to only sleep and hope that the winter recess would never end, and he wouldn't have to wake up from this languid impasse and do something about Helena.

She retained some of the memories of her past life—mere flickers, and sometimes she jolted and spoke of long rooms and silent nurses, and the brilliant flowers of migraines blossoming and bleeding across the left side of her vision; at other times, she seemed to latch onto Sechenov's own, and spoke of Europe and especially France, and both of them craved brioche then—brioche and sunlight. The bakery downstairs offered only yeasty bread that stirred up the nostalgia with its heavy smell.

He couldn't understand, now more than ever, how such things were supposed to work: a creature such as Helena, so menacing and unnatural, so impossible—how could one care for such creation? Was Pygmalion completely insane, was he convinced that the statue he had carved really was more than a slab of matter, any more a woman than a scarecrow? What sort of mind did it take to love this mock-up of a person?

He found out the day he decided to finally share his secret, to relieve himself of this unsightly burden—he did not expect to gain recognition or understanding, but a mere acknowledgment of the peculiarity of his circumstances and a bit of outside reassurance that his predicament was indeed worthy of concern. He had invited Konev, the doctor who had performed H.L.'s dissection, to bear witness to his sad decline.

Instead, the moment Konev's eyes met Helena's, deep and unkind, he seemed to have lost interest in Sechenov's explanation about growth of the cancerous cells in glass flasks, and the mysterious catalytic role the frog's and human nerves played in the process of bringing this mass to life—in congealing it, like bolts of electricity, into the present whole. Instead, he wanted to ask Helena about her thoughts and about how she felt living above the bakery, and whether she had any interest in the balls and society life. It turned out that she had, and she smiled at Konev, with her curling closed-mouth smile.

Sechenov thought of warning his colleague, but Helena's selfish regard already seeped into him, and he merely shrugged and waved them along when Helena rose from the settee (for the first time as far as he could remember), and put her arm under Konev's. Sechenov couldn't help but notice its sinuous, jointless motion— it seemed a tentacle more than a human limb; Konev was oblivious, and even as Sechenov felt a small pang of guilt at not screaming into Konev's face and shaking him out of his foolishness, it couldn't dampen the huge sense of relief that washed over him the moment the door latched shut behind the monstrous creature. Free of its hypnotizing gaze, Sechenov reeled at the thought of what horror he had endured—for weeks!—until the fatigue felled him and he slept, his face resting on the settee where Helena's body left an impression.

He saw her rarely after that, at the university functions where she glided, silent and mysterious, sparkling with jewels, next to Konev, smiling all the while. He suspected that Konev's suicide a few months later had probably something to do with her uncanny influence. At his funeral, Sechenov saw Helena's deathly eyes as they flashed at him from behind her black veil. She left flowers on the cover of the coffin and looked pensive until they covered it with earth—sickly yellow clay of the cemetery. It was a cold day, unusual for May with its biting wind, wet and heavy as it whipped across the mourners' faces. After the funeral, Sechenov stood by the grave, regret and shame prodding him in equal measure—was it his fault for not having warned Konev? Even though he told

Konev about Helena's origin, could he possibly have done more? And, most importantly, was there anything that he could still do to save others? He knew there would be others because of what she was—Helena was spreading, bodies like flasks to her growing appetites.

He didn't notice her approaching him—she glided silently, and he only became aware of her presence when she hissed in his ear, 'What are you doing here?'

He wanted to remind her of the person she once was, of the headaches becoming more and more frequent and the nurses who grew more and more silent and withdrawn, of how she watched her arm—her human forearm, with bones and joints and veins—grow thin and translucent before her eyes, melting into the covers like an icicle in April. Instead he whispered back, 'I came to ask you to come back with me.'

Her breath—rotting apples, sweet cider—lingered on his cheek. 'Did you miss me?'

'As much as I miss brioche.'

She sighed, wistful. 'I am hungry.'

'I can take you to the university. No one is there today, and you can have the frogs and their spines, maybe even bones and spleens.'

'I hate that place.'

He feigned indifference. 'As you wish then. But there's nothing but bread at home.'

She walked silently next to him to the gates of the cemetery, where he hailed a cab. 'Where to?' he asked her.

She hesitated only a moment. 'To the university.'

It is never easy to destroy something one had created so meticulously, worked so long to bring into being. He toyed with the idea of not killing her, only threatening her back into the glass flasks with the tip of his scalpel, but decided against it—who knew what Konev was feeding her, how strong she had grown. A scalpel securely concealed in his sleeve, a distraction—that would be enough. That had to be enough, he thought. He tried not to think about the consequences in case he had failed. *Ergo*, he reasoned, *he couldn't fail.*

———

Grigory, the night watchman who spent his nights dozing in the reception and who unlocked the university doors in the morning was the one who found them. At first, he squinted and shook his head and wondered if it was still a dream—professor Sechenov, a quiet and kind man who always said hello to Grigory, sat motionless in a chair by his bench, as if lost in thought, but his eyes were wide open and unmoving, staring at Grigory in a way only a dead man's eyes could. There was something wrong with his face and neck—long purple and pink and white strands stretched from his cheeks and his windpipe to the shattered glass flask; it was as if the bloodied treacle inside it came to life and twisted itself into hundreds of tiny nooses, except that they entered his skin and flesh seamlessly, growing out of and into it like roots entering soil, smoothly and invisibly. His hand lay limp in his lap, and his fingers were smeared thickly with blood; a broken scalpel lay on the floor, clean and shining, just a few paces away from Sechenov's foot.

Once Grigory managed to convince himself that the sight was neither his imagination nor trick of light, he sighed and went to the vestibule to find someone to fetch the police, too preoccupied to notice thin pink threads sticking to the bottom of his shoe and the nascent headache that just started to throb in the upper left corner of his vision.

EKATERINA SEDIA *(b. Moscow, Russia, 1970) lived in Russia until she was 21, attending Moscow State University before moving to the US. She received a PhD in Ecology and Evolution from Rutgers University. She is an Associate Professor at The Richard Stockton College, where she teaches genetics and plant ecology. She is married to Christopher Sedia.*

Her first story, "Alphabet Angels", appeared in Analog *in 2005, and won that year's AnLab Poll. She's since sold more than 40 stories to various magazines and anthologies, including* Baen's Universe, Fantasy Magazine, Clarkesworld, *and* Dark Wisdom, *as well as* Haunted Legends *(Tor) and* Magic in the Mirrorstone *(Mirrorstone Books). Her first novel,* According to Crow, *appeared in 2005 from Five Star, but she made a bigger impact with literary fantasies* The Secret History of Moscow *(2007),* The Alchemy of Stone *(2008),* The House of Discarded Dreams *(2010), and* Heart of Iron *(2011, all four from* Prime*). She also edited the World Fantasy Award-winning* Paper Cities: An Anthology of Urban Fantasy *(2008, Senses Five Press),* Running with the Pack *(2010, Prime), and* Bewere the Night *(2011, Prime).*

About the possibilities of fantasy, she shared these memorable words in a Locus *interview, 'People say, "There should be rules to magic." Why? It's magic. I understand you shouldn't be able to do anything you want, necessarily, but it shouldn't be like the laws of physics laid on magic. I'm much more interested in surreal kinds of things, where you don't know how things work but you don't care. It's like the Celestial Cow in* The Secret History of Moscow*—she has no rules; she's a cow.'*

Commentary on "Helena": *Russian history is a recurrent inspiration for my stories, so here I go once again. This is a very liberal take on Ivan Sechenov, a renowned Russian physiologist, as well as some fantastical speculation on early successes of cell cultures. The female protagonist's name, Helena, is derived from HeLa—an actually existing immortal cell line that originated much later than the story is taking place. I hope the readers will forgive me this anachronism, as well as sneaking science fiction into a Gothic book.*

Rusalka

Anna Taborska

Full fathom five thy father lies;
Of his bones are coral made;
Those are pearls that were his eyes:
Nothing of him that doth fade,
But doth suffer a sea-change
Into something rich and strange.

—Shakespeare, *The Tempest*

I ALWAYS LOVED SHAKESPEARE AT SCHOOL. NEVER WENT on to college. I guess the possibility just didn't figure on anybody's radar. Once I turned sixteen and school was over, I went straight back to work on my parents' farm. But I didn't stop reading. The number of times my father caught me stretched out under the oak tree at the far end of the north field with a copy of *Macbeth* or *King Lear* . . . Once, in a fit of rage, he swore he'd cut the old tree down, and he did too. But don't think that my father was a bad man—not at all. He just worried that he would die and leave my mother with no-one to take care of her. He loved my mother, you see—loved her like a man possessed. He wouldn't let her sew at night lest she strain her eyes; he wouldn't let her help in the fields so she wouldn't become all hunched over and sore-backed like the other women in the village. He wouldn't even let her milk the cow in case she got cow pox and her dainty little hands grew blistered and calloused. Very delicate she was—my mother. Pale-skinned and raven-haired, with haunted green eyes. My father always said that she'd married beneath her, and that he was the luckiest man in the world.

But my father shouldn't have worried; it was my mother who died first. Cancer, the doctors said. Her cheeks grew gaunt and her whole face appeared to recede until her huge frightened eyes seemed to be all that was left, like a pair of emerald moons shining brightest before their eclipse. Her slender body shrivelled away to nothing. And her raven locks became streaked with white, then fell from her scalp after the hospital treatment—like discarded angel-hair once the festive season is over and Christmas trees are thrown on the compost heap to rot. My father's cries were pitiful to hear. His violent episodes became more frequent as his drinking increased; my mother—the only thing that had stood between him and his baser nature—was gone. He didn't hit me—as even through the veil of cheap whiskey he must have remembered my mother's screams the one time he'd laid a hand on me—but he found my books and burned them. *Coriolanus*, *Hamlet*, *As You Like it*, all the tattered copies of the histories and tragedies I had acquired from second-hand bookstores in the nearest town with the pennies my mother had slipped me out of her housekeeping money. All gone up in smoke. Only *The Tempest* escaped annihilation. I think my father simply hadn't seen it—for there is no other explanation as to its survival. It was as if Prospero had come out of retirement and conjured up a supernatural mist—shrouding the small volume and rendering it invisible for five long minutes while my father rampaged through my tiny room. Or some such thing. When my father finally fell asleep on the kitchen table, tears in his eyes and an empty whiskey bottle in his hand, I picked up *The Tempest* and left. I never saw my father again.

———————

Four years later, aged twenty-two now and having worked my way across Europe doing odd jobs, I found myself in Eastern Poland. I'd wanted to come here for some time, as my mother had mentioned that her mother came from a village in this part of the world. I hadn't pushed her on the subject, as it always seemed to make her sad; I gather that the family had fled some pogrom or other when the Russians occupied the region. But I regretted not having asked exactly which village it was. . . .

The country was beginning to recover from forty-five years of communism, but nobody had told the peasants in its easternmost areas. Here people still scratched a meagre living from the difficult soil.

I'd saved some money working as a hotel receptionist in Lublin, and I knocked around the countryside, half-heartedly looking for my grand-mother's village, and whole-heartedly enjoying the exotic landscape of ramshackle settlements and unspoilt forests.

I fell in love with the little village of Switeziec at once, and took up temporary residence with an old lady who let rooms and cooked a great breakfast. To my delight, her grandson Piotr—a friendly young man of eighteen or so—knew a little English; and what he didn't know, he made up for in enthusiasm, expansive gestures and an easy laugh, which the world around him seemed unable to suppress for long.

'They start to teach English in school as soon as compulsory Russian was kicked out,' laughed Piotr when I expressed my surprise at his linguistic skills. I couldn't help but think that he made a nice change from the serious, somewhat gloomy majority of young Polish men I'd come across so far. Young men who reminded me too much of . . . well . . . me. Yes, I realised that laughter was something that didn't come easily to me, and I often chided myself for my inability to kick back and have fun.

'You come to Switeziec at good time,' Piotr flashed a full set of healthy-looking teeth at me. 'We have big party tonight.' I waited for Piotr to continue, then realised that he was awaiting my response.

'Oh, I see. Well. Thanks for mentioning it, Piotr, but I've got to get an early start tomorrow if I'm going to get to the next village . . . ' Piotr blinked uncomprehendingly. 'You remember what we spoke about?—I'm trying to find the village my grandmother's family came from?'

'Oh, I see.' Piotr looked crestfallen for a moment, but the teeth were out again soon enough. 'But tonight is very special night. It's . . . longest day. Very special.'

'Oh. Midsummer's Eve? . . . So it is.'

'Yes. We have very special party. It's tradition. We have fire and the girls make . . . out of flowers . . . and light candles . . . and put them on river, and the boys have to catch them.'

'What?'

'I not explain well . . . ' Piotr's frustration was painful to watch. 'It's tradition . . . You will like . . . Please, you come with me.' Whether it was a chance to practise his English, or to show off his foreign friend to the other villagers, or just his innate friendliness and desire to be a great host that rendered my presence so seemingly important to him, I don't know, but when Piotr's smile started to waver, I gave in. And so later that evening I found myself following him and a group of his friends to the Swita River, which flowed west of the village.

Twilight had been slow in coming. Beyond the various shades of grey, an orange glow emanated from the riverbank. As we got closer, the sounds of singing and laughter steadily grew. There was a large bonfire on the nearside. Young men sat around, drinking beer and talking excitedly. On the far bank, and about fifty metres upriver, was another bonfire.

'The girls are making . . . erm . . . out of flowers,' Piotr tried to explain, following my gaze. 'Like this.' He used both hands to draw a circle in the air.

'Wreaths?' I suggested.

'Yes, wreaths . . . Normally you put on head, like this,' Piotr demonstrated by lifting the invisible circle and placing it on his head, 'but today they put candles in them and put them on river.' I nodded, doing my best to understand.

'The boys catch the . . . wreaths. And when a boy catch the wreath, he can kiss the girl who made it.'

'I see. . . But how do you know whose wreath you've fished out?'

'Oh, I think the boys—they just kiss the girl they like.'

'That sounds like cheating to me,' I quipped. Piotr looked at me, worked out that I was joking, and chuckled.

There was a flurry of giggling and excited shrieks from the far side of the river.

'Look!' cried Piotr, 'Girls put wreaths on water!' And sure enough, a dozen or so little lights came floating in our direction. Some went out almost immediately, others sank without a trace, but a few continued to float and burn, carried downriver by the strong current.

Piotr's friends giggled no less than the girls, and rushed down the bank with the other youths.

'Come on!' Piotr called out as he hurried after the others, who were braving the freezing water to intercept those wreaths that hadn't already drowned.

I followed cautiously, afraid of slipping and falling in. I'd always been scared of water; even before the time when my father had tried to teach me to swim. He'd used the same method his father had used on him: he'd rowed us out to the middle of the lake near our farm, and pushed me out of the boat. I don't remember much after that, except that he'd had to fish me out himself; his anger at having to get wet tempered by the fear that he'd actually drowned me and that the shock would kill my mother. He never gave me another swimming lesson, evidently deciding that having a pathetic runt of a son was better than having a dead one.

The mirth on the riverbank was infectious, and I couldn't help but smile as Piotr beat his friend to a wreath and pulled it out of the water, waving it in the air and whooping in triumph. Then I saw something that stopped the breath in my lungs.

She was standing between the willows on the far bank, a little aside from the other girls. The light from the bonfire seemed to die before it reached her, and she was bathed in shadow. At first I thought that one of the willows had moved, and I felt startled and disorientated. As I peered into the gloom, my eyes adjusted, and then I saw her quite plainly ... no, 'plainly' is the wrong word— for there was nothing plain about her at all. The bonfire, the singing, the shouts and laughter—everything subsided and disappeared for a moment. All I was aware of was the girl on the other side of the river. She was tall and slender; her dress as pale as her delicate features. Her waist-long hair was so fair it seemed to glow blue in the twilight. As I stared, the girl turned to face me, and I finally understood what people meant when they said that their heart had skipped a beat. I paused, steadying myself, and inhaled deeply. She smiled at me and, despite the distance and the scant light, I could tell that her lips were the colour of coral. Every detail of her form was etched into my memory from that moment on, forever. The only strange thing was—perhaps because she tilted her head down shyly, perhaps because a strand of flaxen hair fell across her face—I couldn't see her eyes.

The girl waved at me; her hand small, with long, tapering fingers. I looked around to see whether she could be waving at someone else, but there was no one behind or next to me. Hesitantly, I waved back, and she waved again, beckoning me to join her on the far bank. My heart beat so fast I could hardly breathe.

'Piotr!' I ran up to the boy and grabbed his arm.

'Hey,' he turned towards me and grinned. 'Look! I have a wreath.'

'Where can I cross the river?'

'Huh?'

'Where's the nearest place I can cross the river?' I slowed my words right down, articulating each one as clearly as I could.

'Just there, to the right,' Piotr's confusion was replaced by mere surprise, and he pointed downriver. I peered into the darkness, but saw nothing. 'There are logs put on river. About twenty metres that way,' continued Piotr, adding: 'Hey, why do you want to go to girls' side anyway?' Then he grinned, 'It's cheating!'

'The girl,' was all I managed by way of an explanation.

'It's cheating,' Piotr repeated, laughing. 'You're supposed to catch a wreath first . . . Anyway, which girl it is you like?'

'The girl,' I pointed across the water, but she was gone. An indescribable, overwhelming feeling of loss and longing came over me; I felt like I'd been kicked in the stomach and I figured I must be having a panic attack of some sort.

'What girl?' grinned Piotr, then stopped grinning as he saw the look on my face.

'The blonde girl,' I tried to explain, my eyes scouring the opposite bank. 'Look, Piotr, thanks,' I stammered. 'I've got to go.'

I staggered off in the direction of the makeshift bridge, leaving a perplexed Piotr muttering to his friends—something about the lovelorn foreigner, no doubt.

Soon I was standing next to the bridge—a couple of logs thrown over the fast-flowing river. I stared down into the murky water.

Full fathom five thy father lies;

If I had any chance at all of finding the girl, I'd have to get a move on. I placed my right foot on one of the logs, then, checking to make sure there was nobody watching, I got down on my hands and knees, tested the logs and started to crawl along them; one hand and knee on one log, one on the other.

The gushing noise of the current made me feel giddy. I determined to crawl straight over to the other side, without looking down. I made it about half-way across, but then I caught sight of something white in the water to my left.

Of his bones are coral made;

I came to an unsteady halt. I could hear my breath coming in short gasps and my heart beating—a blessing, I thought, as it seemed to drown out the hiss of the river. Holding onto the rough bark of the logs, I glanced down to my left. Nothing: only blackness and the rushing, spuming water.

I took a deep breath and moved off slowly. It came again: a silvery flash in the water, caught out of the corner of my eye. I jerked my head in the direction of whatever it was, digging my fingers into the wood and flattening myself against the logs for fear of falling in.

And I saw it: a pale shape floating just beneath the surface of the inky water. In my fear, I thought I could make out a human face, and for a moment I believed I was looking at a corpse.

Those are pearls that were his eyes

But then the thing disappeared upriver, apparently swimming against the strong current. Once I stopped trembling, I crawled as quickly as I dared to the far side. I stood up shakily and looked upriver. Nothing there. As my heartbeat returned to normal, I told myself that I'd imagined everything; that my innate fear of death by water had conjured up visions of corpse-like monsters to torment me.

Then I remembered the girl, and that unbearable feeling of sadness and yearning returned. I hurried up the grassy bank, unnerved by the willows, which looked like frozen human forms in the half-light, and headed upriver.

As I approached the girls' bonfire, I looked in vain for the girl with the flaxen hair. The other girls didn't notice me at first, but as my search grew more desperate, a couple of them spotted me. They approached, giggling, and searched me for any sign of a wreath, telling me off and shooing me away amicably when they found no sign of one. I stumbled past the bonfire and into the dense forest beyond.

The forest was a frightening place at night. The darkness was full of noises—rustling and scuttling, as startled animals fled before me into the undergrowth. Never for a moment did I stop to think about what I was doing. I only knew that if I didn't find the girl, my heart would break—indeed, it was breaking already.

'Hello?' I called out, peering between the ancient trees. 'Are you there?' Only the wind answered, sighing in the branches. For a moment I thought I glimpsed something white flitting in between the trees nearest the river. 'Hey!' I called out, and tried to run, but tripped on a protruding root and almost fell. I righted myself by grabbing hold of a tree, scratching my hand in the process. When I looked up again, there was nothing between the trees, but shadow. I stumbled on in this inept and idiotic way, imagining from time to time that I could see a wisp of blue-white hair ahead of me, stopping only when the dawn chorus broke through my desperate reveries and a rosy glimmer appeared in the east. Defeated and exhausted, I turned around and headed back along the river.

The shouts and laughter, and glow of the bonfire reached me before I broke clear of the tree-line. I was surprised to find the young villagers still partying. The boys and girls had largely paired off, and were holding hands and leaping across the fairly feisty remains of the fire. Had I been in a fit state to appreciate what was going on around me, I would no doubt have concluded that their stamina and party spirit was something to be admired, even if the local vodka was contributing.

'Hey!' someone called, and then Piotr was patting me on the back, with a relieved kind of laugh. 'Where have you been? I been worried for you!'

'I'm sorry, Piotr,' I muttered gloomily.

'Where you were?'

'I was looking for the girl,' I told him, but didn't expect to make him understand.

'What girl? All the girls are here ... ' I must have looked as shattered and distressed as I was feeling, because Piotr put his arm around my shoulders and said, 'Come on, my friend, we go home.' I protested weekly, mumbling something about having to look for the girl. 'Come on, man,' Piotr steered me in a friendly, but firm manner away from the river. 'You look terrible. You need sleep.'

'But ... '

'I help you look for girl tomorrow ... or actually, later today.' Piotr winked at a pretty red-haired girl and whispered something to her which made her smile, then led me back to his grandmother's house.

I fell into an exhausted sleep—punctuated by dreams of floating corpses, dark forests, and the girl disappearing among the trees—and woke at lunchtime. I got dressed and sloped downstairs, presumably looking awful, as a worried look appeared on Piotr's grandmother's face when she saw me. She asked Piotr a question and he shrugged her off, in a not unfriendly manner. He pushed an empty chair away from the table, inviting me to sit down. I forced myself to sit, but every nerve in my body was crying out to get back outside and look for the girl.

Piotr's grandmother busied herself at the stove, and moments later set a bowl of hot hunter's stew down in front of me, along with a small basket of fresh rye bread. I hadn't eaten since the previous evening and yet, when Piotr's grandmother gestured for me to eat, I found that I couldn't.

'I'm sorry,' I said, feeling miserable and ungrateful.

'You feel bad?' asked Piotr, the concern in his face echoing that in his grandmother's.

'The girl,' I said. 'I have to find her.' I rose swiftly, apologised again to Piotr's grandmother, and headed for the door.

'Wait!' Piotr got up and ran after me. 'I come with you!'

A couple of hours later, Piotr persuaded me to return to the house for fear that I would pass out. Reluctantly I succumbed, drinking a cup of sweet tea and packing a chunk of bread, before heading back out, much to the chagrin of Piotr's grandmother.

'I come with you,' said Piotr, somewhat less enthusiastically than earlier.

'No,' I insisted. 'You stay here; your grandmother looks worried.' I left quickly, hearing Piotr and his grandmother arguing as I walked away.

I spent the rest of the day following the Swita River first one way, then the other. Once or twice I thought I saw something pale shimmering in the water, but when I turned to look, it was gone. When my feet grew too sore to keep walking, I returned to the house and tried to sleep. I tossed and turned, and attempted to free my mind of thoughts, but whenever I closed my eyes, I saw the girl waving to me from the row of willows. The terrible yearning and hopelessness gnawed away at me, and I'm ashamed to say that

I cried into my pillow. I finally dozed off a little before dawn, and got up late again.

As I entered the kitchen, Piotr's grandmother eyed me with unease.

'*Piotrusiu!*' she called, and a moment later Piotr appeared, smiling at me in a worried way that I was coming to dislike. There was a brief exchange between the two of them, during which the look on the old woman's face became progressively more alarmed. She said something to Piotr, who laughed, causing her to brandish a wooden spoon at him in a less than friendly gesture. She cast me an extremely troubled glance, then returned her attention to the frying-pan.

'Are you okay?' asked Piotr.

'I'm fine,' I said, forcing myself to smile at the old lady as she set a plate of ham and eggs down in front of me before sitting down opposite and staring at me intently.

'What you are going to do today?' questioned Piotr with feigned cheerfulness; then added doubtfully, 'You are going to look for your grandmother's village?'

'No.'

'You are going to look for girl?'

'Yes.'

Piotr's grandmother evidently asked Piotr what I'd said. The boy translated, and the old lady leapt up from the table, glanced at me, then let out a tirade at her grandson, who was looking more and more embarrassed.

'What did she say?' I asked.

'Nothing,' said Piotr.

'Tell me, please.'

'It's rubbish. Stupid story.'

'Piotr!' I pleaded, and the old lady interjected on my behalf.

'OK,' Piotr finally gave in. 'My grandmother says your girl is Rusalka.'

'Who?'

'Rusalka. A bad spirit.'

'What do you mean?'

'It's an old story that the peasants tell.'

'Go on.'

'They say that if a girl dies before . . . her wedding day . . . she becomes Rusalka. They live in water and in trees.'

'Like nymphs?' If I hadn't been in such a sorry state, I probably would have found Piotr's story entertaining.

'Yes . . . Typical stupid story.'

'Yes,' I agreed. Then I noticed Piotr's grandmother still staring at me and nodding her head gravely. 'But please tell your grandmother not to worry. The girl I saw isn't a . . . Rusalka. She's just a girl, and I'm worried that something might have happened to her. I need to find her.' I got up and headed out, stopping Piotr from following me with a staying hand gesture.

The day passed much as the previous one, except that the sadness and feeling I can only describe as emptiness was even more draining than before. It was as though I'd lost a limb, but could still feel the ache of where it had once been.

I went home when it got dark, and went to bed without speaking to
Piotr. I couldn't face his questions or his grandmother's look of concern. I lay awake for a long time, looking at the ceiling. When I finally closed my eyes, the full moon rose outside my window, its light unnerving me even through closed lids. I could swear I heard someone whispering my name, and I turned to the window. The moonlight was silver-blue, like the girl's hair. The whispering came again and the sighing of the wind in the branches of the tree outside. Eventually I could lie there no longer. I got dressed, crept as quietly as I could over the creaky wooden floor, and headed for the river.

The fields were a pale grey, and beyond them the river sparkled silver. I planned to start at the makeshift bridge, then work my way upriver and into the forest. I walked along distractedly and didn't notice that I was approaching the water a little upriver of my chosen starting point. In fact, it wasn't until I was at the river's edge that I noticed I'd come out amidst the willows—in almost the same place as I'd seen the girl. Startled out of my stupor by that thought, I looked across to where she'd stood. I thought I heard my name whispered on the wind, and then I saw a willow move in the pale light. No, not a willow—her! Standing on the opposite side of the river, now as she had the first time I'd seen her, but even more beautiful in the moonlight, even more heart-stopping. A shiver ran down my spine and goose bumps appeared on my skin despite the warm June night. The girl's hair was so pale that it glowed blue in the moon's rays, and her lips were the colour of coral. I tried, but I couldn't see her eyes. She smiled at me and waved, beckoning me to join her on the other side of the river. Mesmerised, I took a step forward, then stopped as my foot slipped on the soft mud of the riverbank and I nearly lost my footing. I looked down at the rushing, roaring current and felt dizzy. But I would get to her somehow.

'Wait!' I pleaded. 'I'll cross over the bridge!' But she was already moving off in the opposite direction. 'Wait, please!' I ran a few steps towards the bridge, then turned quickly and ran after the girl, keeping track of her across the river as she moved in and out of the willows, smiling wanly and motioning to me. Each time her slim form disappeared from my field of vision, it was like a stab to my heart. I'd missed my opportunity to cross the bridge to her side of the river, but I wouldn't let her out of my sight for more than a split-second.

'Hey, slow down! Please!' I followed her upriver. The solitary willows gave way to clusters of birches, oaks and pines, and soon we were in the forest; the river between us all the while. She was the most beautiful thing I had ever seen; she was a silvery-blue angel, shining among the dark monoliths of the trees. I panicked as she disappeared from view, and quickened my pace.

'Where are you?' I practically begged, hurrying deeper and deeper into the forest. 'Please! Where are you?' Light-headed with anxiety, I stopped and peered across the river. For a while all was still and I was alone with my own heartbeat once again. That overpowering sense of loss assaulted me for a moment, and then I saw her. She moved from behind a tree and stood directly opposite me on the far side of the river. Naked. The moonlight reflected off her lily-white skin and blue-blonde hair. Her body was perfection, and she stood quite still, gazing at me, frozen like the alabaster statue of a goddess. I heard my name whispered in the air, and the girl moved so gracefully that she seemed to float down to the water's edge. She waved to me, beckoning me to approach the river on my side. I got as close to the water as I dared, then stopped and watched the girl go in.

'No!' I called out in alarm. 'Don't!' But the girl merely laughed and immersed herself in the river; the water covering her nakedness. She waved to me to join her, and I waved back, pleading with her to come to my side. The girl laughed and swam over to my side, then swam leisurely back to the middle of the river and floated there. The ease with which she swam and floated in that rushing water made me wonder whether perhaps the current was less strong that it looked and sounded. Perhaps the water wasn't as deep as I'd thought.

The girl beckoned me again and I shook my head, indicating for her to swim to me and come out. I held a hand out to her, and eventually she swam towards me, stopping just a little out of my reach. I extended my hand out further, and she pushed herself up from the water and reached out to me. As she did so, the drops of water on her breasts sparkled. I couldn't take my eyes off her. She moved away again and I lost my balance, toppling into the icy water.

Fear—all the more dreadful for its long-forgotten familiarity—seized me as the dark waters closed over my head. I flailed my arms wildly, managing somehow to right myself and get my head above the surface. Eyes screwed shut against the lashing current, I coughed up water and finally managed to scream for help. Then I felt arms around me—arms colder than the river against which I fought.

'Help me,' I begged through the roar of the raging water—water that
no longer looked silver, but black and threatening. I felt the brush of wet hair on my face and of icy lips against my ear—lips colder

than the spray that blinded me. The girl whispered my name with tenderness, and her voice was the sigh of the wind and the murmur of the sea. For a moment I remembered my mother and how she would hold a large shell to my ear when I was little, and say, 'Listen, my love, it's the sound of the sea.'

The girl's grip on me tightened and I prayed that she would save me, but the water closed over my head once more.

I try to draw breath, but swallow river-water instead. I don't understand. I kick and writhe, but cold hands pull me down and hold me firm.

Gradually I weaken and stop fighting. My terror subsides and I open my eyes. In the blackness, the girl's face looms white before my own. She lifts her heavy lids and I see her eyes clearly for the first time. Fear seizes me once more; the last of my air escapes in a flurry of bubbles as I panic. She holds onto me and smiles, gazing at me with those eyes—a corpse's eyes: milky, opaque ... like pearls.

My lungs swell with water. A strange calm descends on me and I stop struggling for the last time. The girl cradles me in her arms.

I wonder if the current will carry me down to the sea.

ANNA TABORSKA *(b. London, England, 1969) studied Experimental Psychology at Oxford University and went on to gainful employment in public relations, journalism and advertising, before throwing everything over to become a filmmaker and horror writer.*

*Anna has directed two short films (*Ela *and* The Sin*), two documentaries (*My Uprising *and* A Fragment of Being*) and a one-hour television drama (*The Rain Has Stopped*), which won two awards at the British Film Festival, Los Angeles, 2009. Anna has also worked on seventeen other films, including Ben Hopkins'*

Simon Magus *(starring Noah Taylor and Rutger Hauer) and Neil Wassell's* Number One Longing. Number Two Regret *(starring Jenny Agutter).*

Anna served as a researcher and assistant producer on several BBC television programmes, including the series Auschwitz: The Nazis and the Final Solution *and* World War Two: Behind Closed Doors—Stalin, the Nazis and the West. *Anna's feature length screenplays include:* Chainsaw, The Camp *and* Pizzaman. *Short screenplays include:* Little Pig *(finalist in the Shriekfest Film Festival Screenplay Competition 2009),* Curious Melvin, *and* Arthur's Cellar.

Anna's short stories include: "Halloween Lights" *(in And Now the Nightmare Begins: THE HORROR ZINE, 2009),* "Picture This" *(52 Stitches, Year 2, 2010),* "The Wind and the Rain" *(Daily Flash 2011: 365 Days of Flash Fiction, 2010) and four stories published in* The Black Book of Horror, *vols. 5-8 (2009-2011). Anna's short story* "Bagpuss" *was an Eric Hoffer Award Honoree and is now published in* Best New Writing 2011. *Poems include* "Kantor" *(*Journal of Dramatic Theory and Criticism, *Fall 1995),* "Mrs. Smythe regrets going to the day spa" *(*Christmas: Peace on All The Earths, *2010),* "Song for Maud" *(*No Fresh Cut Flowers, An Afterlife Anthology, *2010) and three poems in* What Fears Become: An Anthology from the Horror Zine *(2011).*

You can watch clips from Anna's films and view her full resume here: http://www.imdb.com/name/nm1245940/

Commentary on "Rusalka": *A rusalka is the unquiet spirit of a young woman who died a violent death; a nymph; a she-demon . . . or perhaps all three. My story was inspired in part by visits to Poland, the country in which my parents were born and which, I have learnt, has changed beyond recognition as a result of the Second World War. WWII saw the destruction by invading forces of entire communities in Poland, such as the Jewish minority which numbered 3.5 million before the war and 250,000 after it. When* interviewing Polish peasants for a BBC television series on Auschwitz several years ago, I was struck by the trauma among the elder generation, and the sense of loss for a Poland that would never be the same again. I wanted to tell a story of loss and longing for something that can never be (re)captured, through the eyes of a stranger, but one who has a bond with the place through which he journeys. The watery theme of the story was inspired by the stunning and intensely creepy 'sea-change' passage from Shakespeare's The Tempest, but also by the writing of the Polish bard Adam Mickiewicz, whose long and beautiful poems occasionally contain mysterious water maidens, betrayed lovers and watery graves. In his poem "Świteź", Mickiewicz writes about a town that was attacked by an enemy army while the men were away at war. The women preferred to die rather than succumb to the invaders, but were reluctant to damn their immortal souls to hell by committing suicide. Their prayers were answered when a huge lake appeared from nowhere and the town sank to the bottom of it; the women, children and elders being turned to flowers that grow in the lake to this day.

CANDY

NICK ANTOSCA

1

'... LOST HIS MIND,' MEGAN IS SAYING. 'BUT GRADUALLY.
Nobody noticed at first. His wife told the cops all he did last week
was sit in the Jacuzzi and read *Teen People*. Then he started following kids home from school.'

She's driving. I'm looking out the window, hardly listening, as
scenery slips by: a slideshow of our childhood. Gingerbread houses
with glimmers of blue behind them. The sky, sagging over us, is
ashes and papier-mâché.

'Where did all these swimming pools come from?' I murmur.
'These are all new.'

'I don't know,' she says. 'I noticed the same thing.'

It's good to see Megan again, now that we've finished our fresh-
man years at separate schools, but there's no excitement. I spent
all high school lusting after her. It's never going to happen. I've
come to accept that.

Rain begins falling. The automatic windows slither up. Up ahead,
my house appears.

Megan glances at me. A spread of freckles like butterfly wings
under her eyes. 'Isn't that Harry?' she asks with a toss of her jaw.

I look. The sight of my disheveled Chesapeake Bay retriever

digging a hole in the neighbors' lawn, snout crumbly with dirt, makes me chuckle.

'Yeah,' I answer. 'He's getting senile.'

The Audi crawls into our driveway. I hesitate before getting out.

I ask, 'Do you want to hang out?'

'No, I can't.'

'Where you going now?'

'Jessie's.'

'Jessie?' I suck my lip. 'Aren't you a little old to hang out with her?'

'Don't be obnoxious. She's almost sixteen.'

'And you're almost twenty. Grow up.'

'What? There's no reason I shouldn't hang out with her, she's very smart for her age. And she's my cousin. *What*? Get out, you're irritating me.'

I get out. Her car glides away in the gray drizzle.

M y house is museum-quiet. Like a slender, tense insect, my mother flits from room to room. Later, as she stands folding and unfolding a section of newspaper with trembling fingers, I ask if anything's wrong. A fly creeps across a silk lampshade and she kills it.

Afternoon grades into evening. I wander the house. The silence is stifling. I think of Megan—brown eyes, pecan-dark hair, almond freckles. Looking into the blue dusk beyond the patio doors, I watch the lights go on in the swimming pool.

The twilight thickens. In the kitchen I fix a chicken salad sandwich dripping with mayonnaise. I slice my finger deeply with the bread knife and have to clean blood away at the kitchen sink. I bandage the wound. Then I wash the sandwich down with a glass of white wine. The phone rings as I lick my fingers. An anxious voice talks into the answering machine, asking Dad, who is president of the homeowner's council, to do something about something. The voice is odd. I trudge upstairs.

A TV mumbles from Dad's study—something with a languid, sleazy saxophone.

2

Megan arrives at three with her 15-year-old cousin Jessie. Yesterday's grim drizzle is forgotten—sticky sunlight drips over everything. Jessie looks like she's trying to be some Italian model in those sunglasses, leaning against the car and eating Lifesavers.

My dog, Harry, prances nearby, nosing Jessie's apricot knees, chewing his own haunches, begging for something.

I meet Megan and Jessie at the door. Sunlight knifes off Jessie's sun-glasses. A drab green helicopter slides across the sky.

In the kitchen we eat cold steak sandwiches while the dog gnaws his foreleg. I pick open the half-healed cut on my finger. My parents are not in the house.

Like a bear cub looking for honey, Jessie lowers her russet-blond head to lick mayonnaise from her sandwich crust. 'I want to go swimming,' she says. 'Don't you, Megs?' Megan nudges her elbow. She nudges back. Some inside joke. Annoying.

Megan finishes her sandwich, licks her fingers. A black fly crawls across the white cabinet behind her head, trying to get at hidden sugar. Jessie murmurs again (mouth stuffed) that she wants to swim, and I wonder out loud, 'Why does everybody have pools now?'

I wipe an oily palm on the cover of this week's *Gazette*, whose headline reads, 'Homeowners Quiz Merrick Brass On Dementia.'

'It was a dick-measuring contest,' Jessie says, casual. 'Like every family got a pool this spring. Everybody that works at North Capital got a Christmas bonus, and in March the Lamberts got a new pool, then like three other families did, and then the Walcotts got one bigger and nicer than anybody's.'

'I saw it when we drove past,' says Megan.

'They threw a party to show off, but it was too drizzly to go in the water. That was the irony: everybody got pools, but it's been so rainy, you couldn't really swim until last week. We already had a pool, so we just got a Jacuzzi.' She giggles. 'Dennis is scared of it.' Dennis is her brother.

Harry the dog is laboriously licking kitchen tiles, table legs. The sun burns bronze outside the window. My fingers feel bloodless, anemic, dreamlike. Something is—

'Let's go swimming,' Jessie says.

I slide swim trunks on and, from my bedroom window, watch Megan and Jessie. Huddled in the back seat of Megan's car, getting changed into their bathing suits, they're partially obscured by sun and shade on the rear windshield, but now and then I get a flash of bare shoulder, an imagined giggle, a penny-colored nipple.

We meet outside on the deck. The dog tags along, tongue dangling. The sun hangs in the west. Megan sheds her towel and slices the water with a smooth, clean dive.

She surfaces, ripples spreading around her like ruined halos, and shouts, 'Come on! Get *in*!' She's looking at Jessie, not me. And now Jessie dives too, turning into a sleek, flowing, flesh-colored thing under the surface, leaving me alone.

I get in the water.

The water's cool. It makes the cut on my finger tingle. I surface, suddenly sleepy and peaceful, and watch Megan and Jessie swimming together.

How lovely. The tension and glacial boredom of late afternoon melts away and I feel something I can't explain—a small euphoria in my chest, an incipient orgasm.

The sun gets lower as we swim. An hour passes, two, and my fingers prune. A glorious and malevolent orange glow rusts the sky. Dad appears at the glass door, half-hidden behind reflections of burnished light. Then he's gone. Black silhouettes of birds cross the sunset. The girls laugh and splash like harp seals.

They float in the deep end, paying me no attention. I watch their shimmering, naked, dream-strange legs in endless slow motion. The closeness of Megan's friendship with Jessie has always seemed a little strange to me.

Dusk comes. I feel nourished. Revitalized. The underwater lights throb on and our lower halves glow aquamarine. As twilight thickens, filled with crickets and distant, chuckling sitcoms, Megan drifts up, kisses me, then scissor-kicks away, giggling.

I heave myself out of the water. My fingers are soft and wrinkled, purple flesh fringed with dead white skin. How long was I in the water? Hours, hours—had to be. I could go for hours more. Feels like something is taking place inside my brain, some chewing away of membranes.

The dog circles me, lapping at my trunks.

I look around. And seem to teeter at a delirious height. My senses are limp, or limpid, with overstimulation—the sky, its razory stars like diamonds in folds of black satin; the air, its wine-like sharpness; the night, its promises.

My skin tingles. I turn to the girls. They float, suspended in the luminous water, their pink outlines quivering beneath the surface.

'Hey,' I shout, 'you guys—I have an idea.'

Gliding poolside with languid kicks, they grab the concrete lip.

'Let's go to *all* the pools.' I'm panting. 'Come on, out of the water. Let's go. We'll go to every pool in the entire neighborhood. I mean the *entire fucking neighborhood*. All night.'

I pause. All three of us are panting. Tired but unspeakably alive. Torn gloriously open, changed somehow.

'That is a fucking great idea,' gasps Megan. The girls drag themselves out of the pool. Megan's long bikinied body stretches on the concrete, and she struggles to her feet, giggling. 'I'm a sponge,' she mumbles. 'Look at my hands.'

Jessie collapses on the grass, laughing. My skin hurts. These girls are beautiful. Nobody moves for a couple minutes. We breathe. What's happening to us?

3

I watch Jessie's bare, pruned, perfect feet crossing the grass. We traipse across the front lawn and I'm floating, doped up with laughter and gladness, and I can't keep my eyes off Megan's glistening calves.

No cars in sight. The asphalt feels almost soft underfoot. We cross the street, cross the Rossdales' lawn.

The backyard is gated, and the gate is locked, and, giggling, we lean against the fence, which is made of fresh cedar boards. Soon we stumble away into the darkness, sucking slivers and splinters from our palms.

As we cut across the Bartons' dark yard and the Talbots' leafy garden, I notice I possess astonishingly pristine vision—the night environment, with its veins of shadow and inky niches, seems hyper-real.

Megan's vanilla arms brush her naked hips with each step, swinging with the dumb rhythm of lovely, drunken, pale pendulums. I think of licking them.

We meander across backyards, stubbing pink toes on secret sprinkler heads and parting the lukewarm darkness of the suburbs. We pass satellite antennas that squat like odd black flowers, and suddenly I remember (getting a headache) the plan, so we claw through a gap in the Lawfords' dense hedge.

Several awful moments later (my head suddenly pounding) we emerge with the Lawfords' pool before us on the lawn like a large, dreamy emerald. 'Let's go swimming,' I mumble. I'm bleeding, scraped badly on my arms and hands.

'Come *on*,' I say. I lead them to the luminescent water.

Plunging in, my body seems to open up. Pores dilate, muscles slacken. Opening my eyes, I see the girls, smeared and otherworldly, trailing sheets of white bubbles. I stay under for a while. Finally I burst up for air.

The headache is gone—I'm made of velvet and Novocain. Spectral jetliners scrape thin, precise lines across the night sky. Jessie clings to Megan's arm and hiccups, laughing. I'm inhaling fumes and I can see for miles, a million miles.

Nobody notices the dog at first. Not until he's almost in the water. Then Jessie stops pawing Megan long enough to gurgle, 'What's wrong with him?' and a mottled, hairy thing falls from the dog's mouth into the pool with a flat splash and cloudy blood billows out. The water's turning brownish red.

'What was *that*?'

Now the dog laps obliviously at the bloodied water, and we glide away, our happy trance-like moment ruined, and crawl out of the pool. From the far side, we stare at the hunchbacked dog. He drinks, drinks.

We stumble into the feverish night.

In another yard, two obese women in white cotton underwear wade in the water, eating pieces of raw meat with their hands. A yellow Styrofoam tray drifts in the pool.

They look alarmed when we appear over the fence.

'Get away,' one blubbers. 'There's nothing for you.'

'Sorry,' Megan says, and we clumsily retreat back over the fence. Jessie is getting agitated.

'I want to go swimming again,' she whimpers, clawing Megan. 'My head hurts. *My skin is shaking.*'

'Shut up,' I tell her. 'It is not.' I resist the weird and rapid desire to turn around, stick my fingers inside her mouth, and squeeze her tongue.

We pass a house where lights blaze behind broken windows.

Before we reach the Walcott's fence, we hear voices. I recognize my mother's among the puppy sighs of the conversation. Green light, misty, hangs in the air above the unseen pool.

Kneeling, I stare between fence posts. There's my mother, in her gold and green bikini, with sun-fried wrinkles and a skinny waist, soaking in the green water. A wattled man, not my father, holds her. Old people crowd the pool. No one seems to care that Mrs. Mehl has taken her top off, and her aged, deflated breasts are floating on the water in front of her. An elderly man drinks pool water like a dog.

'Not here,' I mumble, skull thudding. 'We'll find another one.'

The next pool is kidney-shaped, with a diving board on one end and a kiddie pool on the other. We climb the fence, and by now Jessie needs help, she's trembling. The thudding in my head has become cymbals.

We wade in. The water laps hungrily at our naked legs. Once underwater, eyes closed, I soak. The headache goes away! I resurface. The house—which belongs to a family called Ames—is dark. We can stay here all night. I hear a radio, which is somewhere in the darkness beside the pool. It mumbles . . . '—research at Fort Merrick. The Fairfax Homeowners' Council filed a freedom of—'

Then I notice our audience. Dr. Ames sits, half-naked, in a patch of shadows by the pool house. A long dark-colored cigarette dangles from his lips, smoldering. Water glistens in his thistle of white chest hair.

Now the girls notice him too—watching us.

'Oh, sorry,' Megan says slowly, 'we didn't realize . . . ' but she trails away, because it's plain that Dr. Ames isn't interested. He doesn't stir. The radio murmurs, 'Major Collins denied the accusation, saying that chemical and biological research is primarily conducted at Fort Detrick, Maryland, and that Fort Merrick has no such facilities. Still, Fairfax residents who spoke to reporters yesterday—'

Dr. Ames's nose starts trickling blood.

'—sudden onset of dementia in the six cases—'

Dr. Ames's voice, when he speaks, is like porridge.

'I'll warn you once,' he grumbles, 'and not once more—don't move my cigarillos. Or I'll fix you good. I warned *her*, too.'

He sniffles. Blood drips over his upper lip, and he licks it away. 'A hundred times I told her.'

'—*exhibited inconsistent physical symptoms, including severe rashes and swollen extremities, but*—'

The brown cigarette glows when he draws on it, and ashes tumble dangerously into his thicket of chest hair. 'I said don't move them. How hard was that?' He pauses, frowning. 'Maybe I overreacted.'

'We won't bother you,' says Megan.

'That's why I got that drill in the first place,' he says. 'To fix things around the house.'

Turning off the radio, he walks over to sit by the pool, soaking his tanned old feet in the water. He flexes pruned toes.

'I don't mind if you use my pool. Nothing better than a swim and a smoke. Like heaven.'

He sits and smokes for a while. Close by, invisible crickets play their raw violins. The girls swim lazily, and the stars are clear and bright. Megan emerges for air, glittering with droplets. Her eyes are vivid and rich like caramelized candy; damp hair clings erotically to her throat. Like a mermaid she drifts to Megan and whispers in her ear.

The evening hums enchantingly. I close my eyes and see a vision: the suburbs at night, bejeweled with swimming pools. They speckle the dream landscape like unwrapped candy, glistening rectangles, Jolly Ranchers.

'Hey,' I say.

The girls look at me, laughing in duet.

'Get serious.' I say, suddenly irritated. 'There's a thousand more pools to go. Come on. Let's move on to the next one.' I am making my way, in half-submerged slow motion, to the side of the pool. 'Come on, out of the water. Quit fucking around. Let's focus on the, you know, the task at hand.'

Megan murmurs something about skinny dipping. An insectile helicopter crawls across the prehistoric sky. I get out of the pool. Jessie nuzzles one of Megan's creamy arms, whispers to her. Inside joke. Suddenly I lose patience.

'*Fuck you!*' I scream. 'Fine, don't come. I'll just be out there'—I make an expansive gesture, capturing euphoric possibilities—'conquering *every fucking pool in the neighborhood.*'

I stagger away. Somehow I drag myself over the fence. My feet are numb as I cross the street. The night is dizzy, gone all blurry and dark—that extraordinary clarity of vision I experienced earlier is fading. A naked man sits on a front lawn. Some mailboxes have been smashed. Like a zombie I go down the street, all smeared vision and molasses knees. I'm thinking of Megan naked; she's *mine*. I'd like to strangle Jessie.

Pressure in my skull, eyeballs popping out. I find myself on mulch—rough edges stabbing my feet. The playground. I think about Megan and there's a rise in my trunks. So I lie in the mulch, but before I can do anything, a white hot needle penetrates my skull.

Sometime much later, when I can see again, when pastel dawn clouds are just beginning to appear, I find myself staring into the plastic, sneering face of a horse with handlebars jutting out of its petrified mane. I want to get up and go swimming, but the pain is so bad I can't.

5

Dawn arrives . . . or maybe it doesn't, and I'm imagining some things, like the bedraggled and dripping Dalmatian that limps by with a kitten in its jaws. Or the naked twin boys with bloody hands, stumbling around the playground. Maybe seven or eight. They try to climb up the hard metal slide, then topple like animatronic dolls. They wander away, grunting about ice cream.

My mouth is hot and horrible—I must have vomited a bitter trickle while blacked out. That's fine. I think of glistening swimming pools and smooth feminine legs and a blood waterfall. How long have I been here? A day? I close my eyes, and, some time later, open them.

Darkness. It's *night* again.

Arguments, epithets in the distance. Barking radios. The dark seeps into me, and I get sucked under the pounding waves again.

When I wake in the soft grayness of dawn, I'm gnawed by a bad headache and my skin feels like it might slough off, but some raw semblance of cognition has returned.

Awkwardly, I get to my feet. I've been lying on the playground for—almost *thirty hours*. Questions—*why didn't anyone* find *me?*—stir in my brain. I untie the drawstring on my bathing suit and try to urinate, but only a few drops come out. Sapped, drained.

I stumble away from the playground.

6

As I walk home, skull aching, I ignore a half-naked housewife in her forties who tries to follow me down the road. She collapses.

People sleep on lawns or in the street. The dawn is warming up, and I see my house ahead. I cross the front lawn. Megan's car is still parked in our driveway. Another vehicle beside it, a blue SUV that I recognize.

Disinterested, I tiptoe in the front door and go upstairs. In the upstairs bathroom, I search on a whim for prescription drugs. But every RX bottle has been emptied, as if drug fiends have been scavenging.

Harry, my dog, floats in the pool, dead. The sun looks raw like a freshly peeled fruit.

I jump in the water and my nerves start buzzing. Harry's corpse drifts too close and I push it away, then slip underwater. Eyes closed, I open my mouth and drink some of the water. My pores dilate.

With my fingernail, I tear my scabs off. They're soft and come away easily. The cuts tingle.

I float, and when I close my eyes I see funny things.

A large, glistening, Megan-shaped lozenge. A piece of peach or butter-scotch candy with Megan's shape. It gleams a sticky pink, as if it's been licked or sucked on.

'Marty.'

I open my eyes.

A woman, standing beside the pool.

'Aunt Carol,' I mumble, spitting water.

'Get out of the water, Marty,' she says. 'Have you seen the news? Come on, *out*, now.'

Blissed out, I allow my eyelids to slip closed. Stars unfold like flowers. Soon I feel bony fingers snag my armpits and drag me backward until my head thuds gently against the sky blue tiles.

'Come on, get out. Where the hell have you been? Come *on*. Now.'

After a laborious, dragged-out struggle (to me it's just slowly exploding lares behind my eyelids) my upper body is beached on concrete, my feet still soaking. Cautiously, I let my eyelids rise. The sky looks vibrant, prideful.

'Do you know where your mother is?'

My head feels happy. 'Swimming?' I venture.

9

She's talking as she helps me down the steps, pulling me toward my dad's car. 'We're going to the medical center. I'll take the Volvo, I'm low on gas.'

'Oh, then . . . I want to drive . . . I like to drive . . . the Volvo.'

'No. Get in.' She's holding the passenger door open. I climb in. Aunt Carol gets in beside me and starts the car. Because we're blocked in by the SUV and Megan's Audi, she just drives across the lawn.

What I see on the way to the medical center:

Pieces of sunlight like razors, glinting off mailboxes. Birdshit on a mailbox. A Lexus with a broken window. Songbirds. A man with a scarf made of dead cats. Red and white flowers in a flower garden.

The questions that my aunt is driving as she asks, asking as she drives I mean, are easy to ignore. ('. . . seen her? *Any* idea where she might. . . ') Apparently she's worried about Mom, who is missing, but what I'm preoccupied with is the thudding in my skull, and the tendency of sunlight to flow across windshields like quicksilver and form puddles that look like a girl's naked shoulder or pale ankle.

On a hill overlooking the high school sits the medical center. Peppermint ambulances crouch by the entrances.

We park. Aunt Carol helps me walk barefoot across hot pavement.

Inside, a guy has a seizure. My head hurts. Police are everywhere. The waiting room is crowded. 'Wait here,' my aunt says. Nurses try to stop the man's seizures. I stare at a wall-mounted TV.

'. . . *exploded yesterday into an epidemic . . .*'

A little boy next to me chews his fingers.

'. . . *spokesman for Russell & Gimbel, the manufacturer of Sani-Tide, blamed the illnesses on mass hysteria, but officials were adamant that . . .* '

Somebody better stop that kid from eating the potted plant.

'... *believe the first six cases of dementia that stunned this Virginia suburb were allergic reactions to the chemical ...*'

The kid is choking now.

'... *Fort Merrick rumors were false, it was in fact a pool-cleaning agent ...*'

I'm surrounded by flesh-colored chaos. A piece of it breaks off in front of me. My eyes try to focus on this fragment, which is my aunt, saying something like, '... no more room ... across the street.'

My headache makes things blurry and blood-tinged as we return to the Volvo. We drive across the street to the high school.

'I don't want ... school ... I want ... Megan ... ' I'm saying as she parks.

The cafeteria has been turned into a crisis center. Green-jacketed people rush around. My aunt talks with a paramedic, gesturing in my direction. I feel a doctor tugging my elbow.

Head roaring. We're in the all-beige teacher's lounge which has been converted into a medical headquarters, one bald doctor sitting across from Aunt Carol and me, a vein thudding in his forehead. Questions, questions. I try to answer. How long was I where? In the water? What?

The doctor keeps grabbing my hand. A stack of romance novels sits on a side table. Brunette on a paperback cover. A hand grabs mine.

'Listen to me. Are you listening?'

His eyes gleam. Jessie lives on Wintergreen Lane. The room smells of coffee beans.

'You've absorbed a massive dose ... I'm going to try to explain ... know it's hard to focus, but try, okay?'

Giving up, he just talks to my aunt instead. I'm trying, but little creatures with ice picks chip at my skull from inside.

'... through the skin and probably ingested some as well ... his mucus membranes ... might have been ... in Sani-Tide—it's a pool cleaning agent, like chlorine ... because everybody in this area who went swimming in the last few days ... best guess is that something in the Sani-Tide bonded with something external ... formed a highly unstable ...'

A hand clutches mine, urgently. I look at the hand. It is large and warm.

'Try to pay attention. This is important. You ...' Megan has the prettiest eyes. '... different receptors for different neurotransmitters, and each one is specific to a single function. Drugs work by filling those receptors ... trigger specific responses. But *this* ... so unstable it breaks apart when it hits a receptor too ... so it can fit ... called Serotonin 5-HT2, which ... stimulating endorphin and opiate ... but a large dose ...' *God, my head hurts.* '... means it can attack multiple receptors of different sizes ...'

I am dimly fascinated by what he is saying. Also by the path of an insect across the windowpane behind his head. Everything turns me on, makes me think of Megan.

'... universal symptom is lack of impulse control. Inhibitions become ...'

The insect pauses, then starts zigzagging again.

'... in the hospital at least a few days... hopefully out of your system....be painful, like a bad hangover, for about thirty-six ... Okay? Marty?'

The doctor sighs when I tell him I've got to piss. I see the haze of pain that surrounds me vibrating when I speak.

'The nurse will take you.'

A white blur leads me past a row of lockers. It stops to help a heaving man while I go into the bathroom. I breathe and lean against the wall. Then I piss on the floor (I'm horribly dehydrated), tie my drawstring, dry heave, and climb out the window.

M y bare feet are raw and chapped. Fireworks explode behind my forehead as I wriggle my arm into the small opening in the Volvo's window and unlock the door.

I see a lady stagger out of her car and sit dumbly on the sidewalk. I get into her Pontiac and start driving.

I scrape a parked car and nearly hit a few people. It isn't far to Jessie's.

There are people around. A guy my dad golfs with is shitting in a driveway. I drive across lawns. The sky is cloudless and blue.

Things I hit on the way to Jessie's house:

A brown dog. Hedges. Mailboxes. A red Corvette parked in a driveway. A kid's tricycle. Another brown dog.

F inally I brake to a stop. Parked on someone's lawn, ball peen hammers destroying my skull. Jessie's house is down the street. I need to do something first.

In agony, I get out. With cement feet, I stumble around the nearest house. Collapse against the gate. Open it. Stagger into the backyard. Collapse. Get to my feet. Wobble-stagger to the pool's edge. Topple into the water.

Bliss.

15

O penmouthed like a guppy, I gulp several gallons of water. I surface, eyes open, seeing lights explode. The universe is flushed and ripe. Everything's saturated with luscious color.

I tear off my scabs again and soak, tingling. Bliss. Glory. I swim to the ladder and climb out, glittering like a god. I walk across lawns to Jessie's house.

Her house is large, formidable, elegant, surrounded by flowers and shrubs, now trampled. I feel a rush of sexual desire so powerful it makes my fingertips tingle. From the front yard I can see that Megan and Jessie aren't in the pool.

The front door is open, though.

The interior is cool, airy, spacious. An air conditioner humming in the lungs of the house makes me want to sleep. Instead, I drift to the staircase and go up. The upstairs hallway is long, with many doors. Water's running in the bathroom. That door is cracked—I can see a slice of glinting mirror, a hint of flesh-tone reflected in it.

I open the door.

The bath roars. There's no one in the water.

21

Cautiously, I walk down the hall. Jessie's door is closed. Behind it, I hear low, unstable voices. Viciously excited, I ease the door open. Still glistening from the pool, they turn to look. Their eyes are alien and dead.

'How come the bath is running?'

They don't answer. Jessie, in her lime bikini, is lying on the waterbed. She's licking a giant, ridiculous red-white novelty lollipop, gripping it by a long wood handle that has snapped at the end, leaving it jagged.

She passes the lollipop to Megan, who's wearing a damp black t-shirt and nothing else. She has been cooked by the sun. The skin of her face, garlanded by dark tangles of drenched hair, is violent red. A purplish smear darkens her inner thigh. There is a dull lostness in her brown eyes and her face looks softened, childlike.

'Megan,' I say solemnly, 'come with me.'

Jessie interrupts with a laugh, undulating on the waterbed. 'We're married now . . . we had a ceremony. In the bath.' She giggles. 'You weren't invited. Right, Megs?'

Jessie scratches her bare, red thigh as Megan walks dazedly past her. 'We,' Jessie says, 'are in love.' Megan, in a fugue state or something, wanders to the window forgetfully. Jessie leans forward and takes the giant lollipop back out of Megan's unresisting grip. 'Thank you, sweetie,' Jessie says. Megan looks confused.

Blood pounds behind my eyes. Rage wells in me.

37

There is a struggle.

My hand claws at wet tangles of her hair—my mouth tries to bite.

Megan fights, panicked—but I've got her by the arms, by the breasts, I've got my hand—

Deep pain buckles my leg. I'm yelling as I turn and swing at Jessie. She falls. My leg is slippery. Blood. I grope at my wounds. The giant lollipop stick, jagged end now red with my blood, is thrown on the white rug. I stagger across the room past Jessie—she bares her teeth at me.

The wounds in my leg are deep and messy. I limp into the hall, trying to stop the blood with my hands.

I break fingers when I fall down the stairs. But it's my left hand, and I'm right-handed. My pounding head is a bigger concern. I get up, reeling, hearing the girls upstairs. My shoulder brushes the wall and a strip of skin peels off.

Suddenly, I realize I'm nightmarishly sunburned. Blistered. The color, literally, of a pomegranate.

The hallway is swaying as I stagger toward the glass doors, leaving spots of blood on the floor.

Clutching my hand, dragging my gushing leg, I stagger toward the pool. It crosses my mind that I probably shouldn't soak puncture wounds in bleached water.

Never mind.

I wade into the shallow end, cradling my hand.

As soon as my leg slips underwater, blood billows and the wounds start stinging.

Never mind.

I wade in above my waist, dazed and peaceful, although the pain in my leg is kind of strange, warm but also cold, as if the water's turning to ice inside the wound, and freezing tendrils are crawling up my veins.

Never mind.

73

B liss beyond bliss. What a world, all in glorious Technicolor. Can vision be *too* clear? Can you overdose on clarity?

I close my eyes.

Nearby, I hear Jessie and Megan at it again, splashing. I don't open my eyes. I am thinking great thoughts. My veins scream. My skin is peeling off, floating in strips.

Crowding my skull are the beautiful, candy-colored girls that I want.

I want everything

women, cigarettes, salmon, vanilla ice cream, Vicodin, chocolate
éclairs, oysters, cookie dough ice cream, bacon, cheddar cheese,
a deep dish pizza with every topping, a pizza with cheese in the
crust, spaghetti and meatballs, surgical scissors, mayonnaise,
dinosaurs, bluebirds, supermodels, nosebleeds, lobster bisque,
sushi, gasoline, coffee flavored ice cream,
butter, sushi, a burrito,
& naked sisters.

NICK ANTOSCA *(b. New Orleans, Louisiana, USA, 1983) is the author of the cult novels* Fires *and* Midnight Picnic *(winner of a 2009 Shirley Jackson award). His next novella* The Obese *will be published by Lazy Fascist Press. His fiction and journalism have appeared in* n+1, The Paris Review, The Daily Beast, The Huffington Post, Hustler, Nerve, Film Threat, The New York Sun, The Barcelona Review, Bookforum, *and* Interview. *He is the screenwriter of* The Cottage, *a horror movie currently filming in Los Angeles starring David Arquette.*

Commentary on "Candy": *This story comes from a dream I had. I like to swim—I swim almost every day—and I often dream about it. I also dream about the suburbs and about ex-girlfriends. The girls in the story are based on the figures in the dream, which were versions of my high school girlfriend and her cousin.*

Down in the Valley

Joseph Bruchac

Bones, Theo Buck had told him. That was all they found. Sucked clean of every bit of flesh. So white they mistook them for ice when they saw them and the bottom of the stream that led down into the cedar swamp.

How many went missing?

Seven, Theo said, tapping his walking stick on the ground. The Horsemen were no damn help. Just come in and poked around and then said it had to have been a bear. But there was no tooth marks on them bones.

So what can I do that the Mounties can't? John Sundown said.

Since it wasn't really a question, Theo Buck just looked sideways at him and nodded.

John Sundown readjusted the weight of the heavy pack and the rifle as he looked down into the valley. The wind that came up the rocky draw into his face was warm. It carried with it the aroma of new growth, despite the thin snow that clung to the ridges. He recognized the scents of familiar spring plants, the same ones that used to grow near the streams back down on his own reservation— back before the dam was built.

He took a deep breath.

Gettin' too old for this.

Come here, the voice said again.

Not a voice you hear with your ears.

Well, maybe not that old.

 The valley on the other side of the low range of white-capped Ontario hills seemed just as deserted as he'd been told it would be. The streams that flowed down there still had a plenty of trout in them. But no deer sign since he'd started to climb. No rabbits spooked from the brush. And no smells of smoke as there would have been if there were any people still down there. Even though it had been the favored hunting grounds for half the Anish families hereabouts, no one had set foot in the valley since they'd found the bones of Bill Mink and both his boys at the edge of the bigger of the two cedar swamps.

John Sundown raised his chin and drew in an even deeper breath through his nose. And he caught the faintest trace of another scent, a scent that was *majid*. In English *majid* might be translated as bad. But English didn't do the old word justice.

The eight years he'd been forced to stay at the Indian Industrial School hadn't taken away his language or dulled his senses. They might have split him from family, cut his hair, stuffed him into a uniform and thrown him into the guardhouse every time he forgot and spoke a word of Algonquin but all that were able to strip away from him was on the outside.

They thought he'd been civilized. Even the English Master, Mr. Asa Poundshaw never suspected. Boston-bred, the meanest teacher at the school, bald Poundshaw whipped any brown-skinned boy or girl who failed to show proper respect or mispronounced a word. But John Sundown learned fast. He knew who to be afraid of and what he needed to do after his first brutal beating, followed by three days in the cold guardhouse on bread and water. By the time Sundown had been at school for two months, whenever Poundshaw turned his cold fishy gaze to look down his long nose at John, all he saw was a little Indian boy nodding his head in what seemed to be perfect agreement. It was not easy for John to swallow down his anger, to hide the fear that the terrified beating of his heart would give him way. And perhaps Poundshaw suspected that John Sundown's conversion had been a little too fast. But there were far too many other obviously recalcitrant Indian boys and girls for him who needed to feel the civilizing stroke of his cane.

His last two years there, John Sundown had been more than a model example for the civilizing hand of at the government boarding school. A true dawn-of-the-20th century-Indian. Perfect class attendance for four straight terms, second string running back on the Indian football team, member of the school orchestra (playing the cello). One of John Sundown's poems extolling his teachers was published in the *Monthly Arrow*—whose Boston-born editor apparently not only lacked an eye for irony but also had not (like John Sundown) looked up the word 'acrostic' in *Webster's Dictionary*.

For all that school has given freely
Unto this red lad forest bred
Callow before he did receive
Kind instructions, a pat upon his head.
Yea, let me heap up grateful praise
On those who generously granted
Unto me kindly Wisdom's gaze.

He hadn't even spoken a word of protest when he was sent out—like all the other able-bodied Indian students—to be a low-paid field worker at one of the white farms in the countryside around the school that made use every summer of cut-rate red labor. Where sometimes a vulnerable young native boy or girl might be used in another way.

John Sundown shook his head at that memory.

Figured for sure school had killed the Indian in me.

That had been the mistake of Old Hans, the hulking owner of the farm where John had been 'outed,' as they called that system of semi-slave labor. He'd assumed that John Sundown was just another little Indian boy he could take advantage of out behind his cow barn. But John's being quiet and reliable at his chores hadn't meant that he was either vulnerable or slow. One of the little tricks you learn playing football against Ivy League boys—Harvard linemen who knew where to jam a knee at just the right time—had come in handy when he felt the ham-like hand of Hans on his shoulder.

John Sundown smiled at the thought of how Old Hans had limped for a week afterwards—and kept a respectful distance away from him for the rest of that summer.

He shaded his eyes against the rising light of the late June sun with his left hand. This valley was at least a mile wide, maybe four miles long. A river flowing through it. Marsh lands and a little lake at the far end where the cliffs came down. Spruce, hemlock, balsam and pine on the higher slopes, then birch and beech, cherry and oak and maple. Everything here seemed just about right—at first glance—for him to locate what he was looking for. He'd find the useful plants his grandmother had taught him about when he was little, before the Indian agent had him shipped off down to Pennsylvania. The land down there ought to be right for all kinds of medicines, even the ginseng that they'd pay a hefty price for back down in the States, and then ship it off to the Far East where it was used as a medicine for just about any ailment. Ginseng roots were worth their weight in gold. And just like gold, ginseng drew greedy men to Indian lands to dig it out. So now it is rare and worth even more.

They never gathered medicine the way we do, John thought. He touched the tobacco pouch at his side. He was only four when Grama Sabbatis put a handful of tobacco in his palm.

Put that down there by the roots. Don't hurry. Show your respect and thanks. Explain how we need its help. Ask permission before you pull it up.

That plant had seemed to jump into his hand after he did that. And they only took that one plant, not even the biggest one of the family of plants they found growing there. That way there would always be more of that medicine when they needed it.

Healing was like that. You had to take it slow, be patient. And there was a lot of healing he had to do. It was hard to believe how much he'd seen in the last few years. Two years of college at Dickinson after Carlisle. Then enlisting when America entered the war.

He'd been in France, a member of the Expeditionary Force, when it had come to him. Came to him after the blast deafened him and threw him twenty feet through the air. Come while the shrapnel was still so hot in his thigh he could smell his own flesh burning.

The voice came. He'd never heard it before, but he recognized it. It was the same voice his Grama told him she first heard when she was twelve winters.

Wake up, it said. You have a job now. You must help heal the people.

A voice as everyday and as matter of fact as that of one of his superior officers. But an inhuman voice, one without breath, spoken inside his mind.

First, stay alive. Lead your men.

He had done that. He got up. Moving faster than any man should with German steel lodged in his thigh, he'd roused his company. Black men, every one of them. The Army would never have assigned white men to be led by an Indian, even one who was an officer and had gone to engineering school. Then John Sundown had led them down the trenches, across the no-man's land of night, safely away from the gas attack that flowed in behind them like a yellow burning fog over the flat marsh land, its long fingers strangling and suffocating those who had not followed him.

The armistice came a week later. Like tens of thousands of other soldiers in a dozen different uniforms, he had limped away from the bitter land they'd watered with their blood. Packed his kit bag, threw in a few souvenirs, boarded a troop ship at Brussels. A month later he was back home in Maine on his grandmother's porch.

Slowly he drank the tea she'd made for him from the same tin cup given him since John was a little child.

I'm here to help, Nokomis, he said. They both smiled after he said that. Even though she had ninety winters, she could still split wood as good as a man half her age, and there were as many on Indian Island who feared her as there were those who respected her.

If a bear in the woods runs into Grama Sabbatis, it was said, that bear turns and runs for its life.

It's good you come here for help, Nosis, she said.

Then they both sat for a while listening to the river . . . and his breath which still rasped every now and then.

You heard the voice, she finally said.

He nodded.

Good.

Summer began to walk away towards the south and the wind held a hint of the northland's breath. The leaves were falling. John hunted birds and small animals for food. Deer were all gone now from around Indian Island. He worked a few odd jobs in the town to get flour, sugar and coffee. Cut wood, kept the stove burning, grew stronger. By the time of the Freezing Moon, his lungs were clear again. His hip no longer ached every time he drew a breath. That was when the moon was as full of light, as a wise old woman's face. His grandmother told him stories as she had done when he was little. Her words were as healing the clean air, the familiar land beneath his feet, the music of the good river flowing near her cabin.

When early the Moon of Maple Sugar came, they tapped the seven maples by the edge of the road that led to home.

First medicine gift, Grama Sabbatis said, handing him a cup full of the sweet sap before they began boiling it down in the old iron kettle to make syrup.

Drink it.

He drank. It washed away the last of the darkness stuck in the center of his chest.

Then it was the Moon When Frogs Sing. She handed him his pack. Go. Gather medicines along your way. Help the people. Heal when you can. And when the need arises—as it will—use those other skills you learned at war. You will know when.

He hadn't told her about the letter in his pocket from his old school buddy. A letter he had picked up that morning from the store where mail was delivered. Hadn't mentioned he would be leaving.

But of course she knew.

John Sundown had nodded, shifted the strap of the Winchester over his right shoulder. Then she wrapped her strong old arms around him and held him tight for a long time. An embrace that was, he knew as well she did, the last his fierce old grandmother would ever give him.

So, after two months of steady travel he had come here. He'd traveled some by wagon, some by train, more by walking. Then a week on the waters of the big lake and then upstream on one of its tributaries by canoe to reach Theo Buck's reserve. Theo had been the right end on their team at Carlisle.

He found his old friend sitting on the front step of the trading post, holding a walking stick with a bear's head carved on top of it. Theo had always been good with his hands. Best student in the art classes at Carlisle. Pop Warner, the school's football coach and a lover of art, had bought half a dozen of Theo's paintings.

Theo raised the stick in greeting, pointed with his chin to the steps next to him. John Sundown sat.

You got my letter, Theo said.

Ayup.

Theo cleared his throat, spat.

Remember the stories you told me about your grandmother?

John Sundown nodded.

Turns out, Theo Buck continued, my own grandfather knew her. Turns out a bunch of our old people knew her. Knew about her. Knew that she could, he paused, tapped the stick against the steps, handle things.

That is true.

I have heard, Theo said, his voice cautious, that you can handle some things.

I can try, John Sundown said.

Then Theo had told him about the valley.

B elow John Sundown, the next day, the valley was quiet, mostly.

You come.

That voice again. Were the silent words said in Indian or in English? Or neither one?

Setting up his camp took no more than the time for the sun to travel the width of one hand down the sky. He'd learned to travel light when he was a boy. Never carried a tent or all the camping equipment the weekend outdoorsmen seemed unable to live without. Just an oil cloth to stretch over the lean-to frame of straight limbs he'd cut, stripped and erected against the side of the big boulder that blocked the northwestern wind at his back. If a man had a good knife, he could make about anything he needed from the woods. He'd allowed himself the luxury of a cooking pot, a spoon, and his grandmother's tin cup—which he'd found in his pack. But nothing more in the way of cooking supplies. Left more room for the other things as well that he'd stowed in the heavy pack on his back. Things that might save his life or make a difference. The pot hung now over the small fire he started with flint and steel. His coffee would be ready in another minute or two.

No animal tracks, he thought, chewing on one of the pieces of venison jerky he'd brought.

No birds singing. Not one.

Why am I doing this?

Because I can.

The dark came quick, rippling along the valley like dark water filling in a pool. He'd gathered enough wood to keep the fire going through the night, dry logs laid up so he could just shove their ends further into the fire as they burned. He checked his rifle, making sure it was loaded. A good gun, this lever-action Winchester. Better than those they'd given them to use in Belgium and France. He could get off a dozen shots from it in as many heartbeats. He laid it close at hand on his side away from the fire. He could roll to it and have it up and ready to shoot in a heartbeat. Then he reached under his shirt and pulled what looked like a thin black rope. In the old days, when a man went to sleep in a strange place he would tie a little of his own long hair to a tree root. That way nothing could come in the night and take your spirit. After his years in the boarding school and in the army, where barbers held just as much sway, the hair on his own head had still not grown back much further than his shoulders. But this rope of hair that he carried with him was even better than his own. His grandmother had braided it from strands of her own hair, hair that had never been cut but flowed down, still dark as midnight in the forest, even though she had now seen more than ninety winters.

John Sundown tied one end of the hair rope around his left wrist and then tied the other to one of the gnarled fingers of the venerable cedar tree that had wrapped its roots like an elder's brown hand around one side of the boulder.

I tie myself to the earth, he whispered. I cannot be taken from this place.

Something called from the far end of the valley.

You come.

A breathless call. Not a song. Far from that.

Nope, John Sundown said.

He wrapped his fingers around his grandmother's hair and slept.

He woke up before dawn. Took a pinch tobacco from his pouch and offered it with a prayer to the rising sun, dropped it into the fire.

Then he checked his gear. He had all he needed. And he was hearing it again.

You come.

I'm coming. But you might not like what I'm bringing.

As he made his way along the trails that were overgrown now, no sign of deer tracks or any other, he thought. Was it new here? Had it come from some other valley that it stripped of life? Or had it been here a long time sleeping, then woke up hungry, ready to eat until it was time for another long sleep?

He leaned back against a big stone

Can I do this? he said to himself.

Don't ask if you can. Just try. That will be good enough.

He grinned at the memory of her words, so strong that they came clearer to his mind than that call—which was not so far away now.

Okay, Nokomis. I try. He straightened up and began walking again.

It'll be a pond or a deep spring. Like in the old stories. I'm almost there.

You come.

Hurry. Hurry.

Don't be late for roll call.

You are going to get demerits in my book, young man.

A ruler across your knuckles will remind you not to be a lazy savage.

Quick time, march!

Whoa!

John Sundown stopped himself.

He was so close now that the breathless voice had almost overwhelmed his senses. Not just one voice now but a passel of them.

Using my memories against me, eh?

John swung the gun off his shoulder and squatted down, still a hundred yards from that pool of water that had seemed so enticing just a moment ago. A shiver went down his back at the thought of what lay below the placid surface.

Listen.

He heard it. Below the imagined sound of human speech. A hunger, cold and wet. Deep as dark water, full of its own greedy cleverness, its guile that of the stickiness of a spider's web spun across the paths of insects blund-ering into that fatal trap.

Cold, hungry, dangerous. And so sure of itself that it is stupid.

He pulled out the other rope from his pack. Not the one of woven hair, but the thicker one that had a woven core of wire within it, strong enough to pull a Model T up a hill without stretching or breaking. He took out the block and tackle. Could be used to hang up a moose carcass, but it could take a much greater weight. He tied it to the trunk of a black ash that looked to be deep rooted enough in the moist soil, threaded the strong line through it. He'd be able to more than double his own strength when he pulled that line. Mechanical advantage. One lesson he was glad he took away from the school shop.

He pulled out the old shirt. Sweat-soaked, it would have his smell. Just in case smell was what drew the thing. A few sticks tied right, leaves stuffed inside to give it shape, stones to give it weight. A passable dummy. Then, last of all, the big three-barbed hook. Designed for catching sharks, he had picked it up in a port town on his way back from France. Just because he'd had a feeling he would need it sometime. The kind of feeling Grama Sabbatis had taught him to always listen to.

A loop in the rope above the decoy's headless body, a long pole through the loop and now he could walk it out in front of him toward the deep pool of water, the weight of the stones in the cloth like the thump of feckless feet.

Keep your mind clear now of any thought of resistance.

Think just that **Yes, Sir,** he'd been taught to say at the industrial school

The same **Yes, Sir,** that had served him just as well in the army. No matter what his soul was saying.

You come.

Yes, Sir.

Come.

Yes, Sir.

Thump, thump of the manikin's stone feet closer and closer to the edge, the rope playing out behind it back to the tree.

No more than twenty feet from the edge now.

Come!

Yes . . .

KER-WHOMP!

It struck so hard and fast that his heart jumped in his throat. Dummy, pole and line whipcracked forward. Water kicked up into a froth by the big head that arced up with open jaws, and snapped, hurled itself spinning back. Though John Sundown let go as quick as he could, his palms were skinned and he was dragged forward a step.

A death roll like an alligator's. He'd seen that once while sitting at the edge of a pasture a stone's throw from a Louisiana bayou. The big old gator's green head shot out of the water to grab the chestnut foal, yanked it down, tearing flesh and cracking neck bones as it whipped its ridged tail and rolled its massive body. So fast there was nothing he could do to save the young horse. Gone under the weedy surface before he could stand up.

This thing was faster than that gator. So sudden in its attack and retreat that he wasn't quite sure what he'd seen other than gaping jaws and dark shiny skin, maybe pale-bellied like a frog.

He didn't let himself be frozen by the fury of that attack. He stepped quick back to the tree, watching the line that had grown taut, tight as a bowstring. But the tree was strong in the earth. Though the line sawed back and forth as the creature under the surface tried to break free, both the metal-threaded rope and the big swamp ash held against the strain.

John Sundown picked up the Winchester. Gun cradled in his arms, he stood still.

Watching, waiting, slightly disbelieving.

When the sun was in the middle of the sky, the frenzied motion back and forth of the line slowed. He slung the gun over his shoulder. Holding the part of the rope threaded through the block and tackle, John Sundown pulled on the loop to untie the coil around the tree and began to haul in.

No, let go.

Nope.

Let go. Let go. Let go.

Nope.

Though it had swallowed the dummy, lodged the hook somewhere down its throat, it didn't come out head first. It had rolled its body around the rope, tried to pull itself away. What emerged first, covered with mud and weed, was the creature's back side, a snaky tail whipping back and forth. Then short, thick hind legs with webbed feet, a glistening body dark on top and frog white on the belly. He'd been right in what he thought he saw.

Bigger than a gator. But built unlike any alligator or any other critter other than itself.

There were names for this thing in the old languages of the land. *Aglebemu ... Mannigbeskw ...* The Old One Who Swallows Us. Swamp Caller.

That breathless voice was speaking to him again, still trying to find an edge to confuse him. Draw him near enough so it could get him.

No hurt. Let go. Come here. Help.

John Sundown tied off the rope. Unslung the Winchester. Safety off.

It began to turn its head toward him.

Careful. If the old stories were right, now was when the creature would chill the blood of anyone who dared look directly at it. It would hypnotize its prey with terror. It would show John the most fearful and evil visage it could dredge up from his own memories. Then, when its prey was frozen in fright, it would attack, and it would devour.

And, sure enough, the most evil, cold blooded thing in his memory was there.

That was what John Sundown saw.

And that was why he let out a chuckle as he lifted his gun and blew a hole square between Mr. Asa Poundshaw's eyes.

JOSEPH BRUCHAC *(b. Saratoga Springs, New York, USA, 1942) is a gentle, soft-spoken, large and muscular man, whose 35 years of studying various martial arts has earned him the rank of Master and given him the practical knowledge of several hundred ways to kill or maim an opponent with his bare hands (or feet). He has also spent a lifetime practicing wilderness survival and learning the traditional knowledge and history that is part of his heritage as a person of Abenaki Indian ancestry. Thus, if he writes about skinning a deer or engaging in hand-to-hand combat, rest assured that he is not writing speculatively. That said, he has loved fantasy literature since his childhood and has written as good bit of it for both adults and younger readers, including his newest novels* Dragon Castle *and* Wolf Mark.

A native of the Adirondack region of New York State, where he still lives in the house his grandparents raised him in, he and his two grown sons James and Jesse engage in traditional storytelling, perform original and traditional Native music, and work together teaching the Abenaki language and Native wilderness awareness at the Ndakinna Education Center (ndcenter.org). (Since all three of them are mixed martial arts instructors, it is advisable to listen closely when they are performing).

Commentary on 'Down in the Valley': *I like to bring the monsters from our northeastern Native traditions into modern times in my fiction—as I did in my best-selling novel for young readers* Skeleton Man. *There are traditions about creatures such as the one featured in "Down in the Valley" among all of the Algonquin and Iroquoian nations, as well as a number of stories I've heard about present-day encounters with such Lorelei-like monsters.*

I've chosen to place this tale in the early 20th century, however, a time not often written about in terms of American Indian protagonists. It is also a time when American Indian cultures all over the continent were under siege—the languages, religious traditions, and every aspect of the old ways of every one of our more than 300 tribal nations were under attack and our children were being forced into far-away boarding schools with the motto 'kill the Indian and save the man'. My hero is a survivor of that system who not just held on to the knowledge of the old ways, but has taken things a step further by using what he knows and risking his life to help others.

WANISHIN

CHERIE DIMALINE

I HAD A STRANGE DREAM THAT I GAVE BIRTH TO TWINS.
Not sure of their sex; the subject never came up and I didn't
think to ask. Besides the nurse wasn't very attentive. She couldn't
have had many other things to do, though. The hospital was hope-
lessly Dickensian, cold and drippy and dark and full of clutter
thrown into corners—nightgowns, eyeglasses, old newspapers and
empty cigarette packages, but not another person in sight. She
seemed distracted, half erased. Her eyes were dead and the auburn
curls pinned up under her dingy paper cap looked acrylic. There
were unfiltered cigarettes tucked behind each ear and a jagged
scar ran along the top of her starched collar. We were in Ontario,
it was cold, and I was a mother.

The first child was born without pain and carried off, naked and
pensive. I assumed it was brought to some sort of nursery where it
would be wiped and given a blanket. Its skin looked orange against
the pale grey of the nurse's hands and a waxy muck clogged its ears
and nostrils. It seemed no time for celebration or concern and I
watched it being carried away without anxiety. After all, it was the
second child that was significant, the second child that held my
attention.

This child burrowed its way up, tearing through the top of my
uterus, squeezing through the labyrinth of intestines, pulling its

limbs across the soft sacs of my lungs—first left, then right. This child was born through my breast, the left one. I cried and was sure I was having a heart attack like my father and his father before him. The pain was new and shocking but utterly familiar. Then the child was there, pressed up against my torn nipple, and unmoving. It was more statue than child, a calcified baby with fossilized eyes left closed, open instead towards some other place.

The nurse was there at my elbow then, her dead eyes looking past us, through the greasy window scratched by skeletal branches, the etchings of which spelt out words I'd never read but whose sounds I saw shaped by the lips of my nokomis, my grandmother:

wanishin, biish, bawaagan, waniikese . . . lost, water, spirit, forget

In the dream she spoke more deliberately than I ever remembered in life. 'When a spirit forces reincarnation through a fetus, it's still attached to death. Too attached, and it ends up destroying the new life, riding it like a boat over the falls.' Her teeth were chipped and jagged. I watched them cut slits in the skin on her lips as she spoke and I understood why she had been silent till now.

'And it's usually born backwards, up through the mouth or chest, because it moves forwards in a backwards process. It grows ancient through birth.'

Her eyes snapped to life for one moment, long enough to notice the baby, to slide up to my face. I wished they would die again.

'They get lost.'

The alarm clock woke me from the dream warning. In the shower, a slow drizzle of blood-tinged milk washed away down the drain.

This was the beginning of the haunting.

Outside it was cold and wet, the moisture hanging in the air but not actually falling out of it. I was happy for the cover of fog. Sometimes fog can be comforting, making you feel a centimeter tall in a basket of cotton balls. I walked all the way to the used bookstore, unlocked the front door and flipped the sign that hung against the glass to OPEN. Settling in behind the desk, I clicked on the computer and straightened the stacks of books to be shelved into three tall, straight piles on the otherwise clear cherry desk. Then I retreated behind the beaded curtain to the back room to boil water for tea. This was one of my pleasures: the empty store on a rainy morning, and strong black tea drank out of a purposely mismatched cup and saucer. I wound my long dark hair up into a bun, secured it with a ballpoint pen and plugged in the kettle. Then I leaned against the counter to wait.

An ache in my chest and a word from the dream reached me at the same time. I whispered it out loud.

'*Wanishin*. Lost.'

H earing the unmistakable *thunk* of book spines smacking the floor, I jumped. I pushed aside the beads and peered into the store. 'Hello?'

The consonants tumbled to the ground, the vowels mixed with the dust motes kicked up into the air. The sign on the door was still; the bells hadn't sounded. The rows were clear and the tables were still empty. But at the front desk, the three piles of books now lay in a pulpy heap, the volumes sliding over one another like a collapsed house of cards, with one exception. At the top of the heap stood a red hardcover, standing upright at an impossible angle. I thought of the Portuguese busker who stacked rocks into insane inukshuk down on the Lake Ontario beach during the summer. Balanced with Zen-like practice, he'd stack all day for the dollars tourists tossed into the empty butter cookie tin kept on the side of the boardwalk for just that purpose.

I walked towards the desk, stepping over the hardwood on the balls of my feet. What if someone was hiding there? What if I interrupted a robbery and the intruder was still here? I wished I had brought a knife with me, but I didn't want to turn my back to head to the back room now. I inched forward, keeping my eyes trained on the desk and the shadows behind it.

And just then, just as I reached the edge of the desk, the book spun once, like a cubist ballerina on a parchment toe, and then fell. The effect was cartoonish; it jerked up before it fell flat, otherwise it would have just slid down the pile to rest at the base. But before I could stare long enough to trust my eyes in the recollection, a sharp whistle pierced the thick silence.

The kettle. The kettle boiled in the back room. I ran there to unplug it, grateful for the distraction.

Later, after tea and a full read of the newspaper, I shelved the books. The red book was the last to be put away. I couldn't bring myself to handle it after its performance. I read the spine. *Dance Traditions of the Canadian Woodlands Indians*. I filed it in the History section just before I closed up for the night.

Sleep was elusive, slipping ahead of me like an oily trail over the road on summer drives. I chased it with Shakespeare, a proven anesthetic for me. By the time Lady Macbeth broke down, past midnight, I was half dreaming her madness. Then my own dreams took over.

It was the book hitting the floor that woke me up sometime near dawn. The night sky was ripped along its seams and a lighter blue showed through the tears. I leaned over the side of the bed and saw the Shakespeare volume, open and face down, pages fanned out like a dead bird. I reached down and the floor seemed miles away. Eyes still closed, my fingers found the edge of the cover and I pinched it between them. But the grasp was tenuous and it only got about an inch into the air before slipping back down with a splash.

The water was body temperature warm. Tiny flecks of white wax like vernix floated to the surface like bubbles. I cringed, and my hand recoiled from the foot-deep puddle that covered my entire bedroom floor, rippling off into the bathroom and across the threshold into the hallway towards the living room. Habit made me reach down again; I couldn't let a perfectly good book be destroyed. I closed my eyes tight and lowered my hand to the floor. The cover felt dry and I yanked it up to the bed quickly, waiting for the water to seep into the sheets.

I opened my eyes and examined the book. Dry. It was completely dry. I tossed it to the empty side of the bed and leaned over the edge again. The floor was dry, not a drop of water in sight. I rubbed my eyes and checked again. Nothing. Just the floor with my old moccasins tucked under the bureau, the beads worn smooth and dull as cataracts.

Sleep stayed away.

That day at the store, I found myself doodling on the desk calendar, waiting for the sporadic customers to distract me from the exhaustion that refused to commit to slumber. By noon a clear image emerged from the disconnected lines and fanciful curls that found their way across the large calendar, still open to April though it was well into June. It was a shore, the edge of a body of water the stretched off into the curved horizon. Tall shadow trees pushed brush stroke branches into the sky and a half dock snaked out into the still waters. I knew this view. It was back home, not home as in my apartment, but up north by the reserve. It was the shore at my grandma's house. I hadn't seen it in over ten years, not since I stopped off to say my goodbyes on my way into the city for school and a real life, away from this tiny, dying place. That shoreline was twisted into my blood memory, a shade of grainy green on the curve of DNA. I would know it anywhere.

Pain stabbed me in the left nipple and I dropped the pen, gasping at the sharpness of it.

Then a whistle made me jump a second time. The damn kettle. I stared at the beaded doorway into the back room. The kettle was screaming its full boil, waiting for relief. I waited to see the beads sway, but they remain-ed still in the high pitched music of bubbling water and demanding steam.

I hadn't been back there all day. I hadn't plugged the kettle in.

Its scream filled the air, mixing with the dusty sigh of a thousand used books and the big drum bang and ebb of my heart.

The tinkle of bells announced a customer. I looked to the door to the young man who kicked dirt off his sneakers on the welcome mat that showed a cat reading a book on love seat, and smiled.

'Hello.'

I nodded, sure I was still trembling. Then as an afterthought, 'Let me know if you need any help.'

He tilted his head to the right and his body followed in that direction, as if his head were some great weight that determined his course.

The kettle still screamed.

He picked up a paperback and tried to read the back. His forehead broke out in wrinkles and he squinted at the beaded doorway and then over at me, waiting for some sort of response, visibly unsettled by the kettle's steady whine.

I stood and reluctantly made my way into the back and over to the protesting appliance, yanking out the cord with a shaking hand.

I chastised myself out loud, hoping the sound of my voice would clear things up, would make them real. But he probably heard as well—he was walking away past the shop window when I came out.

It was too tiring to walk home at closing time so I hopped on the bus instead. Just after nine I deposited my change and found an empty seat near the back and night had finally wrapped its dark arms around the twinkling city blocks. I rested my head against the window and closed my eyes, just for a moment. The low vibrations of the lumbering vehicle pushed a rumbly lullaby into my head.

I felt uneasy and opened one eye, feeling watched. I caught it staring at me in the window's reflection, its eyes still closed so that the stare was implied by its face, the grey features still and hard. It sat in the plastic curve of the two-seater behind me. Its small, still limbs were ghastly against the red leather seat, corpse-like, in a puddle of dirty blood. It was the second child.

I didn't want to look at it; seeing it through the window was enough. I forced myself to breathe. My breasts ached and a small wet spot appeared on my t-shirt. My legs were dead weight.

I lifted my head from the window and frantically searched the bus. All the seats were empty now, except for me and the dead child behind me. I looked out the window, through the grey reflection and into the night. Where there should have been rows of low-rise apartments, there were trees. The bus jumped and rattled so much I knew we were on a gravel road now.

Where were we?

I looked to the front of the bus, to the driver and saw a petite figure sitting in the big seat, the oversized wheel being guided by pale, feminine hands, and a stack of auburn curls pinned under a bent paper cap. In the large mirror, the nurse caught my eye and smiled her horrible smile full of broken teeth and infected gums. Through the large front window I could see the waters of Lake Huron, and the turn off for my grandma's house.

A movement in the window grabbed my attention and I focused my gaze on the surface of the glass. Now there was only the reflection of an empty seat behind me.

Any relief I might have had over its absence was short lived. A weight pulled down my left shoulder—a cold, heavy presence. It made me think of the tumors that grew in my mother's uterus, the tumors that pulled her away from me, like a weighted body to the bottom of a murky lake.

I turned my head slowly, slowly . . . until my chin grazed the dead skin of a tiny hand and vomit collected in my throat. The child was climbing onto my back. I felt its freezing toes now, digging into the space between my shoulder blades, its other hand reaching up through the tangle of dark hair to rest at the base of my skull.

I was screaming.

'Lady, you okay?' The driver, an overweight man in blue with longer hair in the back than the front, yelled over his shoulder, his suspicious eyes watching me through the slanted mirror.

A half dozen other passengers stared from the front and when I spun around to regard the seat behind me, I startled a short, old lady with a fluffy grey perm, who recovered from her surprise long enough to ask me, 'What in the hell are you looking at?'

'Uh-huh, I'm fine. Nothing. Sorry . . . ' I called to the front.

The driver kept his narrowed blue eyes on me for a bit, and then the bus swung out from the last stop and into traffic. I pulled the cord for the next stop, even though mine was still six blocks away. I stood up from my seat and walked to the back door. And that's when I noticed that the dead child was still on my back.

I felt a sharp pull on my hair and icy toes grip hard in the musculature that spasmed in protest. I reached over my shoulder and ran shaking fingers along my shoulders, which tensed under the weight of the dead, heavy thing. There was nothing physically there. And if I didn't look like a schizophrenic before, screaming in my sleep, then I sure did now, both hands reaching over my shoulders, patting at my back like a congratulatory psycho. I ignored the stares of the other passengers and ran down the stairs and up the sidewalk as soon as the bus stopped.

I was running; my hair was being used as reins and it pulled and tore as the spirit bounced and swayed. I batted at it furiously, my hands uselessly hitting my back, never connecting with the weight that dug in, all the more determined. Two blocks from my house I collapsed on the sidewalk, under a smashed-out streetlamp, and cried. I cried until the tears soaked the collar of my shirt, until an ache pounded its way to my temples from the pit of my stomach. I wiped the water off my face and watched my wet hands fold themselves in my lap like dead birds or dropped books. The light above me buzzed and clicked to life, and its soft orange glow reflected off the wetness streaked across the backs of my hands. I turned them over. In the cupped palm of my right hand, the water shimmered and grew depth. Soon, Lake Huron was sliding along the lines of my palm, sand scratching at my paper cuts, fingers hardening to scabby birch. The stubborn newborn peered over my shoulder to watch; I could feel its breath, or the absence of it, in my ear.

I stopped crying and carried the spirit home. Together, we packed a bag.

Two days later I stood at the edge of my grandmother's shore, the dock writhing and pulling against the drum and ebb of Huron. I watched the dark branches scratch unread words against a turquoise sky.

wanishin, biish, bawaagan, waniikese . . .

A turtle slid under the green waves like a shellacked submarine. A crow clicked across the swollen wood at the end of the dock and regarded me with sharp eyes, its claws clicking like forks on a dinner plate before it took flight, erasing the words from the sky. I opened a hand over the water's edge and dropped tobacco—a prayer for my forgetting, a prayer for my return. I took a deep breath, and the burden floated away from me, like the dry, brown tobacco leaves floating out into the lake, riding them like a tiny fleet of canoes pushing out and over the falls.

CHERIE DIMALINE *(Métis, b. Orillia, Ontario, Canada, 1975) is the writer in residence for First Nations House at the University of Toronto. Before taking this job, she spent time working for the Ontario government, running a Native Friendship Centre, helping at a large women's magazine, curating a police museum, and assisting a magician. Her first book,* Red Rooms, *was published in 2007 and won the Anskohk Fiction Book of the Year Award. Since then, she's travelled the world and written stories that may or may not have to do with the adventures she encountered along the way.*

Her work appears in two 2011 McGraw-Hill Ryerson texts, an anthology of love stories called Zaagidiwin *(Ningwakwe Press), in a limited edition volume of gothic stories about Toronto produced for the 2009 Luminato Festival* (Diaspora Dialogues)*, and will be featured in several upcoming collections including a book of traditional Métis Rogarou tales (University of Alberta).*

Her novel The Girl Who Grew a Galaxy *will be published in 2012 by Theytus Books.*

Cherie lives in Toronto with her 3 kids, 2 dogs, 2 ferrets and 1 blind rat. She is the editor of FNH Magazine *and* Muskrat Magazine, *an online indigenous publication. She collects books, teacups and tattoos.*

Commentary on "Wanishin": *The title is the Anishnaabe (Ojibway) word for lost. After checking with a few community members, I thought it was the best word to describe both the spirit in this tale as well as the protagonist—a young girl struggling to live separate from a world that is unwilling to be separated from her. For many Indigenous people it is a daily reality; living away from your traditional lands and community while struggling to maintain both. Mind you, these struggles don't usually end in being haunted by a dead infant, but, such is the whim of fiction.*

GROTTOR

BRIAN EVENSON

I

A T AGE THIRTEEN, SHORTLY AFTER HIS FATHER'S DEATH from tuberculosis and his mother's removal to the state facility for the insane seventy miles away, Bernt was given to his grandmother. His mother, he knew, wouldn't have wanted this—she had always done her best to keep him away from his grandmother, who she described as *not-just-right*, though without ever explaining what made her so. But his mother, straitjacketed, was not given a choice, was perhaps not even told: Bernt's court-appointed temporary guardian decided this was the option that best suited the state. *It will be*, the guardian declared, *the best for you as well.*

The following morning, before leaving for work, his ersatz guardian stationed Bernt near the curb to await his grandmother's arrival. When morning had become afternoon and she still hadn't arrived, Bernt decided to take matters into his own hands.

H e travelled the first few miles on foot, passing the cemetery in which his father was buried. His feet began to ache as he walked out along State Route 89, along the shoulder where the gravel was fine, almost powdery. Cars passed him but none slowed. It took him two, perhaps three, hours to reach downtown Springville, trudging up over the hill and down past the drive-in, past the grocery store, the town hall. And then he trudged back out the other side, watching the houses thin out and then be mostly replaced by fields. Houses appeared briefly again and he crossed through the four sorry streets of Mapleton, then more fields, nothing but fields. He drank alkaline-heavy water from a horse-pump, his stomach twisting on itself. The road's asphalt sputtered out, became gravel. His feet throbbed, were heavily blistered, perhaps bleeding.

Near dark, he stopped at a farmhouse and asked for directions. 'The old woman?' the man who answered the door asked. 'What do you want with her? Best to stay away.' When Bernt admitted he was her grandson, the farmer stared thoughtfully at him. 'Still better to stay away from her,' he finally claimed, though in the end the man brought him inside and fed him, and then slipped on a jacket and drove him the rest of the way.

B ernt leaned his head against the truck's side window, feeling at once the burnt air of the heater blowing against his face and the way the glass itself was cooled by the night air outside. In the headlights he caught a glimpse of two small white crosses to the side of the road, almost hidden in the grass, and then they were gone.

The gravel road became dirt and then rutted. Along the edge of the road was a running plain-wire line, two barbed top-wires above it. Bernt followed the fence mentally, its regular rhythm, until suddenly it turned a right angle and veered away from the road.

Another half mile and they were turning off the dirt road and pushing along the barest remains of a path, leaves and branches brushing the sides of the truck. They came to a ramshackle gate and stopped.

'She'll be back in there somewhere,' said the farmer. 'This is as far as I go.' He reached over, patted his passenger's shoulder. 'When you need help, you know where to find me.'

Bernt watched the broad front of the truck pull away, backing slowly up the path, its lights distancing, then reduced to a glow through the leaves, then vanishing altogether. He turned to the gate, tried to examine it in the moonlight. There was no latch; it was held in place by a twist of wire looped between the fencepost and the gate itself. He unhooked the wire, somehow slicing open his finger in the process. Sucking on the wound, he wonder-ed how dirty the wire was, whether he needed a tetanus shot.

The land on the other side of the gate was uncultivated, nothing like a farm. There were no lights to suggest the location of a house and the path was sufficiently untraveled to be almost invisible in the darkness. He tried to follow it anyway, pushing his way forward through the grass and then, when he realized he'd misjudged in the darkness, backtracking, trying to find it again.

The moon slid behind a cloud and it became almost impossible to see. He did not know how long he'd been wandering when suddenly he was at the house, sensing it more than actually seeing it at first, and then, as the clouds shifted, catching a flash of the moon's creamy reflection on one of the windows.

He managed to fumble his way to a door, and knocked. There was no answer. 'Hello?' he called. He knocked again, still received no answer.

He groped around until he found the knob and was surprised to find it unlocked. The door slid fluidly and silently open, and he stepped in.

Inside the house was darker than the outside had been. He felt for a light switch without touching anything but bare wall. Trailing one hand along it, he moved deeper into the house.

'Hello?' he ventured again.

He took a few more steps and then stopped, thinking he'd heard something. He waited a moment, listening, but the sound was not repeated.

He had just started moving again when he felt something flick quickly along his leg and away. He stumbled, nearly fell, gave an involuntary cry.

'No need to be frightened,' said a soft, strangely warbled voice.

'Grandmother?' he said. 'Where are you?'

The voice laughed. 'I'm not your grandmother,' it said. 'I'm Grottor.'

'Who?'

There was a scratching sound and a match blazed aflame. In its light Bernt saw, standing behind a table, a boy, roughly his height but very pale, with a doubtful smile. He wore no shirt and his skin was tight to his bones, his muscles nearly as visibly articulated as an anatomy model's. Bernt watched the boy bring the match to a candle, holding it there until the flame caught and doubled itself, then letting the match fall, still smoldering, to the floor.

'Where's my grandmother?' Bernt asked.

'Your *mormor*?' said Grottor, and laughed. 'You want to see your *mormor*?'

Before Bernt could ask what a *mormor* was, Grottor was gone, was leaving the entrance hall and sliding deeper into the house, vanishing in the darkness.

Not knowing what else to do, Bernt waited. There was something on the table other than the candle, a little pile of something that at first he thought to be strange irregular chunks of chalk but realized, once he came closer, were teeth. Four or five of them, almost certainly human.

He was reaching out to touch them when he heard a strange clumping sound and turned to see, lurching out of the darkness, an old woman. She was moving oddly, as if disoriented. She had an odd musty odor to her, strong even from a distance. She stopped at the doorway where she remained hunched over, staring down at the floor rather than looking at him.

'You're my *släkting*,' she said. Her voice was strange, an unnatural falsetto, and seemingly too strong for her body.

'Excuse me?'

'My flesh and blood,' she said. Still staring at the floor, her mouth curled in a smile. 'You have come to me.'

'You were supposed to come get me.'

'And yet here you are.' His grandmother's voice softened. 'My *släkting*.'

'Stop calling me that,' said Bernt. 'I don't know what it means.'

The old lady nodded slightly, stiffly, as if offended. 'There is a room for you,' she said. 'You may stay here. You may help.'

'On the farm?'

'There is no farm. There are only the caves.' She pushed her way out of the doorway and came closer until she was standing across the table from him. She reached out and jerkily stroked his hand, her skin leathery and stiff. 'Grottor will take you there,' she said. 'You must trust Grottor. Trust Grottor in all things.'

'Where is Grottor?' he asked. 'What caves?'

She tightened her fingers around his hand and he was surprised to find her grip so tight. He winced. 'Come,' she said. 'You may take the candle. There is a room for you. I will take you there.'

II

When he awoke, the day was half gone. His room, he saw now in the light coming in through the curtains, was small and the color of a winter moth; the floor of bare, unvarnished boards. His bed was a simple cot. A rickety chair and his open cardboard suitcase were the only other furnishings in the room.

He got up, stretched. After getting dressed he wandered out, limping a little, his feet still sore from the walk.

Nobody greeted him. On the table in the entrance hall someone had left a tin cup of water and a skewer of smoked meat. The meat itself had an almost perfumed taste to it, and was very tough and stringy. He was hungry enough to eat it anyway.

The house itself, he saw by the light of day, was quite old and quite small. It consisted of a pale olive entrance hall, then the umber salon with two doors leading off of it: one to his room and the other to what was, presumably, his grandmother's room. In the back of the house, through the salon, was a humble kitchen with dingy walls, its counters covered with a thick layer of undisturbed dust.

He tried the other door in the salon, found it locked. He knocked, but received no answer. 'Grandmother?' he called, and then, as an afterthought, '*Mormor*?' Where, he wondered, was Grottor's room? Didn't Grottor live here too?

He went outside. He saw the path he had broken through the tall grass the night before. There was another path as well, this one well traveled, leading around to the back of the house. After a moment's hesitation, he followed it.

Once behind the house, this route quickly curved away and toward the mountain. He followed it a little way and then stopped. It switched back and up a slope, he saw, then crossed a flow of loose shale. There, up above the shale, were two dark openings, the entrances to a pair of caves.

Back in the house, he tried the door to his grandmother's room again. It was still locked. *Why does she keep it locked?* Bernt wondered. *Is she in there asleep or is she gone?* He limped outside again, tried to peer in his grandmother's window, but realized he had somehow walked around the house in the wrong direction and was now looking into his own window. There was his cot, his chair, his bloody socks, his small suitcase. He limped further around the house, and found the window of his grandmother's room to be shuttered. Through the slits in the shutters, he could see narrow rectangles of floor but little more. He pushed at the shutters a bit, but they were firmly latched from the inside.

The rest of the day was like that, a slow wandering through the house and around it, trying to figure out what to do with himself. He sat on the couch in the salon, thinking, the air thick with the smell of dust. Should he hike back down, talk to the farmer who had driven him here, try to get his advice on what to do? Should he beg someone to take him away from his grandmother?

He was still turning over such thoughts, vaguely ill at ease, when, late that afternoon, he found his eyes closing. Before he knew it, he had fallen asleep.

Suddenly, Grottor was standing above him, smiling. 'Look,' he said, and held out his hand to show Bernt three teeth. Canine, bicuspid, molar, each broken off roughly, above the root.

'Whose are they?' Bernt asked.

'Now they're mine,' said Grottor.

'But whose were they?'

Grottor shrugged. 'That's all that's left,' he said, and then slipped out of the room.

Bernt awoke in the fading light, in the slow onslaught of night-fall. Even after knowing he had been asleep, he found he could not completely convince himself that Grottor's visit had been a dream.

He got up and found the matches where they lay on the entranceway table, looked through the mostly empty cabinets until he found a new candle.

By the time he got the candle lit, Grottor was there again, standing silently near the opening to the salon, still shirtless, startling Bernt when he turned.

'Don't you own a shirt? Where have you been?' Bernt asked.

Grottor just shrugged. 'Here and there,' he said.

'Where's my grandmother?'

'Your *mormor*? You want to see your *mormor*?'

And then Grottor turned and left the doorway. Taking up the candle, Bernt hurried to the entrance of the salon, arrived just in time to see him slip through his grandmother's door.

He went to the door, listened, heard nothing. He came closer, pressed his ear against the wood. Still nothing.

And then suddenly the door swung open and his grandmother stumbled out, almost knocking him over. She looked even stranger than she had before, was crumpled somehow, her skin loose and saggy. A strange smell rolled off her, like burnt hair.

'Ah,' she said, in that same uneven falsetto, still refusing to look up and meet his eye. '*Släkting.* You wanted me?'

'Um,' said Bernt, still off-balance. 'No,' he said, 'not exactly. Well, I wanted to know where you were all day.'

His grandmother made a strangled sound that he decided must be a laugh. 'For the day, I sleep,' she said. 'As do you. I command it. How are you to go to the caves at night if you do not sleep in the day?'

'What?' he said.

'Have you obeyed Grottor? Have you done everything that Grottor says, as I counseled you?' And then, without waiting for a response she placed a hand on his shoulder and pushed him away from the door to her room. She slipped back inside, closed the door, leaving only a stale, dusty smell behind.

What the hell? wondered Bernt. 'Grandmother?' he called and moved toward the door. He'd placed his hand on the doorknob, was about to turn it, when it opened of its own accord and there was Grottor. He tried to see past him to see his grandmother, but Grottor was already through the door and pulling it closed behind him.

'So, you've seen your *mormor,*' said Grottor, rubbing his hands along his chest and arms as if dusting himself off. 'What did the two of you talk about?'

'Do you share a room with her?' said Bernt. 'Isn't that strange?'

Grottor just shrugged. 'Enough chitchat,' he said. 'Now we go up to the caves.'

Grottor gave him a flashlight and led him up the mountainside, on a steep dry climb to the caves. In the daylight the two openings had looked to Bernt small and shallow, two simple clefts in the rock, but they were higher up than he'd imagined, at the top of a steep, grand slide of shale, and were bigger too.

Up close, the first was a large, sideways bowl hollowed out as if by wind. Inside was a honeycomb of openings, each entrance just a little bigger than a man. All along the walls of the cleft were unknown symbols, some painted in dark reddish-brown pigment, some scratched into the rock. There were images too; crude stick figures of men missing limbs or collapsed in a heap. A strange bulbous shape dominated one wall, beneath it a figure that seemed human but not human, strange rubbery appendages in the place of its limbs.

'What are they?' asked Bernt.

'Would you like to explore?' asked Grottor, ignoring the question. 'Choose an entrance and we'll follow it in.'

Bernt looked at him for a long moment, shook his head.

Grottor shrugged. 'Next time, then. You've seen it at least.'

His eyes kept being drawn to the bulbous shape and the humanoid figure. He had to make a conscious effort to free his gaze and look out of the cave. There, far away and below them, were lights of Mapleton: the real world. His grandmother's house, much closer but unlit, he could not see, nor even guess where it was.

Grottor stood up. 'Come on,' he said. 'There's still the other cave to visit.'

They made their way along the face of the rock, walking on exposed shale that cracked and threatened to give way beneath their feet and send them tumbling down the scree and into the darkness. To bring himself to walk it, even in the dimness, Bernt had to close his eyes, run his hand along the rock wall. The second cave was less rounded than the first, like a punctured and mostly deflated ball, a sort of a sideways wavery slit in the rock, perhaps ten feet tall, twenty-five long. They clambered in.

Against the far wall, beside the one entrance to a tunnel, was a figure. Bernt went toward it, shining his flashlight. It was a body: an old woman, slight of frame, wearing an old and frayed apron. It had been dead a long time. The skin has been eaten away, the eyes were gone.

'Who is it?' Bernt asked.

'Who's what?' asked Grottor. 'That? Don't worry about that, that's nothing.'

'How can a body be nothing?'

'When it no longer holds a person,' said Grottor flatly. 'Then it's nothing.'

'What's going on?' asked Bernt, a little hysterical now. 'What did you do to her?'

Grottor just smiled.

Angry and confused, Bernt came at Grottor, arms out in front of him, but Grottor stepped quickly to one side, fading into the shadows. Bernt struck out, hitting only the rock wall, the sandstone grating against his knuckles. Grottor fell deeper and deeper into the shadows, slipping toward the back of the cave, always only imperfectly caught in the beam of the flashlight.

'Remember your grandmother?' cautioned Grottor. 'Remember what she said to you? You are to listen to me and pay heed.'

'How do you know what she said?' cried Bernt. 'You weren't there.'

And then Grottor's shadow, layered by other shadows, wavered over the opening of the tunnel at the back of the slit and was lost.

Bernt called out to him, but he did not answer. Searching around the slit, then shining his light down the tunnel, he could tell Grottor had crept down the tunnel and was hidden now somewhere back in the caves.

III

At first he thought of leaving, wandering down the mountain and disappearing. But as he shivered his way from one cleft to the other and then picked his way down the path, he began to ask himself, Where would I go? His father was dead, his mother insane, his court-guardian indifferent. Who else was there? There was the farmer, the man who had given him a ride to his grandmother's, but how willing was he to help? Did Bernt want to find out?

In any case, he told himself, coming closer to the house, his flashlight was dying. There was nothing to be done tonight. He would wait. In the morning, if he wanted, he could leave.

Back in his room, the moon came through the shutters to spread dim slats of light along his bed, the floor. Should he stay? Should he go? The dilemma was all around him, solid as architecture, like a structure he was forced to live in or an iron mask locked around his head. He was, he semi-consciously realized, slowly talking himself out of leaving—or at least *something* was, something wanted him to stay.

And then this panic left him, and he was no longer certain what he'd been thinking about, what had happened in the caves or why he'd been worried.

His dreams took him backward along the path down the hill, through the farms, to Mapleton, then South. He walked for days, carrying a knife in his hand. He walked through desert and across blasted, blackened earth. He came to a border town, passed a boy whom he transformed into a corpse with his knife. As this death-change took place, Bernt broke all the teeth out from the boy's mouth with the knife's haft. He was turning and turning the blade of the knife; light caught on it and flashed across his eyes, and then he saw himself waver in the blade. Only it wasn't himself exactly, but who exactly it was he could not know.

H e awoke to find Grottor staring at him, a shape in the shadows, a more tangible gloom. He wanted to be angry with him, but couldn't remember why. All was slowed.

'You've been dreaming,' said Grottor. 'A little nightmare.'

'Why is it still dark?'

'You slept through the daylight,' said Grottor. 'You're learning.'

'Why won't you let me go?' Bernt asked.

He heard the hiss of a match, watched Grottor light the candle. 'Go?' asked Grottor.

And then, suddenly, he remembered. 'Did you kill the woman up in the caves?' asked Bernt.

'Would you believe me if I said I didn't?'

'You didn't?'

Grottor was suddenly touching Bernt's lips with his finger. 'Hush,' he said. 'You've had a terror. Go back to sleep.'

'Why did you leave me alone in the caves?' asked Bernt.

Grottor shrugged. 'Why are you thinking of leaving me?'

'That's different,' said Bernt.

'Remember what your *mormor* said,' said Grottor. 'You must listen to me. When you listen to me, how can you be alone?'

How many days have I been here? he wondered a few days or weeks later, and was puzzled to realize that he could not sort it out, not even roughly. A week or two at least, but perhaps a great deal longer than that, perhaps even years.The dreams continued, filled with a host of people, none of whom he could place. With knives, he and Grottor forced these people up the side of the mountain, to the first of the caves. *Why only the first cave?* he wondered as he dreamt. They killed them there, drew circles around them in their own blood, inscribed on white bodies red symbols whose meanings he did not know. Then they waited until something, a thing that he could never see, a kind of wavering shape that seemed imbued with the darkness between the stars, that slowly dragged them back down one of the tunnels and away. What happened to them after that, Bernt didn't know for certain: shortly after that he always woke up. It was not the killing itself, nor watching the bodies be dragged deeper in, which made him startle awake, but the realization that there was no shock, that it seemed smooth and natural from beginning to end, as if he had experienced the same thing a dozen times before.

Often he woke up to see Grottor in the room beside him, sometimes even in the bed beside him, touching his lips, telling him *ssshhh*, that it was all just a dream. He did not know if it was worse to wake up like that or to wake up alone.

Several times, he had woken up not in his bed at all, but on the slope of the mountain, in full night, his sore body bruised, with no memory of where he had been.

———

Sometimes whole evenings went by without him seeing his grandmother. On the nights when he did see her it was clear that there was something very wrong with her, something not-just-right, some sort of degenerative illness slowly transforming her. She could hardly control her limbs now. Her skin was flabby and hanging in some places, cracked and splitting in others. She no longer allowed him to come close, told him she did not want this to be how she remembered him.

She's dying, Bernt realized. *What will I do when she's dead?* Simultaneously worried and relived, he considered maybe when she was dead he could work up the nerve to leave.

And then she turned slightly and he caught a twitchy flash of something, a rubberiness in her arms as if her bones had started to dissolve. It was so unnatural, he couldn't believe what he'd seen. He involuntarily took a few steps toward her.

'No closer!' his grandmother shrieked and just for a moment looked up and met his eyes, then moved swiftly through the door to her room, slamming it behind him.

Bernt had to lean against the wall to gather himself. What had he seen? Had he imagined it? No, he had seen not the eyes of an old woman but of a young boy. Grottor's eyes.

Quietly, he made his way to his *mormor's* door. He kneeled, pressed his eye to the keyhole. The room was mostly dark inside, lit only by the glow of a solitary candle, but even in that dim light it was impossible to be mistaken. There was Grottor, stepping out of his grandmother's skin, like it was a suit of liver-spotted clothing. And there was Grottor, staring back at the door, staring right at the keyhole, a smile frozen on his lips.

Bernt fled. He ran down the mountain, veering on and off the road, listening for signs of pursuit. He knew what he had seen, but he also knew that if he told anyone he wouldn't be believed. What was he to do? Make up a story, something they would believe? Something, anything. He would escape Grottor. He had to get away, as far away as he could.

He saw headlights far ahead, coming toward him, and he ran toward them, waving his arms. The old truck when it saw him, slowed, stopped.

'My grandmother,' he said when the driver rolled down the window. 'She fell and hit her head. She's dead.' Only then did he realize it was the man who had first driven him to his grandmother's house.

'*Dead?*' said the man. 'Are you sure she's dead?'

'I'm sure,' said Bernt.

'Sometimes people look dead and they're not,' said the man.

'She's dead,' said Bernt.

'Well get in already.'

But once Bernt had climbed into the truck, he was surprised to find the man driving forward rather than turning around.

'Where are you going?' he asked.

'We have to make sure,' said the man. 'Just in case. You'd never forgive yourself if she was still alive and died because I didn't check.'

And Bernt, not knowing what else to do, cried loudly. The man reached over and patted his shoulder, but kept driving toward his grandmother's house. Once the tears dried, he shrunk against the side of the door and stayed there, hugging himself.

When they arrived, Bernt refused to get out. *All right*, the man said, *that's understandable. You saw your grandmother fall and maybe die. I can understand why you don't want to go back in the house.* No, Bernt wanted to explain, it wasn't that, but something syruped his tongue and the man was too quickly gone.

He thought about running toward the house, somehow coaxing the man back before it was too late, but was afraid to leave the truck. He waited, feeling the darkness tuck itself around him.

And then suddenly he was no longer alone in the truck. He knew that there was someone else there beside him despite the fact that the door hadn't opened. He couldn't bear to turn his head to see who it was.

'Nice of you to oblige me by bringing a friend,' said a voice that would stay with him to the end.

Bernt tried to open his mouth, found his tongue to cling to his palate. He made a strangled sound.

Grottor put an arm around his shoulder. He leaned closer until his eyes, shining in the darkness, were inches from Bernt's own. He could feel Grottor's warm breath against his face. 'Who do you listen to?' asked Grottor, 'Who is your god? Who is in charge of you now?'

IV

Before the man was conscious again, Grottor and Bernt gagged him and bound his wrists tightly behind his back, running a lead off the rope as well. Then they went into the kitchen and got a knife, jabbing the man's arms with it until he woke up.

Bernt watched it all as it happened, unable to do anything but what Grottor wanted. He struggled, tried to break free, but couldn't. The man thrashed, and couldn't break free either.

They climbed the side of the mountain, following the path toward the caves. The beam of the flashlight was sharp, all things rendered in crisp and explicit detail. Bernt watched, in front of him, the man pathetically shinnying, his bound wrists flexing against the small of his back. Bernt climbed behind him like a somnambulist, the ground beneath his feet feeling distant, at a remove. Just behind him came Grottor.

They came to the top and entered the first cleft, though Bernt knew this was not where they would remain. They stopped, and the man stood, panting, his gag growing damp. The rope, Bernt could see, was chafing the skin away from the man's wrists. He watched Grottor lean against him, touching slim finger to tight gag.

'Hush,' said Grottor.

The man tried to pull his head away.

He is going to kill him, thought Bernt, yet he could make no effort to stop him.

They made their way out of the cleft and along the face, over the bare, cracking rock. Bernt was first, looking back over his shoulder as he went, shining the light down at their feet. Grottor came behind, holding the man by an elbow to keep him from tumbling down the mountainside.

Bernt clambered up into the second cleft, then Grottor pushed the man up and came in himself. He jabbed the knife into the man's stomach, making him grunt. 'Come on,' he said, gesturing first at the man and then at Bernt. 'Down the tunnel,' he said, and held out his hand to take the flash-light.

Bernt crept first, moving to the back of the slit. *There must be a way out*, he was thinking, even though he couldn't stop walking. This man would die, there was no helping that, nothing he could do now; he had grown willing to sacrifice him if he himself could survive.

Behind him Grottor's flashlight died and all around him the darkness grew palpable, quickly more than he could stand. And then the flashlight reillumined and he saw he had turned himself around in the tunnel and was looking backward into the farmer's pale and terrified face, at the mouth still wriggling against the gag.

'Keep going,' said Grottor, so he did.

The tunnel grew narrow, its floor uneven. They started down a long incline and Bernt found the temperature rising around him, the air thick and hard to breathe. They went farther down and Bernt's feet were now in tepid water and soon the water sloshed up to his knees. The passage began a leftward tilt so he had to lean and push off the rock below him, the other wall slanting to become the roof. Behind him, the man slipped. Though the passage was too narrow for Bernt to quite turn around, he could look back under one arm to see him fallen on his face in the water and, with his hands tied behind his back, unable to get up. And then Grottor yanked the farmer up by the arms, and he arose with water coursing down his face and blood from where he had struck his forehead too, but the gag still in place. Bernt could hear him coughing inside the rag, as if he were choking to death, water coming in gouts out his nose. Grottor, steadying the man and helping him to angle his stance, flashed the light into Bernt's eyes, and said 'Keep going.' *I won't*, Bernt's will resisted, but he kept on.

The angle became severe, the passage tight enough that he had to lie on the slant floor, waist deep in water, and inch along on his back. The passage tightened further, the ceiling coming low enough to touch his chest. He had to let out his breath to move forward. He could no longer turn his head about so had to leave it to one side, looking backward at the man's damp and bloodied face, one hand feeling out blindly in front of him, Grottor's flashbeam behind him and darting all about. He could not see in front of him and could not tell where he was creeping, inch by inch. And then wasn't creeping at all for he saw the man behind him was no longer moving forward, his chest—

'What's wrong?' Bernt asked.

'He's stuck,' said Grottor.

'Stuck?'

'You must be stuck too,' said Grottor.

And Bernt suddenly knew that he was. He could feel the rock against his chest and his breath was with him only in short bursts and he could move neither forward nor back. For an instant, Grottor flicked the flashlight off and for Bernt there was nothing, only an immense darkness, an asphyxiating nothingness. The flashlight came on again and he could see, in the light, the blood beating in the man's neck.

'This is enough,' said Bernt. 'Help me get free. Let's go back.'

Grottor smiled. 'Back,' he said, using *mormor*'s falsetto.

Bernt closed his eyes and tried to think himself elsewhere, but when he opened them, the man was still there, and Grottor too, the latter pushing a knife along the upper edge of the wall, scraping one edge of it along the ceiling, bringing the other through the man's neck.

The man flinched and scraped the side of his head against the rock just above him, the knife cutting deeper. Grottor drew the knife back, the blood pulsing in little jets around it and then spreading in a sheet over the man's shoulders and down his chest. Bernt saw the man's throat tighten as the man tried, under the gag, to swallow. Then the eyes began to glaze, what he could see of them in the dim light. They turned opaque and Bernt knew the man was dead.

He could see through the cleft in the man's neck a section of Grottor's face, the single visible eye pale and hard. Grottor was reaching out with one hand, fingering the man's neck, his sodden shirt.

He began smearing the rock above with the man's blood, writing vague and spindly symbols, muttering as he did so.

'What are you doing?' asked Bernt.'Now it will come for him but take you too. All I need is your skin. Your *mormor* is worn: who better to stand in than her *släkting*?'

And then his hand was withdrawn and Bernt could hear Grottor's body scraping its way back down the tunnel and away, the light of the flashbeam ever more distant. He called out, had no response. The other man's face in the dying light was a solid mass, another rock, inscrutable. *Don't leave me!*, Bernt screamed to Grottor, but there was no response.

He closed his eyes. When he opened them it had fallen dark all around him, more abysmal than he could bear, and then, impossibly, it grew blacker still.

He waited, mind slowly collapsing, for the darkness to take him.

BRIAN EVENSON *(b. Ames, Iowa, USA, 1966) is the author of twelve books of fiction, most recently a story collection called* Windeye *(Coffee House Press, 2012) and a novel called* Immobility *(Tor, 2012). In 2009 he published the limited edition novella* Baby Leg *(New York Tyrant Press) and the novel* Last Days *(which won the American Library Association's award for Best Horror Novel of 2009) and the story collection* Fugue State, *both of which were on* Time Out New York's *top books of 2009. His novel* The Open Curtain *(Coffee House Press) was a finalist for an Edgar Award and an IHG Award. For* Exotic

Gothic 2 *he wrote "The Dismal Mirror," an honorable mention in Ellen Datlow's* Best Horror of the Year, Volume 2. *His work has been translated into French, Italian, Spanish, Japanese and Slovenian. He lives and works in Providence, Rhode Island, where he directs Brown University's Literary Arts Program. Other books include* The Wavering Knife *(which won the IHG Award for best story collection),* Dark Property, *and* Altmann's Tongue. *He has translated work by Christian Gailly, Jean Frémon, Claro, Jacques Jouet, Eric Chevillard, Antoine Volodine, and others. He is the recipient of three O. Henry Prizes as well as an NEA fellowship.*

Commentary on "Grottor": *'Grottor' is Swedish for 'caves' (singular 'cave' is 'grotta'). Probably very few readers will know that, but there's a similarity of his name to the word 'grotto' that made me think readers would make a semi-conscious connection. So, 'Grottor' as a title to me both evokes the boy and the caves. The title I originally had for the story was "The Caves".*

As far as whether the teenage Bernt (whose Nordic name means 'strong, brave bear') and the demonic Grottor are separate or not, I suppose that's the question that I raise in a lot of my fiction. It's very similar to the question that gets raised about Rudd and Lael in The Open Curtain—*even though they're basically overlapped, there are a few moments that can't be explained completely away. Here it's probably the reverse: they're largely separate, but there are a few moments where that separation seems somewhat suspect. Though maybe that's evasive on my part.*

Such a Man I Would Have Become

E. Michael Lewis

The Rainier Club
Seattle, April 1905

'UNCLE HENRY,' CRIED EDWARD (NEDDY) HOLTEN JAMES, 'I do hope our little soiree didn't bore you.'

Henry James frowned at his warm brandy as he swirled it around the snifter. 'No no,' he said with an air of fatigue. 'Dining with a few rustic companions is infinitely better than a banquet in your honor attended by women who remember you only as the author of *Daisy Miller*.'

Neddy laughed and sat in the forest green wingback chair next to his uncle, sipping his own brandy. Before them, the fire roared. The head of an elk of substantial rack, affixed above the fireplace, stared into the room with taciturn solemnity. The parlor smelled of pine smoke and old leather. Across the room, curtains wavered with the breeze from a narrow window, bringing in the scent of rain.

'Tomorrow we shall take the streetcar to Green Lake for luncheon,' Neddy said. 'It is a capital place for relaxation. Beautiful too, even in the rain.'

At length, his uncle said, 'There is a moist ethereal beauty about this land, Neddy. I shall miss it when I go.'

'Your train doesn't leave for two days.' As he replied, a knock, polite but insistent, sounded at the paneled mahogany door.

'Come,' Neddy said. A man entered, tall and thin, with smooth black hair in a sharp widow's peak and a thin dark moustache. His charcoal suit was tailored and fit him well, despite his angular shoulders and sharp elbows. He was a man who, when encountered on the streets of a city on the East Coast, would be looked on as a mountebank—here in the West however, he was seen as an entrepreneur. Henry did not recognize him as one of his nephew's fellows.

'I'm sorry to interrupt,' the man said from the doorway, 'but, if it's not too much to ask of your uncle, may I have one moment of his time?'

'We are waiting for the rain to dissipate somewhat before we drive home,' Neddy said. He glanced at Henry, who remained motionless, then trained his eyes on the intruder. 'We trust to your discretion.'

'Of course.' The man stepped into the room and gave a little bow before the two men. 'I am at your service. I was hoping, Mr. James, that I might ask about one of your works.'

Henry made a noise with his mouth that was not entirely disagreeable.

The angular man sat on the edge of the settee and leaned toward the author. 'I'm afraid that business kept me from your lecture. I'm told you spoke only of *The Ambassadors*.'

'It is my best work, my most complete and satisfactory work "all round".' James looked dismissively from the man to the fireplace. 'Do you not agree?'

'Oh yes, I agree completely. However, I was hoping you'd talk about this.' The man produced a book from inside his jacket. Your nephew has been kind enough to provide the club with signed editions of his famous uncle's work. I want to talk to you about this one.' The man showed them the cover of the volume he carried.

'*The Two Magics,*' Henry read. He looked the disagreeable man in the face. 'Do you wish to talk about *The Covering End* or. . . '

'*The Turn of the Screw,*' the man finished.

With one hand, Henry rubbed his face and looked again to the fire. After a moment, he gestured vaguely to the air and said, 'A bogey tale, a shameless potboiler. A fairy story, pure and simple.'

Neddy watched the interloper's face grow taut and could not decide if he was irritated, annoyed, or merely disappointed.

'Ah, then it's entirely imaginary? There is no truth in it?'

The author's voice edged on interest. 'There is a little truth in everything.'

'See here,' Neddy broke in. 'My uncle is not interested in any spiritualist . . . '

'Of course not,' the intruder quickly agreed, but he pressed the author. 'How much truth?'

Henry smiled a little and said, 'Not a bit.'

'Well,' said the man, leaning back on the settee, 'What if I told you that I possess a ghost story that held the unspeakable truth?'

'My Uncle Henry has no time for campfire stories or sourdough shudder tales,' Neddy said and sat forward. He sensed that the man was about to withdraw when Henry shifted in his chair, removed his thin rimmed spectacles and rubbed the bridge of his nose. He cocked his head, half shuttered his large eyes, and listened to the rain.

'The rain doesn't appear to be in any danger of letting up,' Henry spoke, 'and the fire always has time for a ghostly tale.'

Neddy sighed and settled in, his lips pressed together.

The intruder aligned his posture to the settee and smiled. 'Thank you sir,' he said crisply. 'Mr. James, you have traveled the world, and no doubt have seen a great many things and heard a great many tales, but have you ever heard of a man who killed himself, but lived to tell the tale?'

Nathaniel Gray was a real estate magnate, late of San Francisco. I met him just before the Panic of '93, in the card room of the

Baltimore as we steamed to Seattle from Portland. He was, quite frankly, the best card player on the ship, and it wasn't long before his skills were well known. No one on the boat dared play him. Myself, well, I had won part interest in a coal mine and thought myself something of a gambler. Gray showed me the error of my ways. He took my money unashamedly, scolding me as he did it. In the process, however, we became friends. Gray, I learned, had just sold his business interests in San Francisco, and the smell of money brought him up the Pacific Coast. His wife Alice, who traveled with him, was prudent and respectful, and allowed her husband the social freedom of the card room due to her weakened constitution during sea travel. He had bought land, sight unseen, on the Olympic Peninsula, and planned to build a sawmill.

'Interest in a mine, you say,' he said as we drank coffee in the salon. My cup also contained whiskey, but Gray was a teetotaler. We played cards for sport now, to pass the time since I had lost more than I could afford and Gray knew it. 'Well that's good. A place to start.' There was a smile in his voice.

'Coal,' I said, 'is the driving force of our new economy. Why, everything burns coal. This boat could be powered by coal from my mine.'

'Yes, but can you build with coal? Can you carve it, shape it, make a chair of it and sit comfortably by the fire?' Gray won another game then. I dropped my cards onto the table and could not help but smile at his manner. He continued. 'Now wood—ah, wood is much more valuable. You can power a ship—and build one too. With wood, you can both create and destroy.'

'The mine I now own was once a rich forest. Perhaps under your trees lies coal as well.' I allowed him to refill my glass. 'Perhaps you will think of me when you have cut all your tress down, and sell me the mineral rights.'

'That's what I like about you, my dear Prospector,' He smiled as he reshuffled the cards. 'You think ahead.'

When we reached Seattle, he put me up in a suite for the night before my journey to the Renton Highlands to survey the land I had bought. Mining, I soon learned, required getting more dirt under one's fingernails than I wished, and I soon sold the land and turned my eyes to other misadventures. Streetcars, insurance, fishing, and a little gambling. Gray, however, logged his land and built his sawmill, then bought more land and built more sawmills, but soon gave it up for ship building, and thrived even in the depression. He purchased a mansion on Capitol Hill and his wife turned it into a showplace. I dined with them whenever my business interests permitted. Alice threw lavish parties. It was at one of these parties, rooms brimming with other shameless capitalists, that I met Charlotte Jackson.

Alice Gray, as wan and as pale as when I met her shipboard, greeted me with a jest, as she always did. 'Ah yes, the Prospector.' She smiled as I kissed her hand. This was Gray's name for me now, owing to my start in mining and subsequent risky business ventures. 'You need to find yourself a wife. That suit you're wearing looks like it's been slept in.'

I agreed that a woman's touch might have its advantages, but told her that I was far from giving up my bachelor ways. And who could afford to, with this depression? She laughed at me.

'Go into the parlor and meet Charlotte,' she said, 'and you'll change your mind.'

I resist intrigue less than most, so I did what she said and encountered a scene I could not have imagined. There were dozens of men packed into the room, old and young alike, adorned to the hilt and filled with a particular joy, all facing the center of the room, doting en masse on one woman. Charlotte Jackson was a vision of refinement and ginger beauty, but there was a fierce independence that burned in her, and despite her chaste attire, I could sense immediately what the other men sensed as they laughed with her and raised their port to her. She was a lady full of adventure.

And standing next to that gently rounded femininity, more intent on her every word than any other man, if possible, was Nathaniel Gray.

It goes without saying that we all danced with her, and with each word that fell from her full lips, we each found her more charming and spirited than before. I had never seen such a woman command attention in such a room filled with captains of industry. Born to a fine family from Alabama, she was a widow. Left a fortune by a Kansas cattle rancher, she had come West in search of a new life. What the other women thought of her I can only guess. They dreaded her, I suppose. Nathaniel Gray, though, was far from inscrutable. He played the good host by being so close to her as to practically have her on his arm all evening.

Not many knew Gray as I did. Despite his many dealings in business, he had few close personal friends. I was wont to count myself chief among them, though mostly because he recognized the old fire that, as a young man, had fueled him to become wealthy. And while I knew that all of us loved Charlotte Jackson that evening, I also knew that Nathaniel Gray loved her most of all.

Then the *Excelsior* landed in San Francisco with Klondike gold, and everyone went mad. That day, I was walking through Pioneer Square when Gray found me, newspaper in his hand. He wrung mine vigorously up and down as he met me. 'My dear Prospector, have you seen the news?'

I assured him that I had, and I was prepared to take advantage of this good fortune by outfitting expeditions leaving for the Klondike with my new interest in a mercantile. 'All those miners leaving us for parts North will need equipment,' I told him. 'I think this is only the start of the gold fever.'

He congratulated me on my ingenuity and invited me to dine with him. Afterward, over coffee and Vashon Island blackberry cobbler, he asked, 'Wouldn't it be an adventure? Staking a claim, striking it rich, arriving home a millionaire?' On further questioning, I found Gray wasn't just interested in staking a claim, he wanted to work it as well.

'You may find this hard to believe, as I am past my prime,' he said, 'but I have a wanderer's soul. It was for love of new vistas and fresh challenges that I sailed round the horn from Galveston to San Diego. It made me come alive. While I left with nothing in my pocket, I always believed that my skill in business would see me through, and I was right.' He sighed like a schoolboy. 'But the problem with success is that you always want more.'

I could tell that a Klondike gamble was not all that he meant. I asked him then about his wife. Though she suffered from a weak constitution, nonetheless, she ruled the roost, as they say. She would allow him to fund all the expeditions he wanted, but he could not go himself. She would not let him, as she put it, 'get his hands dirty.' So that was that.

'Charlotte is going,' he said at last. It was not necessary to say more. Her experience in Kansas had prepared her for hardship, and with her tenacity, I was without a doubt that she would prove a success. A woman that could both charm a parlor full of bigwigs and pan for gold in a frozen waste was a prize worth the ultimate risk. Gray told me, 'I often lie awake at night wondering . . . wondering what it would be like, what I would be like, if I hadn't made it big, I mean, if I had had no choice but to seek my fortune in the Yukon. I used to be a solitary and desperate man, you know. To find myself young and in the company of someone so lovely . . . ' He returned his cup to the saucer. 'You are still a young man, my dear Prospector, and not yet old enough for regret, but your day will come, and when it does, you'll know what it's like to be the one on the dock, watching your ship sail out to sea.'

News reached us in a few days that Charlotte had eloped with a man I knew slightly named John Rockwell—a military man, whose family's money also came from cattle. As we had all courted her in our own way, there wasn't a society man in Seattle who didn't wish it were him traveling north with such a prize. Looking back now, I understand that Gray would have forsaken all the gold in the Yukon for the pleasure of her marital affection.

Gold fever continued its grip on the region. That first month alone, ten thousand Klondikers departed from Seattle bound for the gold fields. Nearly one quarter of the police force quit. Even the mayor resigned and bought a steamer to ferry passengers and goods for those seeking their fortunes. Laws were passed requiring each outfit to leave with a year of supplies. In addition to the goods, I invested in a process of evaporation that could reduce one hundred pounds of potatoes to ten pounds. I started an employment agency to capitalize on the labor shortage. In short, though I saw no gold, I still struck it rich during the Klondike Gold Rush.

Gray's shipyards could not keep up with the demand for new vessels, nor with the need to repair the old ones. His enthusiasm allowed him to provide grubstakes for perhaps twenty expeditions. Alice cut back her social schedule and I saw less and less of my friend. Rumors came that doctors made regular appearances at his house.

Word came back of Charlotte Rockwell intermittently, and when it did, we hung on every word. The newspapers dubbed her the 'Belle of the Yukon' and celebrated her both as a rugged pioneer and a merciful beauty, generous with her charity to the other Klondikers. News reached us from Dawson City of her success in the gold fields and the opening of her hotel, immediately dubbed the finest in all of Alaska. She represented all that a good woman, a capable woman, could do. By all accounts, Charlotte was now a fixture in Alaskan life, as constant as the ice and snow. She was our reddish-haired heroine.

I was waiting for a business associate on the docks, when to my surprise, I saw Charlotte disembark a steamer. She was dressed in dark fabrics, clothes as common as any worn by the mass of travelers waiting for the passengers to clear off so they could seek their own fortune in the Great White North. She darted away from the ship, avoiding the press and the onlookers by keeping her head down and hood drawn; but I could never forget her exquisite, genteel profile, and recognized it immediately, despite her reduced circumstances. I forgot my meeting and moved through the crowd to meet her.

Over the throng of onlookers, I called her name, but if she heard me, she gave no heed. When free of the crowd, she bolted into a dockside restaurant, where I found her at a table, bags huddled beneath her like frightened children.

'Charlotte,' I said, touching her on the shoulder, and feeling scratchy Irish wool. 'Mrs. Rockwell. It is you, isn't it?'

She looked up at me with eyes as hollow as any glass-eyed specimen of taxidermy I had ever seen. Her cheek held a deep blush, like a blow that had almost healed. She called me by my Christian name, and took my hand in hers. Her gloves were ragged and threadbare in places. She guided me to the seat across from her as her gaze darted out from under her hood. Those eyes were ringed with black. 'Please don't be a fool.'

I ordered something medicinal from the waiter while her eyes kept dancing furtively toward the entrance.

'What has happened to you?' I asked.

'You shall read it in the papers soon enough,' she said, her voice low with shame. And she related her tale to me, about a man, a scoundrel and a claim jumper from California, who made the public promise that he would have the Belle of the Yukon under his yoke. She told me of the fire that had reduced her fine hotel to ash, of how her husband had done battle with the rogue and gave his life so that she might escape. She finished by telling me that even now, thousands of miles away from the Yukon, she felt his influence, the very presence of this man whom she knew would kill her just as soon as marry her. 'I'm sure he's following me. He knows my every step,' she said, and for the first time, I thought she might cry. 'All that I own is in these two bags.' The waiter arrived with whiskey, and it seemed to revive her downtrodden spirits. I committed myself to helping her, but in truth I was not sure how I could at first. Her staying in my rooms was out of the question, and a hotel would be the first place any cad would look.

'There, there,' I told her. 'You have many friends in Seattle, and we will see you come to no harm. Let's go to Gray's house. He will know what to do.'

'Oh no—not him. Anyone but him, please.'

'Nonsense,' I told her. 'Nathaniel is your staunchest ally. Be not proud. I will take you to him.'

I will never forget that moment standing on the threshold of Gray's door. My knock, though firm, brought no response. After a moment, Charlotte clutched my hand, glanced archly over her shoulder and gasped. I turned and followed her gaze into the street.

At first I saw only a normal everyday street scene. Gray clouds moved low along the horizon, waiting for just the right moment to cast down rain. Trees stirred in a light breeze. A gardener tended a rhododendron in a nearby yard. A middle-aged couple out for a stroll held their umbrellas at the ready. Our cab pulled away from the curb and proceeded to a more populated thoroughfare. Then I saw him.

He was a common, gray, ordinary man, his outfit marking him as a day laborer, or perhaps a lumberjack, but there was something about how he stood still amongst the throng of activity that made me immediately dislike him. In fact, I began to feel the deepest loathing for this man, a rude cipher who seemed to be watching us, even as we watched him.

My 'prospecting' had made me a cautious man. I placed my other hand in my pocket and closed it around my revolver. Its cool metal strengthened my desire to answer to this man. I moved to release my hand from Charlotte's and walk into the street to confront him.

But as I turned, I discovered that the door was open, and there in place of it, was Gray, looking pale and unkempt. Charlotte cried out and held my hand tighter.

I forgot the man at the shock of seeing my friend disheveled. 'Gray! Are you ill?'

'It's my wife,' he said. 'Alice is dead.'

He ushered us into the parlor, where we sat and talked in hushed voices. Alice had just passed, he said. Her heart had finally given out. For weeks, she had required constant attention. The doctors ordered bed rest and sent a nurse to look after her. But Gray, who would not hear of strangers caring for his wife, took over the duties himself. He had watched over her day and night until the end. Gray had sent his servants out and was wont to spend the day alone, planning the last arrangements according to his wife's wishes. The strain was almost more than he could bear, and it showed.

At first Charlotte looked on distantly, even distractedly, as his narrative continued. Then she put her hand on his shoulder—a simple enough gesture—but even in the simple things she had the grace of an angel. As she did, he seemed all at once to brighten. He welcomed her warmly back to Seattle.

'Of course you will stay here. No! I insist. This house has been dreary enough. Stay and lighten it with your red gold hair.'

'I will help you bear your burden, if you will help with mine,' she said, taking his hand.

I must admit to my spirit being dashed a bit by their instant sympathy, an immediate communion I have never attained. I sought to bring the conversation round to Charlotte's troubles and to broach the subject of the stationary man, but Gray would not hear of it. 'No more bad news,' he said. 'Let Mrs. Rockwell have a respite from her worries, and myself as well.'

Finally, I told him that I would have a guard sent over to watch the house and accompany them out. Though he protested, I sent the man anyway, a lanky, no-nonsense Swede named Jorgensen. With a blond head like a chaff of wheat and a tread of quiet Nordic stealth, he fed me reports regarding his duties. Gray himself did not venture out, but received a stream of callers offering sympathy about his dear Alice. Before the week was out, word spread that Charlotte had returned and was staying with Gray, and the traffic into the home increased. Many wanted to hear tales of her adventures in the Yukon and welcome her back into polite society. At this she almost snubbed them, and shamed them for seeking her company when such a man as Nathaniel Gray grieved for his wife. Reporters, I learned, boldly haunted the street night and day in the hope that she would grant them an interview.

Jorgensen told me of their first excursion to the public market after Alice's funeral. 'The woman watched the crowd all the time, like she was looking for someone,' he told me. 'Everywhere she went, she looked behind or ahead.' He told me of a time when she turned deathly pale for no reason, and told Gray she felt ill, and that they must leave. Gray acted with all haste.

I debated the wisdom of telling my friend directly that with a madman loose, he was putting his own life in danger by housing Charlotte. But I knew Gray well enough to know what he would say to this. He hadn't achieved his place in business with timidity, and even in sorrow, I knew that he would be her stalwart advocate. In truth, he seemed to block me at every turn when I spoke to him, as if he already knew she was in danger, but did not dare speak of it.

When I met with the Swede the next week, I asked him, as usual, if he had seen anything suspicious.

'Not likely sir,' he said, but something in his manner made him pause and I asked him what it was.

'Did you see anyone? Anyone watching the house?'

'There are enough people who do that,' he said. 'The papers still send their boys around to alert the reporters should they leave. Still, there is one man . . . '

'Yes?'

'He is awfully queer,' said the man slowly, as if trying to gauge my reaction. 'He just stands there at the edge of the block. Stands there and never moves, for almost an hour and a half. Then, I look away from a moment, and when I look back he is gone.' The man mopped his forehead a little. 'He is awfully queer.'

'The next time you see that man, go to him. Follow him. Don't let him out of your sight. Alert the police to him. He is a murderer and an arsonist. He isn't to get near the house.'

Jorgensen agreed to do this.

My business deals sometimes took me to Tacoma or Olympia, and sometimes I spent as long as a month away. It was after one such incident that, upon my return, I made it a priority to visit Gray and his companion. Through weekly reports from my Swedish hired man, I knew that things had quieted down somewhat, word having spread about Charlotte's desire for privacy and Gray's own grief. But as a result, some of the talk was turning ugly and speculative toward both of them. I decided to pay a call on my friends one evening, with the pretense of speaking to Gray about the quality of the man I paid for. This was in the autumn, with the last traces of summer warming the sound, and the leaves stirring as if the world sighed, resolved to the dampness of approaching winter.

I found the house dark except for the upstairs, and as I approached the front door, Jorgensen was nowhere to be seen. I went to pull back the brass knocker, when the door creaked, and I realized that it was standing slightly ajar.

The only light came from a distant street lamp. I pulled open the door and called inside, but no one answered. I suppose right there I should have involved the police, but instead I drew my revolver and slowly eased through the doorway, into the darkened foyer, where I stood silent and listened.

From upstairs I heard movement, and I crept toward the stairs when I heard a clatter from the kitchen. I walked slowly down the hall and pushed open the door, pistol ready.

The kitchen was in darkness, filled with lesser and greater shadows. No heat radiated from the stove, for I would have felt it; but there was a smell, a vulgar smell that I didn't recognize at first. Wet. Sickly. As I stepped inside, I saw the shadows move. With them came the sound of a struggle, then stillness, and a low moan. The odor, pungent and ammoniac, now filled the room.

But my eyes had begun to adjust, and I could now make out one figure hunched over another across the room.

'Stay where you are,' I said, taking aim. 'I'm armed.'

Then the hunched form straightened and for a moment I saw him in perfect profile against the kitchen window. Before I could breathe, the man—for I now saw that it was a man—turned to me and made to come toward me, a deep, feral growl escaping his throat. I pulled the trigger.

In the moment of the muzzle flash, I saw him plainly. He was coming at me. I saw the Bowie knife in his hands, swung high, ready to strike me down like the point of a lightning bolt. I saw his other hand, balled into a fist, but not like the fist of a normal man, it was somehow altered, smaller, yet still ferocious and as hate-filled as the rest of him. I saw a grin of yellow teeth . . . and I saw something else. Something familiar, something I couldn't believe. At that moment, there was no time for reflection. I knew he would kill me if he reached me, and I knew that he would reach me if I didn't kill him first.

I fired a second time. In the tiny interval between my first shot and my second, I saw that he had closed half the distance between us, that he still held the knife high, his blade arcing toward my chest. His fist was gone now, for his fingers were outstretched and reaching for me, and I knew why his fist had been misshapen. Two of his fingers—his middle fingers—were missing, just worn stubs in the middle of his hand. But that sense of the familiar, that sense that somehow I knew this man, exploded into my mind once again, and I struggled with the pieces of the puzzle, even as he came at me with his strong yet sinister profile and worn face, at once hollow-eyed and emaciated, but twisted sharp like a spool of barbed wire. In my stomach, I felt a blow as if he had already struck me down, for despite the hod-carrier clothes and deformity, this man seemed an identical twin of my dear friend. In the face of the killer, I saw the face of my host, Nathaniel Gray. He leapt at me.

The flash failed to illuminate if I had wounded him, so I fired again despite my revulsion, and though I knew that the man should be upon me, he was not. The kitchen was silent. I moved then, through the acrid gun-smoke to the kitchen light, where I at once activated it, pointing my gun to the floor before me, where I expected my attacker to lay dead.

But my assailant was nowhere to be found. The back door hung open and moved a little in the breeze. Jorgensen lay crumpled nearby, next to a sink, stabbed to death.

I preceded upstairs and found Nathaniel Gray with Charlotte in his room. Charlotte had heard a noise and had retreated there. At the sound of a struggle, Nathaniel had locked the door and armed himself and had to be persuaded to open the door for me. He looked ill as before, pale and unsteady, his grasp on my arm clammy and limp. 'Thank God for you,' he said. Charlotte, too, thanked me, but only furtively, and cast her eyes my way all during the time the police took our statements and transported Nathaniel and Charlotte through the rain, under guard, to a suite of rooms off Pioneer Square. Her eyes held neither a yearning, nor thankfulness, or even gratitude. She was suspicious of me, of what I had seen, though I kept the uncanny details of my encounter from the police. Still, she plainly suffered in mind as Gray did in body, and I knew that despite her unease, they could not afford to forsake my friendship. Her affair had been made Nathaniel's affair and now mine, and I resolved to provide, to the best of my ability, the happy ending they deserved.

In the morning, I met Gray in the hotel lobby.

'My dear Prospector,' he said as he clasped my hand. His eyes were ringed in darkness. 'Charlotte sleeps. Let us eat and talk at length. I have yet to hear the truth of the encounter—the whole truth—from your lips.'

We were seated at a secluded table. Over strong coffee I related the incident, leaving out the awkward sense of familiarity with my foe. 'Still,' I said with confidence, 'The police will easily find a man with such a distinctive deformity.'

'What deformity?' Something about the question itself led me to think that he knew what I was going to say, that he was merely waiting with a doomed sense of certainty to confirm what he already knew.

'He's missing two fingers,' I said. I showed him with my own hand.

Gray's face blanched. His cup jarred into the saucer and he pulled his shaking hands into his lap. 'Now I know for certain what I have only suspected.' He ran his hand over his face as if in an effort to reshape it. 'Charlotte's unhappiness—this current unpleasantness—is all my fault.'

I asked him what he meant. He leaned in then and said, 'I see now that I must tell you everything. Everything as I understand it at any rate. Charlotte is upstairs, almost sick from what I have told her. Still, I believe she will come with me, despite what she knows.'

The narrative he related stunned me. He told me how, as a young man and miner in California many years ago, he had been involved in a barroom brawl, in which his own fingers, the same as my foe's, had nearly been removed. 'The doctor said there was a serious risk of infection to the digits, but I left town the next day rather than have him amputate. Since that day, I have never taken another drink of spirits, nor will I as long as I live.' He wiped the sweat from his brow. 'You remember that brash youth I spoke of, who longed to chase after Charlotte and Yukon gold? Well, such a man I would have become had I stayed in California, poor and deformed and full of drink. I would have not given a second thought to uprooting himself and betting everything I owned on such a gamble. That part of me was a scoundrel and a damnable cheat, and in drunkenness capable of any unrestricted violence. I turned my back on him long ago. But to my shame, I have never stopped thinking about him . . . and the possibilities for his success. I began to think of him as another person, with another life . . . ' Here my friend broke off and put his head in his hands. 'And somehow, I think my yearning, along with some occult agency, has brought him into existence, and now that he has learned of me, all I have he yearns to possess. All I covet he seeks to obtain. All I hold dear he seeks to destroy.'

I must have looked aghast. It is true, I didn't know what to say to him, but sitting there with the rain blowing hard against the hotel's wide windows, and having seen what I had seen, I did not disbelieve him.

'You think I am mad,' he said then, 'and perhaps I am.'

'It is not for me to judge madness in another man. With God as my witness, I believe you.'

'You do?'

'Yes. What's more, if what you say is true, you must leave this place. Go far away before this apparition can haunt you further.'

Gray slipped further into melancholy. 'There is no place we can go. He will follow us. He wants what he cannot have. He wants my life, my fortune, and my dignity, my—well,' he swallowed, 'my Charlotte, to do with as he wills.'

'You can protect her. You will protect her. If you created this phantom in a moment where choices were presented to you, than make this moment the same. Leave Seattle. Find your happiness elsewhere. Anywhere. There is no foreign shore where you and Charlotte could not find happiness.'

'Do you believe it is so?'

I reached across the table and touched my friend's shoulder. 'I believe it. You must take the happiness you have and run away. This creature wants it to steal, but he will not expect you to leave Seattle.'

'He is part of me . . . ' Gray sounded ashamed. 'Will he not follow me until the end?'

'You go armed with knowledge, and that will keep you safe, I know it. I will make the arrangements for it now. Go and tell her.'

'All right. We will leave today. Charlotte and I,' he said quickly. 'We can go to Chicago, where I have some people.' He got up from the table and wrung my hand, just as he had done that day in the beginning of the Klondike gold rush. 'I cannot thank you enough.'

'Leave it to me. The police will protect you in the meanwhile. Go to her.'

I made arrangements for them to take the train to Portland that afternoon, and then on to Chicago the following day. I dared not send anyone to Gray's house to gather their possessions, so I used my influence among the local merchants to outfit them for the journey. I delivered the tickets to the hotel myself and escorted them out before the police could intervene, and before the reporters could seek and find them. Charlotte's color had returned, though she was still nervous, sitting there in a dove-gray dress much closer than necessary to Gray in the cab. It pained me to see such a strong woman on the verge of hysteria, but I knew that escape would revitalize her spirits, and that Gray's presence would fortify her resolve.

On the platform, Gray shook my outstretched hand with both of his, thanking me again. Charlotte stepped forward then and said, 'Dearest Prospector, you have proved your loyalty beyond my ability to thank you.' And yet, as she said this, she leaned forward, planting a small kiss on my cheek, scented sweet cherry. My hand rose immediately to touch the spot and I found my face radiant with heat. I stammered, and she laughed her musical laugh, and Gray his hearty one. I saw them both safely into their compartment and bade them a good journey.

I forced myself into the throng of travelers and out of their view. I paid a man twenty dollars to exchange his traveling clothes for my tailored suit. Fingering the ticket in my pocket, I then boarded the last car and found a seat among the third class passengers. It was too late to hire someone to travel with them, so I would. Once in Portland, I could secure more suitable protection for the rest of the journey.

Once the train was underway and the conductor had been through to inspect the tickets, I went forward from car to car, looking for any sign of Gray's dark twin. I found no one. At each stop I took the time to step out onto the station's platform, to observe any passengers that embarked with us. When I did not see him even then, I felt relieved and resolved to reveal myself to my friends that evening at dinner.

I followed Nathaniel and Charlotte, who walked arm-in-arm and with air of considerable relaxation. With the dining car was reserved for first class passengers, I had to wait until my friends were seated, then I made enough fuss that Gray called out to me and asked me to join him.

Charlotte smiled as I sat down, a genuine smile, as when we first met. 'Well, it's our Prospector. And dressed the part, as well.'

I kissed her hand with thanks. 'Consider this an extended goodbye. I have business in Portland anyway.'

'What business?' Gray asked.

'None whatsoever,' I winked. 'But I'm sure I can find something.'

We ordered a meal and dined like old friends, the terror and fright of the past twenty-four hours falling behind us like landmarks from the train's windows. All was well, until, as we supped, I saw Gray's face turn pale as he glanced behind me. I turned as Charlotte gasped. The maître d' was arguing with a man who was dressed in rugged outdoor clothes, but the sound of his voice was unmistakable, and through I could not see his face, I knew who he was.

Shouting erupted between the two men as Gray haltingly stood. Charlotte blanched and tried ever to camouflage herself by staying perfectly still. I joined her, but I was coiled and readying to launch at the assailant.

'Let me pass, goddamn your eyes!' the ruffian shouted, and drew a Bowie knife. The maître d' stepped out of the way. The other diners erupted with cries of panic. Gray trembled, but marched forward to meet the man. Seeing the two of them together here in the cold daylight of the dining car, it took surprisingly little imagination to see the Gray I knew in the rogue's snaring countenance.

'Stop!' Gray held out his hand. His voice shook. 'You will go no further.'

'I will go as far as I damn well want, and you will not stop me. What you have belongs to me now, and if you don't give it, I will just kill you for it.' He drew back the blade and stabbed at Gray, who sidestepped and grabbed the interloper by the wrist and held the knife away.

As they struggled, I stood and drew my pistol, but I could not get a clear shot at Gray's attacker.

The two smashed into a table, sending flatware, white linens and wine glasses crashing to the floor. Diners rushed to safety amid cries to fetch the railroad detective. I stepped in front of a cook armed with a carving knife and told him to get Charlotte out of here. The cook tugged at her arm, but she remained seated, her eyes trained on the battling men.

Finally, the knife came free, and Gray kicked it away.

'You son-of-a-bitch! I'll kill you with my bare hands!' In a second, the ruffian's deformed hands were wrapped around Gray's throat. Wet noises of pain erupted from him. Here was my chance. As the rogue held Gray down on a table, I raised my pistol and called out, 'Stop!'

The man sneered at me. 'Put down that gun. When I've finished with him, I'll come for you.' His eyes bored into mine like flaming arrows and I felt my spirit weaken.

Gray's arms, having gripped the man to force a release, had started to flail about, but now stopped and fell close in on himself.

The triumphant villain let him go and came toward me.

'Go on, shoot me.'

I wanted to do nothing but that, I swear. But when I turned my head, I saw that Charlotte now stood, and having pushed the cook away, had advanced close behind me. The look on her face held me motionless. She filled my heart with fear. Hers was a face of desire, of want, all and only for him. I blocked her from going forward and said, 'Stay back, or I will fire!'

But it was bravado. As this man approached us, I felt my resolve melt, and in the face of all my most forthright urges, gave myself over to defeat. I know not how, even to this day, the power he had, or how he exercised it upon me.

He reached out to Charlotte and beckoned her to him. 'Give me the gun.'

My grip on the pistol was lessening. Behind me, I felt Charlotte urge me forward.

My eyes sought out Gray. I expected to find the lifeless body of my friend flung over the table where the intruder had left him. But he was gone.

The stranger cried out with a howl of wretched, but unrepentant torment. His twisted features went slack. The rogue lurched forward and careened to the floor at my feet, dead.

I didn't understand. Then I saw that Gray had regained consciousness and had taken up the stranger's knife and stabbed him in the back. A stunned railroad detective stood at his side.

Charlotte who now had an *O* for a mouth, stepped over his body and raced into Gray's arms, sobbing piteously. Gray handed the knife to the detective and said, 'I trust you'll want to arrest me now.'

The detective only managed, 'Who is that man? He looks like he could be your brother.'

Gray swallowed hard. 'I've never seen him before. Not in my whole life.'

I collapsed into the chair where moments before I sat enjoying lamb chops with friends. It was over then, I knew.

When his Uncle Henry did not speak, Edward Holten James laughed. 'That is your tale?'

The speaker, who had been leaning forward and emphasizing his words with urgency, finally relaxed into the settee. His shoulders slumped. 'For my part, yes. That a murder took place in Gray's home is public record. You will find my name and his in the details. The attack on the train appeared in several papers, due to the strangeness and the similarities between the victim and attacker.'

'A man who so boldly asserts his name with pride where murder is concerned is considered suspect in most circles,' Neddy decried.

The storyteller leaned forward again, the slight having stung him into action. Then there was a knock at the great door, followed by the appearance of their driver. 'Sir, the rain has subsided. Shall I pull the carriage around?'

'Please do,' replied the younger James. He and the storyteller stood together, and just as Neddy's lips opened to add another insult, Henry James stood.

'Neddy,' he announced, 'I am ready to go.' Here he offered his hand to the intruder, who took it. 'Yours was a most amusing tale. A pleasant diversion on a rainy night. Yes, a most intriguing tale. Thank you for telling it.'

Neddy seemed to smart with every word. 'Uncle, we must be off.'

'Thank you sir.' The storyteller took the Master's grasp in his.

'Indeed. Thank you and good night.'

The man released his hand, stood awkwardly before the gentlemen, then turned and left the room without turning back.

'Uncle,' his nephew said, as they stood in long black coats under the awning stretching from the Club's wide and elaborately carved wooden doorway to the curb of Columbia Street, 'Did you really like his sordid little tale?'

Henry James put his gloved hand on his nephew's shoulder and motioned him into the carriage ahead of him. 'His tale reminds me of things. Drafts written. Ideas that I had forgotten. It fills me with a most beguiling,' here he paused, then said with emphasis, '*Sense of the Past.*' These words were spoken with wry laughter. 'His tale was . . . inspiring. For example, think of how changed I would be had I stayed in America all those years ago . . . '

E. MICHAEL LEWIS *(b. Seattle, Washington, USA, 1972) is a lifelong native of the Pacific Northwest who studied Creative Writing at the University of Puget Sound. He has spent most of his adult life in Federal Service. His work can be found in* All Hallows, Shadowed Realms, *and* The Harrow. *His story "Cargo" first appeared in the Ash-Tree Press Anthology* Shades of Darkness, *and was reprinted in* The Best Horror of the Year Volume One, *edited by Ellen Datlow, in 2009. His most recent story can be found in* The Horror Anthology of Horror Anthologies, *edited by D.F. Lewis (no relation) in 2011. He has two sons, Michael and Jeffrey.*

Commentary on "Such a Man I Would Have Become": *No one was more surprised than I to find that Henry James, author of perhaps the most influential ghost story in the English language, spent time in Seattle visiting relatives. One thinks of the authors of English ghost stories so trapped by the Gothic that they would never stray from England's haunted shores. Seattle was transitioning from a rude frontier city (population 80,000 in 1900) to a west coast metropolis (237,000 in 1910). Although The Prospector is imaginary, many of the facts about the Klondike Gold Rush's impact on Seattle are true. Those that have read James's other supernatural stories may recognize themes from James's "The Jolly Corner" (1908). In that story, James's protagonist passes out when confronted with his other self, only to awaken in his love interest's arms. At the risk of melodrama (something James abhorred) I made the climax direct. Gray's murder of his divergent self, in full daylight with a room full of witnesses, is a final rejection of his alternate past that James himself never had to make.*

THE UNFINISHED BOOK

SCOTT THOMAS

Massachusetts, 18th Century

W HAT SHALL I TELL? THE WHOLE OF IT? AND WHO WOULD believe if I did? Where then to start? A winter, all but lost, far from the calendar now, a remembrance like a spider's thread glittering alone in a vast, shaded wood. Ahh, I'll tell of it . . . my first chapter. My most early memory.

A small town of roofs and smoke slept beneath the bloodless breast of the moon. It was December, perhaps, or a January, when storms favored the western hills, cleaving down through cedar and oak, smothering pasture and paddock and draping over all with a boundless, final-seeming white.

I, weedy and small, and hardly more flush than the pack on the roof, was fast about my sleep. Contrarily, in the night, the house came awake. It creaked and rattled, the windows chattering a frosty language that only other windows could know. Alternately, or in no particular pattern, the place whined like a babe, or groaned like a dying thing. But you'd have thought it dead already, old as it was.

Well, there was I, under roof and moon, and winds that rushed secrets through the eaves, when a figure came by the side of my bed and prodded me awake. It was a tall, stooped man—my father, likely, though I could not tell his face for all the bandages. He snatched me by the hand.

I was dragged to a door, a heavy batten thing which opened with a rumble that might have passed for the growl of a beast. Dark, suffusing odors drifted up the stairs from the abyss below and wrapped me in miasmic arms. This clammy embracing air fashioned the one sole hug I recall receiving in my childhood.

There were many steep steps and the gangly shadow led me down them all, our progress stingily facilitated by a tin lantern with punched holes too small for a firefly to squeeze through. Once at the bottom I found myself among cider barrels, and draping webs of dusty lace, plunged, as it were, into a silence that made my small heart loud.

Penned in by walls of mumble-colored fieldstones, I took in what the gloom had to offer, which was not much. Central, and somewhat interesting, a mighty heap of rocks spanned from floor to ceiling, forming the base of the chimney stack. But I was not taken down there to view that.

The man directed me to one of the corners. He pointed. *Read the book*, he said, although I had yet to learn to write my own name, let alone read.

A shabby thing, about the size of a man and covered in fur, lay in the corner, fetal on the cellar's dirt floor. Years had flattened it, killed any luster once upon the long, limp hair. The flesh had long since left, but there were bones here and there, discolored white peeking through the frenzy of brown strands.

Of the face I cannot say, there being such mold and shadows, but one of the hands—or the framework of what *once* had been a hand—was clear enough. Long, pale finger bones poked from a sleeve of matted hair and fanned out across the cover of a large flat book.

The face of the tome was slate, or petrified shadow one might suppose. Whatever the surface, it was scabbed with lichens, little colorless blooms that peered at me from between the tapered digits. The book, apparently, was older than the dead thing.

The tall man passed me the lantern and made his hunched,

spindly, spidery way back up the stairs, thumping the door behind him. His footfalls sounded through the floor, a feeble, under-nourished thunder.

There I was left and there I stood, alone with my tears, shivering in the sad colors that shaped damp confines beneath familial rooms. I wept to be sure, but I speak of small, olden tears worth neither time nor coin.

What was there to do but to gaze upon the dead thing, for which I might have felt pity were I not possessed of terror? At length I dared closer and spurred by an incongruous, inexplicable swell of pluck, knelt where the ruin slept in its cradle of shadow. I reached with small white hands, trembling, and took hold of the book.

Oh, it must have been half my weight, and cold as a stone in a stream! And didn't those thorny fingers rasp a wintry sound against the cover as I pulled the tome away?

The flame of my candle, a radiance all but confined in the lantern, provided only restless spatters of light as I sat with the book in my lap. The book opened, exhaled dust, revealed its inky patterns. The letters that comprised the words, seen in meager and shifting luminosity, were as ants that had evaded the prehistoric entombment of amber and now squirmed on pages of a like color. But the pages, unlike the covers of the book, were not in fact stone. They were brittle and thin and smelled of graves and autumn showers. But as I stared the ants became letters and the letters became words and their meaning became known to me.

I read. I read until the candle burnt to nothing, and yet read more. I read in a fever, engorged with secrets, and was ever changed, like one who has nursed at the bosom of the moon.

But for all its wonders and mysteries, the book was incomplete. The words—without explanation—ended partway down a page as if its author had simply vanished, or had met a sudden unfortunate end.

Having taken in all there was to take, I lay on the dirt floor—my mind submerged in an ocean of dreams—and slept. I slept near the dead thing with the book by my side and my hand on its cover. In the morning my father came and retrieved me. Neither he nor

I ever spoke again of the book, and I never had occasion to step foot in the cellar again.

Looking back upon the pages of my later youth, from out the dim majority of days, I find spotty recollections, just dots of light through engulfing murk. Oh, there were noteworthy times to be sure ... the first soft petals of spring that kissed the rain and marked the way to summer and loutish thunderclouds. Beyond that gleamed the frost-gold, rime-rimmed crown of autumn, king of all seasons, and winters heaped and bitterly bright.

But the times between remain largely a haze, and better they do, for they were void of joy, suffused with melancholy too crowding for the size of a boy's heart. I was left to my own company more frequently than not, there in the old family home, which, for all its wood, seemed a thing comprised of dusk. There were parents about, a wilted old hired woman too, and an odd visitor here and there—an aunt once on a rain-silvered Sunday—and occasionally bulky, ominous-looking men that spoke in low rumbles. But, despite the presence of others, I was, in effect, alone.

Of mother I recall little. She was an unspeaking, willow-limbed woman with hair like smoke. I cared little for her gaze (when she looked at me at all) for she bore a filmy eye like a ghostly egg. She came to carry a child in her later days and never had I known a woman in such a condition. I was dismayed to see her belly swell as if she were transforming into a hill.

My sibling was dead from the advent. How could it have been otherwise, looking as it did? The burial was in a pine wood, with trees like skinny legs under frayed green skirts. Crows blossomed above in a garden of wind.

Mother was the next to depart. Father found her in a meadow. The frost had come on and clung to any surface that would have it. It found window panes and bracken and rutted roads where hardened mud seemed treacle under lace. It found mother face down amidst trampled wildflowers.

Years passed. I became a lanky visage in the mirror, my hair and eyes the color of mourning. Though the years had spun their way far from that night in the cellar, the book was with me still. I could see the words when I closed my eyes, vivid words, black branches against moonlight, crow talons against a mist that existed nowhere but for my mind. The book's essence fanned wild currents in my blood and at night the forest inside me hissed with wind that sounded like a sea.

Thirteen summers had passed. Thirteen winters too, to say nothing of springs and autumns. Ahh, autumns . . . always too fast, always on gusty wings of oak leaf and fire. Fast from the eye, the beauty searing the heart deeper with each pass, autumn ghostly behind its veil of smoke and nights as black as a cricket's eye.

It was past the rim of autumn, between November's grey and winter stark as a meetinghouse, when I found my father in the barn. I, sleepless as the moon, had risen from my bed. Something had been braying out in the piney air, something forlorn. I rose up and went to find the source. There was father in the barn—father long and shadowy—an unswinging pendulum hanging from the rafters. I did not cry.

What fate? What road? What tide of unknown turns awaited me? I knew not. But word of my father's passing somehow flew to the ears of a distant aunt, of whom I knew little. Little that made the prospect of residing under her roof sound appealing, at any rate. She was a fearsome woman, so told our old hired lady, and I had no other opinion to measure by.

This aunt, who was of the name Abigail, sent her hired man Jackson to fetch me in a carriage. He brought me to her house, which was wide and tall, a big box of wealth which looked down upon my smallness with many important windows. I felt diminished in its gaze, a peasant, a blight, a ghost stolen from its haunts.

I was ushered into a gracefully adorned parlor and made to wait. Aunt Abigail arrived at last, came into the room like a chilly breeze and planted herself on the baroquely colored carpet. She was strangely angular, towering there with hands on hips, her thin torso balanced on the expensive triangle of her skirts, her elbows pointing sharply to the left and right. She was a severe study if ever there was one, grey of hair and dress, and set with little dark eyes of a frosty, unsettling intelligence. They were the sort of eyes that missed nothing and I was rendered insubstantial, as if those eyes could see into my very being, see the air in my lungs and my blood about its route and deeper yet . . . into the inky whispers of my unborn dreams.

So, you would be my nephew? she said, squinting.

Yes, ma'am, said I, wishing to vanish.

A long moment passed between us, and then, much to my wonder, she smiled.

In the evening she sat me down by candles and hearth and warmed me with tea. There I was captive to her musings and the stars that flickered in the night of her eyes, my ears rapt for the soft, resplendent music of her voice.

She told of girlhood in a dim, loveless house, of a sadness that narrowed the heart, and parents that counted her crimes on backside and bones. She took note of the tears in my eyes.

Why do you cry? asked she.

For the both of us.

Such a strange little family we made: myself, Auntie, Asenath the housekeeper, and the hired man Jackson. We dwelt apart from the larger world, conversant in our small circle, sharing of tasks and mirth. It was the best of days in my estimation, and, for a time, my heart cheered, and sleep was a womb of unfanged dreams.

I emerged from the pall of my earlier days, garnering laughter, singing whatever my blood told me to sing, loving the sun of the passing days as it lit upon me, as it warmed the halcyon naps of cats. It went on this way for a matter of years and before I knew I was perched at the end of my youth.

But I was not the only one to age. Asenath's hair had gone to frost and Jackson, creaking like an old cedar copse, now staggered as if he had bricks for feet. Auntie could no better skirt the sway of time than the rest of us. And while I pretended not to notice, she slowed and stooped and ached. Once, near winter's end, she took to her bed.

It was along the blustery border where March perches between seasons, that I gazed numbly from my chamber. I saw small dun hills beneath the drained sky, afore the jeweled night and the owl's feathery pulse, and future ferns unfurling like the tongues of great buried butterflies. I wished for spring, its rush of green blood, winged and watered, reviving springtide to heal my aunt. But would March usher it in, or bring something else? March was too unpredictable to be accused of lying, you see, too fickle to make promises.

She wishes you not to see her, just yet, is all that Asenath would say.

She will be well again, won't she? I asked.

She will be different, the old servant concluded.

That night I dreamed of bony fingers running through my hair.

Rain wrapped around the house. The coldest rain ever to fall. Its dreary music marched across the roof, a dirge of drops. It prattled at the windows, it wept into the garret and then, just short of midnight, it ended. The moon shed dank gowns and a pale light slithered into Aunt Abigail's chamber. Asenath woke me from my slumber and led me there.

A tangle of high branches bridged the space between the moon and the room and cast a perfect lattice of shadow through the window. This web, these vines of shade—quivering in their delicate disorder—embraced the figure on the bed. Aunt Abigail was all but hidden, heaped with blankets, vaguely lit by the stump of a candle that sat withering on a table. Her face was obscured by a dark veil.

My aunt's voice was not the music it once had been, having greyed like the rest of her, and at that moment it was a whisper.

Dear lad, said she, moving the bedclothes aside enough that the light and my eyes fell on the shaggy grey hair that draped her arms, and the large flat tome clutched with inhumanly long fingers. Her face, vague behind the veil, had lengthened like that of a beast. *It is your time to take the book.*

The candle burnt out and the smoke from the wick was a wraithlike blue, a swirl the color of midnight and rain clouds, of cold, unnamed and forgotten seas.

I t was no little thing, no slight sting, no season of my own devising, that overtook this teller of a tale. I mourned as a sea mourns the drowned and as clouds in their slow flight sorrow for the sun they smother. I was all of pain, and only after a passing of time, after a burial, and a tempest of tears, did I approach, at midnight's call, the book.

My Aunt's secret, no longer under lock, made me to know of my destiny. Had I ever a choice? A winking firefly of memory swam anew in mind as I harkened back to that night in the cellar. But, one may ask, *was she not a monster of fur and talons?* Oh, but a beautiful monster, I avow, with her great flower of a heart, no more a horror than the falling leaf, or the budded rose in seaside mist, no more a terror than deer and sparrow, nor the heart of wildness they ever spur with beating wing and dancing hoof.

The book was waiting in the library. It was as winter to the touch, and heavy in weight and musty odor, the cover hard and grey as slate, and fixed with lichens like minute and calcified blossoms.

Of my reading I can tell little. Was it hours or days, or weeks that I sat hunched above those sallow pages? My mind drank anew of ancient words first seen in youth, and feasted on those penned by my Aunt. She had taken up the task of composing the book, which, when first my eyes dreamed across its mysteries, had rested incomplete. While treasures and marvels had poured from Abigail's pen (her lovely script like fractured black lace) the musings, as before, came abruptly to an end. The book remained unfinished.

I took up quill and took to the world.

———

The year wheeled from seed to ripe to ice-fangs and white, and I was an explorer, masked by dim hours, fey in exulted sunlight. I was a babe again in spirit, bare of foot, wide-eyed, a tadpole in murk, a soft spore on whims of breeze.

The blank pages of the book were a map undrawn and I, the wanderer, alive with senses external and in, groped for the truth through catacombs of sleep, and in the low grey mumbles spoken by stone. It was along the familiar roads of that small town, and where no road braved at all, that winds instructed, their canny breath soft in my own lungs until our sighs were the same.

A year winged by. Hunched by candle, and oak-fed hearth, I added my words to those in the book. Asenath fell sick and resigned to her bed. All the color seemed to fade from her, though in the night I would hear her singing softly to herself up there in the dark, and I took comfort in that, though I hardly know why.

Somehow Asenath hung on for another month or so, miraculously enduring the hired man Jackson's cooking, though she could barely take tea toward the end. One night, while sitting in the library, I heard her singing—a voice as soft as cobwebs. It was lovely, and then it was nothing.

But spring came and I, rapt about my calling, knelt in the shade of graves beneath tangled branches, the known world unraveling its labyrinth, its tenacity, its poem of sun-greened pastures. And on a small hill, beneath bundled clouds and blue, I watched. Bees were in the air like speckles on a trout.

A year and more came to pass, but I was not tallying. I was skirting the world of men, the blind, fettered, inharmonious world of men, who, shrunken at the heart, staggered and hacked their way along, their petty matters and farces bigger inside than the sky outside. Theirs was a realm more of crippled spirits than crippled limbs. No, I was for the serene and noble wood, in wonder of a single drop of rain, which, falling unobstructed, kissed and broke and spoke one fast small secret, into the greater sea of secrets that filled my mind that I might fill the book.

And would you believe that I knew of the dead? The shade beneath all living things, beyond each ebb and flicker? I was schooled in mossy avenues of trees where the dying branch twines with the new, and in the forward dark of October, when the damp hush of autumn gains. By candlelight the shadow of my quill was like shadow on a sundial, ever moving, ever turning, round and round and round.

I buried poor old Jackson in the loveliest spot I could find. He had left me one night in his sleep. It was then that the house seemed mammoth around me, and only sparsely lit. It filled with silence and shadow and webs that never knew a broom. And I, over time, took to greying and stooping, and creaking like the floors of the chambers I inhabited.

Early this evening I sat outside the empty house. I marveled at the deciduous beauty of the stretching hills, their billowing green intact for the time being, though destined for autumn's dismantling touch. The sky shrouded with clouds that did not rain, but hung curtaining, casting a premature dusk. At length I knew it was time to go in.

How the cellar stairs creaked, though I was gaunt and weighed but little. A single candle lit my way as I descended with book beneath arm. My garments could scarcely contain the thick hair upon me, and how long and sharp my face had become! The corner seemed as good a place as any.

While my long, barbed fingers yet have strength to hold pen, and my mind the facility to wield ink, I will tell of what I know. Blank pages will remain—I shall not fill them all—but, I will record what has been prized, and what shall be lost. I will tell of the turnings that no calendar can confine. The seasons that sing in winter's hiss and weep in golden leaves. Seasons of heat and chill, and twining, ivy-kited hours, arcane, impulsive, lush and fleeting, as vital to the heart as they are to the eye.

Now, as a hirsute and snouted creature, I end my journey. But none should pity me that. Call me kindred to the finest beast of all. . . . The great beast Nature, breasted with hills, furred in ferns, weeping her dew in a riddle of mist—all lightness and dark in feral meadows wed—and scribing the breathing myth of the world with a quill born in every thorn.

Would you then believe my story? And forgive me this, our parting? And take pause to read my final sentence.

The seasons, you see, are the pages of a book that none of us shall finish.

SCOTT THOMAS *(b. Marlboro, Massachusetts, USA 1959) is the author of eight short story collections, which include* Urn and Willow, Quill and Candle, Midnight in New England, *and* Westermead. *He has seen print in numerous anthologies, such as* The Year's Best Fantasy and Horror #15 *and* The Solaris Book of New Fantasy. *His work appears with that of his brother Jeffrey Thomas in* Punktown: Shades of Grey *and* The Sea of Flesh and Ash. *Scott and his girlfriend Peggy live in coastal Maine.*

Commentary on "The Unfinished Book": *After reading the tale, someone who knows me and my writing very well observed: 'This feels like one of your most autobiographical stories'. It's a keen and intriguing appraisal. Generally speaking, I'm not one to disclose a great deal of myself in an autobiographical fashion. But, I have to admit that this work defies that inclination, is undeniably more personal than most of what I tend to write. Even so, the me in it is represented in a stylized way, an impressionistic self-portrait. The particulars of the tale are even more inexplicit (my parents are dear to me, for example) so that in this work of revelation I call on implication and metaphor, and apply smoke and mirrors. Perhaps it's a Scorpio thing. The end result is a piece where essence is key. I am every bit the main character in spirit,* *while other abstract elements may or may not evoke or represent aspects of my history. But, for the reader, what is and isn't a part of my life shall remain a mystery.*

CELEBRITY FRANKENSTEIN

STEPHEN VOLK

I N MY MIND THE GAP WAS NON-EXISTENT BETWEEN FALLING
asleep and waking up, but of course weeks had gone by. Obviously. There were many procedures to be done and one had to be
recovered from, and stabilized, groggily, still under, before the next
began. I had no idea of the doctors taking over in shifts, or working in tandem, to achieve the program-makers' aims. I was out of it.
Meanwhile the video footage of the surgery circled the world.
Screen grabs jumping from cell to cell. I learned later that at the
moment the titles began running on the final segment of the
Results show, we'd already had the highest ratings the network had
ever had. *Any* network ever had. This was history, if I but knew it. If
I was awake. Then I *was* awake . . .

Salvator's eyes took a while to focus. Some filmy bits floated in
the general opaqueness like rats' tails which troubled me for a few
seconds. That and a certain lack of pain which came from being
pumped with 100%-proof Christ-knows-what anaesthetic and
various other chemicals swashed together in a cocktail to keep me
stable. The *new* me, that is. If you could call it 'me' at all.

I raised a hand to examine it front and back. It was Murphy's
hand, unmistakably. I'd know that blunt-ended thumb and slightly
twisted pinkie anywhere. The tan ended at the stitches where it
was attached to Vince Pybus's tattooed arm. I revolved it slightly,

feeling the pull in my forearm muscles—not that they were mine at all. Except they were. There was the tremendous urge to yell something obscene, but I remembered being counselled not to do that on live TV for legal and other reasons, not least being the show might get instantly pulled. But the word 'Fuck' seemed appropriate, given a new entity had been given life, of a sort, with no actual 'fucking' involved. As befits suitable family entertainment. Primetime.

Anticipating my thoughts, some guardian angel out of my field of vision put an oxygen mask over my mouth—whose mouth? I felt a coldness not on my lips but on Finbar's, wider and more feminine than mine, a Jim Morrison pout—and I drank the air greedily: it stopped the feeling of nausea that was rising up from my guts. Or somebody's, anyway.

I raised my other hand and it was trembling. It also happened to be African American, muscled and smooth. My man Anthony's. I flattened its palm and ran it over my chest, hairless, Hispanic, down to the hard, defined muscles of Rico's stomach. Maybe alarmingly, I didn't have to stifle a scream but a laugh. And almost as if it wanted to drown me out in case I did, up came the Toccata and Fugue, blasting loud enough to make the walls of Jericho crumble, and my hospital table tilted up, thirty, forty-five degrees, and shielding my eyes with Anthony's hand from the army of studio lights, I blinked, trying to make out the sea of the audience beyond.

'Are you ready for the mirror?' said a voice.

It was Doctor Bob and I saw him now, brown eyes twinkling above the paper mask, curly hair neatly tucked under the lime green medical cap. I nodded. As I had to. It was in my contract, after all.

I looked at Moritz's face as the reflection looked back. Long, lean, pale—not un-handsome, but not Moritz either. Finbar's lips, fat and engorged, maybe enhanced a little cosmetically while we were all under, gave him a sensuality the real Moritz lacked. Moritz, who lay somewhere backstage with his face removed, waiting for a donor. Next to armless Vince and armless Anthony, a fond tear in their eyes no doubt to see a part of them taken away and made famous. I saw, below a brow irrigated with a railway-track of stitches where the skull had been lifted off like a lid and my brain had been put in, Salvator's darkly Spanish eyes gazing back at me like no eyes in any mirror in Oblong, Illinois. Blind Salvator, now, who was sitting backstage, whose grandfather had been blind also, but had only eked a rotten existence as a beggar on the streets of Valladolid. Yet here was Salvator his eyeless grandson, rich and American, and about to be richer still from the story he now had to tell, and sell. Salvator could see nothing now—true, but he had seen a future, at least.

'Wow,' I said.

Doctor Bob and the other Judges were standing and applauding in front of me now, wearing their surgical scrubs and rubber gloves. Doctor Jude's cut by some fashion house in Rodeo Drive, her hair stacked high and shining. The gloves made a shrill, popping sound. Doctor Bob's facemask hung half off from one ear. I was still in a haze but I think they each said their bit praising us.

'I always believed in you guys.'

'You're the real deal. That was fantastic.'

'You know what's great about you? You never complained and you never moaned in this whole process.'

It was the Host speaking next. Hand on my shoulder. Sharp charcoal suit, sharp white grin: 'Great comments from the Doctors. What do you think of that? Say something to the audience.'

With Alfry Linquist's voice, I said: 'Awesome.'

Soon the clip was on YouTube. Highest number of hits ever.

I got out of the hospital bed and they handed me a microphone. I sang the single that was released that Christmas and went straight to number one—'Idolized.' One of the biggest downloads ever. Global.

As soon as I could record it, my first album came out. Producer worked with Frank Zappa (not that I was real sure who Frank Zappa was). *Born Winner*, it was called. The Doctors decided that. Guess they decided way before I recorded it. Like they decided everything, Doctor Bob and his team, the Judges. Went triple platinum. Grammys. Mercury. You name it. *Rolling Stone* interview. Jets to

London. Private jets courtesy of Doctor Bob. Tokyo. Sydney. Wherever. Madness. But good madness.

(The other madness, that came later.)

I wish I could've been me out there watching me become famous. Because from where I sat there wasn't time to see it at all. Grab a burger and Pepsi, then on to the next gig. I was loving it. So people told me. So I believed.

Big appearance was I guested on the next Emmy awards, telecast across the nation, giving out a Best Actress (Comedy or Musical) to Natalie Portman, my Justin Bieber fringe covering my scars. The dancers gyrated round me, Voodoo-like. I spoke and the tuxedos listened. I sung alongside Miley Cyrus and got a standing ovation of the most sparkling people in entertainment. Face jobs and chin tucks and jewellery that could pay off the debt of a small African country.

It was weird to have a voice. Somebody else's voice, literally that voice box in your throat not being the one you were born with. Strange to have a talent, a gift, a kind of wish come true that you carry round in your body and it's your fortune now. Alfry was my voice but I guess I carried him. Without my brain and my thoughts he couldn't have gotten to the top. Without Anthony and Vince's big old arms and Allan Jake Wells's legs and Rico's perfect abs, without any one of those things neither one of us could've made it. But, this way, we all did.

The Judges gave us a name and it was complete and to say we were happy was an understatement. I just knew Anthony wanted to get those biceps pumped right up fit to explode and I could feel Rico's insides just churning with a mixture of nerves and excitement, and I said, OK buddies, this is here, this is now, this is us and this is me. No going back. And I could feel every cell of them saying it with me.

And every night after performing I counted the scars on my wrists and shoulders and round my thighs and ankles and neck and said, 'Doctor Bob, thank you so much for this opportunity. I won't let you down.'

But all dreams got to end, right?

Bigtime.

I appeared on talk shows. Pretty soon got a talk show myself. Letterman eat your heart out. Guests like Lady Gaga. George Michael. (Outrageous.) Robert Downey Jr. (Phenomenal. Wore a zipper on his head to get a laugh. Gripped my hand like a kindred spirit.) Title sequence, black hand, white hand, fingers adjusting the tie, cheesy grin on Finbar's Jagger lips. Salvator's eyes swing to camera. The cowboy-gun finger going bang.

All this while Doctor Bob and his people looked after me, told me what to sign, what to do, where to show up, which camera to smile at, which covers to appear on, which stories to take to court. Which journalists to spill my heart to. Rico's heart. And I did. I did what I was told. Doctor Bob was like a father to me. No question. He created me. How could I say no?

There were girlfriends. Sure there were girlfriends. How could there not be? I was unique. Everybody wanted to meet me, see me, touch me, and some wanted more of me. Sometimes I'd oblige. Sometimes obliging wasn't enough.

That money-grabbing crackpot named Justine, housemaid in some Best Western I'd never stayed at, hit me with a rape allegation, but truth is I never remembered ever meeting her. It was pretty clear she was a fantasist. We buried her.

Like I say there was a downside, but a hell of an upside. Most times I thought it was the best thing I ever did, kissing my old body goodbye. Didn't even shed a tear when the rest of me in that coffin went into the incinerator, empty in the head. Just felt Doctor Bob's hand squeezing Vince Pybus's shoulder and thought about the camera hovering in my face and the dailies next morning.

But the peasants were always chasing me. The peanut-heads. The flash of their Nikons like flaming torches they held aloft, blinding me, bigtime. I had nowhere to hide and sometimes I felt chained to my office up on the 99th Floor on the Avenue of the Stars. Felt like a $1,000-a-night-dungeon in a castle, the Plasma screen my window to the outside world. Doctors checking me, adjusting my medicat-ion so that I could go out on the new circuit of night clubs, appear on the new primetime primary-colored couch answering the same boring questions I'd answered a hundred thousand times before.

Sometimes I growled. Sometimes I grunted. Sometimes I plucked a sliver of flesh from my knee and said, 'I'll deal with you later.' And the audience howled like I was Leno, but they didn't know how bad the pain was in my skull. It was hot under the lights and sometimes it felt like it was baking me.

'We can fix that,' the Doctors said, Doctor Jude with her legs and Doctor Bob with his nut brown eyes. And they did that. They kept fixing it. They kept fixing me, right through my second album and third, right through to the 'Best of' and double-download Christmas duets.

The problem was rejection. Balancing the drug cocktail—a whole Santa Claus list of them—so that my constituent body parts didn't rebel against each other. That was the problem. The new pharmaceuticals did it, thanks to up-to-the-minute research, thanks to a scientific breakthrough. All sorts of medical miracles were now possible. The show couldn't have gotten the green light without them. As Doctor Bob said, 'It was all about taking rejection. All about coming back fighting.'

I told my story in a book. Ghostwriter did a good job. I liked it when I read it. (The part I read, anyway.) Especially the part about Mom. Though Dad wasn't that happy. Tried to stop publication, till the check changed his mind. I did say some parts weren't true, but Doctor Bob said it didn't matter as long as it sold, and it did sell, by the millions. My face grinned out from every bookstore in the country. Scars almost healed on my forehead. Just a line like I wore a hat and the rim cut in, with little pin-pricks each side. Signing with Murphy's hand till my fingers went numb. Offering the veins of my arm for Doctor Jude to shoot me up, keep me going, stop me falling apart. I wondered if anybody had told her she was beautiful, and I guess they had. 'You nailed it. You've got your mojo back. I'm so proud of you—not just as a performer but as an human being,' she said as she took out the syringe.

On to the next job. Getting emails from loons saying it was all against nature and my soul was doomed to Hell. Well, doomed to

Hell felt pretty damn good back then, all in all. Except for the headaches.

But pretty soon it wasn't just the headaches I had to worry about.

One day they held a meeting at Doctor Bob's offices and told me that, 'in spite of the medical advancements,' the new penis hadn't taken. *Necrotis* was the word they used. Bad match. I asked them if they were sure it wasn't because of over-use. They said no, this was a biomedical matter. 'We have to cut Mick Donner off, replace him with someone new.' So I had to go under again and this time had a johnson from a guy in psychiatric care named Cody Bertwhistle. Denver guy, and a fan. Wrote me a letter. Longhand. Told me it was an honour.

I don't know why, and there's no direct correlation, but from the time Mike Donner's got replaced by Cosmic Cody's, things went on the slide.

Maybe it was chemicals. Maybe the chemicals were different. They say we're nothing but robots made up of chemicals, we human beings, don't they? Well if a tiny tweak here or a tad there can send us crawlin'-the-wall crazy, what does it mean if you get several gallons of the stuff pumped into you? Where are you then?

These thoughts, I'll be honest, they just preyed on me. Ate me up, more and more. Maybe that's the cause of what happened later. Maybe I'm just looking for something to blame. I don't know. Probably I am.

Maybe Doctor Bob knows. Doctor Bob knows everything.

After all, before me made us, he made himself. Out of nothing, into the most powerful man in television. A god who stepped down from Mount Olympus after the opening credits with the light show behind him like *Close Encounters* on acid.

I remember standing under the beating sun with four other guys next to a sparkling swimming pool lined with palm trees outside this huge mansion in Malibu. Servants, girls, models, gave us giant fruit drinks with straws and thin Egyptian-looking dogs ran around the lawns biting at the water jerking from the sprinklers. And Kenny started clapping before I'd seen Doctor Bob in his open-neck Hawaiian shirt walking across the grass towards us, then we all

clapped and whooped like a bunch of apes. Poor Devon hyper-
ventilated and had to be given oxygen. I'd felt strangely calm. The
whole thing was strangely unreal, like it wasn't really happening, or
it was happening to somebody other than me. I couldn't believe
that person who was on TV, on that small monitor I was looking at
as it replayed, *was* me. Maybe I was already becoming somebody
else, even then. We toasted with champagne and he wished us all
luck, and I don't know if it was the champagne or the warmth of the
Los Angeles evening, or the smell of gasoline and wealth and the
sound of insects and police sirens in the air, but I felt excitement
and happiness more than I ever had in my life before, and I didn't
want it to end.

We were buddies, that was the fact. Through the entire competition he was less of a mentor, more of a friend, Doctor Bob. Then,
once I'd won, well, our friendship went stratospheric. And I was
grateful for it. Then.

We played golf together. He paid for me to train for my pilot's
licence. Took me up into the clouds. Every week we had lunch at
The Ivy. Hello Troy. Hello Alex. Hello Sting. Hello Elton. Hello
Harrison. Hello Amy. Still at Sony? He wanted me on display. I was
his shop window. I knew that. Sure I knew that. But I always thought
he was watching me. If I took too long to chew my food. If I
scratched the side of my neck. It started to bug me. If I squinted
across the room, or stammered over my words I felt he was mentally
ringing it up. Cutting his chicken breast like a surgeon, he'd say,
'You are OK?' I'd say, 'Of course I'm OK. I'm great. I'm perfect.' And
he'd stare at me really hard, saying, 'I know you're perfect, but are
you OK?' One day I said, 'You know what? Fuck your Chardonnay.'

That was the day I took that fateful walk in the Griffith Park, up
by the observatory. Just wanted to be on my own—not that I could
be on my own any more, there being at least half a dozen of us in
this body, now, that I knew of. Didn't want to even *contemplate* if
they'd stuck in a few more organs I didn't know about. The semi-
healed scars itched under my Rolex so I took it off and dropped it
in a garbage can beside the path. Walked on, hands deep in the
pants pockets of my Armani suit.

You know what I'm gonna tell you, but I swear to God I didn't do anything wrong. I wouldn't do that to my Mom, I just wouldn't. She raised me with certain values and I still got those values. Other people can believe what they want to believe.

She was making daisy chains.

This little bit of a thing, I'm talking about. Three, maybe four. Just sitting there beside the lake. I watched her plucking them from the grass and casting them into the water, just getting so much enjoyment from the simple joy of it, so I knelt down with her and did it too. Just wanting a tiny bit of that joy she had. And we spoke a little bit. She was nice. She said she wanted to put her toes in the water but she was afraid because her Mom said not to go near the water, she might drown. I said, 'You won't drown. I'll look after you.' She said, 'Will you?' I said, 'Sure.' So that's how come there's this photograph of me lifting her over the rail. I was dangling her down so she could dip her feet in the water, that's all. They made it look crazy, like I was *hurling* her, but I wasn't. The front pages all screamed—*People, Us, National Enquirer*—he's gone too far, he's out of control, he's lost it. Wacko. I hadn't lost it. She wasn't in *danger*. We were just goofing around. And who took the shot anyway? Her Mom? Her Dad? What kind of *abuse* is that, anyway?

Parents! Jesus! After a fast buck, plastering their kid all over the tabloids? They're the freaks, not me. And that poor girl. That's what made her start crying. Her Mom and Dad, shouting and calling her away from me. 'Honey! Honey! Get away from the man! Honey!' And I'm like . . .

Doctor Bob want ballistic. Brought me in to the Inner Sanctum, Beverly Hills, and ripped me a new one. (Which he could have done literally, given his medical expertise.) I just growled. I snarled. He looked frightened. I said, 'See those chains over there?' pointing to his wall of platinum discs, 'I'm not in your chains anymore.' He shouted as I left, 'You're nothing without me!' I turned to him and said, 'You know what? I'm everything. You're the one who's nothing. Because if you aren't, why do you need me?' As the elevator doors closed I heard him say, 'Fucking genius. Fucking moron.'

I could do it without him. I knew I could.

But after Griffith Park, it wasn't easy to get representation. I still got by. Put my name to a series of novels. Thrillers. Sorta semi-sci-fi, I believe. Not read them. Celebrity endorsements. Sports and nutritional products. Failing brands. Except I was a failing brand too, they soon realized.

Then this lowlife cable network pitched me a reality series, á la *The Osbournes*, where a camera crew follow me around day in, day out. Twenty-four seven. Pitched up in my Mulholland Drive home for three months. But the paycheck was good. Number one, I still needed my medication which was legal but expensive, and two, I reckoned I could re-launch of my music career off the back of the publicity. So it was a done deal. Found a lawyer on Melrose that James Franco used. The producers sat on my couch fidgeting like junkies, these cheese straws in shades, saying they wanted to call it *American Monster*. I was like, 'Whatever.' The lights in my own home were too bright for me now, and I had to wear shades too. I'd have these ideas on a weekly basis, like my eyes were out of balance and I'd think a top-up from a hypo would get me back on the highway. It did. Periodically.

More and more I needed those boosts from the needle to keep me level, or make me think I was keeping level. Meanwhile the ideas wouldn't go away. I didn't know if the bright lights were inside or outside my skull. The bright lights are what everybody aspires to, right? The bright lights of Hollywood or Broadway, but when you can't get them out of your head even when you're sleeping they're a nightmare. And rats go crazy, don't they, if you deprive them of sleep? Except the drugs made you feel you didn't need sleep.

One of these ideas was there were germs around me and the germs I might catch would affect my immune system and inhibit the anti-rejection drugs. I was really convinced of this. I took to wearing a paper mask, just like the one Doctor Bob wore when he took my brain out and put it in another person's skull. Wore it to the mall. To the supermarket. To the ball game.

Then I guess I reached a real low patch. The reality show crashed and my new management bailed. Guess it wasn't the cash cow they were expecting. Clerval always was a ruthless scumbag, even as agents go, feet on his desk, giving a masturbatory mime as he schmoozes his other client on the phone, dining out on his asshole stories of Jodie and Mel.

Some reason I also got the idea that germs resided in my hair, and I shaved that off to the scalp. Felt safer that way. Safer with my paper mask and bald head, and the briefcase full of phials and pills, added to now with some that were off-prescription. Marvelous what you can find on the internet, hey?

Didn't much notice the cameras anymore, trailing me to the parking lot or to the gym, jumping out from bushes, walking backwards in front of me down the sidewalk or pressed to the driver's window of my Hummer. Didn't care. I guess somewhere deep down I thought the photographs and photographers meant somebody wanted to see me. Someone wanted me to exist, so it was worth existing, for them. How wrong can you be?

It felt like it was all over. It felt like I was alone.

Then one day I got a call from Doctor Bob. No secretary. No gatekeeper. Just him. He said, 'Listen, don't hang up on me. You know I'm good for you, you know we made it together and if I made some mistakes, I'm sorry. Let's move on.' I reckoned it took a lot for him to pick up the phone, so the least I could do was listen. 'I'm going in to the network to pitch a follow-up series. And if they don't clap till their hands bleed I'll eat this telephone. It's the same but different: what every network wants to hear. Hot females in front of the camera this time, and you know what, I'm not going to even *attempt* to sell it to them. The pitch is going to be just one word. We're going to walk in and sit down, and we're going to say: *Bride.*'

I said: 'We?'

He said, 'I want you in on this. You're on the judges' panel.'

And that's what happened. Contract signed, everything. It was my baby. My comeback. It meant everything to me. I went back to the fold. Doctor Jude kissed my cheek. I *did* have my juju. I *had* nailed it. I *was* fantastic, as a performer and as a human being . . .

Overnight, I was booked on *The Tonight Show*. I was back up there. I was going on to announce *Bride*. They wanted Doctor Bob to sit beside me on the couch but he said, 'No, son. You do it. You'll be fine.' And I was fine. I thought I was fine. But when the applause hit me and the lights hit me too I got a little high. I was back on the mountain top. I wanted to sing—not sing, *run*, run a million miles. And I loved Doctor Bob so much, I said it. I wasn't ashamed of it. I said it again. I shouted it. I jumped up and down on the couch saying 'I'm in love! I'm in love!' because that's what it felt like, all over again.

And, though it hit the headlines, I thought, what's the big deal? And, when my security pass didn't work at the rehearsal studio, I thought, what the hell? But when Doctor Bob didn't return my calls, then I knew something was turning to shit. Then I got a text from the producer saying my services were no longer required: there was a cancellation clause and they were invoking it. I was out.

I thought: Screw Doctor Bob.

Screw *Bride*.

I did commercials, appearances, while the series ran and the ratings climbed. If the first series knocked it out of the park, series two sent it stratospheric. I tried not to watch it but it was everywhere like a virus, magazine covers, newspapers. I kept to myself. I sunk low. I shaved my head again. I wore my mask. I took my meds.

Sleepless, I wandered Hollywood Boulevard amongst the hookers of both sexes. They looked in better shape than I did. Scored near Grauman's Chinese. Did hopscotch on the handprints in the cement. Watched the stretches sail by to fame and fortune. Watched pimps at their toil. Sometimes someone wanted to shake my black hand, other times wanted to shake my white.

In McDonald's I picked up a discarded *Enquirer* and saw what I didn't want to see: photographs of Doctor Bob leaving The Ivy with the winner of *Bride* on his arm. Lissom. Tanned. Augmented. A conglomerate of cheerleader from Wichita, swimmer from Oregon and pole-dancer from Yale. There she was, grinning for the cameras with her California dentition, just like I used to do.

Yes, I sent him texts. The texts that they showed in court: I admit that. Yes, I said I was going to destroy him. Yes, I said I was more powerful than him now and he knew it. In many ways I wanted him to suffer. I hated him, pure and simple.

But I didn't kill her. I swear on my mother's life.

Yes, she came to my house. Obviously, because that's where they found the body. But she came there, drunk and high, saying she wanted to reason with me and persuade me to mend broken bridges with Doctor Bob. When the prosecution claimed I abducted her, that I drugged her, that was all made up. She came to me doped up and in no fit state to drive home. I told her to use the bedroom, drive home with a clear head in the morning. It was raining, too, and I wasn't sure this girl—any of her—would know where to find the switch for the windshield wipers. Her pole-dancer arms were flailing all flaky and I saw the scars on her wrists and on the taut, fat-free swimmer muscles of her shoulders.

I put two calls in to Doctor Bob but they went to 'message' so I hung up. She had two blocked numbers on her phone and my guess is she called someone to come pick her up while I was out.

I had an appointment with a supplier because my anti-rejection drugs were low. Maybe I shouldn't have left her but I did. Fact is, when the police found my fingerprints all over the carving knife— of course they did, it was in my house. From my kitchen. Anyway, *their* fingerprints were all over the damn thing too.

I didn't break the law. Not even in that slow-mo car chase along the interstate where I kept under the speed limit and so did they.

I know I was found not guilty, but a good portion of the American people still believed I killed her. Thirty-two wounds in her body. Had to be some kind of . . . not human being. And I am. I know I am.

But the public didn't like it that way. They blamed American justice. Blamed money. Yes, I came out free, but was I free? Really free? No way. I was acquitted, but everyone watching the whole thing on TV thought it was justice bought by expensive lawyers and I was guilty as sin. They near as hell wanted to strap me to the chair right there and then, but there wasn't a damn thing they could do about it.

God bless America.

I had to sell my place on Mulholland Drive. Live out of hotel rooms. Pretty soon I was a cartoon on *South Park*. A cheap joke on Jon Stewart. Couldn't get into The Ivy any more. Looked in at Doctor Bob, eating alone.

Now, where am I?

Plenty of new pitches to sell. Trouble is, I can't even get in the room. Maybe it's true that the saddest thing in Hollywood is not knowing your time is over.

Now the personal appearances are in bars and strip joints smelling of semen and liquor. Not too unlike the anaesthetic, back in the day. I ask in Alfry's voice if this signed photo, book, album is for them. They say, no, it's for their mother. And that's the killer. Nobody wants to say the autograph of the person who used to be something is for them.

Night, I flip channels endlessly on the TV set in some motel, the cocktail in my veins making me heavy-lidded but nothing less than alert. If I see a clip of me I write it in my note book. Radio stations, the same. Any of my songs, I chase them for royalties. I'm human. Everybody wants a piece of me, but I'm not giving myself away any more. Not for free, anyway.

I look in the bathroom mirror and I see flab. Scrawn. Bone. Disease. Wrinkles. Puckers. Flaps. I'm wasting away. I'm a grey blob. What they didn't say when they build you is that you die like everybody else. Only quicker. Six times quicker. The techniques weren't registered and peer-reviewed, turns out. Nobody looked into the long term effects of the anti-rejection regime. That's why I've been eating like a horse and my body keeps nothing in but the toxins. When I was passing through Mississippi and collapsed at the wheel, the intern at the hospital said the protein was killing me, the fat, cholesterol, all of it. My body was like a chemical plant making poison. I said, 'What? Cut the munchies?' He said, 'No more munchies. No more midnight snacks. One more hamburger will kill you.'

I'm a nineteen year old concoction, hurting like hell. Each part of me wants the other part of it back. It's not a spiritual or mental longing, it's a physical longing and it's pain and it's with me every sleepless second of the goddamned day.

My only crime was, I wanted to be somebody.

Trouble is, I was six people.

At least six, in fact.

To be honest, I lost count after the second penis.

Maybe you can hear the music in the background, in the next room. They're playing 'Teenage Lobotomy' by the Ramones on the tinny radio beside my king-size bed.

While I'm here, sitting on toilet pan, coughing up blood.

Truthful? I'd be writing this the old fashioned way, paper and pen, except Murph's fingers are feeling like sausages and I'm getting those flashes again in the corner of Salvator's left eye right now. They're like fireworks. Hell, they're like the fourth of July. That's why I'm talking into this recorder. The one Doctor Bob gave me, way back. The one I needed for interviews, he explained. 'They record you, but you record them. You have a record of what you say. They get it wrong, sue their ass.' Doctor Bob was full of good advice, till it all went wrong, which is why I guess I'm sitting here, wanting to set it all down, from the beginning. Like it was. Not like folks say it was. Not like the lies they're saying about me out there.

Half an hour ago I rang for a take-out and a mixed-race kid in a hoodie rang the doorbell, gave me a box with a triple bacon cheeseburger and large fries in it. Gave him a fifty. Figured, what the heck?

I've got it in my hand now, the hamburger, Anthony's fingers and Vince's fingers sinking into the bun, the grease dripping onto the bathroom floor between my feet, feet I don't recognise and never did. The smell of the processed cheese and beef thick and stagnant and lovely in its appalling richness—a big fat murderer. The intern was right. One more bite *will* kill me. I know it. The drugs were too much. The side-effects, I mean. Like steroids shrink your manhood, this shrinks me. The dairy, the fat. And nobody gave me a twelve-step. Nobody took me in.

I texted Doctor Bob just before I started talking into this thing. He'll be the first to know. He'll come here and he'll find me. Which is how it should be. There's a completeness to that I think he'll understand. For all that came between us, and boy, a lot did, I think we understood each other, deep down.

That's why I know, absolutely, this is what I have to do.

Whether he listens to this story—whether anybody presses 'Play' and listens, is up to them. Whether they care. Whether anybody cares, any more.

All I know is, I'm taking a big mouthful. God, that tastes good . . . A great big mouthful, and I taste that meaty flavour on my tongue, and that juice sliding down my throat. . . . And the crunch of the iceberg lettuce and the tang of the pickle and the sweetness of the tomato . . . God, oh God . . . And, you know what?

I'm loving it.

STEPHEN VOLK *(b. Pontypridd, Wales, 1954) is the creator of the award-winning TV drama series* Afterlife *and the notorious BBCTV 'Halloween hoax'* Ghostwatch. *His latest feature film (co-written by director Nick Murphy) is* The Awakening, *a supernatural mystery starring Rebecca Hall, Dominic West and Imelda Staunton, while his other movie credits include* Gothic, *Ken Russell's trippy telling of the* Frankenstein *origin story and* The Guardian, *co-written with its director William Friedkin. He has also written for Channel Four's* Shockers *and won a BAFTA for* The Deadness of Dad, *a magical realist fantasy set in the town he grew up in. His short stories and novellas, a selection of which are collected in* Dark Corners *(Gray Friar Press, 2006), have earned him nominations for the British Fantasy Award, HWA Bram Stoker Award, and Shirley Jackson Award plus appearances in several "Best of" anthologies. Visit www.stephenvolk.net.*

Commentary on "Celebrity Frankenstein": *As sometimes happens with stories, the title came first, the story and voice rap-*

idly followed. It seemed to me that, of late, almost every television series (here in Britain, anyway) had the prefix 'Celebrity': Celebrity Shark Bait *being the most ludicrous, and least entertaining, example. Clearly, no procedure or abuse was too intrusive, private or extreme to merit attention from programme-makers hungry for ratings. Equally, the public's lust for fame and body image perfection seems to have become ubiquitous in culture as we drown in the spectacle of celebrity suffering, whether on-off relationships, meltdowns, miscarriages, surgery, sectioning and/or ultimately, death. Elvis, Britney, Michael Jackson, Tom Cruise on the sofa, and every* X-Factor *and* American Idol *winner was in my mind when I was writing this, though I'm obviously using Mary Shelley too. Someone who, ironically, knew a little about fame in her own lifetime. (Though never had her own chat show).*

APOLINAR CHUCA, Cover Photographer, *(b. King City, California, USA, 1973) left the heart of Salinas Valley at a young age to be raised in the Great State of Texas, and now resides in Houston. For twenty-two years his talent for conceptual design created award-winning commercial art for a number of U.S. organizations. His ability to combine traditional and digital techniques into a mixed media to arouse desire, emotion and wonderment has set his work apart. Nowhere is this more evident than in his passion for working with brushes and paint. Often he chooses flesh as his canvas, in art projects praised as "darkly romantic" yet "creepy, kinky, and carnivalesque" (recent photos appearing inside Belgium's* Secret Magazine, *volume 33). Chuca relies on his skills as a fashion photographer to document dreamlike women as living (and sometimes morphing) pieces of art, as they celebrate their seductiveness and embrace their role as muses for his Gothic Noir style. More of his art is viewable at www.modelmayhem.com/AChuca and www.chuca.net.*

Commentary on the photograph "Bella Muerte": *Translated as "Beautiful Death" and a tribute to Day of the Dead, this March 2011 portrait modeled by Anna Flores features body painting in a traditional Mexican style of illustrated bones and swirls. It is a celebration of continued growth in honor and remembrance of friends and family who have passed on. It is dedicated in loving memory to Paula Hinojosa, Abuelita (June 18, 1920 – July 25, 2011).*